WHERE THE STATUE WEEPS

The Present is Haunted by the Past

by
Lenn Roberson

Cushing Publishing
www.cushingpublishing.com

ACKNOWLEDGEMENTS

I am forever grateful to my family, who supports me in all I do. I am also indebted to a very special friend, Teresa Mayle, who guided me through the initial phases of this book and helped me become a better writer. I could not have done this without her. I am very thankful to my publisher Rose Cushing and editor, Julia Fisher.

ONE

Spring 2021

I am running away.

But surely this cannot be the place I am going. Pulling off the highway onto the long drive riddled with potholes, I drive under a faded sign that hangs at a haphazard angle. There is a strange looking silhouette of a horse with two faces, one looking in each direction. The rail fence by the road is so old it has rotted through and is completely gone in places.

But underneath the two-faced horse reads a caption, Janus Farms. So, I know I am in the right place.

I shudder inwardly as the sweeping drive curves around the top of the hill and the old mansion comes into view. Partially veiled in the leaves of ancient oaks, it stands vast and rambling, an odd conglomeration of domes, gables, and shuttered windows that stick out at strange angles, a shadowed Gothic monument. It almost looks like a castle from the dark ages, rather than a house.

As the breeze waves the foliage of the trees back and forth the house seems almost alive, like a decrepit old giant. The ground floor is dark in the fading twilight, but I see a figure moving about against the lamplight through an upstairs window on the left wing. As I come closer, I can see that it is a tower room that juts out a little past the corner of the house, rising like a dark steeple, with the third story hovering behind it.

I ease the car around the sweeping drive and stop under the carport. Most of the paint has peeled from the supports and I notice how the roof sags. Maybe I shouldn't leave my car here. It looks as though the whole thing may collapse at any moment. I pull up until I am able to park in the open and sit here for a moment, looking around. If

I had anywhere else to go, I would turn around and drive away right now. Denise Evans, the woman who had hired me over facetime had told me the place was old and sort of dilapidated but that was an understatement. They were fixing it up, a little at the time, she had said. I would hate to see what it had looked like before they started. I am glad for the wheeled suitcases as I pull them up the walkway but so many of the bricks are gone that they bump along behind me, trying to wedge themselves into the holes left there.

I will be filling in for Denise, who runs a therapeutic riding program for handicapped children on the leased grounds here. She had been called away when her mom got sick and will be gone for a few months. I will also be a part time companion to the elderly woman who owns Janus Farms. She has a nurse during the day who administers her medication, helps her with her bath, things like that. She could manage by herself at night, Denise had said but she just didn't want to leave her alone, in case she fell or something like that. The old woman is up in her nineties, I believe she told me.

Climbing the steps, I ring the bell and stand waiting. Thick strands of English ivy climb the side of the wall, tendrils creeping up and across so that you can barely see the wood and bricks beneath. A lizard scampers out of the thick foliage and I jump back as it scuttles across the porch floor, only inches from my feet. Finally, I hear footsteps. The door opens a crack and I see an eye peering through it.

"I'm Jodi Morgan," I say. "Here for the job."

The door opens wide and a middle-aged woman in a nurse's uniform eyes me. She pushes back a tendril of dirty blonde hair, just starting to streak with gray. "You're late. Denise told me you'd be here no later than six."

"Yes, I'm sorry. I got a little lost out here in the country. My GPS wouldn't pick up a signal very well. It kept turning me back towards Roanoke Rapids. I finally had to text Denise and get directions."

She doesn't say anything else, simply takes one of my suitcases and beckons for me to follow her. She leads me through dark, cavernous rooms that echo with our footsteps. She walks so quickly I have to fall into a sort of little trot to keep up. Finally, we stop in a hallway. She presses a button on the wall and a door slides open. An elevator. I have never seen one in a house.

"There's a set of stairs at the front of this wing but Miss Grace can't get up and down them. So, we use the service elevator. I don't know why she won't let us fix her up a room downstairs. It would make things easier on everybody."

The cage rumbles violently as we ascend to the second floor. It makes my legs feel weak. When we come to a stop the door opens with a jerk. We step out onto the hardwood floor of a long, dim hallway, only a little light coming in at the far window. Oil paintings of thoroughbreds peer down from the walls of the passageway like equine ghosts from a time long forgotten.

"That's Miss Grace's room." She points down the hall. "She usually doesn't go to bed this early, but I took her in for a doctor's appointment and she was really worn out. Anyway, your room's right down the hall there."

Opening the door to my room, she pulls the suitcase in and turns to me. She takes the bag I am holding and pulls it from my grasp. Placing it beside the first one she closes the door and says, "Come down with me and I'll show you where the kitchen is on my way out. There's some roast left over from Miss Grace's supper. You can heat it up if you're hungry."

We descend in the elevator, and she leads me down a maze of hallways until we reach a solid oak door which opens into an enormous kitchen. It is filled with hulking appliances that look as if they have been here for the better part of a century. Heavy pots and pans hang from hooks on the wall, so rusted with age that you can barely see the copper color beneath. "You'll find the roast in the fridge. And there's the microwave." She points at the only modern gadget in the room. "There are some greens in the bottom drawer of the fridge too, in case you want a salad."

The whole time she is talking, she is putting on her jacket and edging towards the door. She looks down at her watch. "Sorry, but I don't stay here after dark," she apologizes as she slips out. "I'll see you in the morning, around nine." And she is gone.

Standing here looking at the door as it closes behind her, I wonder what she meant about not being at Janus at night.

Maybe she can't see to drive in the dark, I think. She looks as if she is in her fifties. Sure, that must be what she meant, I tell myself.

I open the rusty refrigerator door and pull the foil back from the old blue and white corning ware dish. The roast peers up at me from the congealed gravy and I close it. I'm not hungry but I do take out a glass of tea. It is sweet and cold, and it slides down my throat smoothly.

I open the door and step out. It is still just light enough to see. Walking across the gently sloping lawn, I can see several large stables and a variety of outbuildings. As I come closer, I notice that, like the house, they are in a state of disrepair. Only one small barn off to the side looks like it is solid and has had work done on it recently.

An old fountain just in front of what seems to be the main stable catches my eye. Rusted and covered over with green moss, it looks as if it has been dried out for many years. But what has really captured my attention is the cracked stone statue that still stands in the middle. It is a horse, large and powerfully built. And like the sign at the road, it has two faces. One face seems to be peering directly into the open doors of the main stable. The other gazes back up at the house. A shiver runs down my spine and I shake my head, trying to clear my mind.

I can make out the outlines of twenty or thirty horses grazing in the pasture as the Roanoke River slides by in the background. Crossing the yard, I whistle softly, and several heads come up, ears pricked forward. Denise had told me they had plenty of grazing with the spring grass coming in and a stream to drink from so all I would have to do tonight was check on them. I will only need to give them grain in the mornings. I walk down to the end of the lane to the spot where the fence stops just short of the river. I stand by the gate, where I can hear the rush of muddy reddish-brown water as it tumbles swiftly over the rocks. Down here, the smell of the water overpowers even the fragrance of the wild honeysuckle that lingers everywhere. It is dark and dank, almost cloying, somewhat unpleasant.

"Huh-huh-huh. Huh-huh-huh." Hearing a horse rumbling in his throat I look up to see a chunky black and white paint coming towards the fence. Not to be outdone, a couple more follow and in a second about half the herd is cantering across the field. I know some of these horses are rescues that came from pretty bad situations and I suppose they are the ones that hang back, watching quietly.

A buckskin gelding reaches the gate first, slides to a stop; and thrusts his head over the top rail, hoping for a treat.

"Sorry boy, I don't have a thing for you," I mutter as I slide my fingers through the black silk of his mane. He tosses his head and then moves over as other horses crowd in behind him. The little herd is quite a mixture. A seventeen hand Saddlebred shuffles up in his flat-footed gait, his movements rapid and elastic. He sniffs at me until a dappled gray pony squeals at him and lays her ears back, chasing him away. Her withers barely reach up to his knees and yet he moves aside and allows her to have his space. I notice that the Saddlebred, majestic as he is, has horrible scars on his face and it makes me wonder what happened to him. A chestnut Haflinger ambles up quietly and his liquid brown eyes peer at me calmly through a shaggy forelock.

Movement a little farther out catches my eye. A gleaming, golden palomino stands back, as if he is not sure whether to approach the gate. The silver mane flows out from the elegantly arched neck, the color as deep as an untarnished copper penny. His ears prick forward, head bobbing occasionally. My heart catches in my throat. He looks so much like my mare, the one I left behind. I shake my head, trying to clear it. Trying to think professional thoughts. Surely, he is nothing like her, full of fire and spirit or he wouldn't be in a program like this. These horses must have a quiet temperament in order to be safe for kids to ride.

WHERE THE STATUE WEEPS

But as I stand here listening to the sounds the horses make; I can't help thinking back to the life I used to have. I competed in reining for almost eight years and there was nothing like it. I loved the thrill of galloping out into the arena, doing flying lead changes, roll backs over the hocks, the three hundred-and sixty-degree spins done in place. Around and around we flew, until even the spectators felt a bit dizzy. Working at it with Cole was what made it seem like a dream come true. We hauled all over the east coast, working the circuit.

Then everything had changed. And now, here I am with no husband and no home. I am drifting: don't really know where I should be or what I should do.

A mosquito lands on my neck and I feel the pinprick. Suddenly they are all over me. I slap at them and shake my head, trying to stop thinking about my problems. Once the horses had seen I didn't have any feed, they had drifted away from the gate and are all grazing quietly. I turn down the path that runs alongside the river and walk downstream, gazing at the dragonflies and back swimmers that hover around the edges. Farther out the murky red water tumbles swiftly over the boulders, rushing through the crevices, making whitecaps rise up towards the middle. Something slithers through the grass, and I stop in my tracks when I see a fat water moccasin plop into the river. I stand for a moment until my heart stops hammering in my chest and then start back towards the house.

Looking up at the enormous old mansion I think for a moment that it almost seems to reflect my emotions. On the right wing, the roof has partially caved in, and a broken window stares out over the grounds. It looks like a festering eye, grayish mold oozing down the walls below as if the old house had witnessed such sadness that it couldn't help but cry tears that have thickened like glue over the years. What secrets does this house hold; I wonder? The opposite wing, the one that contains my room is in better condition and it is easy to see that portion has had work done on it recently. I can only imagine what this place looked like when it was newly built; filled with glamour, wealth, and power.

I don't want to go back up in the elevator, so I search for the stairs at the front of the wing. I lose my way and double back to find myself at the kitchen again. Finally, I find the stairs and go up. I take out my phone and open up Facebook. I have blocked Cole but nearly all my friends are connected to him in one way or another and I keep seeing posts from him, so I put it down. It is too early to go to bed, but I don't know what else to do. It is completely dark now. I would like to just lie back and close my eyes and listen to some familiar show on television but there isn't one in my room. In fact, I haven't seen one anywhere in the house. If I had the laptop, I could stream a movie, but I didn't bring anything that had been a gift from him. I'm sure there's a computer in the office; wherever that is, but I don't feel like traipsing around the old mansion tonight. I could at least listen to some music or pull up a show on my phone, but I can't find the charger, so I figure I better shut it off for now. I don't really care about watching anything but it's good, you know just to have some white noise in the background, voices filling the silence. It makes you feel... well, I don't know. Not so alone.

So, I simply sit here for a few moments in the vast silence. I hear a tiny, scuttling noise. Nothing but a mouse, I tell myself. A mouse isn't going to really harm anything, not nearly so bad as the thoughts that flutter around and around in my head like moths circling a naked light bulb.

But I gradually become aware of other noises, although it is difficult to describe what they are. The hairs on the back of my neck stand at attention as I strain to hear. I know that old houses are constantly settling, shifting, but it seems more than that. Almost as though the walls are breathing. Ker-thump, ker-thump, a pulse that whispers through the house as if the mansion knows things that it wants to tell me.

I shake my head. My own pulse is all I am hearing. I open my makeup bag and take out a prescription bottle. Opioids. The doctor gave them to me a couple of days ago, but I haven't taken any yet. So far, memories of the addiction our last breakup had caused are so frightening they have kept me from using it. But I long for escape, if only for a few hours. How on earth could simple emotional pain turn into such a physical ache, I wonder?

I open the top of the bottle and then pause. I probably shouldn't take it now. What if the old woman woke up in the night and I didn't hear her? I look around at my surroundings and decide I don't care. Here I am in such a strange place that seems to be falling down around me. Out in the boonies, no one else around for miles. I look out the window, accustomed to the lights of Raleigh but only darkness meets my gaze. What on earth have I done? I don't belong here. I don't know where I belong.

Shaking one of the pills out, I pop it in my mouth and take a swallow of the tea still left in my glass. I lie down across the bed and close my eyes. Unbidden images appear before me and the harder I try to avoid them, the faster they come. Images of the first time I had seen Cole at the Equestrian Complex in Raleigh flit across my eyelids. The way he sat so deep in the saddle, he seemed almost an extension of the horse and they moved as if they were one. He was so handsome with that lock of dark hair that fell across his forehead and the open grin that flashed those white teeth. I fell head over heels for him. Sure, I'd had relationships with quite a few men before. But those were nothing like it had been with him. Cole and the horses had become my whole world. And now they are gone. The earth has been tilted sideways; all the solidity of life gone in an instant. I fear that even the ground beneath my feet is nothing but an illusion, like a thin, transparent sheet of plastic that crinkles into nothingness at a whim.

I don't know how long I have been dozing when a noise wakes me. Opening my eyes, I look around, disoriented for a moment. The room is dark, moonlight coming in through the window, just enough to make out the objects in the room. I lie here listening. There it is again. A woman's laughter, deep and sensual, murmuring voices. I can't make out what they are saying. I sit up too quickly and my head swims from the medication. For a moment, all is silent. Then I hear it again, that teasing laughter.

Getting out of bed on unsteady feet, I go to the doorway and listen. The sounds are coming from the end of the hallway. I opened the door and quietly stepped out into the hall. A glow of yellow-orange light emanates from the last room on the right. The strange glow spills out from the door that is partially ajar as it pulsates in its intensity. A shiver runs down my spine.

Go back to bed, I tell myself, but it seems as if some unseen force draws me down the hall. Even though I am afraid, I need to see. I start down the long, dim hallway, hand on the walls to try and steady myself. The shadows reflect off the paintings of the thoroughbreds until they almost seem to be moving. I tiptoe down the hall and ease up to the room. A fragrance wafts out into the hallway, dark sandalwood and jasmine. Now I can hear voices whispering. Slowly I push the door. When it squeals, I stop, my heart pounding in my ears.

There before me lurks an entire suite. Out of the corner of my eye I can see a room off to the right with a tester bed and an enormous chifforobe. Directly across from it is a sitting room. It juts out into a circular shape and I realize it is the tower room I have seen from outside. In the dimness I can just see that the space is dominated by a round table surrounded with high-backed chairs.

I look around the side of the entrance. There, standing by the French doors to the balcony are a man and woman. A field of energy surrounds their forms like an aura of light. It ebbs and flows in multicolored layers, crimson and scarlet bleeds into orange with yellow tips blending into the outer edges.

The man moves towards her and I notice how tall he is. He takes her hand and steps in front of her. Somehow, I can still see the form of her body beyond him, as if he is transparent. He lowers his face to kiss her and their bodies seem to melt into one. When she wraps her arms around him, I can still see the shaggy hair at the back of his neck through the flesh of her arms. The pulsing of the light moves faster now and their bodies glow brighter, the colors of the surrounding aura blending together, faster and faster until they form a vortex of crimson-orange shades. The swirling sensation of the energy field makes me feel dizzy and I stumble backward.

"Get out of this room!"

I have been so entranced with the scene before me that I failed to notice anything else. I turn and there behind me stands a woman that looks as old as the mansion itself. She leans heavily on a cane, pale nightgown billowing out and white hair standing out wildly around her. Her blue eyes are faded and misty in a face like a pale withered pear, but they spark with anger now.

"I...I.." Turning back towards the center of the room, I start to point at the figures by the door, but they are gone. Nothing is here but a swatch of red liquid on the ivory brocade drapes, which seeps down onto the floor. I stand here, looking back and forth from her to the curtains. I take three steps towards the door and then stop, my heart beating wildly. The old woman stands there staring silently.

I put my hand on the drapes, lifting my reddened fingers towards her. "Bloo..." My voice breaks and even to my own ears it sounds high and reedy.

But I can tell she does not see it. "The drapes..." I point towards the ivory-colored material, where the stain continues to spread ever wider. "Don't you...can't you..." My voice trails off as she stares at me. Slowly I become aware that the red liquid on my fingers does not feel like blood. Blood is viscous and sticky, but this is as thin as water. And the smell seems familiar but I can't place it.

Breaking past the old woman, I rush back to my room, slamming and locking the door. I go into the bathroom and scrub vigorously at my hand, trying to remove the red stain.

When I have gotten most of it off, I go back and sit on the bed, shivering. So strange, I think. Surely, I was imagining things. After all, here I am in this weird old house, and I took those sleeping pills. I feel so lost. I don't belong in this place; I just don't belong. But I look down again and see the red color that remains on my palm. It was all real, I didn't imagine it. And the odor, what was it? I know I have smelled it before, just this evening in fact. That's when it comes to me. It's water. Roanoke river water.

TWO

New Year's Eve, 1941

Grace flew up the staircase, her boots skidding on the hardwood floor of the landing. She had planned to only go for a short ride this afternoon. But she had gone down by the river and the weather was so nice she had forgotten the time. Here it was, the last day of December and she had barely needed a jacket. It was a welcome break. For the last few weeks, they had had bone chilling cold, and she had been cooped up inside. And now today, the sun had shone warmly and beckoned to her, almost teasing her to come out and play.

The heels of her boots made sharp rat-a-tats as she walked quickly down the hall to the suite that she and Phillip had made their own. Kicking off her boots and riding breeches, she threw them across the oversized tester bed, opened the door to the adjoining bathroom and turned the hot water on, pinning her hair up as the clawfoot tub filled. Dumping in a little of the bath salts Phillip had given her for Christmas, she swished the water until it bubbled up. It felt so good lying here in the warmth. The muscles from her inner thighs were a little sore from gripping the saddle and the heat was soothing. She wished she could stay until bedtime. To just be up here with her husband, where they could be alone was all she wanted. The bath salts had a deep, flowery fragrance, she couldn't remember what it was called. But it did smell good. And so would she. Phillip always liked for her to wear fragrances that smelled like flowers.

She usually lingered in the tub until the water turned cool but not this evening. She had to get dressed for the annual New Year's Ball. Reaching for a towel, she dried off and brushed her hair, pinning it back with the simple butterfly clasp. She peered at her reflection in the Rococo Revival mirror and sighed. She wished her hair were golden blonde like Phillip's, or maybe dark and shiny. It looked like the hemp-colored twine they used on the farm to hold bales of hay together.

Her eye fell on the gold-rimmed tray, filled with make-up. She hated plastering that stuff all over her face, it made her feel like a clown. But she knew better than to show up at the farm's biggest event of the year without it. Papa would have a fit. She slathered on a thin layer, added mascara and a touch of pinkish rouge to her cheeks. In her hurry, she dropped the tin of eyeshadow and it fell against the silk damask wallpaper, puffing up to make an ugly smudge. No matter, she would clean it up later. She chose the rose-colored lipstick that Phillip liked and dabbed a touch of it on.

Pulling several dresses out of the chifforobe, she threw them on the bed and tried to decide what to wear. She really shouldn't have waited until the last minute, but she hated these social events so. She was always so miserable and out of place.

The periwinkle blue dress. Papa wouldn't be happy because she had worn it before, but she was a little more comfortable in it than most of the others. The neckline wasn't so low and the fit around the hips was loose; it flared out around her calves and didn't cling so tightly. Pawing through the jewelry box, she found the matching sapphire earrings. They dangled too long; she would have preferred the small diamonds. But they did dress up her outfit. And Papa expected that. He always said if she was going to be a Masterson, she had better present herself as one.

She couldn't find the matching shoes. She dug through the bottom of the chifforobe until she had pulled three shoe organizers out. Who in the world needed so many shoes? Suddenly, she thought of the last time she had worn the periwinkle pumps, blushing with the memory. Philip had pulled her down on the loveseat and they had sat there, gazing at the fireplace as he talked about the business deal that he had been able to pull off during the social.

Janus Farms had picked up two of the newer stables in Virginia that would be bringing mares down to breed next month. She had sat with her head on his shoulder, smiling a little at his excitement as he rattled off a list of other owners he was planning to talk to. Finally, his voice had trailed off and he had pulled her close and planted a solid kiss on her forehead. The skin on her neck tightened as she remembered how his warm lips had moved to kiss her there, caressing and teasing until she could hardly stand it. Then his lips had covered hers with a deep kiss that never failed to make her feel light-headed, even though they had been married for quite some time now.

Running across the suite, she dropped to her knees on the Persian rug and peered underneath the loveseat. There were the shoes, still lying where she had kicked them off that night. She put them on and with one last glance in the mirror closed the door behind her.

She pressed the elevator button and waited impatiently. She hated riding in it, but she could hardly walk in the high heels, much less climb the stairs in them.

When the door opened at the marble floor of the third story, the elevator jerked to a stop, throwing Grace off balance a little. The doors opened smoothly and as she looked out at the crowd milling about, her throat tightened. She hadn't expected so many people to be here this early. Looking past them, she tried to focus on the murals that covered every wall in the great room, scenes of horses. They dated back towards the mid eighteen-hundreds when Janus Farms was just beginning to really come into its own. Colts and fillies cavorted around the mares in the gently rolling green slopes of the pasture. Grooms stood dressed in their finest, holding the magnificent stallions on their lead lines with their heads erect in a haughty stance, portraying the regal manner that permeated everything about the place. Scenes of the thoroughbreds battled down towards the finish line, jockeys perched atop them, riding high over the muscular necks. They illustrated such detail that chunks of earth flew up beneath the heavy hooves and clouds of dust trailed behind them. These paintings were the only thing Grace liked about this room.

Milling through the throngs of people, she just nodded politely at the few who made eye contact and made her way around the perimeter of the room, not really speaking to anyone. She always avoided walking beneath the massive gilded and Meissen chandeliers in the center of the ceiling, wondering if one day they may fall, crushing anyone who happened to be standing there.

She didn't see Phillip. Papa was easy to spot, of course. Holding court in the center of the room, surrounded by a group of men, he spoke with that booming voice, grinning broadly as he waved his cigar through the air with a flourish. He was so loud you could hear every word above the laughter that constantly erupted.

"Grace!" She turned to see Mama's eyes on her. She was standing with an attractive older woman. Ashy blonde hair swept up to form a fashionable chignon and a silver fox fur was draped over her shoulder.

"I want you to meet the governor's wife." Turning to the woman, she said, "You remember my oldest son, Phillip? This is his wife, Grace."

Grace nodded at her. She never knew what to say, especially to someone of such important status.

"I'm pleased to meet you, dear." The woman raised her champagne glass. "I wasn't able to make it last year; I wasn't feeling well but I'm sure you met my husband."

Grace nodded and tried to smile.

"Well," the woman looked over the room. "It gets bigger every year. You ladies must come up to see us in Raleigh soon. For the Prominent Ladies of North Carolina. I hope you can make it."

Mama was about to say something, but the band started up and Grace could barely hear. Mama clasped the woman's hand and smiled, then turned and headed for the family table with Grace following close behind. Once they were seated, Grace was a little more comfortable. It was better to simply sit here, silently observing the crowd then to be a part of it. She would rather be flayed alive than to be forced to mix in with all these people, so out of place, never knowing what to say.

She saw Phillip across the room now, talking with a

couple of men she recognized as buyers. They came a couple of times a year to purchase weanlings and yearlings.

She relaxed a little now as she looked out at some of the familiar faces. There was the new minister and his wife. Mayor Sykes. Dr. Joyner was talking to Judge Holders and a couple of attorneys. A few of the jockeys stood together on one side of the room. Buzz, the head trainer for Janus was easy to pick out, towering above the crowd, even taller than Phillip. He mingled with the crowd, laughing easily.

People began to drift towards the tables, seating themselves as they found their place cards. When Papa finally came to the family table, the few who were still scattered here and there sat down. Phillip folded his tall, slender frame into the chair beside Grace and gave her hand a little squeeze, but she knew his mind was on business.

Papa motioned towards the band, and they gave a drum roll, building to a tremendous crescendo. He stood up, cleared his throat, and began.

"I want to thank you all for coming out to Janus Farms tonight for the annual New Year's celebration. "Now, I know there are some who think we should have cancelled the party this year," he continued, shaking his head gravely. "And with all due respect, we did consider it because of what just happened recently at Pearl Harbor."

A murmur rose among the crowd, but Papa held up his hand to quiet them. "But I have to say, we felt it was something we needed to do, our responsibility to the public, you might say. We want to keep things as normal as possible. And we all know in times of war; we need an escape. Something to lift our spirits, to keep us in good morale. So, we decided to carry on. After all, its baseball, boxing and horse racing that keep America entertained."

Applause broke out and Papa raised a hand. "Most of you are familiar with the origins of Janus, but if you'll bear with me, we have a few newcomers here."

Putting his cigar down, he lifted a champagne glass to his lips and took a swallow. "Now I know many people believe that thoroughbred racing began out in Kentucky, but it actually began right here on the east coast. North

Carolina and Virginia. Namely, right here in Northampton and Halifax counties. Part of Warren County too. My many times great grandfather heard about an extraordinary horse up in Virginia, one of the first thoroughbreds imported from Europe. And he went up and brought him back here. The great Janus – the horse who started it all.

"And thus, began the stomping grounds of high society in racing, right here. Janus Farms. Situated halfway between the Belmont Stakes in New York and Hialeah Park in Florida."

He turned to gesture at the wall behind him, spreading his arms with a great flourish. An enormous mural stretched across the perimeter of the room. A horse with two faces lurked there; each looking in different directions. One laid his ears back, teeth bared and smoke pluming from the flared nostrils drifting up towards the ceiling. The other face somehow depicted a younger looking horse, ears pricked forward and a quiet look about the eyes.

He turned back to face the crowd. "Janus was also the name of the Roman god of transitions. The god with two faces; one staring back at the past as the other gazes forward to the future. A very befitting name for the farm, I always thought. All through the years, changing, growing. From a modest cabin to one of the largest farms in the country during the early years of racing. And now, look what Janus Farms has become. No one could have ever envisioned the magnitude of it all. And we will continue to grow each and every year!" Lifting his glass of champagne in a toast, he pointed it from one group to another in the room and stood there, finally silent as a cheer broke out here and there, building quickly to thunderous applause.

As the band started again and people began to get up and dance to the Chattanooga Choo Choo, Grace remembered when she had first come to Janus Farms. Her friend, Mildred Murphy from town had talked her into coming to the New Year's ball here. Invited only due to the fact of her father's position as president of the bank in Roanoke Rapids, she had introduced Grace into this whole new world. Aunt Ada, who had raised Grace in their little cabin downriver had been so angry. The people in their little community followed the ways of their ancestors, living off the land and shunning many practices of what they called "townfolk." They didn't trust anyone who was different and avoided mixing with them. They particularly avoided modern medicine and practiced healing with natural remedies. Aunt Ada believed money was the root of all evil. It had been difficult for Grace to marry into this prestigious family and she still didn't feel as if she belonged. But she had been so in love with Phillip and he was a good man. She still could hardly believe he had wanted her.

Grace tried to shake the memory and her mind drifted to her first night here. She had been so uncomfortable, left sitting alone in a corner while Mildred had danced with one boy after another. Finally, she had gotten up and made her way to one of the many third story verandas where Phillip had found her and taken her down to show her the stables. And then they had danced together, not in the ballroom of the big house but in the wide aisle of the main stable, with only the horses to witness it.

Grace still marveled at the thought that Phillip had chosen her. She did wish he still acted the way he did back then, as if he thought of her every moment, and she was the most important thing on his mind. She glanced over at him now and told herself to count her blessings. Phillip was a good husband, a kind man. He was just so busy because Papa was giving him more responsibility at the farm. Oh, Papa still loved to storm about, puffing, and blowing, especially in front of a crowd but Phillip shouldered the brunt of the responsibility now. And she tried to fit into his world, but it was difficult.

As if reading her thoughts, Phillip reached over and grasped her hand under the table, giving it a firm squeeze. She could feel his warm thigh beside hers and once again, she thought how it would be when the ball was over, and they would go downstairs together. He would discuss the people he had talked with and how working with them would affect the success of the farm. And then he would take her in his arms and kiss her, making the whole outside world of nerve-wracking social events disappear.

Her husband may not have much time for her during his busy workday, but his nights belonged to her.

She watched now as more people ventured onto the dance floor. A couple of the jockeys were out there. Buzz danced well with an easy confidence. She wasn't a very good dancer, but she did wish Phillip would take her out on the floor for one of the slow numbers. The ones where she could simply cling to his shoulder, molding her body to fit his as the band crooned softly. But as usual, his mind was on the business of Janus Farms.

Her eye caught a flash of brilliant red as a young woman entered the room on the arm of a dark-haired man. It was Phillip's brother Frank, and his wife, Lorraine. She pursed her rouged lips, eyes twinkling with delight and scarlet skirts flouncing as everyone in the room turned to stare at them. As always, the atmosphere of the room seemed to change as she swept in.

Dr. Joyner stopped them, and Grace watched him talking with Frank for a moment. Lorraine looked around, tossing back her mane of copper-colored hair, showing off the sparkling ruby necklace that was clasped around her throat.

Dr. Joyner's wife motioned to her husband, and he went to sit with her. Frank led Lorraine through the crowd, smiling and nodding at the guests, even white teeth gleaming beneath his heavy mustache and black hair, slicked back with pomade. He took her to the table, bent down to give his mother a kiss on the cheek and then sat down on the other side of her.

Every young woman in the room had her eye on Buzz. Even the ones who were dancing with other men watched him as he moved comfortably, a different girl in his arms for each number the band played.

One girl in particular seemed to be making eye contact with Buzz. Finally, she stepped up to him, flashing a brilliant smile and batting her eyes at him. He followed her to the center of the dance floor. Everyone watched the swinging fringe of her skirt as he whisked her around the room. She matched him move for move, her gleaming black hair flipping back and forth as she moved with graceful abandon. Grace sat watching, tapping her foot a little in time to the music, wishing she could dance like that.

After that number, the band went into the fast beat of the Boogie Woogie Bugle Boy. The girl stepped back from Buzz and began to twist and turn in time with the music. One leg went up in the air and came down hard on the floor, followed by the other as her hips rolled and swayed with the music, arms flailing out in rhythm.

Buzz grinned and began to copy her movements. Grasping her right hand with his, he whipped her crisply back and forth, twirling her in tight little circles. Gradually, the other dancers fell away to the sidelines and stood clapping their hands in rhythm as the pair ruled the dance floor.

When the number ended, Buzz carved his way through the crowd and returned to the family table. The girl kept staring at him, but he paid no attention. Grace watched her sit down at a table, eyes dark and lips pouting. It was only a matter of minutes before a young man took her back out on the floor but her eyes were on Buzz. It was fairly obvious that he had already forgotten about her.

Phillip slapped the Buzz on the shoulder. "I never knew you could dance like that; you've been holding out on us around here."

A slow grin spread across the trainer's face, and he shrugged his shoulders. "Just never took the notion, I guess."

Phillip laughed. "Yeah, well we never knew."

Buzz winked at Grace. "Lot of things you don't know about me."

Grace blushed and averted her eyes. She fidgeted for the rest of the evening, watching the dancers as Phillip talked with Buzz and different guests who came over to the table. The band began to play Sentimental Journey. They used to dance to that song, Phillip holding her close as they barely moved on the floor. She wished he would take her out there on the dance floor now.

But as usual, Phillip's mind was on business. She knew she should be satisfied, grateful even. Although though her husband was handsome, his manner was quiet, and he always seemed to be thinking deeply behind those calm eyes. He was sometimes overlooked in the presence of Papa and Frank, whose flamboyant ways sought every inch of attention that was to be spared, no matter where they happened to be. He was the kind of man who provided a foundation for the rest of the family to excel. The kind of man who was there, there, always there, whatever the circumstance. He was the one who always made everything all right.

So, she waited patiently for the evening to be over, when she could retire to the tower room with her husband. He would strike a match to the logs that waited inside the carved Breche marble fireplace and she would lie there on the floor, feeling the warmth in the flickering light as he sat, sipping a small glass of cognac. He would talk for a bit and even though she didn't understand some aspects of the business of Janus Farms, she loved to hear him. Papa wouldn't share much of anything like that with Mama. But Phillip was different and she was grateful that he thought she was important enough to have discussions with. She would close her eyes and listen to the rumble of his deep voice, so masculine, so capable. And eventually, the business of the evening would fade away and his mind would be on her.

THREE

January 3, 1942

Grace was the first one in the breakfast room. Phillip had been late last night getting in from town and hadn't gone to the stables, so he had been up well before daylight this morning in order to get an early start. Papa stomped into the room just behind her but as usual he didn't have much to say when they were alone.

Grace heard laughter in the hall and Frank came in with Lorraine and Mama, one arm around each. He pulled out the chair for Mama, then his wife, sat down and poured a dollop of thick maple syrup on a tall stack of pancakes. Papa began to question him about one of the fillies, how she was running. The women sat listening and, in a few moments, Phillip came in. Removing his cap, he sat down beside Grace. His leg brushed against hers and he looked over at her, smiling.

Papa set his coffee cup down. "Phillip, tell Grady he better figure out a way to keep that colt on the inside rail. I've had it with him running wide on the turns. In a tight race that could make all the difference. Just a few seconds can win or lose for us."

"He's been trying," Phillip answered as he slathered a spoonful of strawberry preserves onto a buttermilk biscuit and stabbed a thick piece of country ham with his fork. "We've used all the conventional methods. We're going to have to come up with something else."

"Seems to me like Buzz should get it taken care of." Frank shook his head. "After all, that's what we're paying him big money for. If he can't handle the job...well, why don't we get someone else?"

Papa stopped; his fork full of eggs in mid-air. "I don't want to hear any more of that talk. You know his reputation. He's been the top trainer in the whole country for the last ten years. If we lost Buzz right now, we'd be in trouble."

"But Papa!"

"But nothing." Papa put his fork down and looked Frank in the eye. "You heard what I said. Buzz is the best thing we've had going for us. You keep your mouth shut to him. And just remember, what Buzz wants is what he gets. He's our ace in the hole."

Grace could see Frank's jaw tighten but he didn't say anything. The only sound was silverware clinking on china.

"Frank," Lorraine said. "I'm going to need some money. I want to..."

"Sure, darling. That's fine." Frank picked up a crispy piece of bacon from the platter and dropped it when it burned his fingers. He looked across the table at Phillip. "But about the way that colt keeps drifting out..."

"I saw a dress in the window the other day at Cecilia's shop," Lorraine said. "I can't wait to try it on. And they've got the cutest hat to go with..."

Frank spooned a pile of scrambled eggs onto his plate. "Go ahead and get what you want."

"Well, I need some money. I've got a charge at Bella's Boutique but when I go to Cecelia's, I have to pay."

Frank stood up for a moment, removed his wallet from his pocket and pulled out a thick wad of bills. "Why don't you let Mama go in with you and set up an account at Cecelia's?" Frank turned his attention back to the men. "I don't see why Grady has such a hard time with it," he said. He picked up the bacon again and blew on it to cool it a little. "He ought to be able to handle it. I'm going to tell him we're getting someone else if he can't get it right."

Phillip stirred cream into a steaming cup of coffee. "You know how unmanageable that colt is, Frank. Grady's the best exercise boy we've got. If the jocks can't keep that horse on the fence, you can't expect Grady to."

Frank opened his mouth to answer but something outside caught his eye. Grace turned to look out the window and saw a truck. Hinson's Ferrier Service was printed across the side.

Frank laid his napkin on the table and pushed his chair back. "Hinson's bringing the special shoes I talked to him about." Standing up, he brushed his hand over his wife's shoulder, stopped to give Mama a quick kiss on the cheek and hurried out.

Mama shook her head and looked over at her husband. "Franklin, all this nonsense about those horseshoes," she said. "It's just a waste of money. What if one comes off out in the paddock and you can't find it?"

Papa drained his coffee cup and stood up. "I think we can afford it."

"But it's just silly," she responded. "Besides, it's just showing off a little too much."

"Oh, so the truth comes out. You need to stop worrying about that. You just let me handle it." He shook his head and looked at Phillip. "Women. Always thinking they know something about business and money. Much less how to run the largest thoroughbred racing farm in the whole country." Picking up his napkin, he wiped the coffee off his bushy, silver mustache and laughed. "That'll be the day, when a woman has enough sense to run the horse business at Janus Farms." He put his hat on. "I think it's a good idea the boy had, let's not stifle his enthusiasm. You ready, Phillip?"

Phillip squeezed Grace's hand and followed Papa out the door.

Grace went up and changed her clothes and hurried out to the stables with a handful of apple slices. Strange, she thought. Every pony in the barn was gone except Cloudy. She could see him looking over the stall door by the time she got halfway down the aisle. After he had finished the apple, she wiped her hand on the leg of her twill pants to get the slobber off and slipped the bridle over his head. His small ears curved inward, and she ran her fingers across his face, down to the tapered muzzle to the spot where his fine skin felt like the blue velvet dress that hung in her closet. The little horse followed her out of the stall and stood quietly as she ran a brush over his body. She loved the way the perfectly round, dark splotches ran through his white coat, almost in a leopard pattern. He was an

Appaloosa; Phillip had told her when she first came here. Despite his striking appearance, Cloudy was the most docile horse on the farm. He was one of the lead horses they used to pony the thoroughbreds out to the track, because his quiet demeanor helped calm them down.

Even though Grace's riding skills weren't very good, she loved being out on the back of the farm, just her and the little horse. There was no one to judge her plain appearance or her lack of social skills. She was glad that Lorraine had wanted to go into town today. She felt like these rides were hers and hers alone. It was silly, she knew. But it was her escape, time to be alone and just think. And she didn't want to share it. She had been getting corralled pretty often recently into showing her new sister-in-law the trails around the farm. Even though Lorraine was an accomplished rider, completely comfortable even on the high-spirited horses, she didn't really know her way around yet.

She threw the light saddle over Cloudy's back now and tightened the girth. He stood stone still as she put her left foot into the stirrup and threw her right leg over. She clicked her tongue and he walked off slowly. Once they were outside, she nudged him with her heel, and he broke into a little jog. They started down the path that led to the river and Grace glanced down towards the track. She saw now where all the ponies were. Standing and mounted, in a group in front of the gate. She realized that some of the calmer thoroughbreds were out there too. She had never seen so many horses on the track so she stopped to see what they were doing. It looked as though every hand on the farm was out there, mounted and waiting.

They were struggling to get Runaway Rapids into the gate. Buzz was easy to pick out, with his ever-present Stetson pushed back on his head. He was the only man Grace had ever seen that wore one, all the others wore caps or fedoras. The big, white dog that belonged to him walked back and forth, waiting for the trainer but he never ventured onto the track. She sat for a few minutes watching until the men finally wrestled the stallion inside.

Several of the men were guiding Big Red up towards

the gate, and Grace watched as they struggled to get him in. She could see the big, white dog that belonged to Buzz walking back and forth, waiting for the trainer but he never ventured onto the track. She sat for a few minutes watching until the men finally wrestled the stallion inside. Movement at the far end of the track caught her eye. Phillip was down near the far turn on one of the lead ponies, cantering back towards the head of the track. She loved to watch her husband ride. He never ran flat out the way the jockeys did, the fastest she had ever seen him do was a hand gallop. But there was something about the way he sat in the saddle, head up and heels down, moving with the horses. It always made her heart skip a beat to watch him. She would give anything if she could ride that way.

Pulling Cloudy up, she sat there watching as Phillip cantered up in front of the starting gate and joined the group of men who were waiting there, sitting quietly on their horses. What was he doing, she wondered.

As she watched, the other men pushed their horses up and followed Phillip a little way down the track and stopped. The group sat with their horses turned back towards the starting gate, waiting.

The bell clanged and Grace turned her head to see Big Red burst out of the gate. He immediately drifted towards the outside rail, even though she could see Grady pulling towards the inside. With no other horses on the course, it was easy to see the struggle between them. The exercise boy did manage to slow him down but he wasn't having much luck bringing him back towards the inside rail.

Then, as they neared the far turn, Phillip urged his horse into a canter, then accelerated into a slow gallop, followed by the other horses. They timed it just so all the horses, including the stallion would reach their turn simultaneously and box him in. As they merged, the entire group of horses surrounded Red three and four deep, forcing him off the rail and pushing him gently to the left, towards the inside. He had nowhere to go as they drifted down the track. He was blocked in on both sides, as well as in front and behind.

It seemed the idea was going to work. Around the field

they went, Red sweeping along, stuck in the center of all the other horses. Cloudy stomped impatiently and Grace realized she had been holding her breath. As they went into the far turn, she could hardly tell one horse from another. She could see Phillip out in front, still leading the way. Nobody else sat a horse exactly the way he did.

As they started up the backstretch and back towards the end of the track, Grace could see better. The stallion was still in the center of the bunch, but he was really putting up a fight now. He was tossing his head, veering from side to side and bumping the ponies beside him. This went on for a few moments and she could see that it was gradually getting worse. A chain reaction was getting underway and the horse Red crashed into would, in turn jostle the one next to him, sending a ripple effect through the pack. Finally, the big, red colt found an opening and dived through it, immediately veering towards the outside again.

They were almost home now and Grace watched as Red clung to the outside. He passed all the other horses and began to pull away from them. She could see Grady trying to pull him back but the colt was fighting hard now and refused to slow down. Even running on the outside, he swept farther and farther ahead of all the other horses and Phillip raised a hand in the air. They slowed to a walk and watched as Big Red crossed the finish line, still on the outside rail.

Grace saw Frank snatch his hat off and throw it to the ground. Papa pulled the cigar from his mouth and turned back towards the stables, shaking his head. Buzz stayed where he was, signaling to Phillip to ride towards him.

Grace urged Cloudy forward. She had only planned to go for a short ride but now she decided not to come back for a while. She didn't want to run into Papa because he was sure to be in a foul mood. And Frank. He would be storming around, cursing with every other breath.

If only they would have a little patience, like Buzz and Phillip. Surely this was a tactic that would have to be repeated over and over before they could expect it to work.

She jogged the little spotted horse slowly up the path,

wondering if Runaway Rapids would be ready for the Flamingo Stakes at Hialeah coming up. Racing in Florida was the big deal for the winter months. They would take the train down with the stallion and several of the other Janus Farms horses riding in the baggage cars.

It was all very exciting, she had to admit, even though it was a little overwhelming. First, there was the train ride. When she and Phillip were in their own private car, she was relaxed, able to enjoy her husband's company and marvel at the view of the countryside as they passed by. But they would also be spending a lot of time in the family car. They would take their meals there, the women sitting to listen as the men planned their strategy and spoke detailed racetrack language.

And then, when they arrived at their destination, there was always a great deal of sensationalism to be faced about Runaway Rapids and Janus Farms. The press was always around, taking photographs, lightbulbs exploding into their faces. And you had better be smiling, the entire time. It didn't matter if it all made you nervous or if you weren't feeling well. Papa expected you to put on that front that characterized Janus Farms.

Lorraine had no problem; she was really in her element with it, but Grace preferred the home races that were run at Janus. She would still be expected to represent the family, but at least it was on her home front and that made her a little more comfortable. Janus Farm Racetrack was just as huge and elegant as any other in the country but at least she knew her way around. When they had to travel to all these distant places, she kept a little, gnawing sensation in the pit of her stomach that she would be swallowed up and lost, never to find her way home. That was silly, she knew. But, if she had to pick a track to go to, it would be Hialeah. It was so different down in Florida, so pretty. It seemed more relaxed than a lot of the other big tracks. She loved the sights and sounds there, so different from North Carolina. Even the course was unlike any other she had ever seen; the infield had a little lake where hundreds of pink flamingoes hovered. It wasn't like the other races they went to, where there was nothing but hustle and bustle.

But down at Hialeah, it seemed almost like another world.

Grace turned Cloudy as they came to the river and pulled him down to a walk. The water tumbled over the rocks; a muddy red color stirred by the swift currents. The Native Americans had named it the Roanoke, the word for death. "Don't get too close," she had been told all her life. "The elevation levels drop so fast, just upstream at Roanoke Rapids, it makes the river dangerous," was the way Phillip explained it.

The wide path that ran down beside the river was ideal for riding. You could see the wild, untamed beauty of the river. In places, a huge crevice was visible in the earth that ran by the waters. It had been a canal, one of the few that had been dug in the South. The town of Roanoke Rapids had been built around the transportation made available by the river. But in this section, the river was so dangerous that it was impossible to navigate. So, a canal had been carved out that ran alongside it to bypass the rapids. And this path had been worn by the mule and horse teams that had towed the boats downstream until they could merge back onto the main river and use the swift current to carry them on their journey.

She thought now how the river reminded her of the young stallion, Big Red. Runaway Rapids was his registered name. Sired by the world-famous Renegade Rapids, he seemed to fulfill the lineage of his father. It was true that he was wild, unmanageable, full of fire and spirit. But he lacked the bad temperament of Renegade, he just wanted to run. If only they could harness that energy and keep him running straight, there was no horse on earth that could beat him, Papa always said.

Cloudy fell back into a walk and Grace just let him go at his own pace. Her legs got tired from pushing the little horse forward. Besides, they were in no hurry. It was another warm day, unseasonable for January. The sun beat down through her jacket and the regular rhythm of the horse's gait was soothing. She felt as though it could almost lull her to sleep.

Her thoughts turned to the early part of the previous evening. The family had gathered in the main living room to listen to President Roosevelt's State of the Union Address. Everyone in the room was silent, waiting to hear what he was going to say.

Even though the entire business of war was a little frightening to Grace, she thought the president had done an excellent job with his speech. Instead of using fancy political words he had used simple language that anyone could understand.

She rode along, trying to imagine what it would be like if Phillip had to join the armed services. She could hardly fathom the fear of the young women whose husbands were shipping out, not knowing if they would ever make it home again.

She had watched Papa as he listened, leaning forward in his easy chair, elbows propped on his knees, fidgeting nervously. He would sit back every so often to take a sip of the brandy he had sitting on the coffee table as he chewed on his cigar. She knew what he was thinking; how was this war going to affect Janus Farms? Frank sat by Papa, biting at his nails in that way he had whenever he was required to sit still. Even Phillip sat silently, his brow furrowed, and Grace supposed that was the thing that had actually made her feel so uneasy about it.

As the speech had gotten longer, her mind had begun to wander, and she didn't remember everything the president had said. The one thing that had stood out to her was the fact that he had mentioned these changes were for the progress of all generations to come. As she rode, Grace thought about what a strong statement that had been. Those changes were not only for the present, she thought, but far, far into the future. And she wondered what the future would hold. For the family, for her and Phillip. For Janus Farms.

FOUR

Spring 2021

Holding the halter behind me, I shake a bucket of grain and the horses come trotting up from the pasture, across the carpet of bright yellow buttercups that cover the ground. I have decided to use the Haflinger for this morning's session. He is from one of the smaller draft breeds, I suppose that must be where their quiet disposition comes from.

The medication makes me feel like I am in a constant state of being in a strange zone somewhere between sleep and wakefulness; just hard to function. My head hurts constantly, and the nausea is almost unbearable. I sure don't feel much like chasing horses.

I am hopeful that he will be easy to catch but alas, no such luck. He trots down behind the big barn in the back, where wild kudzu has nearly covered the South wall. I follow slowly, shaking the feed so the noise will tempt him. Finally, the Haflinger walks over, drops his nose into the bucket and I slip the lead line over his neck, but he jerks away and canters off.

Don't want to work today, huh?" I shake the bucket, urging him back. He trots further away, forcing me from the shade of the trees and into the bright sunlight. It pierces my eyeballs, and the heat makes the nausea worse. I rattle the grain, urging him closer. This time I get the rope around his neck, and he follows calmly. He stands quietly as I bridle him, head drooped, and eyes half closed.

I check my phone for the time. My volunteers were supposed to be here fifteen minutes ago. There are special saddles, some with high cantles rising behind the seat to support riders whose trunks are not stable enough to sit up on their own. The volunteers know which ones to use but some of them don't have a lot of experience with horses.

Just then I see a bright yellow jeep bouncing up the path at top speed. It turns in at the stables and comes to a stop with a jerk and a woman steps out. She approaches so quickly that her long ponytail bounces where it is pulled through the back of her ball cap.

"Hi," she says. "I'm Jennifer. Sorry I'm late." The passenger door opens, and another woman gets out. "That's Sandra," she informs me. Sandra's shorter figure approaches a little more sedately and she smiles warmly.

Jenifer glances over at the horse, standing in the crossties, just inside the barn. "How did you know we'd be using Diesel?"

"He just seemed like the safest choice."

Movement catches my eye and I turn to see a maroon sedan driving up the path.

"Here's your first client," said Jennifer. "Landen."

The passenger door opens and I see a small figure sail out. A woman gets out of the driver's side and hurries after him. "Landen! Wait!"

Scuttling off towards the pasture, the child climbs the fence. He reaches the top rail, teeters for a moment there, and drops into the pasture. Jennifer and Sandra are close behind him and Jennifer snatches him up just before he runs behind the big Saddlebred.

"R-i-i-d-e!" he shrieks, arms and legs striking out. "R-i-i-d-e horse!" Jennifer flinches as his heels come in contact with her shins but she doesn't loosen her grip.

"Landen!" his mother calls as she hurries across the field. "Calm down."

"It's okay," Jennifer says breathlessly as they approach the stable. "We've got him."

"I'm so sorry…" the woman begins but Jennifer shakes her head and smiles.

"It's all right. Really. We'll just give him a few minutes."

She and Sandra each take one of the boy's arms and guide him towards the Haflinger. When Landen spots the horse, he tries to jerk his arms loose.

"D-e-e!" he shouts. "D-e-e!"

Yes," Sandra says. "That's Diesel."

"R-i-i-ide D-e-e!"

"We have to put your helmet on," Jennifer says. She nods at Sandra, who moves behind and grasps both arms. His mother holds his head as Jennifer buckles the straps. Landen is struggling but the three women work together until they have him ready.

"Okay," Jennifer nods at me. "Bring Diesel over."

I release the crossties and the horse follows me into the arena. Sandra lifts the child into the saddle and moves to the right side of the horse, placing a hand on Landen's leg. Jennifer does the same on the other side.

"Okay," Jennifer says. Move out."

I lead Diesel away from the gate and sneak a glance over my shoulder. As soon as the horse begins to move, Landen becomes still in the saddle. His hands move to the horse's mane, fingers twining through the long, blonde hairs and his facial muscles relax. His eyes are still now, focused straight ahead. He is making little noises in the back of his throat, but it is nothing like the previous shrieking.

What have I gotten myself into, I wonder as we circle the arena? Me, of all people. I never had much experience with kids, other than a few baby-sitting jobs. And I never knew exactly what to do so the children didn't respond very well to me. I wanted them to like me, but I just didn't know how to make it happen.

And now I am supposed to know how to deal with children who have special needs? I had expected to work with kids who couldn't walk, or...well I don't know what I had thought. But I have never even been around anyone with autism. Surely that is what Landen has. Attention deficit I've seen, lots of kids are hyper, but I don't have any medical training. They need someone that has the knowledge to handle it, someone a lot better than me. My throat tightens. How will I be able to help these kids?

I glance at Landen's mother and wonder what her life must be like. Her face is haggard and worn and I wonder if she ever gets any rest. My heart goes out them both, but I am simply not the person who can help them. I have no skills, no knowledge and surely, they deserve someone better than me.

I'm going to have to find a different job.

A few more kids come, and they are easier to handle. Jennifer and Sandra guide me through it and the session is finally over. But I feel like such a failure.

~ ~ ~

After everyone has gone, I am left alone at Janus. Grace's nurse has taken her into town for a doctor's appointment.

I still feel sick, but the afternoons are better than mornings. The pounding in my head has subsided to a dull ache and the nausea is almost gone. Wandering into the kitchen, I pour a glass of iced tea and take it up to my room. I switch on the laptop I had found in the office. But the service is so slow. I google an article on equitherapy. I felt so inadequate out there. I am the one who is supposed to be in charge, yet I mostly stood around watching as the volunteers took care of business.

The pace of the internet crawls along and I grow increasingly frustrated. Watching the screen as I scroll is making me dizzy. Finally, when I have to quench a desire to throw the computer across the room, I get up. Clouds are coming in and we are supposed to have some showers but no serious storms, so I have left the horses out. They have the run-in shelters, but most horses would rather stand in the rain and keep grazing.

I cannot help but think of my own horse, the training business Cole and I had built. And then came the affair. I left that first time in a flurry of the most terrible rage. I remember, an anger so violent that my vision turned dark and hazy. As the days had gone by, I had become sick. Everything I had eaten had come back up. I was hardly sleeping and when I did, the recurring nightmares attacked over and over. The anxiety medications had made me so sick. Finally, they discovered I had a genetic defect that prevented me from metabolizing them. The only thing I could take were opioids. And I had no idea how addictive they were. I had ended up in a detox center. A living hell is the only way I can think to describe it. I had gotten discharged and lived in a miserable, tiny rundown apartment, slinging burgers. So now, I am struggling to find some medication to help me. Because I am determined I will ever end up in that shape again.

I had passed a room that housed a library this morning. I had taken a wrong turn, ending up in a wing that didn't seem to be in use anymore. I had only gotten a glimpse, but it looked pretty big. When I was growing up, I loved going to the public library and checked out several books every week.

Libraries. I hadn't thought about them in years. With so much information on the web, I guess they are becoming less popular. But now memories come flooding back and I realize that I miss the feel of an actual book in my hands, the smell of ink and paper. Maybe it will help me try to focus on something besides my situation if I go down and explore the library.

The massive oak door stands partially open, just enough to peer through. The hinges groan as I push it wide and step through. There, in the dim shadows I see shelves spanning three of the walls, the fourth lined with glass shelving that contain trophies. Everything is covered in thick layers of dust. The russet carpet must have once been a vibrant red. A table lurks in the center of the room with a beautiful box of rosewood squatting on top, delicately inlaid with ivory. I open it and it is filled with fat cigars. Then I see something moving there and slam the lid shut, realizing it is a huge spider.

I strain to push back the silk brocade drapes and a thin strip of sunlight edges its way in. Using the heel of my hand, I go around the edge of the windowsill, hitting it until I feel it loosen and raise it. Maybe fresh air will help with the musty odor. Most of the books seem to be very old. Jane Eyre and other books by the Brontë sisters, Victoria Holt and Daphne du Maurier. How I used to love those classic gothic novels as a pre-teen. Funny, now here I am living in a house that reminds me of one those eerie old castles in the stories.

In places, the cobwebs are so thick I have to brush them away to read the spines of the books. It is such a dismal place that I am turning to leave when a section along the far wall catches my eye. It is simply labeled JANUS.

The books that actually have to do with Janus Farms are on the upper shelves. Halfway down the wall is a ladder on rollers. I retrieve it and it screeches along in the rusty tracks. Climbing the ladder until I am nearly even with the heraldic stained-glass windows at the top, I scan the titles. My eye stops on a thick book titled, THE HISTORY OF JANUS FARMS by Lorraine Masterson. Pulling it down, I go over to one of the wing chairs by the fireplace and sit down to open the book.

The first thing that catches my eye is a collection of old black and white photos, sepia images, trapped beneath the yellowed cellophane. People peer out at the camera; horses stand with ears pricked and heads held high. Women pose in padded shoulder jackets, classy, wide-brimmed picture hats and men stand behind them in snappy fedoras.

I flip through, stopping to read captions. Some of the races were held at the Pimlico track in Baltimore, a few down at the old Hialeah Park in Florida. It seemed that most of them had been run here at Janus.

A young woman stares out of the page in a lot of the pictures. She is slight of frame with a plain face under a fluff of brown hair and serious eyes. In several of the photos she smiles just a little at the camera, her mouth turned up more on the left side. I wonder if this was Grace. A handsome man with blondish hair swept to the side was usually beside her and I suppose that must have been her husband.

A sudden burst of wind blows the curtain and I look up to see that the shaft of sunlight is gone. I hear raindrops begin to pelt against the windowpane and the wind blows harder.

Many of the photos are in the winner's circle, jockeys astride tall thoroughbreds, necks covered in a blanket of flowers. I keep seeing one man that looks so different. While the others sport the snappy fedoras that were so popular during those days, this man wears a western hat. Usually, he is grasping the horse to help the jockey hold him still. Everything about him exudes a male sensuality. Even from the stillness of the photograph, he gives you the impression of being a man with a very powerful presence.

I try to read some of the captions, but the light is so dim. And straining my eyes is making my headache worse. I'm going up in a few minutes and I'll take the painkiller then. I'll just glance at a few more of the pictures.

Color photos begin to be interspersed here and there. A striking young woman with a wild mane of red hair smiles at the camera from nearly every image. An older woman often stands between the two girls.

A sudden downpouring of rain pelts hard across the window and startles me for a moment but I am so focused on the pictures I barely notice.

In some shots there are two men beaming at the camera, each with a hand on a trophy. The younger man has dark hair slicked back and a heavy mustache. The other man is an older replica of him, with a greyish-black mane of leonine hair brushed back. He always has a cigar in the side of his mouth and a fancy handkerchief tucked into the breast pocket of his suit.

I have a sudden yearning to read this book. I'm going to take it up to my room. But I look back up and see so many more books about this place. I pull out an armful and take them back to the table.

Several are photo albums from the early forties. Amazing, I think, how everything looked so grand. Some of the albums are full to overflowing, pictures falling out that were never fastened in. It seems we have all been guilty of that. Sticking in a little pile of photographs and intending to put them into place later. Then we forget. Of course, now we just click away with our smart phones, taking pictures every day. We plan to store them into electronic files, save them to our cloud, label the card. And we never get it all done. Sometimes, the more things change, the more they stay the same.

I pick up another book and it seems to be a visual record of big wins. Many show the entire family, some show just the horse and jockey. But in each picture, the center subject is a trophy.

Noting the details of the trophies, I look up at the glass

cabinets and am able to match the photographs to the trophies enclosed there. One is tall with colts and fillies cavorting around the base. Another is low and stout, the base made up of three horses, standing at attention in different directions to form a triangle. They support the bottom of the cup on their broad backs while a larger horse perches at the top.

As I turn the last few pages, I see a trophy very different from the others. It is taller and is topped by the same emblem I have seen in various places around the house and grounds, the two-faced horse. The other thing that stands out is the fact that while all the other trophies were gold, this one is a bright silver color.

Turning back to the case, I search for the trophy, but it is nowhere to be seen. Strange, every trophy in the album is on display except this particular one. I thumb through the book again and notice the trophy in the picture sits at the center of the mantel over the stone fireplace. But it is no longer here, the mantle sits empty and dark.

I have been so focused on the pictures that I hardly noticed how much the wind has increased. The change in the barometric pressure is affecting me and my head is throbbing harder than ever. The vertigo is back, and it makes my head feel as if everything is spinning. This is one of the main side effects of the medication. I lean my head against the back of the chair and close my eyes. As long as I am still, the throbbing in my temple subsides a little. I sit here, thinking I probably should have shut the horses up, but I feel so dizzy, I don't think I can go out there now.

I begin to wonder what Grace's life had been like. I felt sure that must have been her in some of these pictures. And that trophy. So strange.

I startle as thunder booms close by and lightning flashes through the window. My head aches so much I don't even feel as if I can put the books back on the shelves. I am certainly not going to climb that ladder. I'll come back later and return the other books to their rightful places. I pick up the book titled Janus and start up to my room.

FIVE

January 12, 1942

Taking a match from the table, Grace struck it and touched it to the kindling under the firewood that had been laid waiting in the fireplace of the library. She curled up in one of the deep, purplish-red armchairs by the stone fireplace and looked out at the rain as she flipped through the book she had chosen. She had read this one but so many of the books on these shelves were over her head. Others were books she had loved to read when she was younger but now, they seemed a little childish. Her Aunt Ada, who had raised her, couldn't read and write. Grace had asked her once how she knew what was in the jars of herbs she kept stacked on the shelves of their little cabin. Everyone in the little community came to her for her healing knowledge.

"Just do," Ada had answered. She had picked up one of the quart canning jars and unscrewed the lid. Holding it under Grace's nose, she said, "Now take a little whiff of that. Mullein leaf. See how they smell?"

Grace had sniffed it and nodded. It had a deep, pungent fragrance.

Ada had pulled a leaf out and crumbled it between her fingers. "You just got to have it all in your head," she had said. "The look, the feel of it all and it won't never leave you."

Grace had finished one chapter in her book and started on the next when the heavy door creaked open. She looked up to see Buzz stride into the room. He looked so out of place in here, with the wide Stetson hat in his hand, boots sauntering across the plush carpet. She had seen him enter the library before. He was the only employee that was allowed to come and go inside the house and Grace knew Frank resented what he called "those special privileges."

Buzz often took meals with the family or came into the living room to watch when they aired special television programs. Phillip had told her Papa was a little nervous that they could lose Buzz if they didn't get back on top pretty soon, so he was inclined to go overboard trying to make the trainer feel as if he was part of the family. Grace had never been in here when he came and she didn't know what to say.

"Morning, Miss Grace." He nodded and the slow, easy smile spread across his face. "It's a good day for reading, not too much we can do out at the track until it dries out some." He shivered. "Cold out there, too."

Grace got up and moved away from the fireplace. "It's warm over by the fire," she said as she turned towards the bookshelf.

"Who's your favorite author?" he asked.

"Oh. I don't know." Her face burned. He would think the books she read were childish. Or too old-fashioned. Finally, she held the book to show him the cover.

"Emily Brontë. I read part of that. More of a woman's story, I guess what with the romance and all. I like Steinbeck, Hemmingway."

Grace stood up. "I'd better get on up..."

"Don't go," Buzz said.

"Well, I don't want to be in the way."

"You're not bothering me, Miss Grace. Fact is, it's really nice to have someone you can discuss literature with." He grinned. "That bunch of knuckleheads down at quarters, I don't think they read anything but the comics. They wouldn't know a good piece of writing if you hit them upside the head with a two-pound book."

Grace smiled. She liked talking to Buzz down at the stables. But the library was just such a secluded place. It made her nervous.

But he moved over to block her way. "Seriously Miss Grace. I don't want to feel like I'm running you away. I'll go if you're uncomfortable."

"No! I don't want you to feel like you have to leave on my account." She sat back down.

Turning, Buzz swept his hand through the air. "All these

books, I never lived anywhere that had such a collection."

Grace nodded. Aside from Phillip and the horses, the library was one of her main pleasures here. "I know. All I have to do is walk right down the stairs and here it all is."

Picking a book off the shelf, Buzz sat down in a rocker, opposite her. She could see the title. Historical Events in Pictures. He flipped through, stopping now and then to gaze at something that drew his interest.

"Do you ever read non-fiction?" he asked.

Grace shrugged. She usually stuck to novels.

"I like to read about things that have actually happened," he said. "Go back and remember the past. The Revolution. The Great Depression. And just think. Pretty soon, people will be reading about the hardships of World War II."

"I know." Grace looked down at the book in her hands. "It all seems a little frightening." She stopped, suddenly embarrassed. "Sorry, I shouldn't go on..."

Buzz smiled. "No, you're just saying what we all feel." Getting up, he crossed the room and returned with a book of poetry. Grace could see that it was fairly new. You could even smell the fresh leather of the cover.

"There's a poem in this collection that really stands out for me." Buzz sat down in the rocker. "I've always liked poetry, but this particular piece touches me like nothing I ever read."

"What's it about?"

"The author talks about things you feel when you are flying a plane, how is to escape from the world," he replied. "Those sensations, they're just hard to explain. But he sure nailed it." Not wanting to reveal her ignorance, Grace simply stared down at him.

"I don't think many people even know about this poem yet. It was written recently by a WWII pilot. He talks about ... well, stuff like I do with my little plane sometimes ...a lot of things that no one but a pilot would really understand. Want me to read it to you?"

Grace nodded. Anyone could see his enthusiasm, to decline would be impolite. She listened as he began to read about the emotions of soaring into the sky. But she wasn't really catching the words. What grabbed her attention was the look on his face. Complete absorption, engrossed in the lilting metaphors, lost to the library around him.

That was the way it used to be with Phillip. He would read to her for hours. The raw masculinity of his deep voice had never failed to send a little shiver coursing through her veins, but when Phillip had read the romantic lines of Wordsworth, Shelly, and Keats, it had taken her to a whole different level. It made her feel as though they were floating along together, hovering above the earth, in a magical realm. That was the way Buzz looked now.

Grace hadn't even realized how much she missed this. Back when they were courting, Phillip would bring a picnic and they would ride out to spread it beneath the big willow at the pond. After they ate, he would pull a volume of poetry out of his saddlebags and lie with his head in her lap, reading aloud as she watched the horses nibble on the tender grass shoots. She remembered now how she used to lay her hand flat on his chest because she loved the way she could feel his deep voice rumble there.

But Phillip never seemed to have time for anything now. During the last year, Papa had been turning over more of the responsibilities of Janus to him. Papa still liked to stride about, puffing, and blowing, great Lord of the manor he had always been. But Phillip took his position seriously. Their overall relationship was still good, in fact it had only grown better over time. Grace blushed as she thought how inexperienced she had been when she first came to Janus as his wife, so fearful at first. But Phillip had taught her things...and it had only gotten better.

But she missed the little things that used to lead up to those nights. She yearned for the way Phillip would talk or read, no one else around, all his attention focused on her. And now, from dawn until past midnight the only times she ever saw him was at meals or the stables, always focused on Janus Farms. The next race. Winning. Growing. Changing. Would it ever be enough? Especially in this last year when the big wins just hadn't been there.

Grace turned her attention back to Buzz just as he read the last few lines. The words were really beautiful, she thought. When it was over, she simply sat quietly, trying to absorb the full emotion of the thoughts.

Buzz didn't say anything either. He got up and went over to the enormous globe that depicted the surface of the earth, opened a little compartment, and pulled out a bottle of brandy. Taking a heavy crystal snifter from the table nearby, he poured two fingers worth and opened the top of the heavy rosewood and ivory box. Pulling out a fat cigar, he struck a match on the heel of his boot and lit up.

"Have you ever heard anything like that?" he asked.

"Not exactly," she said. "There are a lot of poems I love, but that was really sort of different. And to think, it was just written recently. Most of the poetry I know was written long ago and this author seems to be, I guess it's like... almost a part of our lives."

"I know!" Buzz leaned forward, the glow in his eyes almost as strong as the one at the tip of the burning cigar. "Of course, I suppose it's the flying that makes it so personal for me."

Buzz had his own airplane, a little Cessna that he flew just for pleasure. He had told Grace once that his father had been a crop-duster and she asked him about it now.

"Yeah, Dad worked a lot of the big farms down Texas way. Used to take me along pretty often."

"He sounds like a wonderful man."

"Oh, he was the greatest. And between seasons, he would pick up work at some of the big ranches, breaking horses. Worked mostly with quarter horses."

"Quarter horses?" Grace asked.

"They make the best cow ponies. Quick, agile. Really fast to start and stop. Spin on a dime. Calm little critter that can come to life and split the wind like a thunderbolt when you ask him to. Fastest horse in the world for about a quarter of a mile. But then the thoroughbreds will pass them every time. They don't have the size, the long stride and stamina the thoroughbreds do."

"So, you prefer the thoroughbreds?"

"No. Every breed has its own qualities. Take the heavy drafts. Two thousand pounds of muscle, yet they're as quiet as the day is long." He blew out a smoke ring and chuckled. "Nature sure is smart."

"What?"

"Can you imagine if the Clydesdales and Percherons were as vicious as some of the tiny Shetlands can be? Biting and kicking, just when you let your guard down. We'd be in trouble, for sure. Kill us dead as a doornail."

Grace smiled. He had a good point.

"And take Cloudy, that little horse you use for trail riding. Appaloosas, the breed the Native Americans rode. Speed, stamina, loyal to a fault."

"He is a good horse. I'm not such a great rider but he's so gentle."

Have you ever seen a Saddlebred?"

Grace shook her head.

"Peacock of the show ring with that high-stepping action. So collected though, they could canter all day in a spot no bigger than the shade of an apple tree. And the Tennessee Walkers... Sorry. I get carried away. Whether it's planes or horses. Didn't mean to bore you."

"No." Grace shook her head. "I don't know much about planes, but I do love everything about the horses. I never knew about all the different breeds."

"Well, I won't go on. But I will tell you I owe my success as a trainer to the quarter horse. I train the thoroughbreds to get out the gate quick like a quarter horse. That way, we've got the leisure to use whatever strategy we've planned after we get the advantage over the rest of the field. Fall back, stay ahead or run with the pack, it's all easier then." He tapped the cigar over the ashtray, sending ash flying about. "Now if I can just get Big Red to start cooperating."

"I've never known anyone like you," Grace said. "You've had the most thrilling life."

Buzz nodded. "I'm a lucky man. I always had an exciting ride. Whether it was in the saddle or in the sky. But I can tell you this. It ain't ever been boring."

They laughed easily together just as a ray of sun appeared from the tall windows and streaked the carpet. Grace hadn't even realized the rain had stopped.

Buzz stood up. "Didn't mean to go on like that," he apologized. "I hardly let you get a word in."

Grace smiled. "I liked hearing about all that adventure.

And the literature too. Next time it rains, you come back. I'll probably be here."

And any time you want to take a plane ride, just let me know. We'll take off and just 'wander up yonder' for a little while."

Grace blushed a little. She could imagine what Papa would say if she went up with Buzz just for a joy ride.

As if he were reading her thoughts, Buzz nodded, gave her a broad grin, and left.

SIX

January 27, 1942

Grace gazed out the window of the train, watching as the scenery flashed by. The furnishings of the dining car were elaborate, and the filet mignon was so tender that she only had to touch it with her fork, and it fell apart.

She listened as the men planned the strategy for the Flamingo Stakes. Buzz was with them, and the other employees were in a separate dining car. They were traveling with three jockeys and a few of the handlers. Besides Big Red, another colt and a filly from Janus Farms were back in the stock cars.

Buzz cracked open a lobster, picked the white meat out with his fork and dipped it into butter sauce. "The jocks know what the plan is for each race," he said. "Out the gate quick, then each one has his game plan. Jimmy is to hold Red and wait for the straight part of the track. That's where we'll really pour it on."

"What about Charlie?" Papa asked. "Are you absolutely sure he knows how to take Rapid Lady Fire on up and set the pace?"

Phillip broke in. "He does, Papa. We've been over it so many times at home. Buzz has drilled it in his head, and he's got it down pat."

"The one we've got to worry about is Bounty Money," Frank said. "He's the one we've got to watch. And that Manning, he knows exactly how to take Bounty Money through this race."

Buzz nodded. "He's the one, all right. But Red can take him, as long as we can keep him running straight."

The men were still talking when Grace excused herself to go to their private car. Mama went along with her, but Lorraine stayed to listen.

WHERE THE STATUE WEEPS

Grace put her nightgown on and laid down, but she wasn't really sleepy. She was too excited and nervous to go to sleep. Of all the tracks the family went to, Hialeah was her favorite. It had been named the world's most beautiful racecourse. Everything was so different down in Florida. It was enormous, like all the tracks but for some reason, it seemed like a relaxing place. She supposed it was the palm trees and the warm atmosphere. The blue jasmine vines hung from the front of the stands, descending like the fancy folds of a skirt. The balmy atmosphere seemed sort of what a vacation was supposed to be. As the rhythm of the train rocked her gently, she eventually grew drowsy and by the time Phillip came to bed, she was already asleep.

~~~

When the family arrived at the track, the stands were already filling up. Grace looked out towards the center, gazing at the flamingos. She stood underneath a palm tree, taking in the deep fragrance of jasmine, savoring the tropical paradise until the family had to go to their box. It felt so good to be somewhere warm, after the few really cold weeks they'd had in North Carolina. Hialeah, she thought, home of thoroughbred racing for the winter months and the playground for the rich and famous. The track had the reputation of being the most beautiful race course in the world. Movie stars and royalty were often present. The Duke and Duchess of Windsor had been here. And this was where Amelia Earhart had her last public appearance before beginning her flight around the world back in 1937. Buzz had told her that story the day they talked in the library.

After an interminable wait, the bugle calls finally blasted through the air and they could see the horses heading to the starting gate.

"There's Bounty Money," Phillip pointed. "See the one with the blue and white colors of Johnson Stables, number four?"

Grace nodded. The big thoroughbred walked quietly
~~~

through the crowd and that surprised her. "He seems pretty calm," she said. "After all the track talk, I had expected him to be quite a handful."

Phillip shook his head. "That one will fool you. He's pretty steady but when he gets going, he pours it on. He's got a really long stride and they say he just keeps plowing on like a tank. Johnson's been on a winning streak with him for quite a while now."

Then Grace saw the red and gold colors of Janus Farms out of the corner of her eye. She had to strain to see which horse it was. Jimmy was on Big Red with Grady and Cloudy beside him. Red pranced beside his stablemate, shying out from the crowd. She could see Buzz and Grady trying to help the jockey get him in the gate.

"This is one to watch out for, ladies and gentlemen," The announcer's voice came over the speakers from the broadcast booth. "Number seven, Runaway Rapids of Janus Farms. The big, red colt from Carolina. Looks like he's a bad boy when it comes to lining up. He's giving his jockey, Jimmy Brinkley quite a bit of trouble!"

Runaway Rapids was so fractious that the horses behind him had to wait. He reared and plunged sideways. Buzz caught hold of his bridle and the horse took several steps backwards. Buzz walked with him until he stopped, then urged him forward. Then, just as he was about to enter the gate, the colt reared high in the air, lost his balance, and fell backwards.

Grace could feel her heart in her throat as the crowd let out a collective gasp. If Jimmy got pinned under the big horse...

But the jockey was moving quickly, leaping back into the saddle as the horse came to his feet. Grady pushed Cloudy in close until he was nose to nose with Runaway Rapids and the colt seemed to calm down. Cloudy walked quietly up to the starting gate and the big, red horse followed him. Grace held her breath, but the colt continued on into the gate and Buzz slammed the barrier behind him as Grady turned Cloudy to get him off the track.

When Runaway Rapids realized Cloudy was going the other way, he went wild. It was difficult to see exactly what was happening. Phillip, peering through the binoculars, let out a string of curses so Grace knew it was pretty bad. She had her hand on his arm and she could feel how tense his muscles were even through the fabric of his light jacket.

"Stop it, Red," he muttered. "Come on, calm down, save that energy. Papa! He's gone down!"

Grace's heart was pounding. God, they were bound to get hurt. Both of them, horse, and rider. How can a horse go down in the gate without a serious injury? But then, she felt Phillip's arm relax a little and if she squinted really hard, she could see the colt's head.

"Looks like they're okay." Phillip said as he pulled out a handkerchief and wiped his brow. "Wish they could hurry up and get going."

But Red delayed the start for nearly ten minutes. The jockey fought gamely as he tried to bring the horse under control. "Okay, Jimmy, you've got him now," she heard Phillip say under his breath.

The buzzer sounded, the gates clanged open, and she heard the announcer shout. "And they're off and running, ladies and gentlemen! Oh, pay attention here! Runaway Rapids is just getting out the gate, he's a good eight lengths behind the last horse, getting off to an awkward start." The crowd gasped as the big red horse slewed to the right and reared again. It only took Jimmy a few seconds to get him under control and running straight but by that time he was twelve lengths behind.

"Blast it!" Papa shouted. "What the cuss are you doing, boy? Can't you hold that son-of-a-gun?"

"Come on, come on," Phillip said. "Just straighten out."

As if Big Red had heard him, he leaped forward and in a matter of seconds, he began catching up to the rest of the field. His stride was enormous, eating up the ground, gaining on the last horse.

"Well, that was an unruly start for Runaway Rapids," the announcer boomed. "But Jimmy Brinkley finally got him under control, and it looks as if he still may be in the running. Look at that, ladies, and gentlemen. He's really starting to move up. Just watch that Carolina Colt now, he's pouring it on. Beats all I've ever seen!

"Now it's Bounty Money of Johnson Stables in the lead, just as anticipated," the announcer shifted his focus. "We all know he's the favorite here today and I'd be surprised if he wasn't up front. That's the way the Big Cash Bomb runs, he just charges to the front at the beginning of the race and that's where he stays. Always been a front runner. Manning is one of the top jockeys and he knows just how to handle the Cash Bomb. And Crowned Hope is running two lengths behind. The Cincinnati Cyclone is on his tail, looks like he'll be in the money now for sure."

The horses swept down the track, tightly packed except for Red, who was still trailing behind the last horse by several lengths. But he was closing in quickly.

"Now Runaway Rapids is starting to move up," said the announcer. "Look at the big guy go! He's barreling down, about to catch the others as they approach the first turn. Just look at him stretch it out! He's gaining ground quickly now."

"Come on, Red," Phillip muttered. "You can catch them. Go!"

"And now, Rapid Lady Fire, the filly from Janus is pulling up even with Savannah's Sapphire. Look at them hoofing it, they're neck and neck. Now, she's passing him, she's a nose ahead, now half-length. Charlie Rawlings is taking her right on through. Just because she's a filly, doesn't mean she can't run with the boys. Look at her, just gouging great, big chunks out of the air, she's really stretched out. That's what they say about the Janus horses, they all have an enormous stride."

Red was steadily gaining ground. Maybe he *was* going to be in the running, Grace thought.

"And what about Savannah's Sapphire?" the announcer asked. "Looks like he's starting to fall back and Cincinnati Cyclone is coming back up into third place. No, he's not giving it up, he's pulling up behind Rapid Lady Fire again. But One Grand Dude is trailing him, a close fourth.

"Now just look at Runaway Rapids! He's hotfooting it down the track now, pulling even with the rest of the field. It's the Carolina Colt, Big Red! He's knifing his way, watch him now. They're weaving between the other horses, going up to battle with the leaders." Now Phillip was squeezing Grace's hand so hard it was cutting off the circulation. He waved his program through the air with his free hand. She could hear Papa on the other side of him, his booming voice raised above the rest of the crowd.

"The Dude just passed Savannah's Sapphire," the announcer cried. "And he's moving up on Rapid Lady Fire. But she sure is giving him a run for his money. She's starting to pour it on again, now she's pulling away and he's starting to fall back. But just look at her stablemate, Big Red. He's coming on steady, ladies and gentlemen, he's just grinding through the rest of the pack. Passing the Sapphire now and gaining on The Dude.

"Now they're heading into the far turn and Runaway has passed Rapid Lady Fire. He's pulling up even with Crowned Hope and going on ahead. Look at that stride, I think it's the longest stretch I've ever seen. And now he's gaining on Bounty Money, oh boy, he's looking and cooking now! Bounty Money is still a couple of lengths ahead, but Runaway Rapids is steady coming up. Brother, he is killing it! It's a backstretch duel now, ladies and gentlemen; they're matched stride for stride, breath for breath. They're coming on strong, who's it going to be? The Big Cash Bomb or the Carolina Colt?

Indeed, they were running even, Grace thought as they ran the next two furlongs like a pair of lovers locked together. Phillip was still holding onto her hand, nearly crushing it.

"They're running nose to nose! How long can they go on like this?" the announcer cried. "On and on, they're battling down the track, look at them pouring it on. And now Runaway Rapids is starting to pull ahead, inch by inch! Looks like he's leading now by a nose. Still creeping up, he's a head in front, now half-length. And they're almost at the wire. Big Red is still pulling ahead. Manning is going to the bat now; he's lashing Bounty Money, but the Big Cash Bomb is falling back!"

Pulling his hand out of Grace's, Phillip put his arm around her and nearly crushed her in his grasp. Now he was shouting nearly as loud as Papa and Grace lost a shoe as he pulled her off her feet. She glanced down and saw it falling to the ground through the stands, but it didn't matter. They were in first place now; Runaway was going to win this race. This is what they had been hoping and praying for.

Then Grace felt Phillip's body posture change a little, and more than hear it, she felt a little sigh escape his lips. What was wrong, what was happening? As she strained her eyes, she could see that Runaway was drifting out towards the right.

"No!" Phillip shouted. "Not now, he can't do this now. Straighten him up Jimmy! Pull him back to the inside! Don't you do it, Red. Don't you..."

But the colt veered out further as the crowd gasped. "I can't believe what I'm seeing here," the announcer's voice boomed over the speakers. "Janus Farms had it wrapped up, but Runaway Rapids is pulling to the outside and now Bounty Money is moving up on him. The Carolina Colt, he's a wild one, they say. Hard to handle. Brinkley is fighting him, he's pulling over with all his might, but the big, red horse isn't having it.

"And Bounty Money is catching him, he's inching up, they're almost there, they're nearly to the wire, less than twenty yards to go. Neck and neck now, they're coming on in. And the Big Cash Bomb is creeping up and here we go! Looks like Johnson Stables is going to stay on top. IT'S BOUNTY MONEY BY A NOSE!"

~~~

The mood was somber on the trip home. There hadn't been any big wins in over a year now. It was only the long-standing reputation of Janus Farms that was really keeping them in the public eye right now.

Phillip always said not to worry, that every farm goes through its dry spells. Just like any other business, ups and downs. It had been two years since Janus had owned a horse that was really extraordinary. But they did now. And if they could just get Runaway Rapids under control, they would probably be back on top again. Jimmy Brinkley
~~~

was one of the best jockeys they'd had in a long time and Phillip had been counting on his ability to keep the colt on the rail.

Papa was a different story, though. Every time they had a big race coming up, he was so sure that this would be the one. For most of his life, the farm had been on a never-ending winning streak. Just as it had been with his ancestors, dating back into the late seventeen hundreds. And now, the last really outstanding horse they'd had was Runaway's sire, Renegade Rapids.

Runaway was a lot like him, Phillip had told her. The colt was fast as a streak of lightening, unpredictable, hard to handle. The only big difference was that Renegade had possessed an ornery spirit, ill-tempered and sometimes vicious. Big Red had the same fiery passion for running but had never really tried to harm anyone. So, Phillip had assumed that it would be pretty easy to get him under control. But stubborn and strong-willed as he was, the jockeys just couldn't seem to put him where they wanted him. In one race after another, he lost time for them by fighting the jockeys. Runaway Rapids was so gate-sour that even when it opened, he was fighting too hard to start quickly. Determined to run wide, he refused to stay near the inside rail, costing precious seconds that put him behind.

Most owners were pleased whether it was win, place, or show. As long as they were in the money. But not Papa. He always had to be on top, had to be the best. His mood now was so foul that all Grace could think about was how long it would be until she could escape from the private dining car and get away from him. She just hated taking meals on these trips.

The two waiters came in, trays laden with their brimming plates. Grace nodded her appreciation as one of them put her chicken cordon blue down in front of her. She sat, watching the steam rise from it as she waited for everyone to be served.

They ate in silence for a while, the clacking of the train wheels the only sound that filled the car. It made Grace nervous, and the food seemed to stick in her throat.

As they were finishing their desert, Papa slammed his bowl down on the table. "I thought our dry spell was about over. But I guess it's not."

"We didn't do that bad, Papa," said Phillip. "We were in the money. We placed pretty well."

"I know that! But we were always on top. And by God, we've got to find a way to get back up there again. The right jockey, that's what it's going to take. We've got to find someone who can handle that stallion." Picking up his tumbler of bourbon, he strode out the door, leaving the family sitting at the table.

Grace looked over at Phillip, but he was staring out the window as the scenery flashed by. She would be glad when they were home. At least then she would have some space to herself.

SEVEN

February 2, 1942

The family sat in the living room, watching the television broadcast. Frank got up and poured a snifter of brandy, then offered Phillip one. Phillip shook his head. "After supper," he said.

"Do you boys know where your father is?" Mama asked. "It's not like him, being gone at this hour of the evening unless something special is going on."

Frank shook his head and took a long swallow of the amber liquid in his glass.

"He was down at the stables a couple of hours ago," Phillip answered. "Said he was going to meet somebody in town," Phillip said. "I'm not sure who."

Mama smoothed the front of her dress. "I guess he can eat at the restaurant, if he doesn't get in soon."

Frank got up and crossed the room to turn the volume up on the television. The newscaster was talking about the automobile factories. The president had asked them to stop production back in January and frozen the sale of consumer vehicles. They were concentrating on preparing the factories for the building of military weapons.

"It's amazing how quickly this idea is getting underway," the newsman said. "This plan, only a month in the making looks like it will be a surefire success. President Roosevelt has asked the automakers for their help and they are quickly rising to the challenge. They are retooling the factories and preparing for the building of tanks, ships, airplanes and torpedoes." The camera view switched to show a clip of the president visiting one of the factories.

"Look!" Lorraine pointed towards the television screen. "A woman working in the factory! I've never seen that before."

Phillip nodded. "I've been hearing a little about that. The factories are starting to hire a few women because so many of the men are going off to fight. Seems they're doing a good job at it, too."

"Well, I think that's...it's absolutely admirable," Lorraine said. "Don't you, Frank?"

Frank looked over at his wife and rolled his eyes. "Craziest thing I ever heard." He gave a little snort. "Just think, women pretending they can do a man's work. That'll be the day."

Lorraine got up and started out of the room. She stopped by Mama's chair. "I'll be back down in time for supper."

Phillip put a hand on Grace's arm and whispered, "Always got to be a little drama with her. Here we are with our country in the middle of war and even still. She's got to be the center of attention."

Grace gave him a quick smile and turned away. She hoped no one else had heard.

~~~

Papa strode into the dining room accompanied by a slightly built man in a business suit. He pulled his hat off and Grace noticed his hair stood up in little brown tufts all over his head.

"Hoot, I want you to meet my family." Papa extended his arm and the man sat down in the appointed chair.

"You know my son, Phillip here." Phillip reached over to shake hands. "His wife. That's my other boy, Frank and that pretty lady is his wife, Lorraine."

Grace couldn't help but notice that he hadn't even mentioned her name. Each person nodded a greeting.

"And this is our head trainer, Buzz."

The man's eyebrows arched at the mention of Buzz's name. When he spoke, his words were clipped and quick, in contrast to the drawl common to the area. "I know, Buzz Timberlake," he said. "By God, what do you say! I've always wanted to meet you. Your training is pretty much legendary."
~~~

Buzz put his glass of sweet tea down. "And I know who you are. Hoot Harrison. American's number one jockey right now."

Hoot nodded vigorously. "Got lucky a few times, I guess. I've been able to ride a couple of the great horses. It was more of them than me that made those wins."

"Ladies and gentlemen," Papa raised his glass. "The only man in history that has ever won the Derby back-to-back with a horse that was running against the odds. He makes them sit up and take notice."

"Sounds like you're changing your mind about the Derby, Papa." Frank said. "So, are you ready to do that now?"

Papa shook his head. "Just because they're running some fast horses out there does not mean we're going. We're staying on the east coast where horse racing belongs. With the caliber of people that run in our circles."

Grace knew what he was talking about. Phillip and Frank had both been trying to get Papa to enter the Kentucky Derby. But he was determined to stay in the east, where racing had developed among the wealthy. It seemed to her he contradicted himself sometimes. Always talking about change but on this particular matter he was so stubborn he wouldn't even consider it.

Phillip just smiled. "Well, it looks like Janus Farms is pretty well set. We've got the best of the best. And with a horse like Runaway Rapids? These two working together with him? No way we'll ever lose a race."

"Hey, you guys." Hoot threw his head back, clapped his hands together and laughed. It was a high-pitched sound, loud and sort of screeching but pleasant to the ear. And it was infectious. Everyone at the table was smiling now. "I can hardly wait to get started."

"Now that's what I like to hear, a man who's ready to get to work," Papa boomed. "Because we'll be out on the track at five-thirty in the morning."

The jockey raised his eyebrows. "What say?"

"The horses run best early," Buzz explained.

The jockey shook his head and raised his glass. "Always heard you guys down South here get up with the chickens.

Guess now I'll see for myself. Well, if you guys do it, I can too."

"Well, it was cloudy today," Buzz said. "We'll take that as a good sign."

Hoot looked at him and it was obvious he didn't understand the remark. Papa's laughter echoed throughout the room. "Groundhog couldn't see his shadow. That would have meant six more weeks of winter."

Hoot laughed. "You guys have a lot of superstitions down here." He picked up a chicken breast from his plate and took a bite. Big chunks of the crispy, brown crust flaked off and he scooped them up with his fork. Juice ran down his chin. "Mmmm," he said. "Best fried chicken I ever tasted. You guys eat like this all the time?"

"Pretty regular," Papa answered. "Work hard, got to eat hard, too,"

"Could you pass me another biscuit?" Hoot asked Grace. She passed the plate, and he took two, then topped them with butter and added a spoonful of preserves that had been put up from the cherry trees in the orchard out back.

"They put buttermilk in these biscuits, you say?"

Papa nodded. "Didn't know they made them any other way."

"Back home, they just mix a little water in with the flour. They sure don't taste like this." He laughed; that screechy, pleasant sound. "Don't you dare tell my mom I said that."

"What's your real name?" Lorraine asked.

Hoot swallowed the bread he was chewing. "Horace." He made a face. "Guess you see now why I just go by my nickname."

"Never ran into many of you all from up North with a nick," Buzz said. "That's usually something you see down here."

"Actually, it was a guy from Alabama that christened me. Johnny Wood. You know?"

"He was winning big a few years back," Frank said. "Rode some of the great horses. Took Combat General to the top."

"Yeah, he is some good rider." Hoot nodded. "His father rode for Tillery, too. Way back. And his grandfather rode the legendary My General."

"But tell us why he calls you Hoot," Lorraine said.

"Well, I guess it started at the jockey club up in Baltimore." He looked at Papa and Phillip. "You know, the one near the Pimlico course?"

They both nodded.

"Anyway, we were having a pretty good time up there one night. Most everyone was drunk on their...excuse me ladies," he nodded politely. "We were all pretty tipsy. And Johnny, he got laughing and called me Hoot Owl. I'm sure you noticed I blink a lot more that most people. And when I tie one on, it gets a lot worse. The name stuck and that's okay with me." He grinned broadly. "Besides, you got to admit, it's a heck of a lot better than Horace."

As everyone laughed at the story, Grace realized there was a lot of truth to the comparison. With his diminutive size, the little hook nose, blinking eyes and tufts of hair sticking up, he did look a bit like an owl. And when he laughed, he sounded a little bit like one, too.

Paulette came in with a great, steaming dish and put it down in the center of the table. Hoot grinned at the maid, and she blushed behind her Irish freckles and hurried back to the kitchen.

Steam wafted from the dish and a delicate, brown crust covered the top. Thick, golden juice ran down over the sides.

"That looks good," Hoot said. "What is it?"

"Peach cobbler," Mama answered. "It's our favorite. The men would eat it every day. But with the sugar ration, we've had to cut back on deserts a little."

Phillip nodded. "Cook is proud of her cakes and pies. Having to limit them gets that Irish temper up. Makes her so mad, I believe she could fight the war herself, just to get her sugar back. You should hear her when she gets going about it, that Irish brogue she has gets so thick you can hardly understand her."

The little man took a generous helping, then dipped his spoon in and tasted it. His eyes rolled up in his head and he put his hand across his chest. "Man, I never tasted anything like that. I've had peach pie, but this is something out of this world."

"Fresh picked peaches," Mama said. "Right off the tree. Makes all the difference."

"I'll say." Hoot was scraping his plate clean. Think I'll have a second helping."

The jockey kept them entertained for the next hour with outrageous tales of the goings-on in Baltimore and New York. He would stop now and then to rub his stomach and stretch. "I'm going to have to watch out. Looks like Janus Farms can be a pretty dangerous place."

"What do you mean, dangerous?" Frank asked.

Hoot laughed and rubbed his stomach again. "This Southern food. It could be a bad habit for me. I think I'm hooked already."

"Tell us what it's like in New York," Lorraine begged.

"Well, I don't really know what to say. A lot busier than it is down here in Carolina. Especially here around Roanoke Rapids. You know, I've never lived in such a rural place before. But anyway, up in New York, cars all over the place, bumper to bumper. You could hardly get a cat's whisker between them. So many people you can barely get down the sidewalk. I guess it can be a pretty exciting place sometimes. Depends, I guess. On exactly what part of New York, you're in."

Lorraine's eyes grew wistful. "I've always wished I'd been born up. In New York, I mean."

Hoot shook his head. "Not where I grew up, in Brooklyn. Some parts of New York are, well...different up there." He tapped his forefinger to his temple. "Got to have street smarts."

"Pretty tough, huh?" Frank asked.

"A little. But that's what I give the credit to, you know for my winning streak. Got to get out there and fight. On the streets, the track, wherever you are. Just give it all you got. Funny though, most of the jocks, you'd think we were mortal enemies until we'd get back to quarters. Then we're pretty good pals."

After dinner, the ladies retired to the drawing room.

Lorraine sat down at the piano, picking at the keys a little.

"Go ahead and play something, dear," Mama said. "There's nothing more soothing before bedtime than a little music". Mama picked up her needlepoint, swinging her foot gently in time with the soft notes as she worked.

When they heard the men come up the hall and enter the billiards room, Lorraine got up off the stool and flounced down on the maroon sofa. She pouted as she fingered the crushed velvet. They could hear the sounds of the heavy brandy bottle hitting against the glasses and the aroma of tobacco was drifting across the hallway.

Lorraine went over to the doorway and stood, listening. "I don't see why Papa won't let us come in there. I know how to shoot pool."

Mama looked up, raised an eyebrow, and let out a soft sound, somewhere between a snort and a laugh. "Don't you let him know that. Come on over here, the new Sears and Roebuck catalogue came, and they've got some pretty little dresses, just for everyday wear."

That pacified Lorraine and she began to browse through the pages. They could hear a sharp cra-a-ack now and then as the pool sticks connected with the balls over the men's voices. Grace couldn't make out everything they were saying but she could identify the unfamiliar accent of Hoot speaking quite often. Raucous laughter exploded from the room at regular intervals.

"I think our new jockey must have saved some of the more risqué stories for after-dinner talk," Mama said as she got up and closed the door.

EIGHT

Spring 2021

I am finishing the first stall, with a barnful to go. We had some of the horses in last night because it stormed. A few are still in, waiting for the children to arrive; but this morning is beautiful, and the grounds look freshly washed. I just wish I felt well enough to enjoy it. My head hurts, a dull ache that never goes away but it is so bad in the mornings. I feel hot and dizzy, even though the morning is cool.

These drugs the doctor gave me. If I don't take them, I lie awake all night and that makes me feel horrible. If I do take them, they make me so sick. Other people seem to be able to tolerate something to calm their emotional problems. But with this genetic disorder, I can hardly metabolize anything.

And the hallucinations are making me wonder if I am crazy. Maybe I'm not, because the doctors have told me that is one of the side effects of the medicine. But normally, I just have the recurring dreams about leaving Cole. The physical aching to be with him. The fear of being alone and homeless, no idea where I belong or what I should do. But since I have come to Janus Farms...I don't know, it's very different. These crazy things that I am imagining that go on in this place. I have never had upsetting visions unless they had to do with Cole. And it always happened while I was sleeping. I never saw things when I was awake, not until I came here. And they seem so real. But that's silly. They couldn't be.

Probably just because it's such a spooky old mansion, I tell myself. Dark and dreary. Falling down around us. Just like the castles of the old Victorian novels. No wonder my mind keeps playing tricks on me, living in a place like this. I am going to ask the doctor if he can change my medication again. I just wish somebody would do something to help me be able to function like a normal person.

Just as I step into the aisle and turn the wheelbarrow towards the back of the barn, someone calls my name. "Miss Morgan, is that you?"

I turn to see a petite woman walking towards me. She is slender and pretty and smiles openly.

"I'm Laura Britton," she says, holding out her hand. I rub mine on my jeans and stick it out awkwardly, but she grasps it warmly. "I know we're a little early, we usually are."

I open my mouth to respond but a tiny figure catches my eye at the front entrance. It is a little girl, wearing pink western boots. A string of pink flowers is tied around her head.

"That's my daughter, Maggie Mae."

The child continues towards us, stopping to stroke the face of every horse that peers over the stall doors. She speaks softly to each one and I can't make out what she is saying. Finally, she reaches us, looks up and smiles. I can see now that she looks like a miniature replica of her mother.

She waits patiently for a couple of minutes as her mother explains that she had a mild scoliosis of the spine, she is five years old and has been coming to Janus Farms for the last two years.

Finally, Maggie Mae reaches up to tug at the bottom of her mother's blouse. "I'm going to get my pony."

I am surprised when the woman nods, reaches down to stroke the child's head, and continues to talk. I don't want to be rude, but I am watching out the corner of my eye as the little figure marches away. Finally, I turn and grab a lead line from a hook on the wall. "I'll just go with Maggie Mae," I say looking back over my shoulder. "Which pony does she ride?"

"Valentine," the woman calls after me. "But she can get him."

Maybe, I think. But no five-year-old is going loose on my watch.

"Wait, Maggie. I'm coming with you," I call. The little girl stops and waits until I catch up, then smiles up at me as she brushes a stray piece of hair off her face and tucks it under the flowered string. She clutches a couple of apple slices. She chatters about Valentine as we walk down the path that leads to his pasture. She speaks calmly, not what you would expect from a five-year-old.

When we reach the gate, Maggie Mae clambers up on it, reaches up and is just able to reach the latch. She opens the gate, holds it for me and closes it behind us.

"We have to make sure the horses can't get out," she explains, and I nod.

When Maggie Mae spots Valentine behind a copse of trees, she puckers up her lips, frowns mightily, fills her cheeks with air and begins to blow. A little squeak comes out, but it is loud enough for the pony to hear. His head comes up, he turns and walks towards the child. As he approaches, I see that she holds her hand out flat. The proper way to give a horse a treat without having your fingers go along with it. He takes it gently with his soft lips and stands chewing. Maggie Mae puts her arms around his neck and lays her cheek against him. When he is done, she kisses him on the nose.

It is easy to see where the pony got his name. He is a light chocolate color with one white patch on his left flank. It is shaped exactly like a heart.

They stand there for a moment, the child's arm around Valentine's neck and then she turns and marches off towards the gate. The pony walks, not behind her but beside her and I stand here watching, holding the lead line in my hand.

I trail behind as the pair walk up the long path. Side by side. Not like a horse and rider but like two friends. Equals. Just taking a stroll down a little country road.

Jennifer is waiting with Mrs. Britton at the stables. We watch as Maggie Mae walks out to the arena, the pony beside her, unbound, matching her step for step. Jennifer opens the gate and scoops the child up, setting her gently on the pony's back.

Riding bareback doesn't surprise me; children often

prefer it but no bridle? Not even a halter? Absolutely no means of control? But the little girl clutches a handful of mane, clucks, and the pony steps out. He walks slowly down the fence line to circle the arena.

Maggie Mae still holds the hank of mane, but her balance is incredible for a five-year-old. You can almost see a tangible connection between the two. I have seen adults ride bridleless, have even done it quite a few times myself. But this is something else entirely. Not master and subordinate, but a completely equal partnership. Two friends, each taking care of the other, secure in the relationship. And then it hits me. This pony has no idea he is even being ridden.

I can't find the roller bit I am looking for, so Sandra comes into the tack room and opens a cabinet. "It was in here last time I saw it," she says. She pulls several out but can't find the one I was looking for.

We go through the drawers with no luck. Finally, I see an old box that is filled with odds and ends, a couple of rusted old bits lying on top. I dump the contents on the counter, a conglomeration of moldy old halters, brushes that have lost most of their bristles, a couple of bottles of linseed oil that have long since dried up.

Sandra comes over and picks up a small trophy out of the pile. She stands there for a moment. Looking at it. The brassy color is tarnished with age and little pieces are chipped off the edges.

"You know," she says. "My grandmother used to tell me stories of something that happened out here. I was so young I had completely forgotten about it. But now..." She stands there holding the trophy and for a moment it seems she has forgotten I am here.

Then she turns to me. "Someone was murdered here on the farm. A long time ago. And the weapon was supposed to be a trophy."

"That little thing?" I ask. "Why, it's hardly big enough to do much damage with."

Sandra shakes her head. "No, this just made me remember. It was supposed to be a very special trophy. It was solid silver and had an emblem of the two-faced horse on top. You know, like the ones all around the farm."

I suck in my breath. "I saw it. Or at least a photograph of it. In a book in the library. And all the other trophies are there. But I didn't see the one with the two-faced horse anywhere. I wondered about it, but I never would have imagined..."

"I had forgotten all about it," Sandra says. "I couldn't have been more than four or five because Grandma was the one who always told the story and she died before I started first grade. Mom didn't like for anyone to talk about it in front of me because it gave me nightmares." She turns to look at me. "I remember sometimes we would just be out for a drive on Sunday afternoons and pass by here. I would see the two-faced horse up at the highway and it would scare me so much I'd climb up into the front seat between Mom and Dad."

Jennifer is calling Sandra, so she drops the rusted little trophy back into the box and goes to see what they need her for.

After everyone has gone, I go up to take a shower. Then, as I pull off my sweaty jeans and the tee shirt that has horse slobber on the sleeve, I glance over at the bathtub. A huge, claw footed thing, nearly deep enough to swim in. A good, long soak would be so relaxing.

I don't have any bath salts, so I just dump in a little shampoo and soon the tub has risen nearly to the top with warm, fragrant bubbles. I sit down and lean back, the bubbles coming up to my chin. I close my eyes and lie here. I keep thinking about what Sandra had told me but all that had been a long time ago. Enough problems in the present without wondering about the distant past. This feels so good. I try to let my mind go blank, not really thinking of anything. I should learn to meditate, maybe take some yoga classes. I lie here until the water cools off and still, I don't want to move. Lifting my foot, I use my toes to gently turn the knob for the hot water and it trickles in, steaming a little. Closing my eyes, I almost feel as though I am floating.

I must have nearly gone to sleep when the distant memory returns and I jerk awake! No, NO, NO! Stop it, I say out loud, but the images won't go away. It had taken me nearly a year to get over the addiction and my body had begun to adjust. My best friend, Rachel had told me Cole wasn't riding anymore. She had begged me to go with her to a show and I finally gave in. I was standing just inside the entrance watching her perform. I turned to walk out to get my horse and suddenly, there he was. Sitting on his horse, watching me. I had stopped dead in my tracks.

He had cleared his throat. "Hey, Jo. I wanted to talk to you."

He had pulled his foot from the left stirrup and held his hand down to me. Without thinking, I had simply stepped into the stirrup and swung up. God, help me. I never said a word, I just swung up behind him.

My arms had automatically tightened around his waist as he turned and jogged out of the covered arena. He nudged the horse and broke into a canter and then…and then there was nothing else in the world, nothing but the fact that we were together. Loping along in that old familiar rhythm. My breast was pressed up against the thin fabric of his chambray shirt. And I was home again. I had closed my eyes, just feeling the rocking canter of his horse and we were out on the street, weaving in and out of traffic. The iron horseshoes hit the pavement with a sharp sound. Clickety-clack. Clickety-clack. Over and over. The rhythm was so soothing. My heart swelled and I felt as if we were floating, soaring into the sky. After a while, he slowed to a jog and we rode for a long time, never speaking a word.

Finally, after a few miles, the terrain became a little more rural and then suddenly we were coming into a side trail from Umstead State Park, where we had ridden before on so many lazy Sunday afternoons.

Cole stopped at a creek. I slipped off and he dismounted quietly, taking me into his arms and covered my lips with his. I melted. Could hardly breathe. Dizzy with wanting him. The world was spinning, and everything became unfocused. There was nothing but Cole and me.

We barely spoke all evening. He had said he wanted to talk, but there was no need. We just lay on the mossy bank, limbs entwined and holding each other tightly. Any time one of us made the slightest movement, the other tightened their grasp. I wanted to be able to melt, to be absorbed by his skin, to be a part of him so that nothing could ever separate us again, not even for a moment. Towards dawn, he had finally risen to his feet and called a friend to come over and trailer us back to the complex.

And just like that, we were together again. Jo and Cole. Cole and Jo. The way it had always been. We were riding the circuits again and that was when we had started the training business. And I had believed him when he told me it would never happen again.

Shivering now, I get out and wrap the big, soft towel around my middle. I dry my hair and the warm air blowing across my skin feels good to my chilled body, but my nerves are taut.

Slipping into a pair of clean jeans, I sit on the edge of the bed. Why can't I just get over it, I wonder. How in the world can it affect me this way? All the millions of men in the universe. Why does it have to be him that stirs me so? Only him.

The music is so soft that I only gradually become aware of it, and I am not sure where it is coming from. I cannot make out the words, but the tune is just vaguely familiar. You know the feeling, when you hear something your parents or maybe your grandparents listened to when you were really small. It must be coming from Grace's room.

I go over to the window and look down at the horses. My mind goes back to that evening we spent on the creekbank at Umstead. I wish it had never happened. If only I hadn't gone to that show. Or if I'd had the strength to just walk away when Cole rode up. I wouldn't be in this shape now.

The music is a little louder now and I can make out a word or two here and there. Something about a kiss. Like it was nothing special.

Maybe to some people, I think. I used to believe that before I met Cole. Back then, a kiss *wasn't* anything you couldn't live without. I had kissed quite a few men. And lots of boys when I was a teenager. But I could always take it or leave it. Break up and stay friends. Was very fond of one that I had dated. But there was nothing earth-shattering about his touch, his kiss. I had never known what it was like. To have that depth of passion. Until Cole.

The volume of the music is growing louder and louder. Finally, I get up and walk down the hall. It is increasing to an ear-splitting volume. So loud I cover my ears with my hands. The sound pounding so hard now that I can't separate the words. Something about a sigh. As I continue down the long hall, the voice sings something about the passing of time. I reach Grace's room and look in and the music stops suddenly. A screeching noise grates on my ears, the sound that a needle makes when you scrape it across a vinyl record and then all is silent.

Grace is lying on her bed. Strands of hair have come down, loosened from the pins and fine, white wisps spread out across her pillow. She is napping peacefully. Seems like that noise would have woken her. She may be old, but there doesn't seem to be anything wrong with her hearing. I look around the room but don't see a record player or any kind of device that plays music.

I go back to my room and look in the mirror. Dark circles under my eyes. And my jeans are hanging, sliding down, the seat baggy. Most women would love to lose a little weight, but I look awful.

God, I think. I am just hearing things. A kiss. Those words going through my head. I think I have heard that song in an old movie. Don't remember the name of the movie, though. I shake my head, trying to clear my thoughts. I've got to stop thinking about his kisses. It's literally driving me crazy.

Finally, I get up and look at the calendar to see which patients will be here tomorrow. That is what I am thinking about when I hear my phone buzz with an incoming text. I had sent Denise a message with a question about the farrier. He is coming out tomorrow and I know Sundown has to have a corrective shoe. His left front foot turns in, but since they have been using that shoe, he doesn't have any trouble.

Assuming it is Denise, I open the text without really looking.

It is Cole. He has to see me, he says. I lay the phone

on the desk and walk back across the room. I'm just going to stand here and watch the horses a little longer, I tell myself. But I go back and pick the phone up.

"I know there is nothing I can say that will erase what I did," I read. "But please let me come talk to you. I just want you to know how sorry I am. I need to sit down with you, face to face and ask your forgiveness, even if you never want to see me again."

I stand here holding the phone. Staring at the wall but not really seeing anything. Time just stands still. For a few moments, the only thing is the present and I am vaguely aware of my breathing. Breathe in, breathe out.

The phone suddenly quivers in my hand with another incoming text, and I drop it on the floor. I don't know if it is broken, and I don't care. I am across the room in a flash, and I slip through the door. I can hear the sharp clicks my boots make on the hardwood floor, but it seems as if they are coming from somewhere else. The only thing I can think is that I have to leave. Cole has a hold over me, such a strong hold. And I have to get away.

"Just go!" a voice whispers in my head. "Leave, wherever he is, get away. If you agree to see him, you'll give in to him; you know you will."

And I know the words the voice whispers are true. If I agree to see him, there will be no talking. I will simply look at him and he will put his arms around me, kiss me and that will be the end of it all. I cannot let it happen again. I don't understand the hold he has on me; I just know I cannot go through it again. I hear the ring tone of my phone. Now he is trying to call me. I don't want to hear his voice.

Speeding up, I reach the banister and start down the spiral staircase, taking the steps two at a time. I am nearly at the bottom when my heel catches on a piece of loose carpeting. I catch the bottom of the railing but not in time to break my fall. I tumble headlong into the great room, breaking the two-faced horse off the head of the banister. The left side of my face connects with the scarred hardwood floor and for a moment I see stars. I try to draw a breath and it doesn't come. I clamber to my feet and take a step as my lungs struggle for air.

Finally, I am outside. I don't know why, but I just feel the need to keep going. Walking quickly, down past the stables, around the corner of the barn. The horse in the end stall startles, lifting his head and snorting. I turn down the path that leads to the river.

By this time, I am winded, and I slow down to a normal walk. And I realize now that I am still holding the figure from the broken banister, the head of the two-faced horse.

NINE

February 14, 1942

"**W**hat are you going to wear to the show tonight?" Lorraine asked.

Grace shrugged. She hadn't really thought about it. She was just so glad that Phillip had agreed to take time off to go to the movies at the Regal Theater in Roanoke Rapids. She didn't know what was playing. All Frank had told them was that it was a big surprise that he had set up.

"I can't decide." Lorraine let out a little sigh. "I really wanted to wear my pink chiffon. But I don't know, it *is* Valentine's Day. And Frank loves it when I wear red. What do you think about that red one I bought last week? You know, with the full satin skirt and the sweetheart neckline."

Grace shrugged. "They're both pretty." She didn't mention the fact that she had gotten so tired, sitting with Lorraine for nearly an hour, sipping tea and nibbling at the little lemon cakes as they watched the salesgirls traipsing back and forth, modeling nearly every dress in Bella's Boutique. They would come out in the striking outfits, moving gracefully across the floor to glide onto the raised platforms. It was fun for the first ten minutes or so to watch but then it had begun to get pretty boring. And then, when Grace thought it was nearly over, Lorraine had begun to try on her favorites out of the selection.

Dresses, skirts and blouses, jackets, sweaters. Hats, gloves. Shoes to match every outfit. High heel pumps. Low pumps and flats. Matching sets of jewelry: necklaces, earrings, bracelets, and rings. If Grace had remembered how long it would take, she would have stayed home. Bella herself had come out to greet then. She usually stayed back in her offices working, but when anyone from Janus

75

entered the shop, she would suddenly appear. She was always gracious to Mama but when she saw Lorraine, she knew her biggest sale of the day was about to happen.

"You should try on that blue dress," Lorraine had urged. "You know, the one that flared out when the girl twirled around. I know blue's your favorite color and it would look so pretty on you, Grace. I just loved those little pearls around the neckline."

She had kept on until Grace had finally tried the dress on. She stood in the fitting room, staring in the mirror until Lorraine had insisted that she come out. It was pretty, Grace thought, but it was just so fancy. Not quite like those outfits that Papa always insisted she wear to social events, but it just wasn't her.

"But it looks great on you," Lorraine had said. "Now hold your shoulders back, stand up straight." The salesgirl had met Grace's eye and smiled, rolling her eyes a little and Grace was grateful.

But then Lorraine had stepped closer and lowered her voice. "Grace, I think you should try on one of those padded bras. Sometimes they really help, you know?"

Grace had felt the color creep up into her face, wondering if the salesgirl had heard. She had rushed back into the fitting room and put her own skirt back on, then sat in the corner until Lorraine had made her purchases.

"Oh, we're taking that blue one, also," Lorraine had informed the clerk before Grace could protest. By the time she was finished, it had taken two clerks to help them carry the purchases out to the car and the trunk was packed so full they had to put some of the bags and boxes in the back seat.

"Be careful with those hat boxes, please," Lorraine had asked the clerk. "Let's be sure they don't get all crushed. I just love the little turquoise one that has the pearls on the veil."

"You just have to wear that new dress," Lorraine insisted now. "It looks so good on you."

"I don't know," Grace replied. "I thought I'd wear something a little plainer, maybe my..."

They were interrupted by footsteps in the hall. "Where's

Cook?" It was Hoot's voice. They looked up to see him go by carrying a bouquet of flowers so huge that his face was barely visible. They could see the tag from the florist in town but couldn't tell what it said.

Paulette came out from the room across the hall, straightening her maid's cap. "She's in the kitchen. Why?"

Hoot plucked a single flower out of the bouquet, handed it to the maid and put an arm around her shoulder. "How about get her for me, will you? And this one is a peach-colored rose for a peach of a girl."

Paulette giggled, sniffed the rose, and pushed back a tendril of curly blonde hair that had come loose from its bun. "Have a seat in the parlor here," she said. "I'll go get her."

"Hi girls," Hoot looked up when he noticed Grace and Lorraine watching him. "Are you coming out to ride today?"

Grace just shook her head, wondering what he was up to as she followed Lorraine into the parlor. Just as Lorraine started to speak, footsteps came rushing down the hall and Cook appeared in the doorway, pulling at the apron tied around her plump middle, dish towel still in her hand. "Is something wrong?" she asked.

"Everything's right as rain," Hoot answered as he handed her the flowers. "Happy Valentine's Day."

Cook stood there, not knowing what to do.

Grabbing the plump older woman, Hoot spun her around in a little dance across the Aubusson carpet.

Her round cheeks, already flushed with the heat from the stove, turned a deeper shade of pink.

"You're my best girl," Hoot declared. "I don't know how I got through my entire life without ever having any of that food you cook."

"Oh Hoot," she said. "Go on with you."

"I'm serious." He grinned at her and winked back at the girls. "Say, if I get Mom down here for a visit, will you give her some cooking lessons? When I go back up North, I've just got to have someone that knows how to make your Southern dishes."

Cook smiled and flapped her dish towel at him.

"Anyway, I just wanted you to know how much I enjoy

it." Putting a hand on her shoulders, the jockey stood on tiptoe and stretched up to give her a kiss on the cheek. Giving the girls a little wave, he turned and went out the door, leaving Cook standing there, one arm holding the great bouquet, the other hand on her cheek as if to hold the little kiss there as long as possible.

Grace did end up wearing the new outfit that evening. She felt a bit overdressed but as she looked into the mirror above her dresser, she realized how pretty it was. And it was going to be a big evening. Frank had told them it was something really special and Lorraine had kept insisting that they really do it up in grand style. She clipped her hair back and dabbed on some light lipstick. Grabbing her little evening bag, she started out the door and then went back. That perfume that Phillip liked so much. She sprayed a little of the deep, flowery fragrance on her neck and wrists, took one last glance in the mirror and left the room.

Phillip was in the living room with Frank and Papa, listening to another of the fireside chats. Buzz and Hoot were there, the men drinking brandy and smoking cigars. Phillip stood up and pulled a chair out for her without really looking directly at her. But Hoot gave out a little whistle that made her blush. And then she saw Buzz staring at her. She had never had a man look at her that way. Phillip used to look deep into her eyes, so that she could feel his love, but this was something entirely different. Something that was...purely sensual. She had never experienced anything like it, and it made her uncomfortable.

She moved a little closer to Phillip, but as they sat here listening to the radio, she found herself remembering that day in the library. The poem Buzz had shared with her, the passion they both had for literature, even though his knowledge of it was much more advanced than hers. She found herself wishing Lorraine would hurry and come down so they could go. But she knew from experience that Lorraine would keep them waiting until the last minute.

Grace tried to pay attention to the voice coming over the radio, but she was so nervous that she really just caught bits and pieces here and there. Roosevelt was giving a detailed account of the trip he had taken to visit the war factories. He talked about the growing number of women he was seeing at work and even admitted that they seemed more engaged in their tasks than the men. The males usually stopped to see what was going on when he came in, but the women just kept working. They kept their minds completely on the task at hand.

As Phillip leaned forward, intent on Roosevelt's words, Grace could feel Buzz's eyes on her, but she refused to look in his direction.

Roosevelt went on to talk about how high schools were allowing short breaks so that students could help gather crops. In some places every able-bodied man took time from their important jobs to help with the harvest and boost the local economy. Even the housewives were helping.

Grace happened to look over at Hoot when a slight movement caught her attention. He had swiped at his eye. At first, she thought a fly, or some sort of insect had gotten into the house and was bothering him but as she looked closer, she realized he had tears in his eyes. Hoot noticed her staring at him and turned away, turning up the bottle of brandy as he pretended to pour it into his already full glass.

At that moment, Lorraine swept into the room, crimson skirts rustling, rhinestone heels clicking sharply across the hardwood floor. Frank stood up to escort her in. Too fidgety to sit down, she stood beside his chair, his arm around her waist.

Grace sneaked a glance at Buzz. He was staring now at Lorraine so intently that she doubted he was even hearing a word coming over the radio. And she wondered why she felt jealous about it.

When they arrived at the theater later that evening, the parking lot was empty. That was strange, Grace thought. The parking lot was usually full every night. Lorraine turned from the front seat and looked at her, eyebrows cocked. She just shrugged back.

"Frank," Lorraine poked at him with her long, red fingernails. "What's going on?"

"You'll see in a few minutes," was all he would say.

When they got into the lobby, everything looked just as it always did. The fragrance of popcorn wafted through the air as the usher waved them through, without even asking for their tickets. They got their snacks and still, Frank wouldn't say anything.

Finally, they got into their seats with big buckets of fragrant popcorn and fizzing coca-colas. As they waited for the movie to start, Frank finally told them what was going on.

"I rented the entire theater for the evening," he explained. "You see, we're going to get a sneak preview at a big show that's coming out in a few months. They say they hit some hitches, reworking some scenes and it might even be the first of next year. But we're going to see it before it even hits the theaters."

"But how did you..." Lorraine looked up at him as she set her cup into the holder on the arm rest.

"Don't you know, money talks. If you're willing to spend enough, you can get most anything you want. It's something I've heard you girls talking about. So, I contacted a guy who has some connections in Hollywood. At first, he said it wasn't ready so they had to postpone the release date and there was no way he could help me. But when he found out what I was willing to give him, he worked it out. Anyway, I wanted to give you girls something really special for Valentine's Day."

Phillip looked at his brother and shook his head a little.

"What show is it?" Lorraine asked.

Frank grinned at her. "Just wait. You'll see in a minute."

Phillip leaned back and Grace felt his arm go around her. Leaning her head onto his broad shoulder, she began to relax and enjoy herself as she looked around. It was really sweet of Frank. Sometimes he could be a little much but then he would do something like this. You just had to overlook his faults, she thought.

Even though Roanoke Rapids was a small town, the Regal was somewhat elegant. Plush carpeting covered the floor from wall to wall. And the stage. The golden curtain that fell in loose folds until it was pulled back, just making you want so badly to see what it would reveal. She remembered her first real date with Phillip. It had been here, and they had sat in the balcony.

The golden curtain finally opened, and they watched film reels for the first ten minutes. Most of them were short spots supporting the war effort. Then the movie began.

"Casablanca!" a deep voice announced. Grace heard Lorraine give a little gasp.

It really was very exciting, she had to admit. Grace realized that she had seen advertisements that it would be coming out soon. She and Lorraine had both been talking about it for months. It was only now that she realized she hadn't heard anything recently about it.

"Humphrey Bogart and Ingrid Bergman!" the narrator began. He drew the audience in as he talked about the most romantic movie of the year.

Settling in, Grace became so engrossed in the film that she completely forgot about her own troubles and simply sat there, happy to be with her husband. She began to think about what would happen later that night, when she and Phillip would be alone. Phillip kept looking over to smile at her and he even leaned over in the darkness of the theater, his warm lips meeting hers as the music played. She thought how she would never forget the song entitled "As Time Goes By" and mused at how those words were so true. And she wondered; with all the changes that were going on right now, what would the future hold?

TEN

February 15, 1942

Grace sat in front of the vanity, pulling her hair back at the sides and tried to style it a little like Ingrid Bergman's. She let it drop. No use. Too long and straight.

She kept thinking back to the movie last night. Bergman had such class, such style. She always wowed the audience without being overly dramatic. Just quiet and confident. Grace loved the character she had played.

And that voice. The accent. Such a lovely sound. Grace wished she could speak that way. Even here where everyone had a Southern accent, hers was more pronounced. The community she came from had their own way of saying certain words. We drop our endings too much, she thought. When she was growing up, kids from town would tease her about the way she talked. That was one reason she was so quiet.

"Go-*ing, not* gonna" she said as she watched her mouth in the mirror. She was going to practice that accent. "*Go-ing, com-ing, look-ing.*"

She just couldn't get over thinking how kind of Frank to have gone to all that trouble and expense, she thought. No big deal for him and Phillip, it wasn't something men would care about. But for her and Lorraine, that was a different story. Something they would never forget.

She got up and paced around the room. They had stopped for a bite to eat after the movie and by the time they got home, it was so late Phillip had gone right off to sleep. She had felt attractive in her new dress and had been looking forward to being alone. But she knew how exhausted he was from the long hours he had been working.

Opening the door to the veranda, she stepped out. A

light rain was misting. Phillip had gone into town with Papa. They would all be going back down to Florida in a couple of days for another winter race at the Hialeah course, and he had to take care of some things.

A breeze whipped the rain across the veranda, so she went inside. She walked over to the big vase of flowers she had picked from the garden yesterday and buried her face in them. Iris, her favorite. She remembered the time when Phillip had surprised her. She had come into the room to find it filled with bouquets of them everywhere. Dozens of elaborate vases, canning jars and one giant assortment in a water bucket from the stables.

She wished he would still do something like that sometimes.

She wanted to go for a ride, but the rain was preventing that. If only she could get outside.

The library. She could always go down and find something to read. If riding was her favorite thing to do around here, reading took a close second.

She went down and even though it was warm outside, this room always stayed a little chilly. The servants had the wood laid in the fireplace, so she lit it. By the time she had found something to read and settled in the chair that was pulled up close, it was warm and cozy. She sat, flipping through the pages but she couldn't concentrate. She kept glancing out the window. Just checking to see if the rain is stopping, she told herself. But she knew there was more to it.

Buzz. That was what she was really looking for. Rainy days were the times he was most likely to come to the library. She kept thinking how he had kept looking at her in her new dress last night. Every time she thought about it, she burned with shame. But somehow, she wanted him to look at her that way again.

And then when Lorraine had come in and the way Buzz had looked at her. Grace had felt that strange sensation in the pit of her stomach and realized that she was jealous. She had always been a little envious of her sister-in-law. It wasn't just her beauty. She was so comfortable in a social setting, knowing what to say and how to talk to people while Grace would always shrink back into a corner. She could sit a horse almost as well as a man. Why, she could even drive a car. But this was different. For some reason it had bothered her, the way Buzz had looked at Lorraine. There was no mistake about what he was thinking.

She shook her head. This was all just silly. She loved Phillip; she would never even think of looking at another man.

But she *had* looked at Buzz. Even if it was just stolen glances out of the corner of her eye.

"Oh well, she thought. It was only sort of like a special friendship, she thought. It's just because we both love to read. And to have someone to talk with about books.

But she did keep hoping he would come in today.

He didn't. By the time the sun peeked out, Grace went over to the window and saw that Papa's car was back. They must have finished their business and she knew they would be getting out to the track now. It was a little muddy, but thoroughbreds always have to run, no matter what the track is like.

Though it was too wet for her, she decided to go down and give Cloudy a thorough grooming. She stopped by the kitchen and asked Cook for an apple. While the other woman sliced it up, Grace stepped into the pantry and grabbed a packet of fish food to put in her pocket. As she went out the door, she saw Hinson pull up in the farrier's truck. Frank wanted Runaway re-shod with those special shoes every six weeks. She kept thinking what Mama had said. That it was just showing off too much. Not every farm could afford something like that.

She could see Phillip at the track with Buzz. Hoot was breezing a filly. One of the horses they would be taking to Maryland. She seemed to be running well. A couple of the exercise boys were working two of the colts with her.

Grace stopped at the fountain and pulled the packet of fish food out. She sprinkled a little across the top of the water and watched as the enormous goldfish swam to the top. She loved to watch them as they swam, the orange and black bodies gliding through the water. She had been feeding them so often that some would come up to break the surface and she could feel their lips tickling the ends of her fingers as they took the food from her hand. The action was always soothing, watching the fish could be almost put her in a peaceful trance. But then, she would look up at the statue and the enchantment of the fish would disappear. She wished it was just a normal horse. She couldn't quite put her finger on what made her uneasy. It was just something about it, so...abnormal. Apart from the way of nature. Perhaps it had something to do with the look of fear of one of the faces.

"There's my boy," Grace said when she saw Cloudy's head over the stall door. The horse took the apple from her delicately with his soft lips, tickling her fingers. She scratched him in his favorite spot, just behind the withers. He stretched his neck and twisted his head, pulling his lip up in that habit that horses have when something feels so good to them, almost like they are grinning. Grace couldn't help but laugh.

Leading him into the aisle, she hooked him into the crossties, and he stood, stomping at flies. She swiped the shedding rake across his rump and brought off a wad of hair. Black and white strands mixed together. She ran her hand across the perfect, round spots on his flank, thinking how flashy it made the Appaloosa look. She loved the way his head and neck were darker, and the hairs gradually got lighter as they worked their way back to his hindquarters. That was where the spots really stood out with a lot of contrast. A blanket-back App was what Phillip had called him.

Cloudy nosed into her pockets, looking for another treat. Huh-huh-huh, he rumbled deep in his throat. She was brushing his long forelock flat between his eyes when Frank and Mr. Hinson came into the stables. She couldn't make out what they were saying, but they went to Big Red's stall. She could see Frank making gestures as he told the farrier what he wanted.

Then he went to the front door. "Grady!" he shouted. She could certainly hear him now. "Get in here, we're waiting for some help."

Grady and two of the grooms came hurrying in.

"Get that stallion out of his stall," Frank commanded.

Grady managed to get the halter on Big Red but when he tried to lead the colt out and Frank stepped up, still shouting, the horse shied back. The grooms had to help Grady. Even after they got him hooked into the crossties, he managed to half-rear, pawing out and making Frank jump back out of the way.

Frank threw his hands up in the air. "Can't you keep that idiot stallion still?"

Grace had to strain to hear Grady's answer. "You got to go easy around Red, Mr. Frank. You know how excitable he is."

Grace put Cloudy into his stall. She ducked out the back door, put the grooming kit up and returned to the house. Runaway may be getting his special shoes, but she didn't care to be around.

~~~

Grace sat beside Phillip in the stands at the Hialeah Course, watching as the horses began to come out on the track paddock. There were the red and gold colors of Janus, but the horse was a bay, not the bright red chestnut, so that was the filly. Grace hoped she would run a good race.

But Big Red. He was the big deal. She hoped he would stay near the inside rail. Not fight the jockey. Phillip just kept saying if they could get him running straight, there was no horse alive that could beat him.

There were the purple and white silks of Williams Farm. Bronze Force. The colt with the striking looks. The sun was shining on his coat, making him stand out with his metallic brown color. Their biggest contender for this particular race. For the last season, he had kept in the running right behind Bounty Money. She had heard Papa speculating that Johnson was afraid to run Bounty Money against Janus Farms now that Hoot was riding. She had thought he was just bragging but Bounty Money wasn't here today, so maybe there was some truth to it. The entire racing world was surprised by his absence and no reason had been given.
~~~

Several more horses pranced by before she saw Red. There he was with Cloudy walking beside him. Before he had taken ten steps, he spooked out and wheeled around, trying to run in the opposite direction. Hoot brought him under control quickly and Grady steered Cloudy right up in front of him. Hoot put the colt's nose on Cloudy's tail, and he followed docilely enough. Until they reached the gate, that was. Then he put up his usual fight, rearing high and backing away.

"That one sure is gate-sour," Grace heard the man sitting in front of them say. "I know he's from Janus Farms and they're supposed to be the best but I'm glad I didn't put any money on him."

"I put a bundle down on their filly," said the man beside him. "See the bay there in the fourth stall? They say she's a runner. Won a few stakes races. I think she's a safe bet."

Although Runaway tried all his usual antics, Grace noticed that Hoot was able to get him in the stall a little faster than any of the previous jockeys had done. Grady turned Cloudy and got him off the track in just a couple of minutes. The colt was cutting up pretty badly in the stall. Grace held her breath, remembering what had happened when he had gone down in the chute. She could see him, slinging his head back and forth, just frantic to get out of the stall. She reached over and grasped Phillip's hand and he squeezed it tightly.

She jumped as the bell clanged and the announcer shouted, "And they're off! Bronze Force is taking the lead, just as expected. Look at him go, ladies and gentlemen! Taking off right out of the gate! You can't miss him, with that unusual color. And like his name implies, he certainly is a force to be reckoned with!"

The filly got out quickly, well into the middle of the pack. Grace could see the Janus silks bobbing right in the center of the field. But where was Runaway?

Then she saw him burst out of the chute, rearing and lunging, trying to unseat his rider. It was only a couple of seconds before the jockey brought him under control and had him moving forward. The colt ran straight for a couple of hundred yards and then his old habit kicked in and he veered off towards the outside rail.

"Looks like Janus Farms is having a bit of trouble here," the announcers voice crackled over the microphones. "Runaway Rapids was stuck in the gate. Oh, and it looks like a battle between him and the jockey. This seems the course he always takes, gets it from his sire, Renegade Rapids. Now that one was a real fighter."

Phillip put his hand up to his face. Grace couldn't really hear much but sort of sensed him release a sigh of frustration. She couldn't really blame him. All the hopes and dreams, all the hours of hard work and planning. And here they were, watching it go up in smoke once again. Runaway had barely gotten out of the gate and the rest of the field was already approaching the first turn.

They watched in agony as Big Red fought the bit, determined to go wide. But as his pace picked up, he began to drift back to the left, towards the inside rail. Another furlong and he was right on the rail. Just what they had been working on for so long.

But it was just too late. The rest of the field was so far ahead that he wasn't even going to be in the running. The filly was the only chance of a win in this race. And she didn't have the speed of the stallion. The best they could hope for was to show or place. And Bronze Force was still leading the field.

By now Hoot only had Red to the three-quarter pole and the last horse ahead of them was well past the clubhouse turn. Suddenly, the big, red colt responded to Hoot, his stride stretched out and he started coming up on that last horse as if it were walking along. He was giving the jockey his head now and all he wanted to do was run.

"Look at this!" cried the announcer. "Runaway Rapids looked pretty hopeless in the beginning but now he's putting out. He'll be hard pressed to catch the main pack but he's certainly giving it a try."

They were nearly at the far turn when they caught up to the pack. Red began to pass the stragglers one by one.

"Just look at the Carolina Colt!" shouted the announcer. "He's knocking them out, one by one."

Now, as a hundred thousand fans shouted in surprise,

Runaway was plowing through the rest of the field as they swept around the turn. Hoot and the stallion were working their way through, so they were passing the other horses without having to run wide. Each time a hole opened up in the pack they slid effortlessly into it.

"Bronze Force is still holding the lead. He's way out in front and it looks as if Williams Farm is in pretty good shape here with the Force. Rapid Lady Fire is about seven lengths behind, so Janus Farms is still in the money. She's coming on strong, but it doesn't look like she's going to be able to pass Bronze Force.

Now Hoot began to close in on the leaders. Runaway was coming up now on the filly, who was running third. Grace saw her jockey put the whip to her as the colt pulled up even with her haunches, but he was passing her now, she was falling back quickly.

"Now it's the Carolina Colt," said the announcer. "He's gaining ground, just look at that big, red horse run!"

"Now they're coming up on Count's Ruler, and now pulling up even with Pewter Dust, the gray colt from Peterson Farm. And Runaway Rapids is passing the green and yellow colors that represented Peterson!"

"Looks like Hoot Harrison is making a difference for Janus Farms in this race," said the announcer. "They always say he's got a good seat and a light set of hands. And now he's showing us his magic on the Carolina Colt!"

Bronze Force was two furlongs ahead now and suddenly, Runaway leaped ahead, as if he had found a reserved speed that he didn't even know was there. Grace understood at once that Hoot had been holding the colt back a little, keeping his strongest asset in reserve for the finish.

People all around shrieked as Runaway closed in on Bronze Force with a spectacular show of speed and they charged down the stretch with an incredible rush. He was coming even with the favorite now and in three strides, he was at the other horse's head. They went on like that as Grace held her breath.

"Look at that, ladies and gentlemen!" the announcer boomed. "Just how long can they run neck and neck like that? Looks almost like they're hitched together like a harness team! But look at that incredible speed! Bronze Force, the crowd favorite, or Runaway Rapids, the come-from-behind colt from North Carolina, which will it be? Looks like it may be a tie."

They were still locked together, matching stride for stride as the approached the quarter pole. They battled furiously down the track and the suspense was unbearable. Grace could feel the blood pumping in her ears and her heart pounded as if she were the one out there, running. She tried to grab Phillip's arm, but he had it raised high in the air, waving the race program he was holding.

"Now the leaders are at the eighth pole," said the announcer. "And they're still running neck and neck, as if they're fused together."

They were only three lengths from the finish line. The Williams jockey plied the whip to Bronze Force as Hoot simply hand rode Red but now Bronze Force was beginning to falter. Runaway seemed to inch forward the tiniest bit, but it was hard for Grace to be sure. They were still so close!

Two more strides and she heard the announcer shout, "And it's Runaway Rapids, by a nose!"

Grace heard the man in front of her utter a string of curses as Phillip threw his hat into the air and let out a shriek before he turned to grab her and swing her through the air in the kind of embrace that she hadn't felt from him in a long time.

ELEVEN

Summer 2021

"Oh no!" I overslept. I had gone to a doctor in Roanoke Rapids a couple of days ago and got my prescription changed but the new medicine seems to be even worse. It does the job, rendering me unconscious for six or seven hours but there is a hefty price to pay. I feel as though I am swimming through thick mud. Every movement is a huge effort. This is a lot worse than the hallucinations because they only occur occasionally, and this is constant. But the only alternative that I can see is not to take anything. And even though that is tempting, I simply cannot face lying in bed every night, completely sleepless or going through the repetitive nightmares about Cole.

I sit up too quickly and fall back onto the bed, dizzy. I lay my head back on the pillow because the room is spinning. After a few minutes, the vertigo subsides and I rise again, this time more slowly. I set my feet on the floor and linger before I try to stand up. When I do, I have to hold onto the bedpost.

My mouth is dry, parched. I turn up a bottle of water, chugging a couple of gulps. As soon as it hits my stomach, it comes back up. I fall on my knees and grasp the plastic wastebasket, my stomach twisting with one cramp after another as green bile comes up, burning my throat. Finally, I am retching on nothing but air. Dry heaves are the absolute worst.

A light knock comes at the door and before I can get to my feet, Grace opens it just a crack. She stands there leaning on her cane, hair flowing down across her light blue bed jacket.

"Are you all right?" she asks.

"Fine," I mumble.

"Maybe you ought to call off your session."

I shake my head. "I'll be fine."

"I've got something for it, down in the kitchen cabinet. Just herbs. Natural. Not like that stuff with side effects."

"No!" I speak more sharply than I mean to. "It's probably just something I ate."

Grace doesn't say anything else, just closes the door.

Isn't this some crap? I am supposed to be taking care of her and she's about to have to look after me.

I pull the curtain back and see Jennifer's jeep. I send a text, telling her I'll be down.

As I sit on the side of the bed pulling on my jeans and boots, I see a few more vehicles pull in. My heart is pounding and the more I try to rush, the harder it thumps. I make it to the bathroom to brush my teeth and the gagging starts again. Finally, I make my way down the stairs. I pour a glass of tea and carefully take a tiny sip. What I wouldn't give right now to have some ginger ale.

"Miss Jo-Jo, Miss Jo-Jo!" Kyle comes running up as I approach the stables. "Miss Jennifer said I might be able to ride Sundown today! But I have to ask you first."

I close my eyes for a moment. That's right. Diesel has a sore foot. The vet's coming. I don't think it's serious, probably just a stone bruise. He doesn't act like its founder or laminitis.

I try to speak, and nothing comes out. I clear my throat and try again. "That'll be okay. Just remember to sit still and do everything we say. Sunny's sweet, but he's a little quicker that Diesel."

"I know." The little boy flashes me a toothy grin, spins and runs towards the barn.

Sundown is saddled and hooked into the crossties with Peanut and Scooter. They stand calmly, tails swishing, and eyes half closed.

Maggie Mae is already in the arena. She and Valentine are circling slowly, and I marvel again at the relationship. I had seen a photo on the bulletin board. Valentine was lying on the ground with a pink bandage on his foreleg. Maggie Mae was kneeling beside him with her usual pink shirt and boots, her cheek next to his as they both stared at the camera. It made such a striking picture that I had asked Jennifer about it. It had been taken a few weeks after Valentine came here. His mother had died and the man that owned them didn't want to bother with the colt. He nearly starved to death and his growth was stunted. His leg had gotten caught in barbed wire and cut up pretty bad. One of the volunteers had rescued him. Maggie Mae had insisted on helping as they nursed him back to health. His leg had healed but it would never be really strong. And with his tiny size, he wasn't suitable for riding. Maggie Mae was the only one who had ever been on his back.

As I lead Sundown, I turn to look at Kyle, grinning broadly. So are the side walkers. I cluck my tongue and pull until Sundown breaks into a trot. Kyle bounces up and down, giggling so that it is contagious. Even as bad as I feel, I have to laugh. "Let's go faster!" Kyle cries and we speed up a little more. The palomino is now at an extended trot, legs reaching out in front of him, Kyle shrieking with delight. My head begins to hurt again and as much as I want to keep going, I have to slow down.

I want to continue but I feel as though I may faint. I sit panting on the bench, watching as the volunteers finish the session, then watch as Kyle brushes the sweat from Sundown's coat. The golden body gleams in the sunlight, even darker with the moisture and the horse stands, swishing that beautiful white tail, so long it drags the ground.

Kyle says, "I can't wait to tell my Dad I rode Sundown."

More of the children begin to arrive and soon we have eight horses out in the big arena and three in the small one. Saturday mornings are the busiest time. Shouts ring through the air, interspersed with laughter.

I am following one of the kids as they lead Peanut. When we pass Valentine's empty stall, I realize that it has been quite some time since I have seen Maggie Mae. After we finish getting the horse settled, I go look around. I'm not really worried, by now I'm pretty used to the pair wandering all over the stable yard, visiting with all the other children and volunteers.

"Hey Jennifer!" I call. "Have you seen Maggie Mae?"

She stops, resting the saddle she is carrying on her knee. "Yeah, maybe a half hour ago. She was by the watering troughs, talking to that new boy. The timid one, telling him not to be afraid."

"Let's see if we can find her," I say.

Jennifer puts the saddle in the tack room, and I can hear her calling Maggie Mae's name. When she doesn't appear, Jennifer gets more volunteers and soon we are all searching.

After twenty minutes I am feeling a knot of panic in my stomach. I have taken the golf cart down to Valentine's pasture, just sure I would find them there. I start back towards the main stables, not sure which way to turn.

I drive along slowly. I rack my brain, trying to think where she usually goes. I try the arena, Valentine's stall, up by the tack room. We have looked everywhere.

Suddenly, out of the corner of my eye, I catch a glimpse of pink, lying on the ground. There across the east pasture, among a copse of trees. Turning the golf cart off, I hop the fence and walk towards it. The further I go, the harder my heart pounds. What if something has happened to that child?

As I get closer, I can finally make out the tiny figure, lying on the ground. Valentine lies beside her. Dear God, what has happened? As I get closer, I am so frightened I think my heart will stop.

Then I realize what I am looking at. Maggie Mae's back is propped against the trunk of a big oak, surrounded by budding flowers. Valentine's head is in her lap. She clutches a limp bouquet of the blooms in her little hand. They are both asleep, napping in the cool shade, surrounded by the golden flowers that flutter in the light breeze.

I pull my phone out of my back pocket and snap a video of them. Because in my entire life, I have never seen anything that touched my heart quite like it.

~ ~ ~

I am sitting in the office, going over QuickBooks. I hate being in this room, so gloomy with it's dark, oak paneled walls and plasterwork friezes. Thick, maroon-colored drapes that have faded to an ugly pinkish orange. The heavy Baroque mahogany desk and matching carved chair. The Chesterfield sofa was probably a real classic with its genuine leather and brass studding, but the mice have chewed holes in the cushions. The only thing I like about this place is the big painting of the chestnut stallion behind the desk. A grandfather clock looms in the corner, topped by the symbol that seems to be all over the estate. The two-faced horse looks out from the top, chiming on the hour, every hour. All over the house the clocks chime away as the hours pass and one day turns into another. Reminders of time constantly going by.

It is getting late, and I want to go to bed but I have a pile of accounts payable that I have to enter. I can't seem to get organized. If I could just get rid of this headache, it would help. I have let the bills get into a huge jumble with all the other correspondence. I don't have any accounting experience, but the QuickBooks system is pretty easy. It seems like the mental effort of organizing everything is exhausting. It makes no sense. Just sitting here, putting papers into different piles should not make a person tired.

We do payments on the first and the fifteenth. Finally, I get the two piles separated. The feed bill isn't as large as I would have thought for so many horses but then we do have plenty of pasture for grazing. The winter will be a different story, because it will take an enormous amount of hay to feed this herd. Most of the horses just get a little grain in the mornings. A couple of them have to have special feed because they have been foundered in the past, so they can't have too much starch, or their feet will become inflamed again. So, theirs is expensive but thank goodness most of them can do with basic feed.

What with having so many horses the vet bills have been the problem lately. I've had to have him out for several farm calls and usually it's more than one horse. The routine visits aren't too bad; I usually do the worming and the four-way shots myself. It just seems as if we've had a few cases of emergencies with colic and even had to have a couple of after-hours visits.

And the farrier. I always kept just a few horses, but this bunch goes through horseshoes like nobody's business. Instead of every six weeks, we have the farrier out every couple of weeks because all the shoeings don't come due at the same time.

I only have a few more payments to put in when I begin to notice an odor. Something familiar, just vaguely unpleasant. Damp, murky. Then it comes to me. The river. I get up to close the window, but it isn't open. Why is it that I am smelling the river so strongly all of a sudden?

I push the wool and silk brocade drapes aside and when I turn back to the desk, I notice a wet spot on the floor, beneath the painting of the horse. Great, I think. I'll probably have to call a plumber.

But as I step closer, I realize that a trickle of water is running down the wall. Must be a pipe that goes to one of the upstairs bathrooms. But no, the wall above the picture is bone dry. And then I realize the water is actually coming out of the painting itself. How can that be? And it is not clear, it has a reddish tint. Like the water from the river.

And as I stand here, staring at the picture, it moves. Just a tiny movement. Sort of like a 3-D painting when you shift your gaze. But this painting was done long before 3-D even existed. I blink and it moves again. The horse's head comes up, the ears prick forward and the nostrils flare. This is crazy. I am crazy. I am not really seeing this. And then the stallion looks right at me, eyes rolling and showing the whites. Then it lets out a shrill whinny and rears high on its hind legs.

I jump back, my legs hit the office chair and I tumble into the floor. I sit here for a second, my legs curled underneath me. I'm not hurt. But it sure scared the heck out of me. I hold my breath, listening but all I hear is silence.

I stand up, holding the back of the chair for support. I am quivering a little. My pulse is racing, and my breath comes in short bursts. I look towards the painting again and the horse's head has returned to its original position, nothing out of the ordinary.

I sit down, still shivering a little. I had thought I was

beginning to get used to this place but, I don't know... it's just so spooky here. There are always strange noises, the rusty old pipes creaking in the walls when water runs through them, the old wood and mortar constantly settling, the occasional mouse that scurries underfoot. But this... surely, I am imagining things.

I know I have been having emotional problems. My mind doesn't work like it should. But I am tired of all this crap. And I will just be darned if I'm going to keep running away from everything. If I go scuttling off to my room, I'll be a lot more frightened than I will if I stay here and convince myself that it is nothing.

I finish putting the payments in and look at the calendar for tomorrow's appointments. After the farrier, most of the regulars will be coming and there is a new patient.

I need to do something that takes no concentration, so I get a can of lemon pledge and a polishing cloth. As old as this desk is, the shine of the wood still comes alive with a little elbow grease. The shelves could use a little dusting. I begin at the bottom and then get up on the stepstool to reach the higher shelves. I can't quite see over the top shelf but as I reach up and run the cloth over it, my hand connects with something and knocks it into the floor.

It is a picture and I have cracked the frame. The grime on it is so thick you can barely make out the subject, but I can see a car. This must have been here for more years than I have been alive. Running the cloth over it, more of it comes into view but I am smearing it. But now I can make out a convertible. Not a compact one like today's sporty vehicles but a monster of a car, old-fashioned, long, and low-slung. A man sits up on top of the back seat, a wide grin on his face and two gorgeous women on either side, much taller than him. There are other vehicles ahead and behind and a great crowd lines the streets. It looks like some sort of parade. I see a sign for Pritchard's Drugs on a storefront and recognize it, an old-fashioned business that had managed to survive many decades in Raleigh. I barely remember it because it had closed when I was in kindergarten. The only things I can recall are the black and white checkered floor and the fragrance of oranges drifting through the store as the clerk behind the soda counter squeezed them to make the orange aids. The really interesting part of the picture is the caption written in large letters on the side of the convertible. I can only make out a small portion in the center because people standing on the street are in the way. But the part I do see makes me curious and I wish I could read it all.

.... GIVE A HOOT ABOUT ....
..... BUY YOUR .....

Buy what, I wonder. At least I have finally gotten my mind off what happened earlier. Or what I had *thought* happened. Just another stupid hallucination, side effects from the medication. Suddenly the grandfather clock chimes out the hour and I realize how much time has gone by since I came in. I'm going up to bed. And then, just as I lift my hand up to turn the light switch, I see it. There *is* a puddle of reddish-brown water pooled on the floor, right beneath the painting.

TWELVE

February 17, 1942

"Get that filly in the gate first." Buzz gestured to one of the exercise boys.

The filly went into the fifth gate and one of the grooms shut the rear partition behind her. She was a pretty bay with dark points. Long-legged and slender, she was a fairly tall horse but beside Big Red, she almost looked petite, Grace thought. She had walked with Phillip down to the track because he was taking her into town later this morning.

"Bring those other two up," Papa bawled, and the exercise boys urged their mounts towards the gate. Grady, mounted on Runaway hung back, waiting for the others to get into place. Even though another rider was by his side on Cloudy, the big red colt pranced nervously, shaking his head. Suddenly, he reared, front hooves striking out in the air and Grady turned him in a tight circle, bringing him down. Phillip and Buzz walked over to lend a hand and they gradually got him under control. The big, white dog that belonged to Buzz trotted up and Grace put her hand on top of his head. He remained with her, watching the men work with the horses.

"Hoot should be here this morning." Frank spat on the ground, nearly hitting Grace's shoe. "I swear, he misses more practice sessions than he makes."

Papa blew out a cloud of smoke. "Grady can handle it. Besides, it's not like the absences when Hoot's just laying around, hung over. That's a pretty important event he's gone to."

"I know. But what about Janus? What about being on the job when we need him?"

"Relax," Papa said. "What Hoot's doing will be good

99

publicity for the farm.”

“Well.” Frank stabbed at a clod of dirt with the toe of his boot. “It’s a good thing we didn’t have Runaway scheduled for a race this weekend.”

“You know I wouldn’t have let Hoot off if we did.” Papa pushed his hat back. “What are you waiting for, Grady? Bring him on in.”

Hoot had taken the weekend off to go to a benefit show in Raleigh. It was a fundraiser for the war effort, there was going to be a tribute band for the Andrew’s sisters, a party, and a parade. Most of the city was expected to be there.

“Phillip,” Papa said. “How about you riding with Frank to Overton’s? We were going to look at that mare, but I’ve got some other business I need to attend to.

Phillip looked over at Grace. “Well...Papa, I’m taking Grace into Roanoke Rapids. She’s supposed to help the ladies with planting the Community Victory Garden.”

Papa lowered his voice. “You know we don’t want Frank making any purchases on his own. Somebody else can drive her in.”

“This is pretty important, Papa.”

“Oh, just forget it!” Papa bellowed. “Hoot’s in Raleigh, you want to go into town. Every time I turn around, it’s something about this confounded war. I’ll go with Frank tomorrow. Overton’s got a buyer coming to take a look later today but if she’s gone, she’s gone.”

Buzz stepped up. “Phillip, I can ride with Frank.

Papa shook his head. “No, I want Phillip to go.”

Phillip turned to Buzz. “What about driving Grace into town for me?”

Grace started to shake her head, that she would just be uncomfortable, but Phillip wasn’t paying attention.

“Be glad to.” Buzz looked over at Grace. “We’re about done here, Miss Grace. Let us just wind up and I’ll run you in.”

~~~

Grace stared out the window of Buzz’s truck as they traveled down the highway towards Roanoke Rapids. She
~~~

felt so awkward, she didn't know what to say.

But Buzz seemed to be at ease. "Phillip told me about that Community Victory Garden. Seems like a pretty good idea."

Grace nodded. "When the ladies' committee first asked me about it, I wasn't sure what they wanted me to do. Thought I would have to go to some big, fancy meetings or something. But it turned out they just needed someone to help the women in town get started planting."

Buzz chuckled. "Phillip said his mother sort of volunteered you to help."

Grace smiled. "Yes, Mama told them I knew about it. She came with me the first couple of times. She knows I don't like being in a crowd. But I'm really enjoying it. These women are just plain old housewives. Husbands have gone off to war. They know about hoeing weeds, picking vegetables and canning. The only thing they were having trouble with is planting.

"And having that big garden in town, everyone working together. Some of those women live by themselves. Scared about the war. Seems like this makes them feel better. They get to talking and laughing. I'm glad the ladies' circle thought of it."

Buzz wanted to know how Grace had learned about growing things and she spent most of the ride telling him about growing up with her Aunt Ada. They had lived in a little cabin on a couple of acres. She had spent her childhood helping Ada planting and harvesting, it was just the way people in that area lived, nothing unusual.

"The special thing about Aunt Ada was the way she had with growing herbs," Grace explained. "Everyone had a garden. But Aunt Ada, she was a healer. Certain things we would grow and others, we could just go out in the woods and gather. She helped a lot of people."

"`So, do you know all about that too?" Buzz asked.

"Oh, no. At least not like Aunt Ada did. I know the basics for just little routine sickness and accidents, but I could never be a real healer like she was. She had...I don't know. Just a really special gift for it. I always keep a few herbs but they're just for minor ailments. Aunt Ada was different. I've seen her save people's lives. Lots of times. Of course, now we've got a lot more access to doctors. And the new hospital. Not much need for home remedies anymore."

"I'm looking forward to seeing that mare from Overton's," Buzz said. "If they take her, that is. Heard she's a nice one."

Grace looked down at her lap. "I'm sorry you had to drive me. I'm sure you'd rather have gone to get her."

"It's okay," he answered. "I enjoy talking to you."

"It's just..." Grace fidgeted with the packets she was holding. "Phillip told me they don't want Frank doing any of the buying. By himself, I mean."

"I know."

"And I'm glad of it. He doesn't really care if they end up at the slaughter-house."

Buzz nodded. "I know what you mean. I know it's a business but I don't believe in sending horses to the killer. Any horse. If they're not fast enough to win, there's other jobs they can do. Other people that will buy them. And Frank doesn't really know how to choose a runner. He just likes to get out there in the public and try to act like a big man." He snorted. "If brains were dynamite, that boy couldn't blow his nose."

Grace laughed. The trainer always knew how to put her at ease.

"Here we go," Buzz said as they turned into the drive where saw women gathering. "I'll pick you up this afternoon."

Grace was tired that evening. Her back ached every time she went to help at the Victory Garden. She hadn't realized how long it had been since she had done any gardening, or how much she had missed it, either.

After dinner, the family gathered in the main living room. The event in Raleigh was going to be broadcast on the television. Grace curled up beside Phillip on the sofa. Papa fiddled with the television, trying to adjust the horizontal lines. Grace thought about when he bought it last year. They were the only family in the area that had one and he liked to brag about it. Sometimes he would invite people over to watch a special show. As Papa brought the picture into focus, she could feel Buzz's eyes on her. He was sitting across the room in an armchair, smoking a cigar and drinking a brandy.

The picture came into full focus and the parade had already started. Float after float passed by, most of them sponsored by local businesses in Raleigh.

"Look, there he is!" Papa boomed. A convertible came into view, and they could see Hoot sitting high on top of the back seat, grinning, and waving at the crowd. He had a beautiful woman on either side. A banner ran down the side of the car.

GIVE A HOOT ABOUT YOUR COUNTRY
HOOT HARRISON SAYS BUY YOUR WAR BONDS

The news was interrupted be a commercial and when it returned, the camera opened on a large room with crowded tables and a stage. Three women dressed like the Andrews sisters performed their numbers as the audience clapped with enthusiasm. As the camera panned across the crowd, Phillip said. "Look there's Hoot. Right up there at that table, front center."

They could see the jockey up front, clapping along with everyone else. The two women were still there, along with several others seated at the table.

When the singers paused for a break, the emcee came onstage and took the microphone. He talked about how they were raising money for the war effort. "We're trying to take the example of what some of the big celebrities are doing," he explained. "This is a pretty small event compared to them, but we're raising quite a bit here today."

He began to call people up onstage. Several of the prominent businessmen from the Raleigh area got up. No one made any long speeches, mostly just told who they were, the name of their business and went back to their tables.

Then Hoot walked up onstage. "Hi everybody." He gave a little wave at the camera. "I'm Hoot Harrison and I just wanted to...

The emcee interrupted. "The nation's number one jockey, ladies and gentlemen. I think most everyone knows you, Hoot. And we want to thank you for coming out today."

Hoot nodded. "Just wanted to see if I could help a little. Had a pretty good time, too." He grinned. "Just look at all these gorgeous women. That alone is enough reason to be here." The audience laughed.

"Thanks to Janus Farms for letting me off this weekend so I could make it," Hoot said.

The emcee asked a few questions about the farm and Hoot answered casually, comfortable in front of the audience.

"By God," Papa said. "That boy is worth his weight in gold. I told you he was going to get us some good publicity."

THIRTEEN

Summer 2021

I tramp through the tall, damp rye that covers the field on the farm that lies east of Janus, swinging the high-powered flashlight in a large arc, back and forth. Denise had called just after five o'clock this morning. She had received a call from the landowner next to Janus. He had seen a couple of horses out and figured they were ours.

My heart pounds harder with each step. I had shoved a bucket of grain and a couple of halters into my car and driven as far as I could down the path. If they were towards the back of the farm, I wouldn't be so worried but if someone had seen them, chances were pretty good they were up near the highway. I had caught a brief glimpse of the herd out by the stables when I had shone the headlights towards the pasture, but I couldn't see well enough to make out which ones were there.

God, my head hurts. It feels like a pick has been driven into my right eyeball and I wonder if my body will ever be able to adjust to the medication. At least the vomiting has finally stopped. It's been a little better over the last few weeks but having to spring up out of bed so quickly has been a shock to my system. As the tension continues to build, my head throbs harder. I feel so alone, so frightened.

If anything happens to the horses, it will be my fault. Thinking back, I am pretty sure I forgot to turn the electric wire back on last night. The horses had leaned across the boards so much they were breaking them loose. Denise had run a stand of electric wire across the inside of the top rail to keep them off it. The plastic handle to the piece that went across the gate had a crack in it and sometimes you could feel a little tingle when you grasped it to open the gate. Yesterday the ground had been wet from the rain we'd had and when I opened the gate, I had gotten a pretty good shock, so I unplugged the box.

I had been meaning to get that handle replaced. All I had to do was drive to the hardware store and get a new one. Just a couple of bucks. And they certainly aren't very hard to put on, just twist the strand of wire onto the ends. I had just been so sick, I kept thinking; tomorrow. I'll feel better and I'll take care of it.

I wish I could call Sandra. I have no doubt that she would come help me any time, night, or day. But she left yesterday to go visit her parents. They retired to the Outer Banks and have been trying all summer to get her down there. I realize now how much I have come to depend on her.

And now, because I had put off such a simple little task, it could cause a lot of trouble. I don't know the landowner, but horses can do quite a bit of damage to crops. I'm just praying they won't get onto the highway.

I trudge along, thinking about the dream I was having when I woke up. That same hateful dream, over and over. When I had left home again. If I could have one wish granted, it would be that this dream would leave me alone. Leaving home. Leaving Cole.

Cole was fast becoming one of the most renowned reining trainers in North Carolina. Had clients coming in from all over the country. I was the barn manager and we had hired another trainer to work under Cole. I had half a dozen stable workers, mostly teenagers who came in part time.

It had only been two weeks before Nationals. I had gone up to Gloucester, in Virginia to pick up a colt we had purchased. The owners had told me about a shortcut through the back way that would cut off a lot of miles. It was just after dark when I turned in the drive at home and the barns were deserted. I had unloaded the colt, put him in a stall and hung around until he settled down. Then I went up to get Cole to bring him down. I could have just phoned but I wanted to sneak in and surprise him that I got back so early. I had stopped at Colonial Heights and picked up some of that wood-grilled barbecue he loved so much.

Music had been playing and there was a lamp on in the living room. I could see someone sitting at the end of the sofa. Peering closer, I saw long, dark curls spilling over the back of the sofa. "Rachel?" I had called. "What are you doing here?"

I would never forget what had happened when I spoke. Cole's head had popped up suddenly, eyes open with surprise and they had risen to their feet. Completely clothed but it was obvious what was going on.

I had wrenched my shoulder catching my suitcase when it tumbled down from the top shelf. Cole followed me, asking what was I doing, telling me to put the suitcase away. I had filled it with jeans and tee shirts, pushed past him and run down the hall. Rachel was nowhere in sight. Cole followed me to the garage. I had locked the car doors and he was running beside me as I had pulled out. As I accelerated, I could see him in the rear-view mirror, watching me go.

I had found a job in a fast-food restaurant and rented a little flat; refused his calls. Three weeks later he had found me. He cried and promised it wouldn't happen again. Not ever. Just give him one more chance.

I had stopped answering the door and continued to avoid the phone. A few days later, he came in at work and tried to talk to me. That was when I decided I had to get out of Raleigh. And when I had seen the advertisement for this job on Indeed.com, I had applied. It was a little over an hour away, just far enough that he couldn't drive across town whenever he wanted. He wouldn't find me so easily. I have to stay away from him, no matter what it takes. Not that he would ever hurt me, not physically, at least. It is my emotional psyche that frightens me so much. How on earth can it be that one person has so much control over another? Like he is my whole identity.

Now, the light finally reveals hoofprints on the sandy path. I breathe a sigh of relief because they are headed in the right direction, away from the road. I tramp on for about a quarter of a mile before I see two dim outlines against the background of the awakening horizon and breathe a sigh of relief. As I get closer, I can make out the light buttermilk color and black points. Scooter. So surely that would be Peanut with him. Yes, I can see the silky black coat as I get a little closer. Peanut spots me and her head pops up, alert and trying to see what object is moving through the field towards her. I whistle softly but she puts her head down and continues to snatch the short tufts of grass growing between the soybeans. I shake the bucket and the grain rattles. Both horses start towards me, trotting up to dip their muzzles into the bucket and I slip the halters over their heads.

Standing beside the buckskin, I clip the lead line to the halter, run it back to his withers and pull the end back to the other side of the halter and tie it, forming a crude pair of reins. With no bit in his mouth, I will have absolutely no control if he should bolt but he really is a quiet horse. Still, it will be difficult to guide him, turn him in the right direction and all. Standing beside his left shoulder, I grasp a handful of the black mane with my left hand and placed my right on his withers. I leap up, expecting to simply throw my right leg over his hindquarters but it falls short and I am left dangling.

I let out a groan. It has been a long time since I rode bareback. I can't remember the last time. The little horse takes a few steps but stops and stands steady. Finally, I get my right foot hooked over his haunch and pull myself upright.

Grasping Peanut's lead line, I pull her up close to Scooter's flank. I squeeze with my legs, and he moves forward. I squeeze again and he breaks into a trot, bouncing me up and down. With no stirrups to post into his rhythm, it jars my head. Leaning forward slightly, I touch my heel lightly into his side and the buckskin leaps into a canter, slow, fluid and collected. At the end of the row, I move my leg against his flank, and he turns without the slightest hesitation.

Trained to leg aids, this horse is a joy to ride. Nothing as fiery and spirited as the horses I am used to but much more responsive than most of the really lazy horses that are so good for the kids to ride. Jennifer had told me that he and Peanut had been donated by a family whose children had gone off to college. They had been involved in the 4-H program. Peanut had belonged to the daughter, and I could just picture the girl tripping along on the Paso Fino with her fancy gait. The boy had used Scooter for gaming events; barrel racing, goat tying and such. That's why he's so responsive, I think now. I decide I'm going to ride this horse again.

We are just lifting Kyle off Sundown's back a few hours later when I see a car drive up. A middle-aged woman gets out and waits by the car until a pretty teenager gets out. The girl trudges slowly across the yard, posture slumped, eyes downcast. She's new to the program. We met with them a couple of days ago, but this will be her first ride. We usually put the new kids on Diesel, but he is out of commission until that foot heals. So, I saddle Sundown while the girl stands quietly nearby. Then it takes a little encouragement to get her into the saddle. After the first round, we determine that she doesn't need any side walkers. Her balance is fine, and I already know she has no physical disabilities. With her, it's all emotional.

As we fall in behind a couple of the other kids and I lead her around the arena, I try to make a little conversation but so far, we haven't been able to get her so say a word. I guess I wouldn't want to talk either if I had been through what she has. Her mother's boyfriend raped her. Fourteen years old. The thought sickened me. He's doing time at the local prison, has a pretty long sentence. And her mom kicked her out. Claimed her daughter had lied. I wondered if she really believes that or if his six-figure income had something to do with it.

Meanwhile, Drake is living with her aunt who is watching from the fence rail. I can see the concern written on her face. "God, I hope this helps," she had told me. "She won't talk to me, no interest in anything. She won't even cry. I just don't know what to do to help her."

After a few more rounds, I notice this girl has a good seat. She keeps her heels down, puts her weight into the stirrups. She has ridden before. But when I ask her, she doesn't answer.

WHERE THE STATUE WEEPS

The other kids are laughing and chattering as they circle the arena but Drake pays them no attention. A couple of them say hello to her but she keeps her eyes down and doesn't respond. As Sundown walks on, he makes a noise deep in his throat. Sort of a half grunt, half sigh. I feel as if I could do the same thing. I have no idea what to do to help this girl.

Finally, I stop trying to engage her in conversation. I look around at the other kids as we walk. They are having a great time, several of them begging to go faster.

I spot Maggie-Mae over by the fountain with Valentine by her side. She stands there quietly, gazing up at the statue of the two-faced horse. She does this often. The other children don't seem to like it and I suppose I can see why. One of the faces appears to be disturbed. The ears are back and the teeth are bared. But rather than angry, it seems to be more frightened. And I have often noticed that when you look really closely, the eyes almost seem to be weeping. I don't know much about working with mortar but perhaps it had been built on a hot day and some of it had melted and run down the steep lines of the face. But right now, I've got work to do. I turn my attention back to Drake but she remains silent.

As soon as the last patient has gone, I get into my car and drive into town. With hardly any traffic on the road, I don't have to pay much attention to driving and I find my mind drifting. These kids need help so badly. I feel like I am floundering, barely keeping my head above water with this position. I am grateful for the volunteers. I know there is no way I could even hope to manage without them. Right now, they are pretty much running the program. I am just the horse handler. But I am beginning to learn.

I pick up a handle for the gate at the hardware store. I have gotten in line and waited there for a few minutes, then return to the aisle and grab a couple more. No way I'm taking a chance on having to turn the hot wire off again. I've really been incompetent, and I swear I'm going to do better.

Wal-Mart is down the street and since I need a few things I'll just get them now. Then I won't need to come back into town. I throw a couple of pairs of jeans into my cart. They've got a special on plain cotton tee shirts. I sort through, finding my size and choosing a variety of colors. Oh, and I need a couple of sports bras if I'm going to do some riding myself. They give you a little extra support and that helps with the jolt if you're on a horse that's not really collected and smooth.

I'd better pick up a few items from the grocery section. The nurse usually does Grace's shopping, but I get my own food. Since my stomach has calmed down, I've been able to start eating again. An omelet sounds like it would hit the spot for breakfast in the morning. And even some hot, crispy bacon. I browse through the aisle, picking up onions, green peppers and mushrooms, sharp cheddar. I'll make one for Grace, too. She is usually up long before the nurse arrives.

I open a carton of eggs and check to make sure none are cracked. They're brown, free range and extra-large. I am just closing the carton when I hear a familiar noise. It is nothing but a man clearing his throat. But, oh God, I know who it is before I look up.

"Hey Jo." Cole is standing beside my cart, looking at me.

For a moment, I freeze. Then as he starts to speak again, I drop the carton of eggs on the floor. Out of the corner of my eye, I see them splatter as I walk away. Faster and faster, I am striding until I break into a trot and by the time, I reach the door I am running across the parking lot.

FOURTEEN

February 21, 1942

"**B**ut Frank! I don't see what's wrong with it!"

Even though Grace was in the small parlor, she could hear Frank and Lorraine arguing. She had followed him into the billiards room.

"How do you think that would look?" he answered. "The wife of Frank Masterson, working at some menial job?"

Grace could hear Lorraine's footsteps as she crossed the room. "Haven't you heard a word .about what's going on? Women are stepping up to go to work. It's nothing to be ashamed of! People are looking up to the women who are doing it."

"That doesn't mean..."

Lorraine cut him off. "What about the WAACs?"

"The what?"

"The Women's Army Auxiliary Corps! Thousands of women joining. They're doing all sorts of jobs. Some are just doing office work or radio operators. But there are women out there doing really important things. They are doing welding work, being electricians. A couple of the airports have even started hiring women as traffic controllers. All so the men can be released. To go out and fight!"

"I said forget it!" Grace heard the heavy liquor glass hitting wood as Frank slammed it down on a table. "No wife of mine is going to be working in a factory. Or be shipped off somewhere to do what you call the *important jobs.*"

"That's not what I want to do!" Lorraine's voice rose an octave higher. "I just want to work at the bank in Roanoke Rapids. You know I used to help Daddy a little at the bank. I could be so good at it."

Frank snorted. "Yeah, I bet. You don't really know

112

anything about it. You just want an excuse to run up and down the road all day."

Heavy footsteps sounded in the hallway and Grace froze in place. She would know Papa's walk anywhere. He even had an arrogant gait, heel, toe, heel, toe hitting the floor.

"All right, that's enough!" he bellowed. "I don't want to hear any more of this business about a job."

Even though Grace couldn't see, she could imagine Papa waving his cigar, pointing it at Lorraine.

"But Papa..."

He cut her off, his heavy fist pounding on the table. "If you want to work, you can go to the office here a couple afternoons a week and help Artie with the books. Any women that want to continue to live at Janus Farms will *not* be going out into the public to work!"

There was a few moments of silence and Grace held her breath, listening.

Finally, Lorraine spoke. "Well, all right." Grace could almost picture her facial expression, lips poked out. Pouting.

"I'll speak to Artie and let him know," Papa said.

"No, Papa." Frank's voice, usually low, somehow seemed high and reedy.

"Oh, it won't hurt anything. She won't be out in the public. No one will even know she's doing any kind of work. Besides, maybe it'll get her off your back. Give her a little taste of what it's like to work and she'll be glad to get back to the life of luxury."

"But I don't want her..." Frank's voice seemed almost panicky now and Grace wondered why as Papa cut him off.

"She'll come in and help Artie. Just part-time. And I don't want to hear another word about it. Any of it."

No one else spoke and in a couple of minutes, Grace heard Lorraine's high heels tapping sharply down the hallway. She sat where she was, reluctant to move, lest she make any noise that would draw attention to herself. She could hear Papa and Frank talking, but their voices were muted now, and she couldn't make out what they were saying. As soon as she heard the sound of the billiard sticks cracking against the balls, she got up and escaped outside.

~~~

Grace stood outside Cloudy's stall, watching him eat his grain as she polished her saddle. Lorraine thought she was silly to do it when one of the employees would do it for her. But Grace would just always shrug when she mentioned it and not really answer her. The truth was, she just enjoyed doing it. The smell of the special leather oil, mingled with saddle soap. The repetitive motion as the cloth stroked back and forth. The way the saddle looked so shiny when she was finished. Taking care of her tack made her feel good. She was just daydreaming as she worked. Thinking about how Janus Farms had been so successful at the tracks recently. Runaway Rapids was in all the headlines everywhere. The Carolina Colt, the press had been calling him.

When she opened the can of saddle soap, it was nearly empty so she went down to the work room to get a fresh can. The door was open, and Buzz's dog was looking in. She could see that a couple of the men were in there. She hesitated outside the door, then decided she was being silly. She would just get her supplies and be out of their way in a couple of seconds.

"Are you crazy?" she heard Grady say.

"Nope," Hoot answered. "Just a little drunk."

She started to turn away. No way she was going in there if they were drinking. But out of the corner of her eye, she saw that Hoot's arm was bleeding.

"Hoot," she said. "Are you all, right?"

The jockey looked up and grinned. "Not feeling any pain right now, I'll tell you that. Soon as I get this arm sewed up, I'll be just fine."

"What? Who's going to do your sutures?" She thought Hoot must have taken a fall from one of the horses and maybe Doc was on the way out.

"Miss Grace," Grady said. "Will you see if you can talk some sense into this fool? He's trying to sew up his own
~~~

arm."

"Just about got it, too." Hoot raised his right hand, and she could see a needle, threaded with a thick piece of what looked like some sort of plastic string. As she watched, he used it to pierce the skin on one side of the gash in his left arm, pulling it closed, then repeating the action twice more.

"What in the world?" she stood there looking at him.

"We were down at the river," Grady explained. "Fishing a little. You know, the rockfish are running this time of year. Anyway, Hoot slipped of one of those sharp rocks and cut himself. I tried to take him in to let Doc look at it. But I can't do anything with him."

Hoot laughed. "I don't like doctors. Besides, there's no need. I did it myself. With a piece of fishing line. See?" He held it up to show her.

"What a sissy," Grady said. "A man that's willing to get out there and mix it up with crazy horses on the track, but he's scared to death of doctors."

"But Hoot," Grace said. "It might get infected."

"Nah," the jockey picked up his bottle of liquor and took another swig. "It'll be fine." He looked over at the door. "Come here, Spanky. I've got something for you, boy." Reaching up onto the counter, he pulled down a little can. He pulled out something and threw it to the dog, who caught it in mid-air. Then he popped one into his own mouth. "These Vienna sausages," he said. "I don't know who loves them more, me or Spanky." Patting the dog on the head, he kept feeding him until the can was empty.

"Tell you what, Miss Grace. If anything would set me right, it would be a big bowl of that chicken and dumplings we had at supper last night. You think there's any left?"

"I'll go up to the house and see," she answered. As she started up the path, she turned back and looked at the little man. Never, in her life had she known anyone quite like him.

"Oh," he called after her. "Some of that fried cornbread, too. That would really hit the spot!"

~~~
~~~

Grace rode into the stable yard. She had gone out for a short ride after dinner, and it was nearly dark. The only activity she saw was the horses moving around. Most of the hands were probably at the common room, sitting around playing cards.

She dismounted and led Cloudy into the stable, stopping outside his stall. She patted him on the neck and unbuckled the girth.

"Hold on, Miss Grace, I'll get that for you." She jumped a little at the sound of the voice in the empty stable. Hoot stepped up and pulled the saddle off. Hanging it on the side of the stall, he turned back to look at her as Spanky came up to stare at him, hoping for a treat. He reached down and ruffled the long fur.

"How's your arm?" she asked.

Hoot held it up so she could inspect it. "Not too bad. Guess I'm going to have a little scar but what the heck. Not like I'm not covered up with them anyway, what with all the spills I've had on the track."

He patted the spotted rump, and the Appaloosa shifted his weight. "What about you, Miss Grace? Did you and old Cloudy have a nice ride?"

Grace nodded. "I really hated to come in but with it getting so late and all, I..."

"Grace!" Phillip called and they turned to see him at the front door. "I was looking for you. Just wanted to tell you I've got to go into town for a few minutes."

She looked down. "All right." She had been looking forward to spending the evening with her husband.

"You want to ride with me?" he asked. "We can go by the drive-up and get one of those root beer floats you like."

"I sure do. Just let me go get changed. It won't take but a..."

"No need. I'll only be a few minutes and you won't even need to get out. You can wait in the car. And we'll just drive up and get curbside service."

"Go on, Miss Grace," Hoot said. "I'll cool your horse off and put him up for you."

Philip had taken Grace by the arm and turned to walk

off when Hoot said, "Phillip, I've got a favor to ask.

Phillip stopped. "What is it?"

Hoot slid Cloudy's bridle off and buckled the halter around his head. "I need another few days off."

"Well, I guess it depends. When?"

"The eighth through the thirteenth."

"That's a pretty big span. Mighty short notice too," Phillip answered.

"I hope we can work it out," Hoot said. "I've been called to come up to New York."

Phillip raised his eyebrows. "Your family, okay?"

Hoot nodded. "Nothing like that. I've been asked to come up to the All-Star Show. You know, the one at Madison Square Gardens."

"Oh, the fundraiser for the war campaign?"

"Yeah, they're going to have a bunch of movie stars. A real big event. They apologized about contacting me so late. Said they thought of me at the last minute." He scuffed his toe on the ground. "Anyway, I'd hate to turn them down. Besides," he grinned. "It ought to be a lot of fun. "All those good-looking movie stars."

Phillip laughed. "Do you ever go anywhere that you don't run after women?"

"Not much," the jockey admitted.

"All joking aside," Phillip said. "Grady told me you're donating a quarter of your salary to the effort."

Hoot shrugged. "Well ... you know."

"That's a pretty hefty chunk."

Hoot looked down. "Well, it's kind of personal for me. My best friend was at Pearl Harbor."

Grace stepped over and laid her hand on his arm. "I'm sorry, Hoot."

He shrugged. "Yeah, we were pretty much inseparable since we met in second grade. Just two city kids that were crazy about horses. And when we were about ten, we got jobs at a local stable. Mucking out just for free rides."

Phillip smiled. "I can understand that." Grace didn't say anything but so did she.

"Anyway, it just started growing from there. Pretty soon we moved on to the track where they used us for exercise boys and a few years later I got a chance to race. Ben, he was a pretty big guy so that wasn't an option for him. Anyway, he ended up joining the service. Tried to get me to go along but my career was just starting to take off."

"Joining up always seems like a good idea when there's no war on," Phillip said. "You're just going along, building up your benefits and everything's smooth as silk. And then, bam. All of a sudden, everything all goes down the tubes, doesn't it?"

Hoot nodded and swallowed hard. "First time we were ever really separated," he said. "So now you see. I owe it to Ben to do what I can."

Hoot spread his arms wide and grinned. "Besides, wherever I work is pretty much home to me. Sure, I could get my own place, but I like hanging out with the guys. No rent. Always plenty of cars around to drive. All the food I want. No expenses at all. Man, with what I make, there's still going to be plenty left to send my folks a little, put some aside for my long, happy old age."

"What are you going to do when you retire, Hoot?" Grace asked.

He winked at her. "One of these days, I'm going to find me the prettiest woman in the world and settle down. Going to get me one big enough so I can raise a bunch of tall babies. And I'll just sit back and enjoy it all. Yes sir, I'm going to retire really early and have a grand life."

FIFTEEN

February 26, 1942

Grace guided Cloudy down the wide, sandy path that ran towards the back of the farm. She wanted to get as far away from the house as possible. If Papa found out she had sneaked off from Lorraine, he was going to be angry with her. Oh well, she thought. Nothing new about that. No matter what she did he found fault with it, and she just wanted to be alone today.

Especially out here. She felt like these rides belonged to her and no one else. It was just that...out here it was just her and Cloudy. No one looking at her, judging her. No one thinking how she was different or how she should fit in. Just the sky and the fields, the river, the little horse, and her. Fresh air. Movement. She could just let her mind drift and she didn't want to share it.

She heard it just as Cloudy startled. A great who-ooo-sh! A deer stood in the path ahead of them. A large buck, great antlers spread wide, head high as he sniffed the air and blew another warning. The little horse spooked in place but stood steady beneath her and simply trembled a little. Grace let out a long breath. If she had been riding one of the hot-blooded thoroughbreds, she would have been in trouble. She wouldn't have been able to hold one of them.

But the deer wasn't looking at them. It was staring down a little side trail that ran through the wooded area. It stood for a moment, frozen and alert, then bounded across the field; graceful, flying leaps that quickly carried it out of sight.

Glancing back, Grace saw what had spooked it. A horse was coming out of the woods. Big. Black. As tall as the thoroughbreds but much stockier. Heavily built, with long tufts of hair on the huge feet. Carrying a man in a Stetson. And a big, white dog bounded alongside. No mistaking who that was. Buzz. Touching his heels to the horse's side, he reined him towards Grace and broke into an easy canter. Even with the horse's size, he was collected and smooth and the rider barely moved in the saddle.

"Morning, Miss Grace." He touched the tip of his hat as he approached her. "Would you like some company?"

Grace didn't know what to say so she simply nodded. He turned his horse in the direction she was headed and Cloudy followed. They rode in silence for a few moments, then spoke at the same time.

"It's such a nice morning to..." began.

"I don't ever see anyone out here..." Buzz was saying.

Buzz laughed as Grace blushed. "You first."

"Oh nothing. Really. It's just such a pretty day. I'm glad to be out here."

"Me too." Buzz looked at her with a lazy smile spread across his face. "Not too often I get out here on a day like this. We're usually at the track in the mornings. But I told Phillip I was taking a couple of hours."

He looked around for the dog, saw him, and turned back to Grace. "Besides, I had planned to work with Hoot this morning. But he went off into town last night and didn't come back."

Grace nudged Cloudy with her heel. "Shouldn't someone go see if they can find him? Aren't you worried? I mean what if something happened to him?"

Buzz shook his head and smiled. "Pretty sure I know what happened to him. I imagine he tied one on down at the bar. Hoot's a great guy but he sure does love his liquor. He'll be along. Gets mighty aggravating, sometimes. But it did give me a good excuse to get out for a ride."

Grace didn't know what to say so they rode along in silence for a few minutes. Then Buzz turned to look at her. "Read any good books lately?"

"Well...I don't know." Grace hesitated. She knew Buzz was interested in books that seemed more serious than the ones she read. "You know. Just a few novels." She tried to shift the conversation so he would have the opportunity to talk. "What about you?"

Buzz reached back to open the saddlebags that were tied behind the cantle and pulled out a book.

It surprised her and Grace remembered how Phillip used to bring a book along when they would ride together. How they would sit beneath the willow at the pond, his head in her lap as he read poetry to her. She missed it so much.

"A collection of poetry. Shelly, Wordsworth and Keats."

Grace caught her breath. Surely, she had given out a gasp, but Buzz didn't seem to notice. The very same book Phillip used to read to her.

Wrapping his reins around the saddle horn, Buzz thumbed through the book. "This is just one of those books," he said. "You know, one you keep going back to, over and over."

Grace nodded.

"I don't know." Buzz paid no attention to his mount as he flipped through the book and the horse simply walked on. "This is one of those books that I just keep picking up. I might go a few months or even years and not think of it. But then I just kind of get a craving to read it again."

"Yes," Grace said. "Some books just sort of grab you that way." She didn't mention the fact that this was the very book that held so many memories for her. "I guess that's why I keep going back to some of the writing I'm so familiar with."

Buzz put the book back and fastened the saddlebags. Nudging his horse into a slow canter, he looked back at Grace. "You, okay?"

Grace was aware of his riding form as Cloudy trotted to catch up. She was trying so hard to keep her heels down that she forgot about her seat and her bottom was hitting the saddle hard as she flopped up and down. It was such a contrast to the picture Buzz made, floating along on the big, black cloud of a horse. She watched his back as they cantered along, so comfortable in the saddle.

She began to relax and fell into rhythm with Cloudy's stride. Such a steady little horse, solid and dependable. So, what if he did hit the ground a little hard, shaking his rider with his awkward stride? They had ridden so many miles together and she had come to trust him. She wouldn't trade him for any thoroughbred on the farm. And Buzz didn't seem to mind that she wasn't a skilled rider.

Finally, they came to the end of the wide path and the big, black horse slid to a smooth stop ahead of her. Buzz rode so well you couldn't even see the cues he gave the horse, it just seemed as though he would simply think a command and the horse would carry it out. She trotted up beside him and pulled Cloudy gradually down to a walk.

Buzz pushed his hat back. "Nothing like it, is there, Miss Grace?"

She smiled now, thinking he seemed to love it like she did.

"I sure am glad I don't have to spend my days inside, working in an office. Or a factory."

"What breed is that?" Grace nodded at his mount. "I don't think I've ever seen one like him."

"No one has." Buzz reached down and slapped the thick, sweaty neck. "He's a grade horse, not one particular breed. Sort of a mutt."

"Have you had him a long time?"

Buzz nodded. "All his life. He's out of a quarter horse stallion, down at one of the big ranches in Texas where Dad did a lot of work. You see, Dad had this cross-draft mare. No papers or anything but you could look at her and see a lot of Clydesdale, maybe a little Belgian."

Reaching into the saddlebag, Buzz pulled out a jar of water and offered it to Grace. When she shook her head, he took a long swallow. "Anyway, Dad had paid a pretty hefty price for that breeding. He was going to surprise me. 'Course I knew she was in foal; you can't hide a thing like that. Just didn't have a clue about the sire and well...to tell you the truth, didn't think too much about it. Anyway, as luck would have it, this guy hit the ground the night before my eighteenth birthday."

"So, he was a gift to you?"

Buzz nodded. "And we've been together ever since."

Grace pushed Cloudy into a jog because he was lagging behind a little. "I bet he weighs a couple thousand pounds."

"He comes in at just over eighteen hundred."

"And yet he moves like a smaller breed," Grace said. "He's not slow or awkward."

"That's the quarter horse in him." Buzz tapped his forefinger against his temple. "Dad had the smarts all right. Put together the size and strength of the work horse and the agility of a cowpony and look what he came up with. Not to mention the temperament. Can't get much quieter than the draft breeds."

"He really suits you."

"This old boy here has got a head full of sense. When we come up on a creek or a ditch, he won't shove his nose up in the air and get all nervous, prancing around, maybe falling and hurting himself or his rider. No sir, he'll put that big old head down, look at the ground, sniff around. If he can, he'll just walk right on. If not, he'll jump when he needs to."

"I like hearing you talk about your father," Grace said. She had never known her own father. The only thing she had to compare the thought with was Papa. And yet Buzz spoke of his own Dad with such fondness it made her smile a little inside.

Buzz nodded. "I sure do miss him. He gave me a really good life. Best a kid could ever ask for."

He stopped, glancing up at the sun and leaned over in the saddle, digging into his pocket. Pulling out a watch, he exclaimed, "Well, how did it get to be this late?" He looked over at her. "Sorry, Miss Grace, the time just gets away from me when I'm talking with you."

"It's okay,"

"Well, I'm pretty late. Anyway, I enjoyed riding with you, Miss Grace. I'll be seeing you around."

He reined the big horse in the opposite direction, shifted his weight up in the saddle and the horse sprang forward. Grace watched as they pounded away down the path towards the house in a cloud of dust, Spanky following close behind.

~~~
~~~

After Grace rubbed Cloudy down, she went over to the foaling barn. Phillip had told her to come take a look at the colt that had been born last night. He and Papa were there waiting for the vet to arrive to do a wellness check. They also had a two-year-old with a bowed tendon that had to be looked at.

She couldn't help but smile when she saw the new baby, staggering around the big stall, his mother right behind him every time he took a step. A bright red chestnut with a white blaze, tall and leggy. He looked a lot like Runaway.

They watched for a few minutes as the colt nursed, then laid down in the straw, let out a huge sigh and closed his eyes. Then Papa left to attend to a business deal up at the office.

Grace decided Cloudy had cooled off enough to have his grain. She was in his paddock when she saw one of the farm trucks pull up. Hoot got out and she could see he was carrying something. As he came around the back side of the barn towards jockey's quarters, she saw that it was a kitten. How strange, she thought.

Hoot stopped when he passed the paddock and tipped his cap. "Morning, Miss Grace."

"Hello Hoot. Where'd you get that little guy?"

He held the little bundle up and Grace could see him clearly now. A golden tabby, he didn't even look old enough to be weaned yet. "Oh, he was wandering around in the parking lot this morning. Just about got run over." He looked up, a sheepish grin on his face. "What can I say? Guess I'm just a sucker." Pulling the kitten's face up close to his, he looked him in the eye. "Besides, we can always use another mouser around here."

Grace reached over the fence line and stroked the fuzzy head. The kitten turned his blue eyes towards her, opened his mouth and let out a yowl.

"I think this little guy is hungry. Excuse me, Miss Grace. I'm going to get him a saucer of milk and get to work."

Grace watched until Hoot disappeared into the front door at quarters, still stroking the kitten's head.

SIXTEEN

March 1, 1942

"Yoooh-wheeeee!" A loud shriek cut through the afternoon air. Grace peered out the window just in time so see Frank's car pulling slowly down the long drive towards the road. She could see some of the men hanging out the back windows but couldn't tell which ones they were. She couldn't see who was driving because the thick vines of the grape arbor obscured the front of the car, but she knew it couldn't be Frank. "What in the world..." she wondered as she heard more yelling and laughter. Frank was going to have a fit. Then, as the big car passed the grape arbor, the front end came into view. Hoot was sitting on the wide hood. Wearing nothing but a pair of boxer shorts. She closed her eyes immediately, then blinked and walked back over to the bed. But she could feel her cheeks burning with embarrassment and she wished she hadn't seen that.

She finished dressing and went downstairs. Mama was hosting a meeting of the ladies' circle and she was expected to be there. Most of the women were polite but they just seemed so...well, so distant.

Sometimes she wished she could be just a little like Lorraine. Not that she wanted all her sister-in-law's traits, but it would be nice to feel at ease with all the influential people that were always being entertained here at Janus.

Taking a cup of the lime punch, she sat down beside Mama, who was talking to the mayor's wife. The room was buzzing with voices as the ladies clustered here and there. Grace picked up a finger sandwich from a silver tray and bit into it, the slices of cucumber crunching between her teeth, and she felt a rivulet of juice running down her chin. Wiping it with a delicate lace napkin, she cut into one of the little white teacakes and raspberry filling spilled out onto the plate.

Hattie Birdsong, the committee chair, stood at the head of the table and called the meeting to attention. When they went over old business, the Victory Garden was the main topic. The group was full of compliments for Grace's guidance. She sat, blushing as she listened but it did feel nice to be noticed in a good way and it made her feel she was a part of the group.

"Is there any new business?" Hattie asked.

Gladys Shearin stood up. "I've been thinking about what else we may be able to do to support the war effort. What would you ladies think about putting on a Roanoke Rapids Day? Sort of a little festival to raise funding. You know, we do have quite a bit of interesting history in our area, and I think we could draw in a substantial crowd. Not just the locals, but tourists, people who like to travel. And we're on Highway three-oh-one, the main route from New York down to Florida, it runs right through here."

"That's a wonderful idea," said Ella-Belle Odom.

"We could make it into something like a county fair," Mama spoke up. "Do a cake walk, pickle contest. Sell candied apples and popcorn."

"I could get my husband to bring over his draft horses and give a hayride down Roanoke Avenue," said Martha Strayhorn."

Suddenly, Lorraine sprang up from her chair. "Why couldn't we incorporate Janus Farms into this thing? After all, Runaway Rapids is a big deal with selling war bonds. And we've got the most famous jockey in America."

"That's a wonderful idea," Hattie said. She looked at Mama. "Do you think Mr. Masterson would allow us to do that?"

Mama nodded. "I'm sure Franklin would be delighted."

Lorraine's eyes were shining with excitement. "We could bring people out here. You know, do a little tour of the farm. Charge admission. Get Hoot to do autographs. Put Runaway on display and I bet we could sell loads of war bonds."

Her enthusiasm was contagious and now the room was

buzzing. Bits of conversation floated through the room, voices all mixed together, Grace could hardly tell who was speaking.

"We could have a horseshoe contest. Men love to do that."

"What about a dunking booth? I bet people around here would pay a lot to try that if Mayor Sykes would get in."

"Maybe a pie-eating contest. And we need to get to work right away on making some arts and crafts to sell. Do some needle work, homemade doilies, things like that."

"I know!" We could make a quilt to raffle off. Put all sorts of things about the town on it."

"Hey, pictures of things like the mills, the river, our canal trail. Historical things."

"And let's put Runaway Rapids right in the middle. Oh, the farm too."

Lorraine had been quiet for a few minutes. Grace could see the wheels turning in her mind. Now she spoke up. "I'm going to write a book about Janus Farms. We can sell copies. I bet people would stand in line for them."

Everyone was quiet for a moment. Then Mary-Frances let out a little giggle. "You? A writer? Are you actually going to sit down and be still long enough to be an author?"

"Well...." Lorraine stammered. "I can do it. Besides," she looked over at Grace. "Grace will help me. She's the literary person in our family. She always has her nose in a book."

"But I don't know anything about writing," Grace protested. "Just because you like to read...well, that doesn't have a thing to do with writing." But her voice was drowned out under all the excited comments.

"Well, you all know my husband owns the printing press," said Alice Clay. "I'll get him to print the books at no charge to us."

"And we've got the photography studio," said Lucille Edwards. "I'll send Herman out to do the photos. People love historical books with pictures."

Grace sat silently in the midst of the excitement. She knew what was going to happen. Lorraine would go right on with her constant socializing and Grace would be stuck doing all the work. She loved helping with the Victory Garden but writing a book? That was completely beyond her capabilities. How on earth was she going to get out of this?

After the meeting was adjourned, Lorraine took some of the younger women across the hall into the drawing room and Grace could hear her playing popular tunes on the piano. Grace stood in the hallway for a while, watching. A few of the girls gathered around the piano but most of them simply re-organized into tight little groups and continued with the small talk. Grace stood, peering through the doorway, and feeling like an outsider in her own home.

Slipping out to the side porch she sat down in the swing. This thing that they wanted her to help Lorraine with. She had no clue how to go about it. She had tried to tell them she couldn't do it, but they just wouldn't listen.

She sat there, gazing out at the horses. Taking her shoes off, she pushed the swing with her foot, and it moved gently back and forth as she sipped her punch. Twilight was just descending, and lightening bugs glowed here and there through Mama's flower gardens. The fragrance of gardenias drifted up onto the porch.

Funny, she thought, how the birdsong was drifting gradually away, and the crickets were becoming louder. And the dandelions. The yellow flower she had seen this afternoon had turned itself inward as the sun faded. The feathery spikes floated now in the evening breeze.

The chirrup of the crickets had nearly taken over completely when she saw Phillip's car coming up the drive. Her heart thumped a little like it always did when she saw him come home. Soon now, he would be upstairs with her. All alone in their suite. She would lie with her head on his shoulder, and he would tell her about his day. But he had been so exhausted recently that he would often fall asleep mid-sentence.

Phillip pulled around to the carport at the rear of the house and she could barely see the car. She heard the doors slam and Phillip came around the corner, followed by Hoot and Grady. Hoot had on a pair of pants now, but they looked about four sizes too big, and he was holding then up as he walked. One of the cuffs that was rolled up came loose and fell, tripping him. Stumbling to his knees, he let out a string of curse words but began to giggle as Phillip scooped him up onto his feet. Grady followed behind them and Grace could tell they had both been drinking. Heavily.

"Don't ever dare Hoot to do something," Grady chuckled. "He'll do it or die trying. You should have seen Sherriff Walker's face when he pulled us over." Grady slapped his thigh. "I swear, he didn't know whether to laugh at Hoot or throw him in jail."

"You're lucky he knows you, Grady." Phillip turned Hoot in the direction of the stables. "Or you two would be down there cooling you heels in a cell all night."

Hoot stumbled again and Phillip hoisted him up just as another car turned into the drive. "Here Grady," Phillip said. "Get Hoot on down there and see if you can get him in bed."

Papa's car pulled up. Three more of the hands got out, laughing a little but Papa sat there for a moment, chewing on his cigar. Frank's car pulled in behind him and Frank got out. Three steps and he was on Hoot. Grabbing his arm, he spun the little man around.

"Hi-ya Frank," Hoot said. "We're just going down to quarters and have another little drink. You want to come?"

"You idiot!" Frank jerked the jockey so hard that the pants started to slide down. Phillip stepped over and pulled them up.

"Come on, Frank," he said. "You have to admit. It was pretty funny. They did shake Roanoke Rapids up a little this evening."

"Made fools of us," Frank sputtered. "What would you say the town thinks of us now?"

"I guess they probably think we have a lot of fun out here." Phillip turned Hoot towards the stables. "Go on with Grady."

"They stole my car! And riding all over town nearly naked! Bunch of fools."

Frank reached for Hoot's arm again, but Papa walked up. "Settle down, boy." Pulling the cigar from his mouth, he twirled it, pulled a lighter from his pocket and lit it up.

Frank's head jerked around. "You don't care that he made fools of us?"

"Oh, I don't believe anybody thinks that," Papa answered. "The men have to get out once in a while, sow a few wild oats."

"But Papa, he ought to be fired."

Papa stepped up to Frank and looked him in the eye. "Hoot's the nation's number one jockey right now, Frank. He's not going anywhere."

Frank turned on his heel and stalked away, disappearing into the garage. Phillip and Papa went around to the side entrance and Grace lingered in the shadows. She didn't want anyone to know she had witnessed all this. If Phillip mentioned it later tonight, she would just pretend she didn't know anything about it.

SEVENTEEN

Summer 2021

Drake has arrived early this morning, nearly an hour before anyone else will be here. I am sitting on the veranda with Grace, having a second cup of coffee when I see her aunt drive up and let her off. As the car drives away, I start to get up but then I settle back again. Some deep instinct tells me to leave her alone for a little while. There is a reason she is here early. She wants her time alone with the horses.

Grace lays her hand on my arm and nods. Such a strange old woman, so intuitive. Sometimes I think she can see right through me, knows what I am thinking, almost before I know it myself. Always looking, listening, never talks much at all.

We watch as Drake leads Sundown out of the stables. She ties the horse to the hitching post, and we watch as she pulls out the shedding rake, runs it over his coat, then stops to pull out the long hairs it has collected. She falls into a rhythm: rake, pull, repeat. Sundown stands hipshot, right hind foot cocked at an angle, hindquarters on that side drooped into the most relaxed position a horse can assume.

We sit, not talking as we watch for about fifteen minutes. My mind wanders a little as I think about how many clients, we will be working with later this morning. Thank goodness Sandra is due back today. It's been tough without her help. I hadn't realized how much I depended on her until she was gone. Finally, Drake stops, gives the palomino a little slap on the rump and goes to return the grooming kit to the tack room. She returns with a wheelbarrow and pitchfork, so I know she is going to clean Sundown's stall. We see her appear again in a few minutes, pushing the load of dirty straw down to the compost heap behind the back shelter.

I have been watching Drake closely for the last few weeks. She always looks comfortable putting the palomino through his paces, the slow jog, leading into a working lope. I have noticed how she will reverse directions and cue him to the correct lead, inside leg reaching out first. And if he takes the wrong lead, she stops and corrects him. I can tell this girl has done some show ring work, probably the Coastal Plains circuit. She knows how to ride pleasure classes. Not really an advanced rider, but I certainly would say she is intermediate.

When we begin to see the others arrive, I take Grace inside, make sure she has everything she needs, and head down to the stables. Maggie Mae goes off to get Valentine while Jennifer and Sandra take Landen to get him ready.

As I lead Diesel around the arena with Landen sitting fairly still on his back, I watch Drake. She is in the lower arena, cantering easily and Sundown is responding well.

From the corner of my eye, I see Maggie Mae and Valentine, walking up the path, side by side. I am finally getting accustomed to the sight, marvel that it is. Horses are like people, I think. They would rather stand around and eat than work, but Valentine doesn't know he has a job. All he knows is that he has a little friend who gives him treats and keeps him company. When she sits on his bare back with no means of control and he simply goes where he chooses, you could hardly call that work. He's probably happy to have her there, swatting the flies away. A symbiotic relationship if I ever saw one.

I had sent the video of them sleeping to Maggie's mom. She posted it on Facebook, along with a link to our website. It went viral. Millions of likes and shares. And it has changed things around here. There has always been help from local sponsors but suddenly we are receiving donations from all over the country. Substantial donations. Several of them have contained notes that mention how deeply the video touched them. Denise is thrilled and we have had several conversations concerning how to direct the money to the improvements most needed.

Sandra drives up and is barely out of the car before she is bombarded with kids running up to greet her. It is plain to see that I am not the only one who missed her. She turns back to the car and takes out several large boxes of pizza. By the time the volunteers have everything spread out on the picnic tables, kids are coming from all directions, tying their horses up at the hitching posts so they can ride again later. Diesel comes trotting up with kids spilling out of all sides of the cart.

By the time I get to the picnic tables everyone is grabbing pizza and they are all talking over one another until you can hardly make out what they are saying. But it is a happy noise.

Maggie Mae is just beginning to eat. Suddenly she looks up and points down the length of the table.

"Can I have some of that Farmer John Cheese, please?" she asks.

"What, honey?" Sandra asks.

"That Farmer John cheese."

The adults look to the spot she is pointing at, and we begin to laugh. Maggie's mom picks up the jar of *parmesan* cheese, smiles and nods at us as she passes it down the table.

After we are done, Sandra and I help Maggie's mom clean up the mess while the volunteers are supervising the children who are riding again. Quite a few of them are just goofing off, hanging out together. When the last of the trash is bagged, I go back to the arena and watch.

Sandra comes up to lean on the fence beside me.

"How was your trip?" I ask.

"Oh, it was great to see my folks. They want to come spend a weekend with me. I was telling them about how the program is growing and they want to come out and see it." She pauses and looks back towards the house. "And Jo, I was asking Mom about what I had told you. You know, about the murder here, way back."

"Did she remember it?"

"Well, it happened before she was born so she didn't know too much. Just that someone was killed, bludgeoned to death with that trophy. You know, the silver one with the two-faced horse." She shudders. "Said they found little chips of silver in his skull."

"You mean…right here, on the farm?"

Sandra nods.

"But who was it? Why did they…"

Drake rides up and stops at the fence, so Sandra simply shrugs her shoulders, and we change the topic of conversation to how well Drake is riding. But as the day goes on, I continue to wonder about it. All the strange things I have seen and heard around here. I shake off the thoughts. Silly. Just my imagination. Besides, whatever happened out here was a long time ago. Over half a century.

"Hey Jo!" Jennifer calls and I turn to look. It is getting to be nearly dusk, and I have hardly noticed. "Maggie's mom left about a few minutes ago and I'm taking her home a little later. Have you seen her?"

Oh, no, I thought. Here we go again. I signaled to Drake to come in and then I leave in search of Maggie, knowing Drake will cool the horse off and put him up properly.

We begin our search but we're not really worried. By now I have become accustomed to Maggie's little disappearances. I wander through the stables, looking as I hear Jennifer and Sandra calling for her.

"I saw Maggie Mae and her pony a little while ago," Drake says as she walks past me, leading Sundown.

"Where's that little rascal got off to this time?" I ask.

"They were going up the path," Drake says. She points towards the house.

Sure enough, I can see tiny little hoofprints leading up the path. They were probably somewhere up there under the cedars. Or maybe at the grape arbor. I quicken my pace. I hope she's not feeding grapes to Valentine. He eats everything she gives him. I don't want to have to call the vet out for colic.

I put my hands up to shade my eyes, but they are nowhere in sight. I'm not going to panic though. I have learned how those two have a way of being in the least expected places.

Then I notice something. I'm no tracker or anything but the little hoofprints are here, plain as day and they are leading right up to the side door of the house. The one that opens into the kitchen.

I open the door and step in. There they are, Maggie Mae sitting at the table, Valentine standing beside her munching on apple slices. Grace, seated on the other side of the table looks up at me and I see a smile on a face that is usually somber. The nurse is standing behind Grace, wedged into the corner, holding a broom.

"Look, Jo-Jo," Maggie says. "We're having a party with Miss Grace."

"Maggie said she was sorry that I couldn't come down to the pizza party," Grace explains. "So, she brought Valentine up to visit with me." She tips a glass at me, filled with Kool-Aid, and pushes a plate towards me. "Have a cookie with us."

I don't want a cookie, but I stand for a moment, watching them. Grace passes the plate to Maggie-Mae. "Want another?" she asks. Maggie takes a cookie and nibbles it as Valentine finishes his apple slices. He nudges her and sniffs around the table, looking for more, then starts towards me to see if I have anything to offer. As he passes the nurse, she draws the broom back.

"Don't you dare hit that pony!" Grace says with fire in her eyes. "He's not hurting a thing."

The little hooves clomp across the faded old tile with a loud ticking sound and Maggie laughs. "Isn't this a good surprise, Jo-Jo?" she asks.

And I have to admit that it is. Sort of out of the ordinary but it is good, nonetheless.

The nurse, still holding the broom, scurries to the door. "It's nearly time for me to go. Since you're here, Jodi, I'm leaving."

Maggie doesn't notice anything, but Grace and I smile at each other as a look of conspiracy passes between us.

"I told Jo-Jo I'm going to be a barrel racer when I grow up," Maggie tells Grace. "Like the ones I saw on television. I'll have a fast horse and we're going to be big stars. It will be the biggest show you ever saw."

Grace's eyes mist over for a moment. Then she clears her throat and says, "I knew a really big star once," she said.

"Was she a horse rider?" Maggie asks.

Grace nods. "Sure was. Only it was a he. Not a girl but a young man. Probably the best rider I've ever seen in my life." She put her glass down. "And believe me, honey, I've seen the best."

"Tell about him," Maggie begs. "Was he a barrel racer, too?"

"No honey. He was a jockey. And how the people did love him. He was probably the most famous jockey that America ever saw."

EIGHTEEN

March 8, 1942

"**T**he most exciting nightspot in the whole world!" Lorraine exclaimed as they walked down fifty-third street in New York. "That's what my fan magazine calls it."

Phillip looked down at Grace and rolled his eyes. Lorraine had insisted on bringing eight bags of clothing even though they were only going to be here for three days.

Grady and the grooms were taking care of Runaway where he was stabled down at Madison Square Gardens for the upcoming show tomorrow. A temporary stall had been put up and someone would be guarding him at all times.

To tell the truth, the heart of New York City was all a little overwhelming to Grace. She had become accustomed to going to big places for the races, but this was different. Bustling with activity, the street was filled with lights, car horns blared incessantly, people jostled each other on the sidewalk. She was glad to have Phillip's arm around her.

Hoot led the way, having been to the Stork Club before. Buzz really looked out of place up there beside him with the wide-brimmed Stetson and western boots. He did have on a suit though because the dress code here was really strict.

An awful racket permeated the air as they neared the building. A loud, rhythmic clanking noise that rose above all the surrounding sounds. Then Grace saw what it was. A man and woman were outside the door, metal spoons in their ands beating on a collection of pots and pans.

The woman stopped and smiled at then. "Admission price is one piece of aluminum ware," she explained.

Suddenly, Grace understood. The aluminum drive, of course. To convert to armaments for the war.

WHERE THE STATUE WEEPS

They hadn't brought any pots and pans along, so Papa pulled the roll from his pocket and peeled off a hundred-dollar bill for each person in the party. Eight of them. The couple thanked him as he said, "Guess you can get a few pieces with that," and strutted up to the door.

The doorman presented each of the women with a live orchid. Phillip stopped to help Grace pin her flower on.

"Look, girls," Mama said in a low voice. "A whole room full of movie stars! There's Myrna Loy and Loretta Young." The two women passed by and the family watched as they returned to their table.

Everywhere Grace looked, she saw gorgeous stars in full evening gowns and silk gloves accompanied by men in tuxedos. It *was* hard to believe they were in the same room with all these famous people.

The waiter arrived just then to escort them to the table. "Mr. Hoot Harrison and Janus Farms party?"

Hoot nodded. "Follow me, please. We have one of the best tables reserved for you."

As the family followed him, they recognized celebrities scattered throughout the room. The Stork Club was known as the place for the rich and famous but tonight, familiar faces were everywhere. Movie stars were gathered to prepare for the WW11 Relief Show that Hoot had been invited to.

Just as the waiter placed a plate of filet mignon in front of Grace, the shimmering pink stage curtain opened, and the floor show began. Women in brilliant costumes of every color tapped out onto the floor, whirling in perfect sync. Such a large group of them, Grace counted fifty. Suddenly, they parted in the center and a woman stepped through them to the front of the stage. She trailed a long, scarlet-colored scarf ten feet behind her. The elaborate dance number ended with a fan blowing the scarf straight up as the other dancers swirled around her.

Lorraine, sipping her lobster bisque, put down her spoon and clapped enthusiastically. Her cheeks were flushed with the excitement. Papa signaled for the waiter. "Another bottle of champagne!" he demanded. "Your finest."

The floor show ended, and the curtain closed. Grace noticed the house photographer moving across the floor, stopping at the tables where stars were seated. She was surprised when he made his way towards them.

He paused for a moment. "May I?" he asked.

"Certainly," Papa agreed. "Please do."

After he snapped a few shots and moved away, Lorraine let out a little squeal, "Who would ever have imagined we would be here?"

Hoot grinned at her. "Next time you come, you'll probably see your picture right up there on the wall, alongside all those Hollywood stars."

The stage curtain re-opened, and the band began to play. They were watching when the head waiter walked up to the table and cleared his throat. "Mr. Harrison?"

Hoot looked up. "Yes sir, what can I do for you?"

"A newspaper columnist has requested your presence in one of the private rooms. He would like to do an interview." He turned to Papa. "Mr. Masterson, I presume? Of Janus Farms?"

Papa nodded. "That's me."

"He would like you to accompany Mr. Harrison, please."

As Papa and Hoot got up to go with the waiter, Frank followed them.

As the band began to play Moonlight Cocktail, Buzz got up and held his hand out to Lorraine. "Could I have this dance, please?"

Lorraine followed him onto the floor. And there, dancing even among all the Hollywood celebrities, all eyes were on them. Lorraine was just as glamorous as any starlet in the room. And Buzz. Well, none of the actors could hold a candle to him for looks and just pure, raw, male sexuality. At least, that was what Grace thought. He took Lorraine in his arms and swept her through the crowd, towering a head above the other men.

As Grace watched, her stomach tightened. At first, she thought it was just the excitement of it all but then she realized she was a little envious. She didn't really understand it. Here she was, sitting with her husband, so handsome, so kind. Not just a good man, but sincere in all things. How could she possibly be having thoughts like this?

The song ended and the band broke into Don't Sit Under the Apple Tree With Anyone Else But Me. Grace watched as Buzz swung Lorraine around and she smiled up at him. Phillip looked over at her, and for just a split second she thought she saw something a little different in his eyes. She couldn't really put her finger on it. Not angry. Not really sad. Just...serious. Could he somehow sense what she had been thinking? Probably just her imagination. Her guilty conscience.

The mood was broken when the waiter came up to pour more champagne. When the band moved into the slow melody of String of Pearls, Mama waved a hand at Phillip. "Go on, son. Take your wife out there on the floor. I'm fine. I just enjoy sitting here and watching it all."

Phillip took Grace by the hand, led her out and began a slow waltz step. He was such an experienced dancer that he could even lead a bashful klutz like her around the dance floor. She laid her head on his shoulder and let herself relax, moved by the gentle force of her husband's tall, strong body, and melted into the music. Even among all this glitz and glamour that made her feel so out of place, he made her feel comfortable. Made her feel safe.

After a few dances, they sat and watched. It really was fun, Grace thought. This was something most people would never hope to see.

When the band took their break, the emcee took the stage to announce the balloon drop. "This is something for ladies only," he instructed. "If you'll look up into the ceiling, you'll see that net filled with balloons. Each one has something in it. It may be a little prize, or it may be a number for the drawing. When we release them, I want you to be ready to grab one. After all, you never know what you may get!"

Grace sat there, reluctant to get up. Lorraine was already out in the center of the floor, surrounded by women. Mama got up from her seat. "Come on, Grace. Let's see what we get. Evidently this game's not just for the young women, I see a lot of older gals out there."

Mama took her hand and pulled her out on the floor. She looked back at the table. Phillip and Buzz were watching them, amused smiles on their faces.

"All right, ladies! Are you ready?" The emcee strutted back and forth on the stage, fueling the excitement. The women moved about, vying for the best vantage point.

And then the emcee took hold of the golden cord hanging in the center of the stage and gave it a mighty heave. The net released and hundreds of balloons floated through the air. The room turned into a squealing mass of feminine flesh, jostling each other.

Grace caught a white balloon and wasn't sure what to do. She stood there, holding onto it until Mama got one and they returned to the table. Lorraine was there, waving her red balloon through the air victoriously. They sat watching, until every woman on the floor had grasped a balloon.

The emcee was up at the microphone again. "Now, ladies! On the count of three, I want everyone to pop their balloons. Are you ready?"

Shouts of YES went up and he began the countdown. "ONE! TWO! Are you sure you're ready? All right, THREEEEEEEE!"

Balloons popped throughout the room amidst a great deal of shouting. Several of the women got up to chase their balloons across the floor.

Grace had number fifty-two and Lorraine had thirty-six. Mama's balloon contained a hundred-dollar bill. She had folded it with a smile, tucked it into her bosom and said, "Don't even tell Papa. We have all those charge accounts at home, but it's sort of different to have my own money."

There was a great deal of excitement as the prizes were handed out. All kinds of jewelry, bracelets, several necklaces, a bottle of perfume eau du jour. When Lorraine's number was called out, she marched up onstage and came back with a five-hundred-dollar gift certificate for Macy's.

Finally, the emcee called number fifty-two and Phillip had to give Grace a little push. She felt so self-conscious walking up onstage. She stood awkwardly, waiting.

"And what is your name, sweetheart?" he asked.

"Miss Grace Masterson," he repeated into the microphone after she told him. "It looks like she picked the right balloon. Twice each year, we have a really big prize, and this lady is our winner. Are you ready, Grace?"

She nodded and he raised an arm to beckon to someone beyond the curtain. "All right, let's bring it on out."

Grace didn't see because she was looking at him, but the crowd let out a gasp and she turned to look. There, rolling slowly across the show floor was a pink Cadillac convertible. She blinked her eyes. Surely, she wasn't really seeing that. Why, she didn't even know how to drive a car!

But it was a car. A pink car. She had never seen such a thing before.

"What do you say to that, Grace?" the emcee asked.

She turned to look at him. "I... well...I..."

"Look at that, ladies and gentlemen. She's speechless. Let's give Grace a hand."

The audience went wild with applause until the emcee held up his hand. "It's last year's model. The automotive factories aren't building them this year. The war armaments, you know. Anything we can do to help the war effort. But it's practically new. Hardly has any miles at all on it. And now, let's get your family up here, Grace."

Lorraine came bouncing up onto the stage, grabbed Grace and whirled her around. Phillip came up the steps with Mama on his arm and shook hands with the emcee. Grace looked out and she could see Buzz, grinning at them.

The emcee took the keys out of the ignition and handed them to Grace. She didn't know what to do. She had never thought it was a big deal that she didn't know how to drive but suddenly she was ashamed. As usual, Phillip came to her rescue. He took the keys, escorted her to the passenger side and opened the door for her. Going to the driver's side, he started the car and Grace could still hear applause as they drove behind the curtain and down the ramp. A man brought out a clipboard with paperwork to be filled out. Grace just sat there, waiting for Phillip to do it but he handed it to her and said, "Oh, no you don't. This car belongs to you."

LENN ROBERSON

~~~

HOOT HARRISON SAYS GIVE A HOOT ABOUT YOUR
COUNTRY
BUY YOUR WAR BONDS!

A corral had been set up near the entrance of Madison Square Gardens. Runaway Rapids pranced back and forth in it behind the banner, throwing his head and snorting. Hoot sat at a table in front of the corral, signing autographs as stewards sold bonds and collected money. He managed to smile brightly at everyone but Grace knew he was hungover from last night at the club. Phillip, Buzz, Grady, and the grooms stood at the corners of the corral, their eyes on the big stallion.

After people purchased their bonds, most of them walked up close to get a good look at the famous horse. A few were trying to pet him, but the men were keeping them well back. Cloudy stood quietly near the stallion in the corral and Grace knew that was the only thing that was keeping Red manageable. Even through all the excitement, the colt was feeding off the other horse's calmness.

It seemed to Grace that every single person that came in was going over to see Runaway Rapids. And it looked as if they were all buying bonds, too. As soon as they got an autograph from Hoot and took a look at the racehorse, they moved on over to the stewards to purchase their bonds. This was going to be a huge success.

"Come on, Grace." Lorraine tugged at her arm. "Let's go back and watch some more of the show."

As Grace followed behind her sister-in-law, she turned to look back at Phillip. He smiled at her and nodded his head.

Returning to their seats beside Mama and Papa, the girls settled down to watch more of the entertainment. Grace reached up to cover her mouth and stifle a yawn. This was the most exciting thing she had ever seen but the show had been going on for hours and hours. Over fifty stars were making an appearance, the emcee had announced and it
~~~

was all quite grand. Singing, dancing, comedians. Here she was in New York City, seeing celebrities in person. So many that she had seen at the theater in movies and on special television programs. Never in all her wildest dreams would she have imagined it. Myrna Loy was just starting to dance and Grace realized that she had been in the same room with this gorgeous starlet just a couple of nights ago. Jimmy Durante came out and joked about his big nose.

Grace didn't know how long she had been dozing when Lorraine gave her a little shake. She found herself leaning against her sister-in-law's shoulder and struggled to sit upright. She looked around and rubbed her eyes.

"How on earth could you ever sleep through this?" Lorraine half-whispered. She pointed at the entrance to the arena below. Suddenly, Grace was wide awake.

The crowd let out a collective gasp as Cloudy jogged in, followed by Runaway Rapids. When the stallion saw them, he reared and pawed the air. Grady and Phillip came in, one on each side, taking hold of the bridle and helped Hoot get control. Finally, after Buzz brought Cloudy over to stand beside him, the colt calmed down a little. They walked the horses out onto the floor, Red spooking at the slightest movement.

A hush came over the crowd when the emcee announced them as the grand marshals. "Ladies and gentlemen," he roared. "We give you; Hoot Harrison and Runaway Rapids of Janus Farms!" The national anthem began to play and Cloudy stepped out calmly. Hoot followed on Big Red and the colt matched his stablemate, step for step. Grace could tell the jockey was having a hard time, it was all that he could do to hold the horse as they went into a canter. The only thing that made him manageable at all was having Cloudy by his side. Every eye in Madison Square Garden was on the big, red thoroughbred but Grace was so proud of Cloudy.

Three times they circled the arena, as Runaway Rapids cantered a half-length behind his stablemate. As the song came to a close, Buzz pulled Cloudy into the center of the arena and Hoot followed close behind on Red. As they stood there waiting for the last chords of the song to end, the horses suddenly became very still. The stallion's head was up, ears pricked but he remained motionless.

The applause was deafening as the crowd cheered for the country's favorite pair as the last line of the song rang out. A deep shiver reverberated down Grace's spine as she looked around at all these patriotic people. Some could well afford it but there were plenty of common people here too. Even those everywhere out there who had so little, giving freely to the effort, doing so much to support their country on the Homefront. This, Grace thought, really was the nation of the people who were free and brave.

NINETEEN

April 6, 1942

"**H**ey, how would you girls like to go wander up yonder with me?" Buzz asked. Grace and Lorraine had just saddled the horses. Frank and Phillip had gone to Warren County to look at a mare.

"Wander where?" Lorraine asked.

Grace smiled a little inside because she knew exactly what Buzz was talking about.

But Buzz was grinning at Lorraine. "Fly off into the wild, blue yonder. Escape from this sorry old earth for a little while. You know, just float around up there among the clouds and get away from it all."

"There'll be none of that." Papa walked up, scowling. "If you girls are going to ride, mount up and get out of here. Otherwise, get on back up to the house."

As they rode away, they heard Buzz yell, "If you girls change your mind, I'll be leaving in about an hour."

They had only ridden about a mile when Lorraine said. "Let's go back and ride with Buzz. I could tell by the way Papa was dressed up; he was going into town."

"I don't know," Grace nudged Cloudy to catch up with Lorraine's horse. "Phillip did say Papa was going in to see how the progress was going on the special trophy, with the two-faced horse. But what if he comes back early? Anyway, we're supposed to work on the book when we get back."

"Why are you so scared of Papa? Besides, no one would dare tell him."

Grace didn't say anything. She knew she was a coward, but it still stung to hear someone say it out loud."

"Stay here if you want," Lorraine said. "But I'm not missing out on a chance like this." Turning her horse, she dug her heels into him and galloped back towards the house.

Grace rode on down the path, following alongside the river before she pulled Cloudy up and looked back in the direction Lorraine had ridden. She could hardly bear the thought of Buzz and Lorraine, alone in his little plane.

Cloudy tossed his head, impatient to go and she turned him back towards the stables, pushing him into a canter. She was going to defy Papa and go with them! She didn't care how angry he got.

As she rode, she thought how someone around here was always arguing. Her thoughts drifted back to the previous night. She had gone to give Cloudy a treat, thinking everyone was gone. She could hear Phillip in the tack room and as she went past, she caught a glimpse of Frank there with him. She didn't pay a lot of attention until Frank had raised his voice.

"Look Phillip, I'm just asking you for a loan, I'll pay you back."

Grace's grip had tightened on the apple she was holding. She didn't want Phillip to look out and see her. But she could still hear them even from the back of the stable.

"Why don't you take an advance on your salary?" Phillip had asked.

"Papa might find out. This is the last time I'll ask you. I swear."

Cloudy had nickered and the voices were muffled. Then she had heard Phillip.

"You go around spending money like crazy."

"You got to spend it to make it."

Grace saw Phillip step out of the tack room and into the dim light of the aisle. "If you'd stop buying those horses that can't run, you wouldn't have any problem."

Grace had known what he meant. Phillip had finally broken his silence and given her what he thought was good news. He and Papa had decided not to let Frank do any more buying unless one of them approved it.

But that hadn't stopped Frank. Instead, he had gone out and spent his own money to purchase new horses, with the same results. He had been borrowing from Phillip to cover his losses.

"We're not losing that much," Frank had said. "We can afford it."

"That's not the point. Doesn't it bother you to see those horses go to Bullock?"

"Well, that's the racing business. Either they can run, or they end up in the slaughter pens. It's not just us, it's standard for the entire industry."

Cloudy had snorted and Grace couldn't hear Philip's response. A moment later, he had come out and gone towards the house.

She kept nudging the little horse forward now. At the edge of the woods, the stables came into view. Cloudy picked up his pace, eager to get back to his stall.

But just as she rode into the stable yard, the roar of an engine filled the air. Most of the horses in the paddocks spooked and ran in circles, heads high and snorting. Even Cloudy startled a little underneath her and took a couple of steps sideways. Grace looked up as the rumbling grew louder and saw the tiny plane fly over the stables. All the hands came out and looked up just in time to see Lorraine lean out of the passenger side and drop something. A red chiffon scarf floated down and one of the grooms caught it. Spanky cavorted around Hoot's heels as he snatched it and draped it across the boy's head. There was a great deal of laughter and joking about the fragrant perfume.

"Looks like Miss Lorraine might be slipping out of the traces a little bit here," one of the men said.

As she brushed Cloudy, all she could think about was what Buzz and Lorraine were doing. She should have just come back when Lorraine did. What would it be like, she wondered? To just go out and grab onto every experience that life afforded you.

~~~

Later that afternoon, Grace looked out to see Frank and Phillip unloading the mare they had bought. She wandered down to the stables to see the new horse. The stable boys had put down a thick bed of fresh straw and Phillip led the mare into her stall. Frank dumped a bucket
~~~

of grain into the feeder and Grace filled a hay net and hung it on the wall. They watched as the mare paced, then settled down and began to chew on the grain.

Two of the hands come in, carrying saddles towards the tack room. "That Buzz, I bet he had himself a good time with Miss Lorraine today," one of them said.

The other one laughed and let out a whoop. "Don't you know it! How'd you like to be in his shoes? Or maybe I should say, in his airplane?"

Frank whirled and swung the stall door open. "What did you say?"

The two men stopped in their tracks, staring open-mouthed. Frank stepped up to face them. "Don't just stand there, I want to know what's been going on around here!"

They both took a step backwards and Grace could see the color rising on their faces.

"It wasn't really anything, Mr. Frank," said the one holding the saddle. "We were just kidding around...you know..."

"About my wife!" Frank's voice was rising. "I want to know what was going on.!"

"Just...well Buzz gave her a ride. Just flew over the farm. I didn't...well... there wasn't any harm. Really, it was nothing. We were just making a little fun, you know..."

But Frank cut him off. "Get out of here. Both of you."

Phillip stepped up and took the saddle. "Go ahead to quarters. I'll get this."

Frank stood, glowering as they scampered out of the stable and disappeared. Then he stalked off towards the house, leaving Phillip and Grace to watch as he went to deal with Lorraine.

~ ~ ~

The gates of Janus had opened up for the race and Grace walked down towards the stables. Papa was so sure they were going to win. But what if they didn't? Someone else would be taking the trophy home. The silver one, with the two-faced horse on top. He would be so angry. Just as she came around the corner of the main stable Frank led Runaway out. The wind caught her skirt and blew it, making the stallion spook. Frank cursed and snatched the reins, tightening the bit until it rode up and dug into the roof of the horse's mouth. He rose on his hind legs, pawing at the sky, nearly hitting Frank with his front hooves. Frank ducked and struck the horse against the chest with a heavy whip. The horse scrambled backwards, and Frank braced himself to pull against him but even with the steel bit he couldn't hold twelve hundred pounds. His feet skidded across the ground as the horse dragged him.

Buzz appeared in the doorway of the stable and strode across the yard, Spanky trotting at his heels.

"Ease up, Frank!" he called. But Frank ignored him.

The stallion reared again as Buzz took the reins. Now he was running backwards but Buzz simply walked with him, holding the reins as he kept pace with the horse.

"E-e-e-easy there, now." The voice was low and soothing.

The whites of the horse's eyes still showed as they rolled back in fear. The trainer continued to go with him, never forcing him. Gradually, the horse's movements slowed, and all four feet were planted firmly on the ground.

Buzz spoke to the horse again and Grace couldn't tell what he was saying. The horse snorted, great whooshing sounds of air exploding from the flaring nostrils. He took a few more steps backwards and the man gave him free rein, walking along with him. Reaching up, he laid one big hand on the gleaming neck and his touch seemed to soothe the horse. Finally, the trainer brought him under control and Runaway stood, prancing nervously in place, the delicate hooves beating out a staccato sound as his special shoes hit the hard ground.

Hoot scampered up, dressed in the red and gold silks that represented Janus Farms. "Buzz! We're late, it's nearly time for the first heat."

Buzz put the reins over the horse's head and held him in place as the jockey leaped into the saddle. Keeping his hand firmly on the bridle, he led the horse, prancing and jumping towards the grandstand area. Runaway lunged and reared again, and Hoot pushed forward with his weight over the muscular neck, forcing him downward.

Buzz kept his hand on the bridle, turning the horse to the left in mid-air, working with the jockey to bring him down. Now the horse was headed in the right direction, tossing his head, and snorting as he pranced beside Buzz. The trainer motioned at the exercise boy who waited nearby, and he urged his mount forward, jogging slowly beside the stallion. The pony horse's quiet demeanor calmed the big horse a little and Hoot brought him under control now.

Buzz turned back towards the stable, but Frank stepped into his path, dark eyes flashing.

"You don't just come in and push the owner out of the way." Frank's teeth were gritted, and his right cheek twitched furiously.

Buzz stopped and looked down at Frank. "Sorry Frank, but we need to get on out there."

"You don't talk to your boss that way," Frank said, his voice hoarse with anger.

Buzz pushed his hat to the back of his head and gazed at Frank calmly. "Excuse me, son. But your Daddy's the one that's always been my boss. And I'll take care of things out here as I see fit. You can't man-handle that stallion." He tapped his finger beside his head. "You got to out-think him. Think like a horse. Come on, now, let's all forget about this and get down there before we're late."

But Frank reached out and grasped Buzz by the collar and Grace heard a growl. A low rumble, deep and throaty, like far off thunder rolling.

Frank heard it too. He looked around to see Spanky creeping up behind him, crouched low to the ground, ready to pounce.

"I think you better get your hands off me, boy." Buzz reached up and pulled his shirt out of Frank's grasp. "Looks like Spanky don't care much for your little temper tantrums."

Frank backed away and the dog placed himself between the two men, still growling, ears flattened against his skull, lips pulled back to show long white fangs. Frank raised the whip in his hand and stepped towards him. The dog sprang forward, growling furiously.

"SPANKY!" The dog stopped in mid-air as Buzz yelled at

him. "Get over here!"

Spanky returned to his master's side, still growling. Buzz stood watching as Frank started down the hill towards the grandstands. The hands that stood against the stable wall snickered.

"That Frank! What a wimp!"

The men stroked the dog. "I wouldn't give a pretty penny for getting to see that," one of the grooms said. "Frank sure got what he asked for that time."

Grady walked over to where Buzz stood, watching. "You best watch that son-of-a-gun. Once you've crossed him good, it seems like he doesn't ever forget it."

"It'll be okay," said Buzz as he scratched Spanky behind the ears.

Grady's eyes were a little worried now. "He's a sneaky piece of work though. You never know what he'll do. Always been like that. He'll start something and doesn't have the guts to finish it. Then, he'll go behind your back and cause all kinds of trouble."

"Oh, he's all vines and no 'taters," Buzz answered. "Just a big-mouth."

"Grady's right, Buzz," said one of the grooms. "Frank's always been one that's…what's the word for it? Always wants to get back at you for the least little thing."

"Vindictive?" Buzz asked and the groom nodded.

Buzz snorted. "Just like I always say, If brains were dynamite, that boy couldn't blow his nose. Don't worry, it'll be okay." He started down the hill behind Frank towards the track.

Grace watched a few minutes later as she slid in beside Mama in the owner's box. As usual, they were having trouble getting Bid Red in the gate. Each time Hoot pushed him forward, he reared and whirled away. Finally, with Phillip on one side and Buzz on the other, they managed to get the stallion in and slam the gate behind him.

"Ladie-e-ss and gentleme-e-nn!" the announcer cried. "The winner of the race today will be taking home the most coveted trophy of the year. The Janus Farms trophy. It is pretty unusual, I have it in my hands here now. Strangest looking horse that I ever saw on top. It has two faces. I am told it stands for Janus, the Roman god the is supposed to be looking at both the past and the future. And they say it is made of solid silver. Now! Let's get this race going!"

Starting from the fifth stall, Runaway leapt out as the bell clanged. He was fighting hard, trying to drift out but Grace could see Hoot working to bring him back to the inside. The other horses swept down the track bundled together as Runaway trailed behind but suddenly, he gave to the jockey and Hoot was able to pull him over to the inside. Then Hoot gave the big horse his head and the two of them came together. The jockey's body fell into perfect rhythm with his mount, arms reaching out with every stride. The stallion had his legs well under him and he poured on the speed.

"Looks like Hoot Harrison has been able to get Runaway Rapids out of his usual pattern," the announcer said. "Now he's coming up strong and if he stays where he is, no doubt he'll catch the rest of the field, fast as this guy is. Now it's Cincinnati Cyclone in the lead, followed closely by Bronze Force. Thundering Victory is in third place and then Knight's Destiny. Looks like two of the horses from Janus Farms are coming on up, Grand Rapids right in front of Rapid Lady Fire.'

Mama was sitting beside Grace and she reached over now to squeeze Grace's arm. Grace knew what her mother-in-law was thinking. If Janus lost this race, the trophy would be gone. She didn't think Papa could bear that.

"Brother, look at the Carolina Colt," the voice came over the loudspeaker. "He may be a wild one, but Harrison got him straightened out and right now, he's cooking with gas! I'm telling you; he is sure killing it. He's caught up with the pack. He's passing Savannah's Sapphire and coming on up beside Crowned Hope. Now he's even, neck and neck with One Grand Dude and he's coming on, coming on, now he's passed The Dude."

Grace turned to look for Phillip and she could see him now, down in front of the starting gate with Buzz. He had one hand in the air and even from this distance, she could see his excitement. She watched as Red plowed through the field, now he was catching up with the leaders.

"Grand Rapids has passed his stablemate, Rapid Lady Fire and now he's about to catch the Cincinnati Cyclone. But wait a minute, he's slowing down, looks like he's starting to give to his right hind end a little. Yep, the jockey is pulling him down, something's wrong here. And it doesn't look like Rapid Lady Fire's going to catch them. If Janus Farms wants to keep that trophy it looks like it's going to be up to Runaway Rapids.

"And he's still coming on strong, ladies and gentlemen. Just look at the Carolina Colt. Is he a jim dandy of a runner, or what? I tell you; it looks like Hoot Harrison has about gotten him broke of his old habit of running wide. He is beating it down now. Coming up on the leaders now, passing his stablemates. Grand Rapids is still slowing down and now the Carolina Colt is coming up on Lady Rapid Fire and the Cincinnati Cyclone. They're running neck and neck. Now Runaway is passing them and he's catching Bronze Force, who is in the lead."

Grace could hardly breathe from the tension. She looked over at her mother-in-law. Her face was red and Papa had both hands in the air on the other side of her. He was sort of hopping from one foot to the other. They were almost at the wire.

"Only a hundred yards to go!" shouted the announcer. The Carolina Colt and The Force. Running even and they're almost there. Which one will it be! Is Runaway Rapids going to be able to keep that trophy for Janus Farms?"

Grace looked down towards the gate for Phillip. She saw Buzz, picking him out from his height and the Stetson hat but she couldn't see Phillip.

"And they're still running together. Matching stride for stride and the rest of the field is falling back. Look at these two go, they're pouring it on. Now twenty yards, come on, come on. Now only ten yards to go and they're still neck and neck. As close a call as I've ever seen, looks like they're fused together. And here they come, up to the wire. And it's...it's Runaway Rapids by a nose!"

The crowd went wild. Papa threw his fedora into the air, grabbed Mama, whirled her around and gave Lorraine a kiss on the cheek. He even gave Grace a thump on the back, nearly knocking her out of the stands. Climbing down the steps, he turned to motion them to join him on the way to the winner's circle.

Red shied away as the blanket of red roses was placed across his neck and it took both Phillip and Buzz to help Hoot hold him in place. The race steward stepped up to hand Papa the special trophy for Janus Farms Race. Papa stood grinning, unlit cigar in his mouth as he held the silver trophy, depicting the two-faced horse. Cameras flashed all around.

"Smile, girls," Mama whispered.

Grace tried to pull her face into a pleased look, but she glanced over towards Runaway and all she could think about was the look of rage on Frank's face as he stood shoulder to shoulder with Buzz.

TWENTY

April 30, 1942

"**N**ow push the clutch in with your left foot. Keep your right foot on the brake and turn the ignition key."

Grace did as Phillip instructed but as soon as the Cadillac started, her foot slipped off the clutch and the car cut off.

"That's okay," he said. "Let's try again. After the engine starts, don't do anything until I tell you."

She pushed the clutch back in but forgot to put her other foot on the brake and the car rolled forward.

"The brake, Grace! All you have to do is hold it until you're ready to pull off! I don't see why you're having such a hard time with it."

Stabbing her right foot at the brake, she forgot to hold the clutch in. When her foot slipped off it, the car lurched forward, throwing Phillip into the windshield for the third time.

"I swear, Grace! If you would just stop being so nervous, it would help."

But the more he told her to relax, the more her muscles tightened up. He had been patient with her, but he was beginning to get really irritated. He didn't usually lose his temper with her like that. Or anyone, for that matter.

They went down the path that ran behind the back pasture. There was nothing out here that they could bump into, he had told her.

But she was so nervous. She wanted to show Phillip that she could do it. Sure, a lot of women couldn't drive, but many were beginning to.

Just look at Lorraine. She could drive anywhere she wanted. She would just put those flashy sunglasses on, sit right back and steer a car like a man. She could even

156

drive with one hand and smoke a cigarette with the other.

Phillip had finally had enough. Getting out of the passenger side, he came around and opened the driver's door. "Move over."

Grace did as she was told, sneaking little glances over at Phillip to see if he was angry. His bottom lip was set. She knew it took a lot to irritate him but she had finally done it. He turned the car around and headed back up the hill.

Grace knew she should consider herself fortunate. Just suppose he was like Papa or Frank? At least he wasn't always stomping about, yelling, and cursing.

The path curved back towards the stables, and they passed by the old willow tree. The spot he used to bring her to. Back when they would pack the saddlebags with a picnic lunch and a bottle of wine. And a book. Back when he took time to sit in the shade and read aloud.

She glanced over at him now and wondered if he may be remembering. But she knew he wasn't. If he were, he would look over at her and take her hand.

He had his mind on business, she knew. Hoot had gone up to Washington for the Army and Navy Relief show that was being put on by the Hollywood Victory Caravan. Fifty of the most popular movie stars were making a cross-country trip, putting on a musical revue extravaganza in twelve cities to raise money. The had left Los Angeles and tonight would be the last show. This afternoon, they would be stopping for a tea party on the lawn with Elanor Roosevelt.

Lorraine had a fit when she found out the family wasn't going. She had pouted for weeks. But this party was strictly by invitation. Since Hoot was the only one going, Buzz had flown him up. The party was going to be broadcast live on television this afternoon.

Phillip looked over at her as he parked. "Want to go and see the new three-year-old?"

"Sure. I've been wondering all morning what she looks like."

"She's a gray." He took her hand and they started down the path to the stables. "Tall, sort of raw-boned. We'll see what she can do when Hoot gets back."

The mare was still nervous in her new surroundings. She paced in the stall, strewing the fresh straw underfoot. Grady came up with a scoop of oats and dumped them in the feeder, but she wouldn't be still long enough to eat.

"She'll settle down in a bit," Grady said. "She calmed down some while there was no one in here. But every time anybody comes through, she gets a little antsy again."

The mare let out a shrill whinny and the horse in the next stall answered her.

Everything was quiet for a few moments and the mare turned to the corner feeder and began to eat. After a few bites, she raised her head and neighed but started eating again immediately.

Phillip reached in and gave her a pat. "She'll be fine. I'm looking forward to seeing what she can do."

"Want me to saddle her up and breeze her a little?" Grady asked.

Phillip shook his head. "No, let's wait. We won't have time before they air the White House event on television. You coming up to the house to watch with us?"

"You bet," Grady replied. "Can't wait to see my buddy up there. You know he'll be the life of the party."

Phillip grinned. "I'm sure he will. That boy has a good time, I don't care where he goes. All those starlets. He'll be right in the middle of them. I just hope he stays sober until it's over."

"I wish I could get women like he does," Grady said.

"I bet you do. Anyway, we've got about an hour. Cook will probably have some snacks put together, so come on up before it starts."

"Wouldn't miss it for the world," Grady called as they started back towards the house.

~~~

Grace dumped a box of photographs out on the table in the library. She still had a half hour before the program. She had already gone through dozens of photo albums. Yesterday Mama had given her three boxes of loose
~~~

pictures.

"I keep meaning to get them organized and see which ones I want to put into albums."

"Well, I can sort them into groups, if you want," Grace had replied. "And after we get this book finished, I'll help you get them put into albums."

"All right," Mama had replied. "That reminds me. I need to get some albums next time I'm in town."

Grace pawed through the pictures now. It would be fun to just look at them. But as for working on this book, it was making her really stressed. She just didn't know what to do.

I'm a fool, she thought. Here I am and Lorraine's off on a shopping trip. But she sure will be there when it's time to take the credit.

But as long as they had started it, Grace wanted to make sure that it would be something that Janus Farms would be proud of. Phillip had promised that he would sit down with her next week and give her some information they could use.

She picked up a picture of a small boy, with blonde curls tousled all over his head and smiled. This had to be Phillip. Wearing a pair of knickers. It aroused her interest, and she became so engaged in looking through the photographs that before she knew it, it was time to go.

Phillip and Grady were in the main living room, discussing plans for next week's race. In a few minutes, Frank came in with Mama on his arm and she went about making up plates from the big, silver platters on the table.

Grace was biting into a cracker with brie cheese and cranberry when she heard Papa's voice out in the hall. He came bustling in.

"I couldn't find Lorraine," Frank said. "Has anyone seen her?"

"She went into town," Mama said. "Wanted to find a new outfit for next weekend."

As if on cue, Lorraine burst into the room carrying two large packages. "I didn't have time to go upstairs yet," she explained. "I didn't miss anything, did I?"

"It's just about to start," Mama said as Papa turned the

television on.

They sat, watching commercials for a couple of minutes. Then, a huge band stood and played. After they were finished, the camera moved to the announcer.

"We're gathered here on the lawn at the White House," he began. "The Hollywood Victory Caravan arrived just a little while ago for a tea party with First Lady, Eleanor Roosevelt." The camera panned over to show the president and his wife beside him.

The announcer walked over, looking back at the camera. There, on the steps sat dozens of people, so crowded together that you could hardly tell who they were.

"Ladies and gentlemen, you see here before you two dozen of the most famous stars that Hollywood has to offer. The Caravan has come all the way across the country to provide funding for the Army and Navy Relief Society, doing shows every night. These humble stars have taken time out of their busy schedules to come out and support the war effort. They started out from Los Angeles two weeks ago on the Santa Fe Railroad. Yes-sir, seventy-five people will be on stage tonight along with these stars for the last leg of the act at Loew's Capitol."

He walked over to the two men standing in front of the others. "Oh, my gosh!" Lorraine gasped. "Cary Grant! I could just die! We should be there."

"Now, Bob Hope and Cary Grant here are sharing the honor of Master of Ceremonies," said the announcer. The two stars waved at the camera.

The camera panned across the group and the family was able to pick out more stars.

"Look," said Mama. "There's Charles Boyer. I always loved his movies."

"Claudette Colbert," Grady stood up and moved closer to the television to see better. "Boy is that Hoot one lucky guy."

"I don't see Hoot," Papa said. "He needs to be closer out in front there, make sure Janus Farms is represented well."

Mama shushed him. "This is a big event, Franklin. All those movie stars. You can't expect Hoot to just waltz right in and take over all the attention."

The camera had just stopped on Mrs. Roosevelt and the announcer was asking her who was her favorite movie star. Before she could answer, her voice was drowned out by the sound of a loud motor. Everyone looked around, trying to see where the noise was coming from.

The camera tipped upwards and at first Grace thought the cameraman had done it by accident. Perhaps he had fallen down or something. But then a small airplane came into view. As is flew over the White House, they could see a long banner trailing behind it.

JANUS FARMS

"No need for alarm, ladies and gentlemen!" the announcer shouted to make himself heard. "I thought we were about to be bombed but it's none other than Hoot Harrison, America's leading jockey. But I sure thought he'd be down here with us."

The little plane circled twice as the camera moved back and forth. First, upwards to show the airplane gliding through the air and then panning down to catch the expressions on the faces of all those present. The movie stars stood, shading their eyes, looking upwards at Hoot and Buzz.

Then, the side door opened, and the camera caught Hoot leaping out of the plane. Grace's breath caught in her throat and the family could hear all the guests let out a collective gasp. Suddenly, a parachute opened, and the jockey floated slowly towards the White House lawn, dangling from the red and gold colors of Janus Farms. There was a message painted in three-foot-tall, blazing scarlet letters on the chute.

GIVE A HOOT ABOUT YOUR COUNTRY!
BUY YOUR WAR BONDS

"By God," Papa said. "That boy's done it again. He's stealing the whole show."

TWENTY-ONE

May 15, 1942

Grace was in the bedroom changing clothes when a soft tap sounded at the door.

"Miss Grace?" Paulette's voice called.

Grace opened the door and the maid stepped in, pushing her dark blonde hair up where it was coming loose. "Grady just came up and said Buzz wants to see you down at the stables."

"Why?"

"Grady said his dog's not acting right. They think he's sick. I hope it's nothing bad.

"I'll be right down," Grace said. She finished dressing and went downstairs.

"Paulette?" She peeked into the dining room where the maid was polishing silverware. "Have you seen Mama?"

"She's taking her afternoon nap. Something I can do to help you?"

"Oh, no. I just...well Phillip's gone into town. I didn't want to go out there with all the men by myself. All the hands will probably be hanging around. I usually wait until they're at the track before I go. But I'll just..."

Lorraine walked into the room. "I'd go with you, Grace. But I really don't feel like riding today. I wanted to go shopping but Frank wouldn't let me take his car. Last week, I saw this dress in the window at..."

"I'm not riding," Grace replied. "Spanky's sick and Buzz though maybe I could do something to help."

Suddenly Lorraine was alert. "Oh, I hope it's nothing serious. I love that big, old goofball." She was at the door before Grace could answer. She poked her head back in. "Well, come on. What are you waiting for?"

Grace followed close on her heels. Lorraine, still in

her formal skirt and red high heel pumps, picked her way between the piles of horse droppings. They saw Hoot coming from the barn out back.

"Hoot, where's Buzz?" Lorraine shouted.

Hoot hooked his thumb behind him. "In there, by the tack room. Spanky won't eat. I've got some Vienna sausages in my room. I'll get a can and we'll try him on that."

They found Buzz in the wide aisle of the bar, surrounded by a group of the men. They stepped aside to let Grace in, and she saw Spanky, lying on his side, panting. Buzz, kneeling beside him, looked up. "I think something pretty bad is wrong, Miss Grace."

Grace knelt beside him and stroked the big head. "How long has he been sick?"

"Couple of hours now, I guess. He seemed a little off at lunchtime. I always give him a couple of bites, you know, whatever I have, and he didn't scarf it down like he usually does. Just kind of picked at it."

Grace rubbed her hands over the big body as the dog turned his head to lick her hand. He didn't feel hot. She pulled his eyelids back, no jaundice. But he was panting hard, in obvious discomfort. Grace forgot her own bashfulness because something was clearly wrong.

"You noticed him having the trots, or vomiting?" She looked over at Buzz.

He shook his head. "Just wouldn't eat. Then, about twenty minutes ago, he laid down there and wouldn't move."

Hoot came in and Grace heard the top of the can click as he pulled out a fresh Vienna sausage. He bent over and offered it to the dog. "Come on boy, you know you love old Hoot's viennas. You usually eat more of them than I do."

Spanky sniffed at the meat and turned his head away.

"What do you think it could be?" Buzz asked.

"Well, I'm not a veterinarian or doctor. But I'm wondering if he could have eaten something that made him sick."

"I don't know," Buzz answered. "He's been hanging around the stables all day."

Grace palpated the big dog's abdomen and he groaned.

"He's pretty young and I don't think it could be a tumor or anything. And looks like if one of the horses had kicked him, somebody would have heard the ruckus. I just have a feeling he ate something that made him sick."

Spanky groaned and laid his head on the dirt.

"I really think you should call the vet," Grace said.

"I already did." Buzz stroked the white forehead. "He's out at a calving. They're sending him over as soon as he gets in, but...I don't know. I wish he could get on over here. I think we need to do something pretty quick." He looked at Grace. "I know you're pretty good at helping people with your natural remedies. Isn't there something you can do?"

"I've got some emetic up at the house. Makes him vomit. I guess you're right, if it's something in his stomach making him this sick, we can't wait for the vet. We need to get it out quick as we can. I'll run up to the house and get it."

"I'll go, Grace," Lorraine said. "You stay here with Spanky. Where is it?"

Grace had forgotten Lorraine was there. "It's in my bedroom. Look in the trunk. There's a little green bottle. Got bloodroot written on it."

"Be right back." Lorraine turned, her skirt flying out and ran out of the barn. Grace crouched there for a moment, staring after her.

"Anything we can do, Miss Grace?" asked Hoot.

"Get me a syringe from the tack room," she answered. "And I'll need a little water. Just get me a cup or jar, where I can mix the bloodroot up."

Hoot opened the door to the tack room, and they could hear him rooting around in the box where the medications for the horses were kept. He poked his head back in the door. He was holding a twelve-cc syringe with a long needle. "Will this work?"

Grace nodded. "Just the syringe, we don't need the needle."

Grady handed her a tin cup filled with water just as Lorraine came running back. Taking the bloodroot powder from her, Grace shook out a little and measured it by guess in the palm of her hand. Dumping it into the cup, she stirred it until it dissolved.

"Can you sit him up?" Grace looked at the men.

"With Buzz on one side and Hoot on the other, they lifted the dog's body upright. Grace dipped the syringe into the cup and pulled up ten cc of the viscous liquid. She stuck it into the corner of the dog's mouth and started to depress the plunger, but Spanky shook his head, pulling his lip back in disgust. Grady stepped up and cradled the big, white head in his strong hands.

"Try again, Miss Grace," he urged.

Pushing the syringe further back, Grace put her thumb back on the plunger and pressed again. Quickly, until it went all the way down. This time, with all three men holding the dog, she was able to get him to swallow it. As soon as Grady loosened his hold, Spanky shook his head violently, spraying them with what was left of the mixture.

"Well," Grace said, wiping her face. "I think we got enough in him."

"What now?" Buzz asked.

"Just got to wait. See if he throws up."

Fifteen minutes ticked by with agonizing slowness. And the big dog had still not vomited. He lay on the ground, head down, panting hard.

They repeated the process and before two minutes had passed, Spanky sat up and began to heave. His stomach contorted and he gagged several times. Suddenly, the contents of his stomach spewed forth, spilling across the barn floor. After several minutes, the vomiting stopped, and the dog reached up to lick Buzz in the face.

"Good boy," Hoot urged as he clapped Buzz on the shoulder. "You're going to be okay."

Grady picked up a rake and pulled it through the wet mass on the floor. "Look there," he said as he pointed towards bright green granules scattered through the vomitus. "Rat poison. Where did he get that?"

Buzz stood up. "Mr. Franklin doesn't allow rat poison around here. Says the horses could get into it. Says that's what the barn cats are for."

"Somebody must have fed it to him," said Hoot.

"I can't believe that." Grace turned to see Lorraine;

hand clutched to her throat. "Nobody would hurt Spanky. Everyone on this farm loves him."

~~~

Grace led Cloudy into the barn. Hooking him into the crossties, she loosened the girth and stroked the spotted cheek. "You're such a good boy," she crooned.

She was just lifting the saddle down from the sturdy back when the door of the tack room opened, and Buzz stepped out with Spanky at his heels. "Here, Grace. Let me get that for you." Lifting the heavy saddle with one hand, he swung it across his shoulder and carried it inside. Grace was going over the little horse's sweaty coat with a rubber dandy brush when he came out.

"Spanky still feeling, okay?" she asked.

"He's been fine," Buzz answered as he reached down and patted the big head. He looked back at Grace. "I sure appreciate what you did to help him yesterday."

Grace blushed. "I'm just glad it worked. I don't know all the cures like my Aunt Ada, but she taught me some of it."

"Good day for a ride," Buzz said. "Did you go down by the river?"

Grace nodded. "I rode past the rapids, all the way down where that old trestle bridge was. You knew, where you can still see pieces of it just before you get to the new one."

Buzz released the clasps on the crossties and handed her Cloudy's lead line. "That's some pretty country out there, where the river calms down. Gets so quiet out there you could almost..."

They were interrupted by voices at the front end of the barn. "Haywood, get that bay colt out, and warm him up. Let's put him on the track and see what he can do." Frank continued to shout orders as he came down the wide aisle. They could see him but Cloudy was between them, blocking his view. As he pushed past the little horse, Grace saw his eyes drift past her and land on Buzz. Then they moved down, and she saw the surprise in them when he saw Spanky standing there. If there had been any doubt in her mind it was gone now.
~~~

Buzz stepped around her and walked up to Frank. "I been waiting for you," he said.

"I...what?" Frank's gaze darted nervously to Spanky. The dog stood quietly beside Grace, and she reached over to rest her hand on top of his head, hoping he would stay calm. Haywood had stopped and stood, watching.

"I know you're the one that did it, Frank," Buzz said in a low voice.

"Did what?"

Buzz stepped closer and tapped his forefinger against Frank's chest. "You...! Why don't you grow up and act like a man instead of a spineless coward? Sneaky jerk!"

"What are you..." but Buzz cut him off. "I'm giving you fair warning right now. If something happens to anything of mine; my truck, my plane, and especially my dog or my horse – I'll stomp a mudhole in your hind end and walk it dry! You hear me, boy?"

"You've got a lot of nerve," Frank answered. "I don't know what you're accusing me of but you're going to be..." Spanky was growling now, and Frank took a step backwards.

"I'll be what?" Buzz asked, stepping forward so he was face to face with Frank.

"You'll be looking for a job, that's what."

"So be it," Buzz said through clenched teeth as he grabbed Frank's collar. "But let me tell you something, boy. All the money your Daddy's got won't save your sorry butt. Now you just get out of here and think about that!" He shoved Frank backwards and he stumbled as the back of his knees hit a wheelbarrow that was sitting in the aisle. His eyes dropped to the pitchfork beside it. Grady and a couple of the other grooms had come in and stood, waiting to see what was going to happen.

"Come on," Buzz said. "I wish you would come after me. That would give me just the excuse I need to beat the living tar out of you."

Frank looked over at the men who had gathered to watch. "Get back to work!" he shouted. "Or I'll fire every last one of you." The group dispersed and the men drifted slowly out of the barn.

Frank straightened the lapel of his suit, turned on his heel and stalked off silently. But as he went, he threw a backward glance that frightened Grace even more than all the shouting and angry words had done.

TWENTY-TWO

June 23, 1942

Grace had gone along with Mama and Lorraine to a Ladies' Circle meeting in town. They had taken Grace's car. "Oh, please, Grace." Lorraine had begged. "Let me drive it in. They'll all be green with envy."

Grace didn't care about making anyone envious, but Lorraine just wouldn't stop until she agreed.

The meeting had gone well. The quilters guild had gotten off to a good start. Every section for the Roanoke Rapids Day had a chairperson and each one had made her report. Materials for games were being gathered and Mrs. Anderson's husband had agreed to store them in one of his warehouses. After much urging, Mayor Sykes had agreed to sit in the dunking booth. The ladies had cackled with laughter, just trying to picture him all soaked. It really was fun to be a part of all this, Grace had thought.

Until the subject of the book had come up, that was. Mama had given a report on what was going to be done at Janus. "Franklin was all for it," she told the other women.

"How's the book coming along?" Mary-Frances Grant had asked.

"Well...." Lorraine had looked over at Grace. "My sister-in-law is in charge of the research. And well...I have to have that before I can really begin." Mary-Frances looked sideways at the girl sitting beside her as if to say; I told you so. Grace, in turn looked at Lorraine, trying to send a message that she would like to throttle her.

"But it won't be long."

"I hope so," Mary-Frances answered. "You better get a move on."

"Have all you ladies heard about the WAVES?" asked Hattie. Grace could tell she was trying to smooth over the irritation. "The women's group, to help out with the war."

"Actually, the name is WAACS, "Lorraine answered.

Hattie shook her head. "No, they're paid employees. This is Women Accepted for *Volunteer* Emergency Service.

Lorraine perked up and Grace knew what she was thinking. If it were only on a volunteer basis, Papa would encourage it. Because it would look good for Janus Farms. Frank now, that was a different story. He wanted her right there at the house all the time, under his thumb.

Lucille spoke up. "Ladies are doing so many things. Some of them are even going into the military. My father knows a woman who's assisting with bombing calculations."

Hattie banged her little gavel on the table. "All right, ladies. Let's get back to business. The Roanoke Rapids Day Celebration will be here before we know it."

When they had left, Grace was still seething with anger. All that talk about the WAVES hadn't made her forget about being put on the spot with the book. Her sister-in-law had a lot of nerve. And Lorraine knew she was mad.

Mama kept leaning up from the back seat, talking about the meeting. She knew they were at odds; Grace could tell. "Let's stop by Bella's Boutique while we're in town," she told the girls. "We'll see what if she got a shipment in this week."

Lorraine bought a new outfit. Mama wanted to look for something for the celebration. Bella told them she was expecting a shipment in a couple of days.

When they went out to get into the car, Lorraine said, "You drive home, Grace."

Grace shook her head. She remembered how it had gone when she had tried on the farm paths. How she just couldn't get the hang of that clutch.

But Lorraine pushed her now into the driver's seat. "Come on, Grace. It's the middle of the afternoon. There's hardly any traffic on the street. Come on, I'll show you what to do."

Grace got the car started with no trouble. It sat there, in the parallel park on the avenue, the motor purring so quietly you could hardly hear it run.

"Okay," Lorraine said. "Push in on the clutch, step on

the gas. Just a tiny bit, you know. Then, ease up on the clutch. Real slow."

Grace tried but the car lurched, and the engine cut off.

"Come on, Grace. You can do it. Now this time, pretend you're riding a horse. You know how you ease up with the pressure on the bit, let the reins out a little. And you push him with your legs? Well, it's practically the same thing with driving a car. Pretend the clutch is the same as the reins and let it out just a little. And the gas pedal. Think how when you're riding, you push with your legs at the same time. Just don't be so nervous."

Grace tried again and this time it worked. The car bucked and jumped but it continued on down the street, wobbling from one side of the road to the other. They only had to make one stop and turn right, then it was a straight-a-way to the farm. All three women started laughing and couldn't stop. After one particularly sudden lurch, Grace looked in the rear-view mirror to see Mama's hat knocked askew, sitting sideways on her head. She took one hand off the wheel, pointed back at her and ran off the road, skimming the ditch bank. By the time they turned in the drive at home it was going a little more smoothly.

But they couldn't stop laughing. Mama got out and held onto the side of the car, bent over double. Lorraine came around, giggling and took her by the arm. Grace was grinning impishly as they started up the steps.

Henry and Louis were trimming the azaleas by the side of the house. Grace heard them as she followed Mama and Lorraine inside.

Henry scratched at the blonde curls under his cap and stared at them. "I tell you what, if I didn't know better, I'd swear them ladies been boozing it up," he whispered.

~~~

Grace was in the library, working on the book when Lorraine came in with a box of photographs. Grace looked up from her notes and riffled through a few of the pictures.

"Where did you find these?"

"Frank got them out of the attic for me. I thought you
~~~

could put them in some kind of order," Lorraine said as she plopped down.

"How about *you* see if you can figure some sort of order," Grace said. Lifting the box, she carried it over to the long table where there was room to spread them out.

"But I thought you could..."

"I'm working on these notes." Grace was beginning to get really irritated. "Phillip's told me a lot. But it's just different stories. I'm trying to figure out a way to put the dates together. Besides, I've already gone through hundreds of pictures."

"Phfffft!" Lorraine blew out her breath. "I just don't know where to start."

"Well, neither do I! You're the one that wanted to do this, not me."

"Hey!" Lorraine pulled out a photograph. "Here's one we've got to use."

It was a brilliant color Kodachrome, taken last year. The family was standing in the winner's circle with Runaway. You couldn't see Grace very well; Papa was standing in front of her. Lorraine was out in front, Frank's arm around her. A scarlet skirt flowed out around her calves, the wind blowing it up a little and a wide-brimmed picture hat framed her delicate face. Her even, white teeth gleamed, and she smiled as though she had won the race herself.

"There's something else you need to do," Grace said. "We need to get Papa's viewpoint. Things he remembers about his own father and grandfather."

Lorraine sighed and looked down at a red fingernail that she had chipped. "But Grace, you're so good at it. Can't you..."

"No! You're the one that wanted to do this book. But I've been working on it and you...you just haven't done a thing."

"All right." Lorraine got up and started out of the room.

"You might want to take a pen and some paper. You know how Papa loves to talk."

Lorraine threw her a pained look and Grace had to laugh.

Grace pulled the typewriter out of the closet and carried

it to the table. She put in a sheet of paper, and it got all twisted. The second try was a little better and she was able to get it lined up. With her handwritten notes in front of her, she began to type.

But forty-five minutes later, she didn't even have one page completed.

"Evening, Grace." Startled, she looked around. Buzz was standing behind her. She turned away, embarrassed that he had seen her, trying to type with two fingers.

He sat down across the table. "Working on the book?"

She nodded, her cheeks flushing.

"How's it going?"

"To tell you the truth, it's not."

He raised his eyebrows. "Not what?"

She threw her arms up in the air. "Not going, that's what."

"What's wrong?"

"I'll tell you. It's all Lorraine's idea. But you know how she is."

Buzz chuckled, pulled a cigar out of the box, and lit it. "I know. But what can you say? She's just...well, she's just Lorraine."

"I know." Just saying it out loud made her feel better. "And when the photographer came, she had made an appointment with him. But was she here when he came? Of course not. I had to take him up to the ballroom so he could get photographs of the murals and then..."

She stopped suddenly, realizing how trifling she had sounded. "I was thinking this book would be sort of a partnership. I dreaded it when I first got dragged into it, but you know, then I thought having someone to work with would make it fun. But I'm pretty much on my own here." She rolled her eyes and laughed. "I guess you saw me picking at that typewriter."

"Well, make the ladies' circle help. Surely in that crowd, there's one or two who can type." He picked up a stack of photographs and began to sort through them.

"This was a great day." He laid a picture on the table. "Our first win after I came here."

She looked at the picture. The men were standing with

a big, chestnut horse. The first thing she noticed was how much younger Phillip looked. Then she peered closely at Buzz in the picture and saw that he was fresh-faced too.

"That was Renegade Rapids," Buzz said.

"Runaway's sire?"

`Buzz nodded. "Toughest horse I ever had to deal with. I sure am glad Big Red's not like him. He's high-strung and he can be a little ornery. But Renegade now, he was a different story."

Grace started jotting down notes. "Do you mind?" she asked.

Buzz shrugged. "Sure, maybe I can help you get it laid out. But that Renegade, he was one dangerous stallion. He could be vicious. Never been around but a couple of horses that you could call mean-spirited, but he was. And with the size and power he had, you really had to watch yourself."

Buzz looked through some of the pictures. "I can tell you about the beginning of thoroughbred racing in this country, if it would help."

"It would," Grace answered. "I'm going backwards here, starting at the tail end."

Buzz sat down, put his cigar in the ash tray, leaned back and crossed his arms behind his head. "It actually started right here in this area. They called it the race-horse region of America. Halifax, Northampton, and Warren counties. Up across the Virginia line, too. The most noted horse breeding and racing section of the entire United States."

He leaned forward and stared intensely at Grace. "The thoroughbred named Janus was imported here to this farm in the seventeen-hundreds. I forget exactly what year it was. I think this was a really small place back then."

Grace was writing as fast as she could, trying to keep up as he spoke.

"Later on, the place had really grown. Between the time of Revolutionary America and the early nineteen-hundreds, horse racing was the biggest past-time in the United States. By the late eighteen- hundreds, all the big farms were really into racing. It was regarded as high fashion. Especially in the East. From New York straight down to Florida was considered the stomping grounds of what you would call their high society folks. You know how Mr. Franklin is. Won't even consider going out to the Derby. He thinks all the what you call elite should remain here on the east coast."

Grace was pressing down so hard on the paper that the tip of her pencil broke, and he had to wait while she stuck it into the sharpener and turned the crank handle.

Buzz poured a generous shot of brandy. "They just kept raising horses here and Janus sired so many winners that they kept breeding them back into the line. After a few more decades, Janus Farms became the most prominent thoroughbred family in the country."

Buzz want over to stare out the window at the river in the background. "And it's been that way all these years. Sort of ebbs and flows. You know, a long winning streak and then a few lean years. But with Hoot riding for us, we're sure at the top again now."

Grace put her pencil down. "Is that why you came here? Because Janus has been on top so long?"

He nodded. "I'd been training for a few years. At first, I could hardly believe my good fortune. To be working here at the most prominent racing farm in America."

Grace looked down. "I know. That's how I felt when I first came here. Still do sometimes. Like I don't belong."

Buzz looked her in the eye. "You do, Grace. And don't let anyone tell you different."

He pulled his out his pocket watch and shook his head. "Didn't realize it was this late." He stood up.

"Here, let me help you put these photographs away."

They were nearly finished, and Grace slid the box down the table where a couple of stray pictures lay side by side. As Buzz put one in the box, she reached for the other one but so did he. Their fingers touched and Grace felt a prickle run through her hand and up her arm. Pulling it away, she dropped the picture in the box and put the lid on.

Buzz put his hat on. "I can come back and help. We'll get everything lined up. Make a rough draft for you to work by."

Grace nodded. But as she watched him leaving, she knew she should have told him no.

TWENTY-THREE

August 12, 1942

Grace was in the bedroom when she heard Lorraine come upstairs. She knew it was her because of the way her high heels made sharp, little clicks coming down the hall. She caught a glimpse of her as she passed by, then heard the door to her bedroom close. Strange, Grace thought. Lorraine was always down in the office on Monday afternoons, helping Artie. She's probably changing clothes, Grace thought. She sure did love that little job. You would think she was a bank president like her Daddy or something.

Grace turned back to her flower arrangement. She had picked some roses from the garden. She placed the pale, yellow flowers in an oversized cut glass vase. They were just opening up and the pink edges of the petals made them look, oh so delicate. She buried her face in them and breathed in their fragrance. They smelled just like the tea rose perfume Phillip had given her for her birthday.

She fussed with the furnishings a little, straightening the satin spread on the big, tester bed. She ran her hand over the smooth satin and fluffed up the matching pillow shams. She liked to keep everything just perfect in here and she cleaned this room herself. She couldn't really explain why, but she didn't want Paulette or anyone else to come in here. It was such a private place to her; she just couldn't bear the thought of anyone in here.

She was just straightening a picture of herself standing with Phillip on the tableside when she realized that she had been hearing a sound for a few moments, even though she wasn't paying it any mind. Sniffling, a sort of muffled, low sobbing.

That had to be Lorraine. Probably not a big disaster, she certainly did love drama.

Picking up a book, she sat down in the rocker and tried to read. The crying was still annoying. Probably just another one of her spats with Frank and Grace was getting a little tired of hearing it. He would probably come up in a few minutes and they would make up, as usual.

Grace had finished three chapters before she realized how late it was getting. She'd better get ready for dinner. She went to the closet and pulled out a dress. Then she realized she had never heard any movement out in the hall. Lorraine had probably fallen asleep.

Crossing the hallway, she tapped gently on the door. "Lorraine," she called. "We'd better be getting down for dinner."

Opening the door, she saw Lorraine, staring out the window. "I'm not going," her sister-in-law said.

"But you know Papa. He'll have a fit."

"Tell him I'm sick."

"What is it? You got the monthlies? I can get you some raspberry leaf."

Lorraine shook her head. "No, I'm fine."

"Well, you know Papa will ask me."

"All you have to say it it's female trouble. He won't say another word."

"All right." Grace started out into the hallway.

"Grace, wait. Do you...do you think the family is okay?'

Grace stared at her a moment; brow furrowed. "What do you mean?"

"You know. Like...if everyone is working together, all trying to...I don't know."

"I don't understand what you're getting at."

"I'm not going to be helping with the bookwork anymore."

"Why, did you make a mistake and get in trouble?" Grace wanted to be sympathetic but that inner, nasty part of herself almost wanted to be glad because everything about Lorraine was always so perfect. She tried to squelch that feeling down.

"Something funny is going on."

"What do you mean? Artie made a pass? He's always so quiet."

Lorraine waved her hand through the air. "I'm used to men doing that all the time. This is something really serious. You know when the men go to the different racetracks, out of town?"

Grace nodded.

"Well, they keep all the receipts. You know motel rooms, gas, and food. Stuff like that. And Artie re-imburses them."

"That's what he's supposed to do, right?"

"But Frank's been collecting all the receipts and making Artie write a check to him. Pretends he's been paying for it. Thousands of dollars, nearly every week."

"Well, doesn't he?"

Lorraine shook her head. "The employees pay for it. And then they come in, demanding their money back. Artie tells them he paid Frank and they'll have to talk to him. But Frank sends them right back to Artie, like he doesn't know what's going on."

Grace was beginning to understand what was happening.

"Frank comes in and tells Artie to pay them cash. Artie tried to talk to him, but you know how Frank is. He got mad and told Artie to just do it and keep his mouth shut."

Now Grace was starting to take it all in. Frank was stealing money. From Papa. From Janus Farms. All those expenses. Going out not once, but twice. Double payments. And evidently, he had gotten himself so far in hock, that he'd had to continue doing it even after Lorraine had started working on the books. So that was the reason he had been against her doing it. Grace remembered now how panicky he seemed when Papa ordered him to allow Lorraine to work in the office.

Lorraine looked up at her. "I can tell Artie's scared. He had a hard time finding a job with that leg of his. The banks don't want him limping around. I feel kind of sorry for him."

"Me too."

"I don't want Frank getting Artie in trouble. But...I'm not sure what to do about it."

Grace stood silently, thinking. She had no idea what to suggest. This was a terrible mess and Lorraine had accidentally gotten involved in it.

Lorraine stood up and went over to the closet. "Well, thanks for listening. But you can't tell anyone." She looked up; her brow furrowed. "Oh God, I shouldn't have said anything. If Frank finds out I spilled the beans, he'll go crazy."

"I won't say anything," Grace promised.

"Not even to Phillip." Lorraine looked panicked now. "Please, Grace. Promise me."

"All right, I promise."

"I'm not going to help in there anymore," Lorraine said as she pulled a dress out of the closet. "I'm not going to get caught up in this any more than I already am."

~~~

"See, like this," Mama said. She reached over and pulled a loop of thread over Lorraine's needle. "Just pull it back through...yes, that's it. Now pull it tight."

Lorraine looked at Grace and made a face. Grace smiled back at her. The ladies' circle had decided at the meeting this afternoon to sell handmade items for Roanoke Rapids Day. Mama was determined to teach Lorraine to crochet. She looked down at her own bundle of thread with a little sigh. She understood how Lorraine felt. Although she knew how, it was a painstakingly slow process.

"No, dear." Taking Lorraine's needle, Mama pulled a stitch out. "Like this, over and then you go under."

Lorraine stood up, stretched, and walked across the room. "This is so boring, Mama. It's just the same thing, over and over. And besides, I'm already doing my part for the celebration. I'm working on the Janus book." She looked at Grace. "Well, I am! I've got tons of notes I took from the things Papa has been telling me."

"But we also promised to make doilies to sell." Mama pulled off her reading glasses.

"It's so useless, though." Lorraine said. "Why don't we just go out and buy them?

"When people go to fairs, they like to buy things that are handmade. Especially in small towns in the South.
~~~

They just think it's quaint..."

Lorraine sighed and flounced over to the window. "But it's just so...mundane. I sill wish I could get a job. Be a part of the world outside of Janus."

Mama put her thread down in her lap. "Well, you know how Papa and Frank feel about that."

"But Mama! With the war on and all, women all over the country are starting to get jobs. It's...it's ...just patriotic. What do you think about me joining the WAVES, Mama? It's just on a volunteer basis."

Mama polished her glasses and put them back on. "That's between you and Frank."

"I still wish I could get a real job in town," Lorraine said. "I'd be so good working at the bank. I really do know a lot about working with numbers. Just for a few hours, you know, to get out and see a lot of people every day.

"Why did you stop helping Artie, dear? I know you like doing the books."

Lorraine shot a look at Grace and their eyes locked for a moment.

"Well, I just..."

They were interrupted by a knock at the open door facing and Grace saw Lorraine's face flood with relief.

Buzz stepped into the parlor. "Grace, I'm sorry to bother you ladies. But I wonder if you could take a look at Hoot. He's not feeling too good."

Grace stood up and put her needlework on the end table. "I don't know if I can help, but I'll come down."

"I appreciate it. Actually, he needs to go in and see Doc Joyner, but he won't do it. Told him I'd get Doc out here, but I can't even get him to agree to that."

Buzz waited for Grace to go up and get her bag. As they walked down towards the stables she began to ask about Hoot's symptoms. She knew how afraid he was of doctors and wasn't surprised that he refused to see one.

"Well, for a couple of weeks now, Hoot just hasn't been himself. You know how Hoot is, always ready to have a large time, going into town, drinking, and gambling. But he's just been sitting around. And I've heard him, out behind the barn, just puking his guts up."

"You think he's caught a bug?" Grace asked. "Anybody else down at quarters been sick?"

Buzz shook his head. "Not as I know of. And it's been going on too long for a flu bug or something like that, right?"

"I don't know. Let's take a look at him."

Hoot was lying on one of the leather sofas in the main room. He sat up when he saw Grace and reached over for the little green bottle of Coca-Cola on the table and took a sip.

"Miss Grace, he said. "What are you..."

"Buzz said you've been vomiting." Grace sat down beside the jockey and put her hand on his forehead. "Don't believe you got a fever."

"I'll be fine, I just..." Hoot winced as he stood up.

"You got a belly ache?" Grace asked and he nodded.

Grace got up and palpated his abdominal area gently and he recoiled in pain.

She looked at his throat and felt his glands. She had expected to find some redness and inflammation but there was nothing there. She peered closely at his fingernails and ran her thumb across them, checking for ridges. He didn't seem to have any parasites.

The only thing she could determine was that Hoot's pulse seemed fast. And irregular.

"I don't know." She went over to take her bag off the table. "I'm not a doctor or nurse. I really think you should see Doc Joyner, Hoot."

"I will if I don't feel better soon.

"Buzz, you come on up to the house with me. I'll give you some tea to bring back. It's got cardamon, fennel and a couple more herbs in it. It might help a little."

She turned back to Hoot. "I'll look in on you tomorrow. But I wish you would go see Doc."

Buzz waited downstairs in the kitchen while Grace went up to her room for the herbs. When she returned, Cook was gone to the pantry and Buzz was sitting at the table alone, drinking a cup of coffee.

"Now, just mix a teaspoon of this with a little water and make sure he drinks it. Don't let him chug it down, just sip slowly on it."

Buzz nodded and stood there, looking at her. "Grace, I..."

"What is it?"

Again, he just stared at her. Finally, he spoke. "There's just something about you. So different. You're not all frills and flounce like most of the women I know. You've got something special, deep down in you. I'm not sure how to say it. A quality, maybe. That most people don't have."

Grace wasn't sure what he meant. She stood there holding the bag.

Buzz stepped over and took it from her. His fingers grazed hers and for some reason, her hand tingled where he touched it.

He lifted his free hand and cupped her chin in it for a moment, then turned and went out the door.

TWENTY-FOUR

Summer 2021

I watch as Drake takes Sundown through his paces. She is good for him; she makes him work. Although he is not a total deadhead like most of these lovable guys around here, he is a little lazy. But then, most horses that have been trained for pleasure classes are.

What a funny thing perspective is, I think. To Kyle, he is a fast, exciting horse. Kyle was used to riding Diesel and you can hardly get him to go any faster than a walk. Compared to that slowpoke, Sunny is a steed of brilliant valor.

Drake still comes early, so she can be alone with the horses. I often watch her from the house, grooming Sunny. She still doesn't have much to say to anyone.

Jennifer and Sandra have Landon on Diesel. He is calm and as long as he is on the horse, you would never guess he has severe autism. Erick is on Peanut, giggling as the volunteers run beside her doing her fancy little gait, making him wobble from side to side. Jacob is on Pokey Joe, following a little more slowly. We have twelve horses in the main arena right now, each one topped by a smiling child.

Maggie Mae and Valentine come walking out of the barn. She has on a pink western hat and is giving the volunteers a hard time about taking it off. But they tell her she will not be allowed to ride without her helmet, so she gives in grudgingly. As Valentine walks away with her on his back, she turns to look at them. "Take good care of my hat. My dad got it for me."

The volunteers nod and one of them sticks it on her own head. She looks ridiculous because it is so tiny. Maggie laughs, faces forward, and doesn't say anything else.

I hear a loud, rattling noise behind me and look around to see a pickup coming up the drive. It is pulling an open trailer with a small John-Deere tractor loaded on it.

A tall, stocky man in faded jeans gets out of the driver's seat and a teen-aged boy clambers down out of the other side.

"Are you Miss Morgan?" the man asks.

"I am," I nod. "And you must be someone's dad?"

"That I am. Got two youngsters. But not your patients, if that's what you mean."

"Oh sorry." But he was grinning in such a friendly way. "What can we do for you?"

"Actually, I'd like to do something for you. For the farm, the kids."

"Oh, well. We appreciate any help we can get."

He stuck his hand out and I shook it. "I'm Ransom Copeland. I'd like to donate that tractor." He jerks his thumb back towards the truck.

I feel my mouth drop. A tractor?

"That is, if you could use it. If you had something to mow these pastures with, you could bale hay for the winter."

"I...I.." I am at a loss for words. Finally, I find my voice. "Well, thank you. But that's such a large gift. I mean..."

He laughs. A pleasant sound. "Yes ma'am, I want you to have it. This one's too little to do much with. I farm the Jones land right down the road, you know. A couple others right up by the county line."

"How can we thank you?"

He waves a hand through the air. "Well, I know you're non-profit, I can do a tax write-off. So, it's a win-win situation. I can come by this weekend and get you started baling. By the way, this is my son, Gavin. My right-hand man. Got a daughter too. Emmerson. She's twelve. She's the one that got me thinking about this. She wants to come out and volunteer."

"We'd love to have her."

"She's the real horse nut at our place. We do a little trail riding, that's what I enjoy. But Emmy, I can hardly get her off the horses long enough to eat and sleep."

I laugh. And then I realize it is the first time in a long time that I have really felt it when I laughed. It felt genuine. For so long now, I have only been pretending to laugh. "I was just like that when I was twelve," I admit.

"Come on, son." He gestures at the boy. "Let's get this tractor in the barn and let this lady get back to work."

He could have sold that tractor for a heck of a lot more than he can get as a tax write-off; I think as I watch them drive back down the path towards the highway. Simply amazing.

Later in the afternoon, I look up towards the house and see the nurse leaving. I take the golf cart and go to see if Grace would like to come down for a little while. Recently, she has been letting me bring her and she will sit here in the seat, watching the kids. She never stays long because she tires so easily.

I drive her through the barn to see the new tractor. She gets that look in her eyes that tells me she is back in the past and sure enough she says, "The men used to mow these pastures and bale hay for the winter. Papa always said this fescue grass was about as good as you can get. We never had to buy the first bale of hay."

She shook her head as if to bring herself back to the present. "It never fails to amaze me; the things people do to help with this program. And it keeps getting bigger and better."

After we have watched for a few minutes, Grace is tired. The volunteers are putting the horses up anyway, so I take Grace back to the house.

I help her to the bed, but she doesn't want to lie down. She sits on the side of the bed, watching out the window as the cars leave. She looks so serious, deep in thought, but I never can tell exactly what is on her mind. After a few moments, she leans over and picks up the framed picture that sits on the bedside table. A young couple stares at the photographer and I know it is Grace and her husband.

She holds it, staring at it for a long time.

"If only I had done things differently." It is a mere whisper and I wonder if I misunderstood her. Something has upset her, and I have no idea what it could be.

I lay my hand on her arm. "Grace? Are you okay?"

She turns to look at me and I can see that her eyes have cleared.

"Did you ever wish you hadn't done something?" she asks.

I nod. "Sure, I think we all feel that way, sometimes."

"No." She shakes her head. "I mean something really important. Something that...well, it changes everything. Just everything." She looks down at the picture again.

Now, I begin to wonder what happened that gives her such deep regret. But she doesn't say anything else and I'm not going to push her.

~~~

I am restless after Grace finally lies down. I go downstairs and wander out to the stables, hoping Jennifer may still be around but her jeep is gone.

I get the bridle for the Saddlebred and walk over to the pasture he is in. He walks up to me and stops, standing calmly as he swishes his tail. I scratch the place behind his left ear that seems to be his sweet spot and he curves his neck in towards me. Taking my thumbs, I massage the pockets over his eyes, and he stands, head drooped, eyes half-closed. My fingers trace the scars on his face.

Boogie was a rescue; I had found out after I had been here for a while. Boogie To The Beat was his registered name. Abused by his previous owner. The man had beaten him with a piece of chain. Not because the horse had done anything wrong but simply because his owner had no idea how to handle horses. It is difficult for me to imagine anyone striking this sweet boy. Inquisitive and friendly by nature, he follows me through the pasture and paddocks while the other horses are busy grazing. He constantly noses my pockets looking for a treat. Ears always pricked forward, and a kind look in his eye. So tall that his looks are a little imposing, but such a gentle boy.

I take him up to the barn and saddle him. I have been told that he has been standing in the pasture, never ridden since he came here but he stands quietly while I mount. I
~~~

squeeze with my legs, and he moves out at the flat walk. I guide him into the arena and urge him into a trot. He steps high and I post, rising out of the saddle on every other step. When I signal to him to go into the special four-beat gait of the Saddlebred, each foot meets the ground at equal, separate intervals. I can feel the high knee action as he holds his head high and pricks his ears. The up and down motion is exaggerated but extremely smooth and now his name seems to fit perfectly, Boogie To The Beat. He does seem to be dancing beneath me, performing the special moves unique to the Saddebred. When I push him into a canter, it is so slow and collected it feels like riding on a cloud.

"Let's get out of here and go down by the river, boy. What do you think?" Turning out the gate, I walk the big horse down the path behind the stables. Several of the other horses whinny as we go by, and I brace for a little fight. But Boogie does not seem barn sour at all. He pays no attention to the other horses, just puts his head down, ears pricked forward and gives me not one speck of trouble. He feels good under me, just solid and ready to do his job. I urge him into a canter again and when we reach the river, we turn and follow it.

This really is a beautiful place; I think as I ride along quietly. Even though that damp, murky odor lingers in the air, I like riding here. The water tumbles swiftly over the rocks, stirring the reddish river into huge whitecaps, creating a roar that drowns out other sounds. We come to a rocky vine-clad cliff that scales steeply down to the water. Wild kudzu covers the trees like a dark green dressing-gown. The trail we follow is wide and flat. I have heard that it is a historical canal trail. These waters were so dangerous that back in the eighteen-hundreds when it was used for transportation, they had to dig the canal to bypass the rapids.

As we continue downriver, the water calms and runs smoothly. The slope is gentler now and makes no sound. A sudden noise crackles in the brush and I look up to see a red fox scramble across the path and disappear into one of the cut-out gorges. I brace for the horse under me to shy out but he only spooks in place. Stops with a quick jerk and raises his head to watch them go. Never have I seen a such a calm Saddlebred and I decide I'm going to start using him. And I know exactly which patient I'm going to put on him.

I've been enjoying the ride so much; I hadn't noticed the sun was beginning to set. I push Boogie into his fancy gait and now we are covering ground swiftly.

Twilight is just settling when I turn off the river path and head towards the barn. I can see the great house on the hill and in silhouette, it is easy to imagine how grand it used to be. The photographs I have seen, the articles I have been reading online are a testament to how magnificent the place was so long ago.

I cool Boogie off and put him in his pasture. He lies down and rolls, scratching his back where it had gotten sweaty, then wanders off, nibbling at the grass. It's so nice out, I don't want to go inside. I wander into the back of the main stable, where a dozen of the horses are shut up. We have an early session in the morning so we left them in. Every one of them sticks their head out, hoping for a treat. Moving towards the front of the stable, I walk up to Sundown's stall and hold out my hand. His soft lips nuzzle it, tickling my palm.

Diesel has his head over the stall door, making that little whinny sound, huh-huh-huh; and I know what he is really saying is feed me. I look down the wide aisle of the barn and a head is looking out over every door. "I swear, you guys never get full, do you? I'll give you all an extra scoop of grain."

I stay in the barn for a little while, just watching the horses eat. I love to listen to the crunch of teeth on grain and smell the fragrance of the hay. Finally, I lock up and start towards the house.

A light is shining dimly in Grace's bedroom window, and I remember what she said earlier. How she looked at that picture of her with her husband. I wonder what she had meant when she said she had done something that she shouldn't have. I shake my head, trying to clear my thoughts. Rumors, old stories. Sure, Grace had seemed a little strange when I first came here. But at her age, who wouldn't be. I just couldn't believe Grace was capable of ever hurting anyone. Or any creature, for that matter. I have a feeling that she wanted to tell me something. But I don't think she's ready yet.

TWENTY-FIVE

September 8, 1942

Grace sat beside Lorraine in the autograph booth. People were lined up all the way out to the sidewalk for the book signing.

"And this is my assistant, Grace." Lorraine stopped writing and put her hand on Grace's arm. The woman who had just bought a book smiled and nodded at Grace.

"I don't know what I would have done without her help," Lorraine gushed. "I could have never gotten my book to the press in time."

Lorraine looked over at Grace. "Don't forget to give her a ticket."

Grace handed the woman a ticket. "Thank you for buying the book. That entitles you to one free ticket to get in for the tour at Janus Farms today."

Lorraine held her hand out and the woman shook it, then moved aside as the next buyer stepped up. Grace watched her as she flipped through the book. She could see over the woman's shoulder which pages she had flipped to as she looked at the pictures in the center and Grace did feel a certain satisfaction with what she had done. Throughout the morning, she had become so jaded with her sister-in-law's little speech about how it was *her* book that it hardly bothered her anymore.

She stood up. "I'm going to get another lemonade. You want one?"

Lorraine shook her head. "I'm not done with this one yet."

Grace shrugged and started down the path. They were set up in the center of the town square. She wasn't hungry but those roasted peanuts smelled good. She bought a bag and munched on them as she took in the sights of the festival.

Mama was at the canned goods table, working with ladies from the church. Tourists were purchasing quart jars of the colorful vegetables, pickled peaches, and pepper jellies.

She was just eating the last handful of peanuts when a motor droned overhead, and she looked up to see the little plane circling. Buzz was taking tourists up for an aerial view. He would fly them around town, then down along the river, circle Janus Farms and come back to land on the football field on the schoolyard, a couple of blocks away from the town square.

The color guard from the high school led a parade down the avenue. A float swept down the street, carrying the homecoming queen and her court. A man dressed like Uncle Sam towered over the crowd on stilts. The school band marched behind him, horns and drums blaring in perfect symphony.

"Miss Grace!" She turned to see who was calling her. Cook and Paulette were coming down the sidewalk. "Look what I got," Cook declared. She held up a blue ribbon.

"Oh, Cook! You won the cake-making contest."

Cook nodded. "One of my hummingbird cakes. The judge said it was the best he ever tasted." She made a face. "I don't care what the government says, I was going to use my sugar and I wasn't going to spare a drop. Used every bit my recipe calls for."

Grace gave her a little hug. "I never doubted you would win." She had had that cake enough times to know. Thin layers with creamy coconut, sour cream, and toasted pecans. It would melt in your mouth.

Paulette held up a plate with a generous piece. "She made me save a slice for Hoot. We're on the way back to the farm. Are you coming out?"

Grace nodded. "Later. Oh, there's Miss Dot. I'm going to see the rest of her tour."

The town librarian shuffled along on her short legs, looking back at the group of tourists.

"Wasn't that big house just magnificent?" Grace heard one lady say as they passed the post office, where teenagers were sitting on the low stone wall out front.

The group followed for a few blocks, until they came near the river and Miss Dot led them to a blocky building. On the near side, the ground was hollowed out in graduated depths.

"Is this a canal lock?" asked a man with a Northern accent.

Miss Dot smiled, eager now that she saw curiosity in her favorite historical interest.

"It certainly is," she nodded. "The river was actually the reason a town was formed here. For transportation back in the seventeen hundreds. Goods were shipped by boat back then.

"But the elevation line drops so fast along here, it made the river dangerous. The rapids flowing along the rocks would smash the boats to bits. So many people drowned here, the Native Americans called it the Roanoke River. The word means death."

Murmurs came from the crowd as they stood by the canal, eating their treats.

"So, the settlers were forced to dig a canal along this part. Had to dig it out by hand, can you imagine? Seven miles long. Then mule teams that would tow the boats along the canal, back and forth.

"And then, when the elevation really dropped drastically, the boats would have to go through these locks. They would keep going down, a little at the time. Then they would open the next gate and drop it a little more until they could get back to the main part of the canal. And eventually, after they passed through Weldon a few miles downstream, they merged back into the river after the waters calmed down."

"Very interesting," said the man with the Northern accent. "Took a lot of ingenuity to do something on such a large scale back then. And a lot of manpower."

Miss Dot beamed, clasping her hands under her chin. "I've been talking to the town council for years now, about converting this little building into a museum. And we could actually turn the canal itself into a wonderful hiking trail," she said. "And who knows, one day maybe they will actually do it. It's really our biggest claim to fame. And all to think, just because we live alongside such a dangerous river."

~~~

Vehicles were lined up for nearly half a mile, waiting to pay their admission to get into the gates at Janus Farms. Phillip and Grace could see the front pastures crammed with cars, filling the overflow from the parking lots. Phillip smiled over at her.

"A pretty big success you ladies have put together."

He put his hand on a copy of the book that was lying on the seat. "And this book. You did a really good job, Grace. I'm proud of you."

She looked out the window. "Well, I had some help, you know."

"Phfffft!" He blew the sound out of pursed lips. "Not from the one who has her name all over the cover."

Grace shrugged. "But the ladies did help. Martha Strayhorn did the typing. And Mr. Clay from the printing press helped me lay everything out."

"And what about Lorraine? She didn't really do anything, did she?" He put the car back in gear because the line was starting to move again.

"She did help some." Grace made a face. "Of course, it was only because I finally forced her to. And the ladies were really getting on her back about it."

They were finally able to get down to the stables. They could see Red in the front corral and Hoot sitting up on the stand that had been placed in front of it. The stallion paced back and forth in the corral. A big banner covered the front of the booth where Hoot sat.

HOOT HARRISON SAYS GIVE A HOOT ABOUT YOUR COUNTRY
BUY YOUR WAR BONDS!

As they walked up, they could hear Hoot talking to the fans. Grady and two other hands stood behind him,
~~~

keeping an eye on the horse and selling bonds.

"Now, what's your name, sweetheart?" Hoot asked a young woman.

"Make it out to Mary-Margaret," she said as her cheeks turned fiery red.

"All right." The jockey scribbled on the paper and handed it to her. As she reached out, he took her hand and gave it a little kiss. "Thanks for coming to visit us," he said.

"Good turnout, huh?" Papa's voice boomed as he walked up behind them. "We've got some crowd."

Phillip nodded and raised his eyebrows. "Well, with a team like Hoot and Red..."

"Yep." Papa stalked off and Grace watched as he worked his way through the crowd, stopping here and there to shake hands with the visitors, then turned back to watch Hoot.

"Hoot, how about something cold to drink?" she asked.

"Now that sounds exactly like what I could use," he answered as he signed for an elderly couple.

She went over to the concession stand and waited in line behind the visitors. She overheard one woman say to her husband, "I just can't believe we're actually here. At Janus Farms. It's so exciting."

He pushed his hat back off his forehead and nodded. "Sure is. I enjoyed seeing Runaway Rapids. And that Hoot Harrison." He stopped and shook his head. "That guy is really something. America's favorite hero, I guess you could say."

Grace turned and looked back at the autograph line. All those people waiting to get up there and speak to Hoot. The man was right, America did love him. Funny, she thought now. How Hoot had been getting sick each time a race was coming up and then he always got better a couple of days later. Maybe it was just nerves, she thought. He never seemed to be anxious about racing or anything else, but some people could put up a good front. And stress could really affect a person's health, especially anything to do with the stomach. Maybe that's all it was.

She finally got up to the concession stand and got

Coca-Colas for Hoot and the rest of the guys. They gave her a box to put them in and she made her way back over to the paddock.

Hoot was talking to a little boy. The child's face was shining with excitement as he grinned up at the jockey, his mother's hand on his shoulder as if he might get away from her. He was so small that it was hard for him to see. Phillip picked him up, putting him on his hip so that he was nearly even with the stand. His shining eyes never left Hoot.

"I'm Carson Turner," the little boy sputtered. "My dad was your very biggest fan. Ever. In the whole world."

"Well, where is he?" Hoot asked. "Did he come with you today?"

The boy's head dropped, and he was silent.

His mother stepped up and said in a voice so low that Grace could barely hear, "His father passed away a few months ago. I thought bringing him out here would be good for him."

"Well, sure it will." Hoot turned back to Carson. "So, you like the races?"

Carson nodded. "It's my favorite thing. Dad took me to see you last year."

"Really?" I hope you had a good time."

"Oh yes. Dad loved horses, just like me. He used to ride when he was little."

Carson's mother reached up and put her hand on his arm. "Honey, we have to move on. All these people behind us are waiting to see Hoot, too."

"It's okay," the jockey said. "We've got all afternoon."

The little face looked up at Hoot. "Can I tell you a secret? You're not supposed to tell your birthday wish. But...I don't see how it's ever going to happen if I don't let you in on it."

"Well, you tell old Hoot and I'll do my best."

"My wish was to ride Runaway Rapids! Could I?"

The smile melted off the jockey's face and he was quiet for a moment.

"I'm sorry, son. He's a racehorse. And he's pretty hard to handle."

The boy's face dropped. "He's mean?"

"Oh, no." Hoot shook his head. "Nothing like that. Just high-strung. Nervous. He's been taught to run fast and that's all he knows how to do. He's not a horse for kids. He wouldn't hurt anyone on purpose but you can fall off a horse like him pretty easy."

The boy's lower lip trembled but he didn't say anything. Finally, he looked up and said, "Well, thanks anyway. It was really nice to meet you."

Phillip set the boy back on the ground and his mother started to lead him away.

"Hey, Carson! Wait a minute. Come back."

The boy pulled away from his mother and turned back, looking at Hoot.

The jockey turned to Grady and one of the grooms. "Hey, you guys. Saddle Cloudy."

Grady's face lit up with a grin and he headed towards the stable.

"You guys just stay here for a couple of minutes," Hoot instructed the boy's mother. "Let me get a few more autographs signed for these folks here."

He had only signed three when Grady came out leading Cloudy.

Hoot looked out over the crowd in the long line and shouted, "If you folks will just excuse me? I'll be right back."

Jumping off the stage, he mounted Cloudy and motioned to Phillip to hand the boy up to him. Phillip put him on the horse in front of Hoot and the boy sat there, smiling.

"What's going on?" a heavy-set man asked as he turned to look at his wife. "We've been standing in this line for an hour."

The woman standing a few places up in line turned and Grace heard her explaining what was happening. The story seemed to be traveling down the line, as people strained to see.

Hoot pulled off his jockey's cap and put it on Carson's head. "We're going for a ride on the track."

"The race track? Really?"

"Yes sir, we are. This is Cloudy. He's sort of like

Runaway's best buddy."

"Wait until I tell my friends I rode on the racetrack!" The boy tipped his head back, trying to see Hoot's face. "Horses have best friends? Just like kids?"

"Well, kind of. Cloudy's really calm, a little bit lazy. All he wants to do is walk along. You have to really push him to get him to go any faster. And when he's with the race horses, that makes them calmer, too."

The newspaper photographer snapped a few shots as the boy's small face peered out from under Hoot's cap. Phillip was writing down Carson's address. "We'll get a dozen copies and send them to you," he said to the boy's mother.

She caught him by the sleeve. "I can't tell you what this means to us."

"All right," Hoot said. "Let's ride!"

The little face took on a look of extreme concentration as Cloudy walked off. But his eyes were bright, and the tiniest smile played on his lips. The crowd stood, watching as Hoot walked Cloudy down the hill. They broke into a jog, and she could hear Carson giggling as he bounced around a little. Hoot guided the horse onto the track and pushed him into a slow lope.

Grace wondered if people would really be irritated now, they had been standing in line so long. But when she turned back to look, nearly everyone had a smile on their face as they watched. And the few that didn't were busy wiping off the tears that rolled down their cheeks.

TWENTY-SIX

October 11, 1942

Grady and one of the grooms led Red out of the stables. The colt was excited and flighty, but Grace could tell he was becoming a little more manageable. He spooked a couple of times but stayed in place, dancing nervously. Hoot came around the corner of the stable, fastening his helmet strap.

"All right, Hoot," Frank said. "You know how much we've got riding on this race. I want you to give it all you've got. But do it just the way we planned."

Hoot nodded but didn't say anything. He gathered the reins and put them over the horse's head, stretching high on tiptoe to reach up. He tried to put his foot in the stirrup; but slipped. Grace noticed that he swayed for a moment.

"Are you okay?" Grady asked and Hoot just nodded.

"You don't look like it." Grady took the reins from the jockey's hand. "You look mighty pale."

"I'm okay. Just give me a minute."

Grady held the colt while Hoot stood there for a moment. He was breathing heavily and somehow his eyes didn't seem quite focused. He leaned against the stirrup fender for a moment.

Phillip and Buzz walked up just as the jockey lifted his head.

"What's going on here?" Phillip asked.

"I don't know," Grady answered. "But something's up with Hoot. He's not acting right."

"I'm okay," Hoot croaked. "Just got too hot for a minute there. I'll be fine."

Grady caught Phillip's eye and shook his head.

"Hoot, if you're sick, maybe we need to scratch the race," Phillip said.

The jockey looked up at him and the relief written across his face was obvious. "Maybe you're right...if I can't do my best...I don't know... suppose we don't win it."

"We're not scratching." Frank stepped up. "As much as we've been putting into this race, I'll be damned if we're going to just give up and quit!"

"Calm down, Frank," Phillip said as he stepped up and took the reins from Grady. "Hoot has got a point. If he goes out there without being a hundred percent, we could very well lose this. It would be a lot better to just scratch."

"No!" Frank looked over at Hoot. "Janus Farms never scratches."

Hoot walked back over to the horse and put his foot in the stirrup. "I think I'm okay. Just got kind of woozy for a minute there."

"Well...," Phillip looked uncertain. "You sure?"

Hoot nodded and they watched Grady take hold of Hoot's left calf and give him a push upwards into the saddle. Grace couldn't help but be irritated with Phillip. He should have stood up to Frank and demanded to scratch the race. How much would it take to satisfy her brother-in-law, she wondered. With all the wealth, the steady success of Janus Farms. Even if they did scratch or lose today. She knew how important this particular race was to the family, but she was just angry with them all.

Well, it would be over in just a little bit, she thought. And after Hoot came in, she was going to watch over him for the next week or so. She was still going to the kitchen every morning, cooking up a fresh batch of bone broth for Hoot. It was the best thing for him to eat that she knew of. While it didn't have a lot of calories or fat, it was full of the minerals and nutrients he needed.

She wondered what the future would hold for Hoot. She doubted that he would ever go back on an eating binge again and put on excess weight. At least not while he was still young enough to race. It was easy to see how it had happened. Hoot had never had Southern cooking before and he loved it. And those pounds had just sneaked up on him. Anyway, she intended to keep a close eye on him for a while.

She and Phillip climbed the stands to the family's box a few minutes later. Mama and Lorraine moved over to make room for them. Papa swung around to greet Phillip, binoculars bumping against his chest. Pulling the cigar from his mouth, he clapped Phillip on the shoulder. "By God, we got this one wrapped up, don't we, son?"

Phillip nodded. "I hope so." But Papa had turned his attention to someone in the stands beside the family's box. "Good to see you," he boomed, and Grace knew it must be someone he considered important.

They watched as one of the exercise boys jogged a pony horse up towards the track beside Runaway. Hoot was having a hard time controlling the colt. He pranced beside the pony horse, shying out and colliding with the thoroughbred on his far side. Grace could see the other jockey raise his whip to try to fend them off. Buzz stepped up and grasped Runaway's bridle firmly, forcing him back to the side.

They had drawn fifth position. Grady and one of the handlers were waiting there. As Runaway approached, he whirled back, and it took a few minutes until Hoot and Buzz were able to bring him under control. As they approached the gate again, the men took hold of the colt on both sides, working hard with Hoot to get him into the stall.

Frank entered the box just as they slammed the gate shut behind Runaway. Grace could see him rearing in the stall and she hoped he would calm down. She was still worried about Hoot.

"Okay," Frank said. "Hoot knows what to do. Buzz told him to hold back until the quarter pole, then give the colt his head."

Finally, all the horses were loaded into the starting gate and the excitement of the crowd continued to build.

Grace jumped when the bell clanged. Runaway was the last horse out the gate, still fighting his jockey.

"And they're off!" shouted the announcer. "It's One Grand Dude in the lead, trailed closely by the Cincinnati Cyclone. Pewter Dust in third and Bamboozle running on his flank! Looks like the Carolina Colt is up to his old habits, late out of the gate and giving his jockey a hard time."

A few more strides and Hoot was able to get the colt straightened out. At least he wasn't trying to move towards the outside they way he used to, Grace thought.

Phillip squeezed Grace's hand. Hard. "Thank God," he said. "With a start like that we wouldn't have a chance if he went to the outside rail."

"The Dude is still in the lead and Big Mama Maggie is moving up, passing Bamboozle. Pewter Dust and the Cyclone are packed pretty tightly together. Oh look, just as usual, Runaway Rapids is starting to move up! He's almost caught up to the pack. Boy, he's got his wheels in motion now."

Phillip loosened his grip on Grace's arm and she felt him relax a little. Papa was on the other side of him, slapping the racing program against his thigh. She looked back at the track to see Red moving on up towards the other horses.

The family watched, their eyes glued to the track as Red caught up to the last horse and began to plow through the pack. He had passed the stragglers when Papa shouted "What in the world is the matter with that confounded jockey? He's making his move too fast!"

Almost as if Hoot had heard the remark, he reined the colt, and they began to run even with the others.

"Now hold him there, Hoot," Grace heard Phillip mutter. "Just the way we planned."

The horses were all tightly packed now, moving almost as one entity as they ate up the ground, clods of earth shooting out beneath the flying hooves. Excitement continued to mount among the crowd and Grace could see people all around then, jumping up and down, waving their programs in the air, shouting, and screaming.

The horses swept down the track, tightly packed. Then, a little over hundred and fifty yards from the half mile, the red and gold colors of Janus charged forward with a terrific burst of speed.

"What does he think he's doing?" Frank yelled. "It's not time yet."

A gasp rose collectively from the stands and Grace strained to see what was happening. Runaway was on the far side of another horse; a big bay and she could hardly see him. Then, as he pulled ahead, she could see Hoot's body, slumped over his neck.

What had happened, she wondered. "Had the jockey fainted? Her heart pounded against her chest. How on earth was he staying in the saddle?

Grabbing Phillip's arm, she looked up to see his eyes wide with worry. "What's happening?" she tried to shout but he couldn't hear her above the noise of the crowd.

On and on the horses ran, the big, red stallion churning through the bunched-up pack. Now that he had free rein, Runaway was passing the other horses, steadily going for the lead. By the time they reached the half mile mark, there were only two horses ahead of him and he was steadily gaining ground.

Hoot was still slumped over the horse's neck, leaning just a little to the left. He's going to come off any minute, Grace thought. All those horses coming up behind him, surely, he's going to be trampled.

Coming into the backstretch, Runaway caught the horse in front of him. His stride was huge, digging great chunks of earth up into the air. And then he was coming up on the lead horse, quickly gaining ground. Now they were neck and neck for another twelve paces, then Runaway began to pull out in front. They swept across the finish line, the red and gold colors of Janus a full three lengths ahead.

Hoot was still slumped over, and the colt gave no signs of slowing down. Riders standing by on the pony-horses went after him, but he left them behind like they were running at a lazy lope. Riders came from the opposite end of the track and soon had him closed in. One of the men swung in close and grabbed the reins that had gone slack. The stallion put up a fight, nearly jerking the other rider off his horse, but the man held fast. Other riders boxed him in and gradually, they were able to slow him down.

Grace expected to see them pull the jockey off, but they simply gathered around. Runaway was standing mostly still now but the men didn't seem to know what to do. Photographers weaved in and out among the horses, leaping out of the way of quick hooves to keep from being trampled. The race stewards were running down the track to meet the riders who were bringing Runaway in.

They all milled around the big horse and still, no one pulled the jockey down. He remained slumped over. Phillip started down out of the stands and she followed close on his heels.

"You women stay here," she heard Papa bark but pretended not to. If they could just get to Hoot, he needed help.

Unable to keep up with Phillip's long stride, she trotted along, elbowing her way through the crowd. Frank passed her, catching up to Phillip and she could hear Papa behind her, his breathing heavy.

When she finally reached the track, Phillip already had hold of Runaway's bridle. She hadn't seen Buzz coming but there he was on the other side, helping Phillip hold the stallion. Frank stood off a little with the other men.

Papa came tramping up. "What...what's going..." His breath was short, and he was coughing. "What's going on here? Will somebody please tell me?"

The crowd of men parted to let Papa through, and he strode up brandishing his cane around his head. "What ... blast it! Why aren't you getting him down?"

Phillip caught Papa's sleeve with one hand, the other still on the bridle.

"Papa." He looked at his father and didn't say anything for a moment. Grace noticed his face had gone pale, even beneath the flush of excitement and running down the track. "Papa," he said again. "Hoot's dead."

TWENTY-SEVEN

October 12, 1942

Grace woke just before dawn. Even before she opened her eyes, she could tell Phillip was not lying beside her. She had tossed and turned all night but evidently, he had never even come to bed at all.

Obviously, she wasn't going to get back to sleep, so she got up and went out onto the veranda. The sun was just beginning to peek over the horizon, and everything was still. She could see dark silhouettes of the horses in the background, grazing.

Going down to the kitchen, she poked around until she found the big can of Maxwell House coffee and got the percolator going. Funny, she thought. After all the time she had lived in this house, she didn't know how to find a thing in the kitchen. Such a strange thought. Back in Aunt Ada's little shack where she had been raised, she could put her hand on anything she needed to.

When the percolator stopped gurgling, she poured some coffee into one of the fine porcelain cups. Going to the refrigerator she poured in a thick dollop of cream and searched for the sugar but never could find it. It didn't matter. What she really wanted was just the comfort of the hot cup in her hands, to be able to watch the steam rising. If she could just concentrate on that, maybe she could block out the visions of what had happened yesterday.

Carrying the cup, she walked down to the stables. Usually, the hands were at work by this time but there was no one in sight. Phillip's car was parked in its normal spot under the carport, but she didn't have a clue where he could be. She just wished someone were around. Not that she felt like talking. But the loneliness felt so desolate. Almost like she was walking through a different world.

Only the horses seemed normal this morning, she thought as the sun got brighter. She envied them that. The fact that everything was here and now. No thoughts about the past or worries of the future.

Stepping into the main stable she thought surely, she would find her husband there. But there were only the horses to greet her. Big Red stuck his head over the stall door for a moment, then moved away nervously and she heard a loud thump as he turned back, and his broad chest connected with the solid wood again. He tossed his head up and down, anxious for his breakfast, then began to pace the perimeter of the stall again.

All the horses were hungry, but she knew the men would be out soon to feed them. Walking over to the stable that housed the pony horses, she went straight into Cloudy's stall. The little horse stood quietly as she ran her hands over his spotted body for a moment, then leaned into him and rested her weight on the thick neck. They stood like that for a few moments, neither of them moving.

Then, a slight movement outside caught her eye. Phillip was standing in the pasture, down the hill, under a big oak. Just standing there, staring off into space.

She started to go to him, but something held her back. The way he was standing so still. If he wanted me around, he'd be up in our room, she thought. I'll just give him a little time.

No one said much at breakfast that morning. Lorraine's eyes were red, and Grace could tell she had been crying. Papa came in and sat down without saying a word. Just stared down at his empty plate as they waited for the servants to bring in the food. It was the first time she had seen him silent. Ever.

Grace's stomach churned with anger as she looked over at Papa and Frank, wondering what they were thinking. She doubted it was concern for Hoot and his family. More likely, Papa was thinking the winning streak may be over for a while. That the popularity Hoot had brought to Janus Farms would fade away. Frank had actually argued with the stewards. Forced them to look at the rule books. Any horse that crossed the finish line first with a jockey in the saddle took first place. How could he not?

Paulette came in, carrying trays laden with sausage and eggs. Cook was behind her with a plate of country ham. She stumbled a little and nearly dropped the plate. Grace looked up to see her face was red and splotchy and her lower lip was trembling.

Phillip stood up and took the plate from her and she lifted the hem of her apron to dab at her eyes.

"Are you all right?" Phillip asked. Cook nodded but as Phillip stood up and reached for her arm to steady her, she turned and left the room quickly.

The family ate in silence. The only noise in the room was cutlery scraping across the fine china breakfast plates.

Grace didn't eat anything but half a biscuit. It stuck in her throat for a few moments. She was finally able to wash it down with orange juice. But when it hit her stomach, she felt as if she may throw up. She excused herself and left the table.

The rest of the day was pretty much the same. Except Papa didn't even come down to the noon meal.

"Is he okay?" Phillip asked Mama. "Ever since I was little, I've never known Papa not to come to the table."

She nodded. "I know. I tried to get him down, but he's just sitting up in the bedroom. Said to just leave him be for a little while."

After lunch, Phillip got into the car and left without saying a word about where he was going. Grace doubted that it was business. He probably just wanted to be alone too, Grace thought. It must be a thing with men, she thought.

All afternoon, the house was so quiet she finally wandered down to the stables. The men were working, cleaning stalls, soaping down the saddles and polishing the hardware on bridles. But they worked in complete silence. None of the usual joking and laughter. And no work going on down at the track.

Taking Cloudy out of the stall, she put him in the crossties and went to get his tack. She passed a couple of the men on the way back with the saddle, but they didn't step out to help her as they always did. She didn't even bother to groom the little horse first. Just ran the brush across his back a couple of times on the area the saddle would fit and tacked him up. She would give him a good grooming when she got back.

She rode along slowly, letting Cloudy go at his favorite pace, never breaking out of the walk. She felt so exhausted she didn't have the energy to push him. But neither could she just sit up in her room. Her body was so tired, but her mind refused to be still.

How can I feel so tired, she wondered? I haven't done anything. She supposed it was the tension. And how her adrenalin had spiked yesterday, then crashed. Very little sleep, filled with nightmares.

As they walked along, the sun beat down on them and the afternoon heat made her feel nauseated again. She wished Phillip would have taken her with him, wherever he had gone. It didn't matter, she just wanted to be with him. Even if he didn't really talk much. She just needed to be near him. To feel his strength. How he was so steady and solid. How he always made everything turn out all right.

She had missed him last night. She hadn't expected to make love or, anything like that. She just wanted to feel the warmth of his body next to her. Or today, if he would just take a little time, put his arm around her. Hold her for a little while.

She was being selfish, she told herself. She knew how much Phillip was hurting. How fond he was of Hoot. Sure, he bore the main responsibility of running Janus Farms and he had a lot on his plate right now. But she knew he was really hurting inside, and he had to find his own way to deal with it.

Turning onto the path that ran beside the river, she welcomed the shade of the tall trees. It was much cooler here. Cloudy picked up his pace a little and went into a slow jog. She just sat in the saddle, letting him choose his gait and go as he pleased.

She had ridden a couple of miles downriver and was about to turn back when she saw a big, black horse ahead. A heavy horse with feathered fetlocks so she knew it was

Buzz. The horse stood there in the shade with his head lowered, swinging his tail at the flies. She didn't see Buzz anywhere. Surely, he hadn't been thrown. She felt her adrenalin begin to pump and her heart hammered.

Then she saw him. Sitting on a big rock that jutted out over the river. Just sitting there. Staring out over the water.

Grace dismounted, tied Cloudy beside the other horse, and walked down to the river. Buzz didn't say anything, but she knew he had heard her. When she sat down beside him, he finally turned and looked at her.

"Grace." He just spoke her name. Nothing else.

She didn't answer. Just looked out across the place he had been gazing at. Nothing out of the ordinary there. Muddy, red water with occasional whitecaps here and there boiling over.

Finally, Buzz spoke. "I never knew anyone exactly like him."

"None of us did," she answered.

Buzz picked up a stone and plunked it into the water. "The Lord sure broke the mold when he made that boy. I've had a lot of friends in my life, but..." He broke off, unable to speak for a moment.

Grace sat silently, waiting for him to regain his composure. He scuffed the toe of his boot at a scrawny bush that was growing out of a crack in the rock.

"This place never knew a dull moment with Hoot around," he finally continued. "Always up to something. Him and Grady. Some of the other guys. But Hoot, he was always the instigator, the one getting things going."

Cloudy let out a little squeal and they turned to see Buzz's horse nip at him. Just a little thing, the way horses do. Nothing really threatening.

"I know you thought a lot of Hoot," Grace said.

Buzz turned and gave her a little smile. But it only made his mouth turn up at the corners a little. The corners of his eyes didn't crinkle up the way they always did when one of his grins was genuine.

"He did just about drive me crazy," Buzz said. "That drinking problem of his. I never knew if he would turn up for practice or not. Everything Hoot did, he just seemed to…I guess…carry it a little too far. Drinking, eating too much rich food, playing tricks, chasing women."

He shook his head. "But come race day, he never let us down, did he?" His face fell. "I should have pulled him out of that race. I knew something was wrong. He was just so stubborn, sometimes you couldn't tell him a danged thing."

Grace felt her stomach twist. "He had such a kindness about him, didn't he? Everyone here loved him."

Buzz nodded. "I swear, everyone in the whole United States loved that boy," he said. "Generous to a fault, always the life of the party." He grinned again and this time it seemed a little more natural. "How you could put all that energy and charisma into such a tiny, little package is beyond me."

"I know," Grace said. "It's just so hard to believe he's gone."

Buzz turned away and for a moment, she could see the broad shoulders shaking as he choked back a sob. She laid her hand on his back and she could feel him tremble.

He turned back to her; his eyes filled with grief. He stared at her for what seemed like a long time. She just sat there, watching him.

Then he laid his big hand across her cheek, cupped her face in his palm.

"Grace," he whispered, so low she wasn't sure he'd said anything until she heard it again as he pulled her face closer to his.

And even though she knew she should resist, she didn't. She allowed him to keep pulling her closer. Allowed her upper body to lean in towards him. Then his mouth covered hers, his lips so soft. So warm.

And she felt herself melting under his touch. She could smell tobacco on him and the clean fragrance of his cotton shirt. Her mouth opened as she yielded to his touch. Every nerve in her body trembled, tingled so that if felt like the time she had accidentally touched a naked electric cord at Aunt Ada's cabin, and it sent little shocks through her body.

And she simply sat there on the rock, kissing him back as her heart pounded. Every muscle so taut she could hardly breathe.

She felt herself easing backwards until she was resting on the side of the riverbank, her body cushioned by the soft leaves of the thick kudzu vines. He ran a hand down the side of her bare arm, and she shivered, even in the afternoon heat. She felt so helpless to resist, so drawn to him. Nothing existed but the fact that they were together. All this time, it had been coming on and she had pushed away from it. And now, she was finally going to let it happen.

Then, Cloudy squealed again and as she looked over to make sure the big horse wasn't doing him any real harm, the spell was broken. Putting both hands against Buzz's chest, she pushed him away.

"No, I ...Buzz, we can't. Hoot just died, we're out of our minds. We don't know what we're doing."

"We do," he answered. "It's what I've wanted for a long time, Grace. And so have you. Don't even try to tell me anything different." Even as he pulled back, his eyes searched her face.

She didn't say anything else. As much as she wanted to stay, she was afraid. Scrambling up the riverbank, she untied Cloudy and mounted. Digging her heels into his sides, she pushed him into a high canter. Glancing back over her shoulder, she saw Buzz just standing there watching her and she nearly lost her balance as she heard him call her name. Then she pulled herself upright in the saddle and did something she had never done before. She kicked the little horse with all her might, sending him into a fast gallop, and all she could hear now was the sound of steel horseshoes clacking sharply on the stones of the river path as he carried her towards home.

TWENTY-EIGHT

November 22, 1942

Three races since Hoot had died and not a single win. The best Janus Farms had done with Runaway Rapids was second place in one of them. Phillip and Buzz had gone through strategy after strategy, racking their brains night and day. They had switched jockeys several times but so far, none of them had been able to put Red just where he needed to be. He wasn't veering to the outside, it seemed Hoot had cured him of that. But the colt just fought the jockeys so hard, he didn't have his mind on the game.

The entire nation had grieved over Hoot's death. Every time you turned on the television, the screen was filled with images of him. Perched on top of Runaway in the winner's circle, beaming down at the audience. Selling war bonds, signing autographs. Footage of him at all the fundraisers he had done for the war effort. Grinning at the camera with tall, beautiful women on his arm. The one they ran the most was when he had been filmed floating down on the lawn of the White House in the parachute with the lettering:

GIVE A HOOT ABOUT YOUR COUNTRY!
BUY YOUR WAR BONDS!

And the radio. Interviews with Hoot, coming over the airwaves. You could close your eyes and listen to the clipped, Northern accent and swear the little man was right there in the room with you. The local stations had taken call-ins for several weeks and hearing average citizens talk about Hoot made it clear how people had felt about him. He was a national hero, and they were missing him as if he were one of their own family. The newspapers too. The headlines for weeks had been about the jockey.

Each time they lost a race, Papa would throw a tantrum, stomping about, cursing anyone who crossed his path. "Just give us a little time," Phillip tried to encourage him. "Buzz and I will come up with something."

And Frank. He just seemed to grow more agitated day by day. Extremely ill-tempered to the help. Fighting with Lorraine more. Grace heard them every night. She couldn't always make out the words, but she could hear the angry tones. It seemed as if she could actually feel the vibrations of anger, lingering in the air, to eventually be absorbed by the thick walls.

At first, Lorraine had flared out against him. But after a few weeks, she refused to rise to the challenge and Grace could see something change in her. Her eyes. They slowly stopped sparking with anger, and she would drop them, looking down when Frank spoke harshly to her. She didn't have to admit that she was afraid of him, it was easy to see. And more than once, Grace saw bruises on her.

Grace felt as if she didn't really know where to be. Papa was staying in the house more, wandering about, just gazing down at the tracks through the windows. Having to sit through meals with him had always been uncomfortable but then he had always left for the stables or town. Now the only place in the house where she could avoid him was in her suite and she couldn't stay cooped up in there all day.

And down at the stables. It was better there, but Phillip and Buzz were under so much pressure. Last week was the first time Grace had ever heard Phillip really speak sharply to the hands. Everything was different since Hoot had been gone. Everyone worked hard but there was no laughter. No joking. You could feel the tension in the air.

She went down anyway. She would just get Cloudy and get out of there before anyone saw her. The little horse nickered when he saw her coming. She stepped into the stall, and he nuzzled at her, hoping for a treat.

She was glad she had come. Being with the horse made her feel a little more normal. Cloudy behaved the way he always had. Nothing ever different with him. Always the same. And with a horse, that was a very good thing. They were the safe ones. The horses that were the same, day in and day out. You always knew exactly what they would do. No surprises. No danger. No fear.

She had gotten saddled and mounted without seeing anyone up close. But as Cloudy started down the aisle, he felt a little bit off. She stopped and put her weight into her right foot, pushing down to shift the saddle over a little that way. Sometimes when she mounted, the saddle would slide that way a little and become unbalanced.

But when they started out again, she could tell something was wrong. The horse seemed to be giving a little on his near foreleg. She dismounted and ran her hand down his lower leg. She didn't feel any heat or swelling, so she tried to lift his hoof to get a look at the frog.

But he wouldn't budge. He was usually good about giving her his feet. He must really be sore and now she was worried.

"What's wrong, buddy?" she asked. "Come on now, let me take a look." "Need some help, Miss Grace?" She looked up to see Grady coming up behind her, carrying two heavy saddles. He draped then across a stall and walked over.

"I guess so. He seems a little off. Not really lame, but…I don't know. Just sore maybe. Like if he was stove up. I can't get his hoof up to take a look."

Grady came over and put his hand on the horse's hoof, expecting him to lift it automatically, but Cloudy kept it stubbornly on the ground. Grady put his big shoulder into the horse's and pushed him backwards. When the foot came up, he simply caught it and lifted it up onto his knee. The horse began to struggle but Grady caught the foot between his knees and held it there as easily as if he were holding a kitten. Sometimes Grace wished she had some of that physical strength.

Grady reached into his back pocket and pulled out a hoof pick. He dug down gently into the deep groove beside the frog and a small stone popped out. He released his hold on the horse, picked it up and tossed it into a trash can in the aisle.

"There you go, Cloudy-boy." He handed Grace the reins.

"Walk him a little way there, Miss Grace."

"Looks like that's all it was," Grady said as he watched the horse's gait. "A little piece of rock like that sure can make them uncomfortable when they put their weight on it."

He was handing the reins back to her when Frank's voice came from the front of the barn. "Grady! Get your butt over there and get that stallion down to the track. Right now. We're waiting for you!"

They watched as Frank turned on his heel and started down the hill towards the track. Grace could hear Grady grind his teeth together and his face turned a deep purple.

"I hate that...that...!" He shook his head. "Sorry, Miss Grace."

She put her hand on his arm and even through the thick sleeve, she could feel the hard muscles. "It's okay, Grady. I can't say as I blame you, the way he always treats you."

"It's not that. Oh, I've always disliked him. All the years I've been here, I could hardly stand him. But this...God, I never hated anybody like this."

Grace was quiet, waiting for him to continue.

"Buzz and I know what he did to Hoot."

She started to speak but he interrupted her. "Don't worry. Besides the family, we're the only ones that know. "

"But what are you talking about? The family doesn't know what really happened."

"The way Hoot kept ..."

"Grady!" Frank's voice echoed down the aisle of the barn.

Grady turned to leave, then looked back at Grace. "If I have to keep working with him, one day...one day...I'm going to bash his brains in. So help me, that's a promise."

Grace stood there, holding Cloudy's reins and wondering what he'd been talking about. What Frank had done to Hoot. Evidently, he thought she knew what it was. Otherwise, he would never have mentioned it. She stood there wondering for a moment, then Frank came down the aisle and she left.

WHERE THE STATUE WEEPS

~~~

That night after supper, the family gathered with Buzz in the main living room as they had been doing nearly every night. No one had eaten very much, so Cook had sent Paulette in with a special dessert. Her rich, five-layer hummingbird cake with pecan cream cheese frosting.

Even though Grace wasn't hungry, she took a small slice. Cook's feelings would be hurt if the platter came back to the kitchen with the cake untouched. As Phillip fiddled with the buttons on the radio, she took a small bite. And it actually stimulated her appetite. It was so good, with the mashed bananas swirled in with coconut and pineapple and toasted pecans sprinkled on top. You could taste the spices, especially the cinnamon and ground nutmeg, it was strong enough to make your tongue tingle a little. She surprised herself by cutting a second slice. Mama and Phillip accepted a piece and she poured hot coffee and sat, listening to see what the news would bring tonight.

Buzz poured a glass of bourbon for himself and Phillip. Papa and Frank had already been drinking since late afternoon and Frank's eyes were glassy.

Lorraine cut a slice of cake and offered it to her husband. He pushed the plate away and reached for the liquor to freshen his drink. She walked over to the easy chair where Buzz was sitting and handed it to him. He set it on the coffee table without touching it, but his eyes followed Lorraine as she went back over to the sofa. Frank noticed him watching her and Grace saw his jaw tighten and twitch the way it did when he was really angry.

She tried to concentrate on the voice coming over the radio, but her mind was everywhere else. What had Grady meant earlier today when he said Frank had done something to Hoot? Maybe he was talking about the way Frank had practically forced him into riding when he was so sick, he should have been in bed.

She shook her head, trying to clear her thoughts. The memory of what had happened to Hoot was so raw and painful. She tried to push it out of her mind.

Sneaking a look over at Buzz, she happened to catch
~~~

him looking in Lorraine's direction. She remembered how he had kissed her, down by the river. And she didn't like it when he looked at Lorraine.

"The top story today is that further gas rationing will go into effect, immediately," the words came over the radio.

"Blast!" Papa said. "What will it be next? The gas ration is hurting the racing industry plenty already. It costs money hauling thoroughbreds up and down the coast."

"Nothing we can do about it," said Phillip. "Let's just be thankful we can afford it."

"Some farms can't though," Buzz said as he sat forward, swirling the amber liquid in his glass. "It's affecting them. And the spectators, some of them can hardly get the gas to drive to the races. Even if they have the money, there's times they just can't find the gas."

"More reason to keep scheduling races here at Janus," Papa said. "We can usually pack them in."

Phillip cleared his throat. "I've been meaning to speak to you about that Papa. There's been some talk about making parimutuel wagering illegal in North Carolina. Nothing definite. But we need to keep a close eye on what's going on there."

Papa's fist came down on the end table, knocking his drink onto the oriental carpet. "Blast it! That's all we need."

"Calm down, Papa," Phillip said as Mama wiped up the spill. "I don't think it will go through. There's too much money being made. And even if it does, we're right on the Virginia line. Thirty, forty-five-minute drives will get us to some of their tracks. We don't need to worry anyway, we can well afford the fuel, whether it's Kentucky or New York."

"It's just the principle of it," Papa took a fresh drink from Mama and downed a slug of it. "If the government tries to come in and tell us we can't hold races at Janus. Our family has been holding them here since the seventeen-hundreds. Our's was one of the first really big tracks in the nation. What would Janus Farms be, without a public racetrack?"

"Let's not worry too much yet," Phillip said as he picked up his plate and took a bite of cake. "We'd still be fine, even if we had to shut our track down."

Paulette came in with a fresh tureen of hot coffee. She poured some into Grace's cup and you could see the steam rising, along with the delightful fragrance. After she topped off everyone's cup, she put the tureen on the tall end table next to Lorraine's chair.

"You know they've started rationing clothing," Lorraine said. "We're not going to be able to get anything made of silk for a while and I really wanted…"

"You've got enough clothes to last the rest of your life," Frank snapped. "Two big chifforobes full, right there in the bedroom. And then, you've got that whole dressing room packed. You've got more dresses in there than Bella does in her whole shop. I guess if we go broke, we can open up a clothing store out here."

"Oh, lay off, Frank," Phillip swallowed the last bite of his cake and wiped his mustache with a linen napkin. "Have a slice of cake."

"And stockings," Lorraine pulled her skirt up a little and looked at her leg. "They're using nylon to make parachutes for the air force. What if I run out? I hear that in England, they can hardly get…"

"Will you just stop with your griping!" Frank stood up and paced around the room. Don't you see the big picture out there? The important things?"

Lorraine bristled. "My appearance *is* important. To me. It used to be to you, too."

Frank looked at her with glazed eyes. You can't do anything but spend money, can you?" He looked over at Buzz. "And don't think I don't see you staring at my wife!"

"Come on, Frank," Phillip said. "Let's call it a night."

Buzz set his drink on the end table, got up and started out. "I'll see you first thing in the morning."

Frank watched him go. As soon as the door closed, he turned on Lorraine. "I see you making eyes at him. The hired help, for God's sake! Every time I turn around, you're off with him in that stupid plane or down at the stables looking for him. That's why you always want something new to wear. You don't have a brain in your head. All you think about is spending my hard-earned money."

Lorraine was on her feet now. "Well, you won't let me work and make my own money! And besides, what a laugh. Your *hard-earned* money. You better leave me alone, Frank. You don't really have to *earn* anything, do you?"

Frank was glaring at her across the coffee table. "What do you mean by that remark? That smart mouth of yours..."

"I'm trying to tell you," Lorraine said. "If you don't stop being so hateful, I'm going to tell what you did."

His face blanched as he finally understood. "Shut up, you slut. Or so help me, God. I'll shut you up for good."

Phillip stood up and took his brother by the arm. "Come on, Frank. You've had too much to drink. Let's get on up..."

Frank snatched away and turned to glare at his wife again. "You better zip it."

"I'm warning you, Frank," she said. "I'm sick of you on my back every second. And you haven't been working for that money." She looked at Papa. "He's just been taking it!"

Papa looked at her, confused.

"I should have spoken up when you fired Artie, Papa. I'm ashamed not that I didn't have the courage to tell you. Artie didn't have anything to do with that missing money. It was..."

She never got Frank's name out because he lunged across the tall end table at her, pushing her back down. But drunk as he was, he stumbled and fell into the table, knocking the steaming tureen of coffee over onto the sofa. Lorraine shrieked in pain as it splashed across her face.

Mama jumped up and wiped it off with a napkin as Lorraine moaned in agony. Grace handed Mama the ice bucket that held the cubes for the liquor. "Here put ice on it, it's the best thing for a burn."

By this time, Phillip had Frank's arms locked behind him, pulling him away from the sofa. He struggled to get away. "I didn't mean..." his voice trailed off. He stopped for a moment, standing quietly as he watched Mama and Grace minister to the burn he had inflicted on his wife's perfect face. Then he gave a mighty heave and broke free of Phillip's grasp and stalked from the room, the heavy door slamming behind him.

TWENTY-NINE

January 2, 1943

Grace knocked on Lorraine's door with one hand as she balanced a breakfast tray with the other. Since the night Frank had attacked her and left Janus, she wouldn't allow anyone but Grace or Mama to come in. The annual New Year's ball had gone on without her. Grace had overheard Mama telling someone who asked after her that she wasn't feeling well.

Lorraine opened the door just a tiny bit, peering out to make sure Grace was alone. Grace could see one green eye peering out at her. Lorraine opened the door wide enough to allow her to enter, then turned and went back to the chair by the window.

As Grace placed the dishes on the table, Lorraine kept her head down, chin tucked in, eyes on the floor.

"Rapid Charisma dropped her foal last night," Grace said. "A filly. She's the cutest little thing you ever saw."

Lorraine didn't answer, neither did she eat anything. She sat, sipping a little of the orange juice. They had learned not to bring up a cup of coffee.

"She must have been born just before sunrise," Grace continued. "I was down there before breakfast, and she could barely stand up. Her coat was even still wet a little. She's a bay. Four white stockings and a blaze. Why don't you walk down with me?"

Lorraine turned and stared at Grace. The sunlight coming in the window glared across the left side of her face, emphasizing the burn mark that cut across that eye, halfway down her cheek. Not quite as angry looking as it had initially been, it was still raw, red color. It was in such a prominent place that it was impossible not to see it when she looked at you. The delicate features of Lorraine's face made it even more perceptible, Grace realized now. Such perfect beauty now tarnished and tormented. Like a perfect white rose with an ugly blemish right in the center.

"You know I can't do that." Lorraine turned to the window, her hand on her cheek.

"Lorraine, it's really not that bad," Grace lied. "Really. And no one's around. Just the hands down there."

"I said no!"

"Well, you can't just sit in here forever."

Lorraine's bottom lip began to tremble. "I know. It's just...I can't bear for anyone to see me like this." Her hand went to her face again. "I'm so ugly."

Grace put a hand on her shoulder. "You're not. I know how you must feel, but you..."

"No, you don't. How could you possibly know what it's like to walk around with a scar like this?"

"You're right," Grace said. "I don't. All I know is that we all want to help you."

Tears were rolling down Lorraine's cheeks now. "I should have never said anything to Papa. I should have never told him what Frank had been doing. I was just so mad, so tired of treating me like that all the time."

"It was an accident, Lorraine. I know he was mad, but he didn't mean to burn you."

Lorraine glanced into the mirror, then looked away. "You don't know what he's really like. He just has this anger inside him, it's like he can't control it."

"He's just been spoiled all this life," Grace answered. "Papa's eyeball. Papa always thought the sun rose and set on Frank. Let him get away with doing anything he wanted."

"It's not just that," Lorraine said. "Grace, it's like he's just gone insane. Like he can't control himself. He's always had an awful temper. We'd get into a fight and then he'd apologize. But this is different. Like there's this quiet rage seething in him all the time, just under the surface, waiting to come out. And the least little thing can provoke it."

Grace thought about what Lorraine had said. They had all seen it in him, they just turned a blind eye to it. Because he was Frank.

"There's something you don't know, Grace." Lorraine got up and paced around the room. "Remember when Spanky ate the poison, and you gave him that herb that made him throw it up?"

Grace nodded.

"Well, later on, Frank asked me what it was that you gave him. I didn't think much of it, I just told him what it was."

"I don't understand," Grace said. "Why would Frank be interested in something like that?"

"I found a bottle of it in our room. I thought maybe you gave it to him. But I...I'm afraid..."

"What is it?"

"I think Frank got it out of your chest and...I don't know. Maybe I'm wrong. But I think he was forcing Hoot to take it."

"But why?"

"You know how Hoot loved our Southern food. And he was gaining weight, off and on. He was really having a hard time staying under his limit. Frank made him take it for a couple of days before a race. And I think it might have ... I don't know, maybe it made Hoot's heart weak or something. But I've been afraid to say anything about it. I think Grady knows about it. He's always hated Frank. You know how Frank treats him. But now, I don't know, it was really different after Hoot died. I would see the way Grady looked at him and sometimes, I would think Grady was going to..." She stopped and stared out the window.

"What? What did you think he would do?"

Lorraine shrugged. "I don't know. As if, well, maybe like he was just waiting for Frank to do something. You know, to give him any excuse to get into a fight."

Grace didn't say anything. She was remembering how Grady started to tell her something in the stables, but Frank had come in and interrupted them. Could it be true? That knot had come back into her stomach. If it was, she was partially responsible. If not for her, Frank would never have known what to use.

I'm glad Frank's gone." Lorraine looked up at her. "I hope he never comes back."

~~~

Grace kept thinking all morning about what Lorraine had said. After Frank disappeared that night, they hadn't seen him since. Phillip had followed him outside and he just got into his car and drove away. They had all thought he'd be back by morning, but they hadn't heard a word from him. He probably couldn't face Papa, Grace thought. He knew Lorraine was going to tell Papa how he had been embezzling from the farm. But he probably didn't even realize that she knew how he had made Hoot sick. Not that he'd meant for him to die. That would have been like killing the goose that laid the golden egg. But Hoot had died anyway, and she couldn't stop wondering if Lorraine was right.

She thought back on all the times she had felt jealous of her sister-in-law. Her beauty, her social skills and popularity. What an excellent horseback rider she was, the way she could drive a car with such ease.

But poor Lorraine. She had married a man who really didn't seem to love anyone but himself. Grace was the lucky one.

~~~

It was only the middle of the afternoon when Phillip came to the house. At first, Grace thought something was wrong. He and Buzz had been working so hard, trying to get the farm going again. She hardly even saw him at meals anymore. They had been having Cook send trays out to the stables.

But he caught her by the hand and headed upstairs. "We're going to get Lorraine out of that room," he said. "We can't let her keep sitting in there all the time."

Walking down the hall, they stopped at Lorraine's room, and he rapped sharply on the door. "Go in there and make sure she's decent," he said.

Grace did as he asked and just as she suspected, Lorraine was still sitting there in her gown and robe, staring down at the stables.

"You better get dressed," she told her sister-in-law. "Phillip's coming in and I don't think you can do anything about it."

Lorraine started to shake her head. "No… don't let him in Grace."

"I really don't think I can stop him," Grace said just as a couple of loud thumps came at the door.

Grace cracked the door open. "Give us a minute," she said as Lorraine got up and pulled a skirt and sweater out of the closet. Just a plain, nondescript shade of brown. Grace would never have imagined she would wear something like that. But she supposed when you didn't feel pretty, you didn't enjoy wearing clothing that demands attention. That's probably why I don't like fancy clothes myself, she thought.

When she let Phillip in, he took Lorraine gently by the arm and steered her towards the door. "You and Grace and I are going to take a ride."

Lorraine's eyes widened. The only times she had left the house was when Phillip and Grace had taken her in for doctor's appointments. She covered her face now with her hand. "But I don't want anyone to see me like…"

"No one is going to." He urged her down the stairs. "We're just going to take Grace's car for a spin. We'll stop at the Drive Up and get a root beer float or a chocolate soda. You need to get some air."

They all scrunched into the front seat and Grace was a little uncomfortable in the middle. But Phillip had put the top down and the soft breeze felt good on her skin as her husband drove slowly down the long path.

Phillip fiddled with the radio once they were on the highway and finally settled on a station that was playing popular music. "I tried to get Mama to come with us, but she doesn't want to leave Papa," he said. "The way he's just been sitting around the house and all. No mind, we'll bring a soda back for them."

A news bulletin broke in over the radio. "We have word on the war that…"

Phillip switched the station and found one that was

playing music. "We don't need to hear anything about that right now," he said. "This is just a little pleasure ride and we're going to keep it that way.

"On the positive side, though, we got a call from Richardson," he said. "You know, the guy in charge of the Hollywood auction. To raise money for the war effort. Collecting items donated by the Hollywood stars, things like that. They wanted to see if we would send them something. I asked if they'd like to have a set of Red's horseshoes and they seemed pretty excited about it."

Grace nudged Lorraine. "That's a great idea, isn't it?"

Lorraine just shrugged. "Maybe that would finally be of some use. We never did understand why Frank wanted to spend all that money. And now Papa just keeps carrying on the tradition with it."

"Just their weird idea for social status," Grace answered.

Phillip and Grace tried to make small talk all the way into Roanoke Rapids. Lorraine answered when she was asked a question but other than that she didn't say a word. When they got to the Drive Up, Phillip went around to the far side at the back, parked and started to get out.

"Where are you going?" Grace asked.

"No need for the waitress to have to come out to the car," he said. "I'll just run in and get our drinks."

"That was thoughtful of him," Lorraine said as they watched him walk around front. "That's why I didn't want to come, I just don't want to see anyone."

On the ride home, Lorraine was still silent, but Grace could tell she wasn't as tense since she hadn't had to face anyone. And she sat there, feeling the warmth of her husband's thigh against hers on the car seat, she thought how fortunate she was. To be married to such a kind man. She just wished that everything would just be all right again.

THIRTY

When Drake brings Sundown in to unsaddle him, I go over and sit on the bench nearby.

"Have a good ride?" I ask.

She just nods and doesn't say anything.

"What would you think about riding Boogie?" I ask. "He really could use some exercise."

She turns to look at me. "The Saddlebred?"

"Yep. How about it?

"Okay, should I go get him now?"

"Bring him in and I'll help you saddle up."

I watch the girl as she goes. It has taken me a while to decide to let anyone ride Boogie. Saddlebreds are so well known for their excitable temperament. Never mean or vicious, simply so high strung that it makes them hard to handle. But after riding the big gelding several times I am convinced that he is safe enough for a rider with Drake's skills. No spook, no buck, no rear. Just solid.

She comes back, leading the big bay behind her. Nearly seventeen hands high, the tallest horse on the farm. She ties him and begins to brush his coat. Boogie stands quietly. The awful scars across his face and neck are visible, even from where I sit.

We lead Boogie into the lower arena together and I stand by as Drake mounts. Boogie's head comes up and the girl chokes up on the reins, instinctively shortening them so she has good contact with his mouth. But she has soft hands, sensitive to the slightest movement from every part of his body, right down to the ground.

Her cues are subtle, unseen. But the big horse moves forward with his long stride in a springy flat-footed walk. A quarter of the way around, he goes into the elegant two-beat pace at the high trot. Drake posts in perfect rhythm, rising in the stirrups at every other step and coming down in the saddle with excellent timing.

As I watch Drake, I can see Jennifer out of the corner of my eye. She has Diesel hooked up to the cart and they are jogging down the path with three kids. Squeals and shouts of laughter ring out through the air as the children bounce each time they hit a bump. Boogie pays no attention to all the noise of the kids and the rattling cart but simply goes through the paces as Drake cues him. I can tell she is a little nervous; after all she has a lot of horse under her, and they are new to each other.

"Hey, Jo!" Sandra calls. "Haley's mom just brought cake and ice cream. Can you help us plate it up before it melts?"

I am a little reluctant to leave Drake in the arena alone, but I will be able to see her. I keep an eye on them as we prepare the plates for the children, and they seem fine.

Diesel comes trotting up with kids spilling out of the cart. Jenifer leads the pony over to the hitching post and loops a lead line over it.

I hear hoofbeats approaching and look up. It is Drake, walking Boogie to the hitching rail. She pulls his bridle off, puts his halter on and ties him to the rail. She stands with him for a moment, pats his slick neck and whispers, "I'll be back in a few minutes, boy." I pretend to be busy with Diesel as I watch her go over, sit down next to Maggie Mae, and take a bite of cake.

It is difficult to tell who is saying what with all the noise as the children chatter. I don't want ice cream, but I take a small serving of cake.

Sandra's phone buzzes and she puts her fork down to see who it is. Her brow furrows with concentration, then she looks up, eyes wide with excitement.

"Hey, guys! Guess what! The building supply in town is donating roofing materials. I went by and explained that we were going to raise our own hay and had to do some repairs before we would have a place to store it."

There is a great deal of high fiving as everyone congratulates her. I breathe a sigh of relief. I had been nervous about how we were going to work it out.

As we sit; talking and eating, I am watching Drake. Maggie Mae has ice cream running down on her shirt and Drake takes a napkin and cleans her off. Then she gets up and goes over for a second helping. She returns with a huge chunk of cake and a mound of ice cream running over the side of the plate. I make a mental note to tell her aunt because she has been so worried about Drake's loss of appetite. Maggie Mae says something that I can't hear, and it makes everyone laugh. Including Drake. We clean up the tables as some of the other volunteers take riders into the upper arena and start making their rounds.

Drake is riding Boogie again. I walk back down to the bottom arena, lock my left foot into the bottom rung and prop myself on the top railing. If they looked good before, they are absolutely stunning now. She is getting more comfortable with the big gelding and giving him some rein. He, in turn is stepping out, stretching his long legs in that fancy gait that only a Saddlebred has.

After a couple of rounds, I see Boogie tuck his head into his chest, his neck and shoulders rise, his hindquarters come up under him and he goes into his canter. It is breathtaking to watch; he floats elegantly through the air. The up and down action is exaggerated while the forward action is slow and methodical, that spectacular, slow canter of the Saddlebred. Drake's lower body never moves in the saddle, rocking in perfect rhythm with the big horse. It is almost like watching a ballerina and her partner. They are, indeed true to his registered name as they boogie to the beat. I can hardly take my eyes away.

After twenty minutes, I go to help the volunteers. Jennifer is busy so I unhook Diesel from the cart. I can see several of the children over by the fountain. The volunteers cleaned it up a couple of weeks ago. There is no water spouting up like I suppose it did in the past but the pool is clear and you can see the goldfish that come to the top, expecting to be fed each time someone passes by. It's a funny thing. Now that the fish dart back and forth, the statue of the two-faced horse doesn't seem so ominous anymore.

Drake approaches me. "Hey Jo-Jo," she says. "Did you see Boogie?"

I look at her, stroking the fine, velvety muzzle. There is a light in her eyes that I have never seen before. "I did. You two looked pretty good out there."

"Do you think I could take him out again?"

I smile. "Sure do," I said, and she actually smiles back.

The sun shifts and the deep scars on the gelding's face are a little more obvious. As Drake turns to put the horse away, I think how similar they are. Only his scars are much more visible.

~~~

I sit in my room, looking through the photo albums I had brought up. Such a different world back then, all the glitz and glamour. This place will never be the same. But it is so exciting to see the strides we are making with improvements.

I get up and set my alarm. I've got to get that back pasture mowed. We also have to put some tarps on the roof of the hay shed until we can get it repaired.

I go back to the album. Runaway Rapids had been an amazing horse; a legend almost. I am turning the page when I realize that I hear faint music. A long way off. It's that same song again. Words about a kiss.

I open the door. The hallway is dark, just a little moonlight coming in at the end of the hall. It seems to just be coming from everywhere, as if it is pouring out of the very fibers of the walls as it grows a little louder.

Finally, I realize that it is coming from the stairwell. From the third floor.

I put my foot on the first riser. I have never been up there. The nurse had told me there were places where the floors had rotted through. I stop on the second step.

Am I really going to listen to her advice, I ask myself? She always so afraid of every little thing.

The music continues to float down. I continue up the stairs, testing each one before putting my full weight on it.

Something about a sigh.
~~~

Where have I heard this song? I had nearly driven myself crazy the first time I heard it. You know, the way you feel when something is right on the tip of your tongue.

I had thought then that I was really, totally psycho. Like crazy as a loon. Or that I was having hallucinations from the medication. But I know now that wasn't the case. The current prescription I have seems to be working well. And I have tapered down to a very small dose. It's not the medicine. And I'm not crazy. The sound is real.

I am halfway to the third floor when the riser beneath my right foot gives way. I catch myself on the rail and move up to the next one. I test it and it seems solid.

I continue upwards as the music floats down and fills the stairwell. Such a haunting tune. I catch bits and pieces about the future. The words, the melody. I'm going to google it when I go back downstairs. Should have done that the first time but I had just kept trying to put it out of my mind.

I reach the top stair and step onto the marble floor beyond. It seems pretty solid, but I bounce a little to make sure it will hold. It creaks a little but that is all.

Huge windows reach from floor to ceiling of the grand ballroom so that the moonlight filters in. I can see well enough to make out tables and chairs lurking in the center of the room.

I make my way along the wall. The boards underneath the marble creak and groan but they hold fast. In some spots the floor seems a little soft, as if it is giving to my weight.

I notice the music is softer again. Like when I first began to hear it. Almost... I shake my head. No, it is not possible for a song to want to lure me up here.

As I feel my way along the wall, my hand connects with a light switch. I lift it and a dim light fills the room. An elaborate chandelier dangles from the ceiling. Most of the bulbs burned out, probably decades ago, but two are still burning stubbornly, as if they are determined not to give up.

Horses fill the walls. The great, huge murals of the thoroughbreds. I recognize them from the photo albums.

It is so dim and dusty here that it is difficult to make them out. And the cobwebs; so thick that some of the paintings are nearly obscured.

The music is coming from the center of the room. I am making my way to the tables there when my foot sinks into a soft spot in the floor. I shift my weight back onto my other foot and pull it out.

I have to slow down. Pay attention to where I am going. I keep glancing around the enormous room as I take tiny steps. The *grand* ballroom, I think. Even through my anxiety, I wish I could have seen this place while it was still grand.

I make my way around, from table to table. There. The sound is coming from the one that sits crossways, in front of the back wall. A large box sits in the center of the table and as I come closer, I can see that it is an old-fashioned record player. My dad used to have one like it that had belonged to his parents.

I peek into the box. The music is coming from here. The turntable is spinning but there is no record on it. Still, the voice continues the haunting melody.

Those words about time…something about it passing.

I look up at the wall behind the table and there I see the great mural. The one I have seen in the albums. But it looks so different when I actually lay my eyes upon it. Janus. The two-faced horse. One looking back at the past as the other gazes towards the future.

THIRTY-ONE

January 28, 1943

When Cook saw Grace come into the kitchen, she reached into the apple bin, took one out and cut it into slices. "I declare, Miss Grace. You'd think that horse of yours was a child or something the way you mollycoddle him all the time." But she was smiling broadly as she handed her the slices.

Grace ate a couple of slices herself as she walked down to the stables. It was good, not too sweet. She savored the crispness, the tart flavor. She was thinking about what they had heard on the radio last night about the upcoming auction and she was glad they would be able to do something to help.

She and Phillip were taking Lorraine in for an appointment later today. They were going to talk about having her see a specialist. A plastic surgeon. They were beginning to do a lot of that, the doctor had told them.

She could see Phillip and Buzz down at the track with some of the two-year-olds. As Grace approached Cloudy's stall, she didn't see his head looking out over the door. That was strange, she thought. A couple of the hands were cleaning stalls and all the other horses were peering out at them, hopeful of getting fed again.

He was standing in the corner with his tail to the door. She had never seen him do that.

"Here boy, I've got your treat." She walked around and offered the apple slices, but he simply sniffed them and turned away.

Something's wrong, she thought. Horses don't turn down food. Unless they're sick. She glanced up at the hay net and it was nearly full. Walking over to the corner feeder, she saw that his grain hadn't been touched.

Pulling the little horse's head around, she looked at his eyes. She was no horse expert but with creatures of any kind; whether it be human or animal, that was the first place to look. His eyes were dull and listless.

She poked her head over the stall door. "Henry," she called. "Would you run up to the house and tell Mama to call the vet out here?"

Henry nodded, put down his pitchfork and started out of the stable.

"And hurry," she called. "I think Cloudy has colic."

Henry picked up his pace and she saw the other hand heading in the opposite direction. In a couple of minutes, he was back with Grady.

"Let's take a look at you, Cloudy-Boy," Grady said as he entered the stall. Taking him by the halter, he pulled on it but Cloudy didn't want to move.

"Come on, boy." Grady pulled his head to the side, forcing him to move to keep his balance. Once he took a step, Grady was able to get him moving and pull him out into the aisle.

"If he's trying to colic, we don't want him going down in there," Grady explained.

Grace followed as he walked the horse down the aisle and into the paddock. Cloudy put his nose down and sniffed at the tender, green shots of fescue growing there. But instead of grazing, he dropped to his knees. Grady caught him and urged him up before he could lie all the way down.

"Oh no, you don't, Cloudy-Boy. We can't let you lie down."

He turned to Grace. "You're right. I'm pretty sure it's colic. Henry and Tony hadn't gotten to his stall yet, but I noticed there weren't any droppings in there. His bowels are locked up.

"I was afraid it might be something like that. What do you think caused it?"

Grady shrugged. "Hard to tell. Horses have such a delicate digestive system. It's not unusual. He'll be okay though. Doc will get out here and dose him and he'll be fine."

"Is there anything we can do while we're waiting?"

"We have to keep him on his feet. Walk him as much as we can. Sometimes that's all it takes, and the bowel may start working. We can't let him lie down and roll. That could cause his gut to twist and that would mean surgery. Or worse."

Phillip and Henry came up at the same time. "Doc's out at Peterson's." Haywood said.

"They're calling out there to tell him to stop here on his way back in."

Phillip stepped up and put his hand on the horse's flank. "He's mighty tight and bloated. Let's get him moving."

Grady reached for the lead line, but Grace said, "I'll do it." She tugged on the horse's halter until he took a couple of steps. Always slow and pokey, Cloudy just dragged along. They had only walked a few minutes when he stopped and dropped to the ground. Phillip and Grady ran up behind him, but he refused to get up. Phillip finally had to swat at his hindquarters with the halter he was holding to get him up.

They continued in this pattern for the next thirty minutes. By that time, the horse and began to sweat and occasionally he would let out a groan.

Phillip swore under his breath. "I don't think we can keep waiting. We better dose him ourselves." He looked at Haywood. "Run over to the work room and get some tubing and a bottle of mineral oil." Henry was halfway down the aisle by the time he finished the sentence.

"I sure wish Doc would come on, "Phillip said. "I don't like tubing them. If we get it into his lungs, that'll be dangerous."

Cloudy stood quietly as they mixed the mineral oil and water. Grady took a strong grip on the halter as Phillip began to insert the tubing into his nose, but the horse kept snatching his head away.

"Get the twitch on," Phillip said.

Henry stepped up with a long piece of wood that had a little loop of rope attached. He caught the horse's upper lip in the rope and twisted it tight so Cloudy couldn't move without putting pressure on his mouth.

Phillip patted the thick neck as Cloudy's eyes rolled up, showing the whites. "Sorry Cloudy," he said. "Just trying to help you here."

They were able to get the tube inserted and got the mineral oil into the horse's stomach. Phillip handed Grace the lead line. "See if you can walk him around a bit." He and Grady pushed a little from behind and Cloudy followed Grace.

After twenty minutes or so, the horse stopped suddenly and groaned. Terrified, Grace turned to look at him. But his tail was raised, and she saw droppings hit the ground.

"Good, Cloudy-Boy!" Grady shouted.

Phillip walked up and took the lead line from Grace. "He's going to be fine. We'll just keep an eye on him for a little while. Turn him loose and we'll make sure he doesn't want to lie down."

Cloudy walked around for a moment and then dropped his nose to the ground. They watched for a few minutes as Cloudy nibbled a little at the grass.

"Grady," Phillip said. "Grace and I have to take Lorraine in for a doctor's appointment. I want you to stay out here and keep an eye on him." He turned to Henry. "You pick up Grady's chores."

Grace walked over to her horse. "Phillip, I really don't want to leave Cloudy."

"He's fine, Grace. I wouldn't leave if he weren't. Look at him, he's grazing. Grady will keep an eye on him. And Buzz is right down at the track."

"I know. But...that was scary. Why do I need to go anyway? You know I can't drive very well. That's why you always take us in the first place."

Phillip pushed his cap back on his head. "I guess you're right. If you'd rather stay here, I guess it'll be okay. I can run Lorraine in." He kissed her on the forehead. "I'll come down and check on you as soon as we get back."

~~~

When Grace took Lorraine's supper tray up, she had several outfits laying out across the bed. Ignoring the
~~~

food at first, she held up a royal blue dress that had little sapphires attached to the neck. She pulled it tight against her body and looked in the mirror for a moment.

"Do you think Paulette would alter this a little for me? Take it in at the waist." She made a face. "I've lost too much weight. Everything I have looks sort of baggy."

"I'm sure she would." Grace began to lay the dishes out on the table.

Lorraine picked up a fuchsia-colored skirt and matching jacket. "This is one of my favorites. "I think I'll keep it like it is. For later, you know."

She sat down and slathered butter and pear preserves onto a biscuit. Cramming it into her mouth she washed it down with a big swallow of sweet tea. "I've got to put some weight back on. I look like a bean pole."

Grace didn't know what to say. Lorraine almost seemed like her old self.

"Not that I want to get too fat or anything." Lorraine was cutting her steak. "I just want to look like I used to."

"You could stand a few pounds," Grace agreed.

Lorraine shoved a spoonful of mashed potatoes into her mouth. "I can hardly wait to get my surgery. You know, it's funny. But just knowing they'll be able to do it...I don't know. I don't feel so ugly anymore."

"I told you we were going to do everything we can to help you."

"I don't know what I'd do without you and Phillip." Lorraine picked up a dish of cobbler. "Is this blueberry?" She tasted it and smiled. "It's really good to have a family that takes care of you."

~~~

Grace went with Mama into the living room after supper. Papa and Phillip were listening to the news. Papa had been going to the stables, getting involved with business again. He was going with Phillip tonight to a business meeting.

"Come on, Papa. Let's get into town."

As she watched them go, Grace wished he would talk with her a little. But she supposed he was trying to protect
~~~

her and Mama from worrying.

She told Mama she was going down to check on Cloudy once more before bedtime. She had been down every hour on the hour even though Phillip had insisted that he was fine.

It was too early for bed anyway. And she didn't feel like sitting around the house. Taking a brush from the tack room, she went to Cloudy's stall and ran it over his coat. "I'm so glad you're all right," she murmured as he reached his head around to see if she had any feed.

She had been in the stall for twenty minutes or so when she heard someone walk up. She peered out to see Buzz standing there.

"Evening, Grace. I didn't know you were out here."

"I just wanted to check on him one more time," she explained.

"I know. Me too."

Buzz stepped into the stall and ran a hand across the spotted rump. Cloudy turned towards him and tried to rub his head across Buzz's chest. He reached up to scratch under the long forelock. "Got an itch, do you?"

"It's so good to see him well, isn't it?" Grace ran her fingers through his mane.

"Sure is. Colic can be scary."

"Did you hear about the ship that we just lost?" Grace asked.

Buzz nodded. He didn't say anything for a few minutes and the silence was awkward. Finally, he cleared his throat. "I've been thinking..." he stopped.

"What is it?"

"I'm thinking about joining the Air Force."

She dropped the brush into the straw. "You can't. I mean..."

He looked out over the stall door. "Since Hoot's been gone, I've just felt like I should do something." He shook his head. "That boy sure did raise a lot of money for the effort, didn't he?"

"Yes, but I...we need you. What would we do without you? I mean Phillip, the farm." She changed the subject. "And we're still helping them. Donating the horseshoes, you know that will bring in quite a bit of money for the auction."

He took her hand and turned the conversation back into its original direction. "What about you, Grace? Would you miss me if I left?"

She nodded. "More than I can tell you."

"That would make a difference. I've just been restless. Not sure what I want."

"Please don't go. I... we couldn't bear it if you went off to war and something happened to you. We've already lost Hoot. And now, everything with Frank." She began to cry. "I just, well everything is changing so fast."

Taking her by the arm, he pulled her close to him, took his big thumb and rubbed a tear off her cheek. "If I had a reason to stay..."

He was just leaning in to kiss her when they heard several of the horses nicker. Grace looked up and Grady was coming down the aisle.

"Evening, Buzz." Grady stopped and looked into the stall. "Oh, Miss Grace. I didn't see you there."

"I was just checking on Cloudy." She busied herself adjusting the halter so Grady couldn't see her face.

"I guess we all had the same idea." Buzz stepped out of the stall. "But he's fine. I'll see you later, Grace. You coming to quarters, Grady?"

Grady nodded, but as he turned to follow Buzz, Grace caught the look on his face. He had sensed that he had interrupted something. She knew Grady wouldn't say anything, but she stayed in the stall for a while longer, thinking about what Buzz had said.

THIRTY-TWO

February 1, 1943

Buzz was down with the new jockey, Mason Glover, giving him instructions as they waited for the race to begin at the Hialeah course. They had drawn seventh position. Grace sat with Phillip and Papa in the stands. Mama had stayed home with Lorraine.

Glover had been doing pretty well with Runaway on the practice runs. They had been searching for someone with a strong hand and this jockey was known for being an aggressive rider. Phillip and Buzz had been concerned though because Red tended to fight back if a rider got too pushy with him. And they were seeing that happen some now. But none of the jockeys they had tried so far were able to manage the stallion. He would take advantage of them, pulling out to the right to run wide on the outside just as he used to do.

When the gate clanged open and the horses shot out, Runaway was in the middle of the pack, so at least the jockey had been able to control him to get him started. They were holding in the middle of the pack. A hole opened up between two horses and the stallion shot between them, gaining advantage as they got closer to the inside.

"That's it." Grace could hear Phillip above the crowd. "Come on, Glover put him in there. I think we're going to do it this time."

Runaway continued to gain quickly as the pack surged forward. Each time an opportunity came, they scooted between horses, always towards that inside rail. But as Grace looked through her binoculars, she could see that he was fighting his rider. The jockey was pulling him over too abruptly and plying the whip hard. The stallion had always gotten angry when anyone used it on him.

As they went into the clubhouse turn in front of the grandstands, there were only three horses ahead of him. Then, at the quarter pole, he collided with Thundering Crown, slamming him towards the left. Thundering Crown, in turn bumped High Rolling Man and his jockey was nearly unseated. For a few strides he clung to the side of the saddle. By the time he pulled himself upright, Runaway was out in front, and he crossed the finish line a good eight lengths in the lead.

But it was all to no avail. The race stewards called a foul because he had interfered with the other two horse's chances. Papa bellowed and waved his cane in the air, brandishing it over the heads of the stewards in the box but the decision was final. Runaway was disqualified.

~~~

"Buzz and I came up with an idea," Phillip said to Papa at the breakfast table.

"It had better be a good one," Papa answered.

"I think it is. It's a little risky, but if it works, it could get Runaway back in the spotlight again."

"Well, let's hear it."

"A match race. With Bounty Money." Phillip took a spoonful of steaming hash browns, thick with caramelized onion. "That way, there's only the two horses. We wouldn't have to worry so much about fouling against other runners."

Papa put his tea glass down and smoothed a hand across his mustache. "That just might work."

"A win against them would really increase Runaway's importance as a sire," Phillip said. "Raise our stud fee tremendously. Bounty Money. is the only really big opponent we've lost to. I know we could have taken him when Hoot was riding for us. I guess Johnson knew it too. That's got to be the reason he scratched every time he was up against Hoot."

Papa twirled his mustache. "I believe we can take him with Glover up. Let's set up a meeting with Johnson."

"And I'd really like to have it here," Phillip said. "We
~~~

need something to breathe new life into the course here at Janus. If we can work this out, the crowds will keep coming to Janus for years, just as they always did."

~~~

Grace was tense as she rode in the back seat of Papa's car, heading towards Raleigh. Mama sat beside her, with Grady driving. They were due at the Governor's Mansion this evening for a special presentation. The Prominent Ladies of North Carolina were touring through the country, stopping at the capital in many of the states. Mama had been asked to come as a special guest due to all the funding that Janus Farms had raised for the war effort. Grace was beginning to feel comfortable driving the car around Roanoke Rapids. But Raleigh? There was no way. She had been hoping Phillip would bring them. But he was busy, so he had asked Grady to drive them.

The group had been working on a project to send items to the soldiers overseas. A PACKAGE FROM HOME, it was called. All the packages had been gathered from each county and were being delivered to the event to be shipped off. There would be a big party this evening and they would stay overnight. The media would be there in the morning when the trucks were loaded, and the governor's wife had asked them all to stay.

Grace had enjoyed boxing up the items with the Roanoke Rapids ladies. They had put in socks, cigarettes, chewing gum, baked goods, blankets, and autographed photos of movie stars. They had also put together little sewing kits that they called "housewives." They contained needles, small bits of assorted colors of thread for mending clothing and also lint to pack into wounds.

It was the social event itself that Grace dreaded so much. But she couldn't let Mama go alone. Mama did look pretty, dressed in a new lavender outfit from Bella's. Her gray curls were combed back loosely and the veil from her hat fell across her forehead. Her matching pearl necklace and earrings set it off perfectly.

Grace had on her favorite blue dress. Papa's eyes had
~~~

fallen on it as they were leaving and she had half expected him to order her to go up and put on a different dress, one that she hadn't worn to several events in the past. But he didn't say anything. Grace figured he had more serous worries on his mind.

Papa and Phillip had a telephone meeting scheduled this afternoon with Johnson to talk about the match race. Papa was adamant that the race would be run here at Janus, but Phillip wasn't so sure they could persuade Johnson. Grace knew how stubborn Papa could be though.

Mama looked over at Grace. "I wish Lorraine could be with us," she said. "But who knows? Maybe after her surgery, we'll be able to convince her to start getting out some."

The surgery was scheduled for next week and Grace thought Mama was right. Right now, her sister-in-law still didn't want to leave her room much, but she was constantly going through her wardrobe, having certain outfits altered to fit her thin frame. She seemed excited, knowing that in a few months the scars from her surgery would be fading. She had confessed to Grace that she was almost afraid to get her hopes up too much. "If it doesn't work and I still have this horrible scar across my eye, I don't know what I'll do," she had said. "I'm really scared. What if it never goes away? And no one will ever want me again."

Grace felt a little guilty that Lorraine was at home, with her and Mama both being gone. But it was only one night. And she knew Paulette and Cook would take care of her until they got home. It was just that she kept herself so isolated. Oh well, it wouldn't be that way much longer. Maybe next time they had a big social event, Lorraine would feel like being involved again.

Grace sat by herself in the banquet room because Mama was one of the special guests who would be escorted in and introduced. After her speech she would be brought down to sit with Grace. She looked around and it seemed as if an ocean of women surrounded her. Women of all ages; young, old, and middle-aged sat talking as they waited with anticipation, dressed in their finest. Soft music played in the background.

Finally, Kate Livesey, president of the Prominent Ladies of North Carolina, swept through the curtain and went to the microphone to welcome everyone. "I want to thank you all for being here with us tonight," she said as she stared into the television cameras. "And to all the women all over the country who are providing support in so many ways.

"The reason I became involved in this particular project is because I have a son in the navy," she explained. "I don't know exactly where he is right now, but I do know he is at sea, and he may very well be in harm's way at any moment. And many of you out there have husbands, sons, brothers, and neighbors in the armed services. So, you see, we are actually one big sisterhood, trying to support our own as we go about our daily lives on the home front.

"And we also have a lot of women out there, doing so many things to help. Over six million females have joined the work force. All kinds of jobs; steel and munition workers, nursing in the war fields, translators in naval intelligence. Even non-combat pilots. The list goes on and on. Things are really changing for women in a big way."

One by one, she called out the names of special guests for their speeches and Grace thought it really was motivating but it was long and drawn out. After a few speakers, she began to lose focus and her mind started to wander. She couldn't help but think about what was going with the family business and hoping things would start to turn around again for them. She wondered if Papa had been able to persuade Johnson to run at Janus.

Then she heard, "And now we will hear from Mrs. Franklin Masterson of Janus Farms." Mama appeared from behind the curtain and took her place at the podium.

"I think most everyone here knows what Janus Farms has done for the effort," Mrs. Livesey said. "The late jockey, Hoot Harrison has sold so many war bonds and we are forever grateful. And I hear they are donating a set of the famous stallion's special horseshoes for the big auction coming up in Hollywood. That's going to be an interesting night. I know that I, for one, will be glued to the television."

She handed Mama the microphone and Mama spoke with ease and confidence. "Thank you for having me here tonight," she said. "It's quite an honor. And as for the auctioned shoes, that was no hardship for us. Horses have to have their shoes replaced every six or eight weeks anyway, so they would merely have gone to waste. And I'm so glad they didn't. I always did argue with my husband about that wastage for such expensive horseshoes. Just as he has always argued that I had too many shoes in my own closet."

Laughter broke out among the women. When it died down, she spoke briefly of the way Hoot had inspired everyone at Janus to get involved and how much he was missed. "He was the one who really got things going," she said. "A very special young man. Whom we will never forget."

She stepped down to a round of applause and took her seat beside Grace. They listened as Kate Livesey went through some of the packages to be sent, stopping to read a card here and there, thanking the soldiers for the services, for their courage and protection.

As soon as the presentations were over, waiters appeared immediately, serving the guests. Shrimp cocktails were brought out as the main appetizer, and they were delicious. Gigantic, tender shrimp swimming in a spicy, red sauce.

Mama had finished hers and was starting on her salad when Grace noticed her rubbing at the side of her face. It was angry and red, and, in a few moments, she had welts going down the side of her neck.

"It must be the shrimp," Grace said. "I think you're having an allergic reaction."

Mama shook her head. "I've never been allergic to seafood."

"Well, something's going on. I think you're going to have to go to the hospital."

Grace went over to let the governor's wife know they had to leave.

"Oh, we've got a friend who's a doctor. Just down the street. Let me call, I'm sure he'll come over."

The doctor confirmed Grace's suspicion that it was a reaction and gave Mama a shot. "It might make you drowsy," he warned.

The medication not only made Mama feel lethargic, but she was a little nauseated too. She wanted to go home, so they made their apologies and Grady brought the car around. Mama actually dozed a little on the ride home.

It was nearly midnight when they got there. Grady dropped them at the door and took their unused luggage in.

"Just leave it here, inside the door and we'll get it later," Grace said. She walked with Mama to her room, holding her by the arm because she was a little unsteady. When she opened the door, they could hear Papa snoring. Mama insisted she was fine, all she needed was to get into her own bed and get some rest.

The same thing I need, Grace thought as she went back to the door and picked up her bag and started upstairs. She was sorry Mama had gotten sick, but she had dreaded spending the night at the event. She was so glad to be home. She would just slip into bed quietly. She wondered what Phillip would say when he woke up to find her there beside him. She smiled at the thought.

But just as she put her hand on the doorknob of their room, she heard the sound of voices. Low, murmuring. Slowly, she turned the doorknob and opened the door about a foot. A slight noise caught her attention. It was coming from the sitting room. And there by the doors that opened to the balcony stood Phillip and Lorraine.

As Grace watched silently, Phillip lowered his head and brought his lips down to meet Lorraine's. Grace closed her eyes for a moment, thinking the vison would be gone. This could not be happening. She opened her eyes again and glanced towards her husband and sister-in-law as they stood by the drapes, locked in a slow, deep kiss.

She didn't realize she had lost her grip on her suitcase until it hit the hardwood floor with a loud thump. Phillip and Lorraine looked up and saw her standing there. She closed the door and backed away. Halfway down the stairs she noticed a low moaning noise and then realized it was her. She made it out the side door before she stopped in Mama's flower garden. And the moon hung there in the cold sky, watching as she vomited into a clump of winter pansies.

THIRTY-THREE

February 27, 1943

Grace had moved into another bedroom and hadn't come out during the day for a while. She couldn't sleep. Phillip was still there in their room, at the end of the hall. And on the other side, just a little way down, Lorraine was in her room. Grace was staying in the room at the far end, as far away from them as she could get. But she could feel their presence, each in their separate rooms. And the anger churned in her stomach like the choppy waves of the sea in a terrible storm.

She thought about moving downstairs. Nineteen empty bedrooms down there. But as far as she knew, Papa didn't suspect that anything had happened because he never came up to the second floor. If he saw her sleeping down there, he would demand to know what was wrong.

In the beginning, she had even stopped going down for meals. She had heard Papa shouting all the way from downstairs. "What in Sam Hill is wrong around here? Has every dad-blamed female in this house gone crazy?" She couldn't hear Mama's reply.

Mama had known something had happened between her and Phillip. She would bring her meal tray up to the new room and sit with her, encouraging her to eat.

"I don't know what happened between you and I'm not going to push you," she had said. "But I'm here if you need me."

And Lorraine hadn't gone to have her surgery. Grace didn't know what excuse she had given Mama and she really didn't care. She hoped Lorraine would never be able to have her face repaired. That the ugly scar would remain there for the rest of her life. She could hear voices pretty often from the hallway, but she couldn't always tell what they were saying.

And all she could think about was how much she hated Lorraine.

Some nights, if she tossed and turned long enough, she would take her pillow and blanket and steal away up to the third floor. And there she would lie, beneath the great murals on the wall, looking up at them as moonlight flooded in through the windows. Begging for sleep to take her away as she stared at the two-faced horse, thinking how everything did change as time went by.

For the last few weeks, she had been slipping out to go down to the stables in the middle of the night. She would just sit with Cloudy. He would stand there quietly, nudging at her to see if she had something to feed him and her body somehow seemed to absorb his calmness. Funny, every time she was around people, how she became more and more tense, but Cloudy's presence helped and then when she would return to her room, she would drift off into slumber, even if it was disturbed with drifting visions.

Phillip had tried to talk to her. He had come to her door every evening, but she refused to open it. After a week had passed, he finally kicked it in. It startled her so much; it was so out of character for Phillip to do anything violent. It caught her off guard so that she had finally broken her silence.

"What do you think you're doing?" she had demanded.

He had taken her by the shoulders, forcing her to look at him.

"Grace," he said. "I don't really know what happened. I can only tell you that I felt so sorry for her."

"That's not..." she began but he cut her off.

"I know. That's not any reason for what I did. I could never love a woman like Lorraine." He looked down. "She does have some good in her." He stopped and laughed, a short, bitter sound. "Granted you have to look really deep to find it. I know how she can be so shallow and silly. Probably the most self-centered woman I've ever known."

"That's the first thing you said that I can agree with," Grace had answered.

"I know. She's like a selfish child sometimes. But she

was just so vulnerable, so lost and sad these last few months since it all happened."

Grace had turned to the window, and he had come around to face her. "She's not like you, Grace. You've got strength and character. You have the respect of a lot of people. But Lorraine. All she had was her looks. And now she feels like that's been completely destroyed. I guess my heart just went out to her a little too much. And that night. When she came into our room. I know I should have made her leave. At first, she just sat on the side of the bed, crying. Said how much she wished she could have gone with you and Mama. How she felt like she was missing out on everything life had to offer. And God help me, I let her get to me. That's all I can tell you."

He had left the room but the next day, she had started going down for meals again. She hadn't talked much but she could tell Phillip was relieved. He had asked her several times to come down to the stables, but she didn't want to go while all the men were there. She would often watch out the bedroom window as the men were working down there. She couldn't really tell very much about how the new jockey was doing from that distance. And she couldn't bring herself to care so much, either.

On the surface, it seemed that things were gradually going back to normal. Except that she refused to return to their bedroom. And even though Phillip had tried to persuade her to go with him to some of the races out of town, she always made an excuse. Mama and Papa usually accompanied him, leaving Paulette and Cook to take care of the girls.

And last night, she had let Mama persuade her to come into the living room while they listened to the news.

Grace could feel Phillip watching her. She knew he was concerned about what was happening with the war, but he was so different. For the last year, all his attention had been focused either on the war or the continued success of Janus. And now she could tell, he was thinking a lot more about her.

She glanced over at Buzz. He was concentrating on what the news reporter was saying. He hadn't had very much to say to her, except to speak politely. Grace supposed he knew something was wrong between her and Phillip. As she sat looking at him, she remembered the feelings she had had for him. Even though she hadn't acted on them, she *had* thought about it. So, how could she be so angry at Phillip, she wondered. And yet, she still was.

~~~

The media had gotten wind that Janus Farms was contemplating a race with Johnson, and they were playing it for all it was worth. "East versus West," came the voice of the announcer, over the radio. "The Cash Bomb versus the Carolina Colt. Looks like they're trying to line up a match race, Bounty Money against Runaway Rapids. We're just waiting to find out when and where.

Grace thought it was rather presumptive of them to be announcing it all because Johnson hadn't officially accepted the offer yet. She couldn't help but wonder if he was afraid to pit his horse against Runaway.

She heard a lot of the talk, but she couldn't bring herself to care very much. Since that night she almost felt as if she was walking through a fog. It didn't seem real. And she didn't know how to feel or what to do. She only knew it was really difficult for her to be around Phillip.

And Lorraine. She hadn't seen her since that night. Mama and Paulette took her meals in, and Grace hadn't heard the slightest sound come from her room. How long could Lorraine stay in there, she wondered.

She also wondered what she would do if Lorraine did come out. She had thought about almost nothing else since it had happened. She felt as though she should do something about it, but she wasn't sure what it would be. The only thing she was certain about was how she hated her sister-in-law.

She thought of leaving. Being here was so miserable. But she didn't know where she would go. She could go to Aunt Ada's little cabin; she supposed but Ada had passed on and she would be there all alone. She had gone there once before, a few years back. But she hadn't been able to
~~~

stay away from Phillip. This was different though.

Maybe she would go tomorrow, she thought. That was what she told herself every day. But she knew she wouldn't. She should have gone when it first happened. And now she had fallen into her new routine, it just continued, day by day. And the more time that went by, the more difficult it became to do anything.

And all the while, Philip and Papa continued to court Johnson, wheedling and cajoling, trying to manipulate him into accepting their challenge. They couldn't pin him down. He wouldn't agree to the conditions they tried to work out. There were endless meetings with the racing secretaries, never ending debates about the amount of weight each horse would carry, the date the race would be held, all the details.

Johnson insisted they set the race for Pimlico. And that was the one thing Papa refused to concede to. He had agreed to allow Runaway to carry the top weight. Agreed to the date. But he refused to budge on the location. The match race would be run at Janus or not run at all.

It was a Wednesday evening when Papa came strutting into the dining room with a different air about him and Grace wondered immediately what was going on. He seemed so different. Phillip followed him in and sat down quietly. Grace noticed he looked tired, but a little smile played across his lips. Grace realized it was the first time she had seen him smile since that night.

"By God, we've finally done it," Papa boomed. "Johnson sent in his acceptance today. To be run right here."

Mama passed the platter of thick pork chops across the table to Grace. "How did you get him to agree to come here?" she asked. "I thought he was all for the Pimlico Course."

"I agreed to all his other terms," Papa answered. "Just to get it all worked out. "But this is going to be the race of the century. And I'll see to it that it's not going to be run anywhere except Janus Farms Course!"

THIRTY-FOUR

March 1, 1943

The flurry of excitement over the match race continued to grow. One could hardly turn on the radio or television without hearing something about it. There was a great deal of speculation as to which horse would be favored by the public.

Now that the event had been set in motion, the tides seemed to carry then along and there was no turning back. The men had been swept into a never-ending flurry of preparations; interviews and meetings, making sure the track was in shape. Repairs to the grandstands, repainting the clubhouse.

Grace knew how glad they were that things were looking better for Janus. But she secretly thought Phillip was relieved to be so busy. She wished she had something to take her mind off what had happened with their relationship.

She spent the greater part of her days in her room, thinking how angry she was with Phillip, how much she hated Lorraine. She wished her sister-in-law would leave and never come back. Maybe Frank would come and take her away. She knew now exactly how abusive he could be, but she didn't care. She just wished she never had to see Lorraine again.

And when she would lie in bed, trying to sleep, she could feel the presence of her husband and her sister-in-law in those separate rooms just down the hall. It was as if their thoughts and emotions permeated the very air around her. The fibers of her chest wall would draw tightly, and her breath would come in short gasps. The attacks frightened her, made her feel panicky.

She had tried taking valerian root to calm her nerves.

But it gave her such intense dreams. So vivid. So real. Over and over, the nightmare recurred. She would dream of Janus Farms, the upcoming race, the meeting for the Prominent Ladies of North Carolina. But everything was all mixed together. The women's group would be sitting in the grandstands but when the bell clanged and the gate opened, there were no horses. Instead, Phillip and Lorraine would appear beyond the barrier, locked together in a tight embrace. After a week, she stopped the valerian.

She continued to steal up to the third floor on those nights that she just turned and twisted, unable to sleep. The great painting of Janus looked down on her and she imagined how it was watching as everything in her life changed. Turning upside down, inside out util she barely felt like the same person.

Sometimes, she would put a record on the player and sit alone at the table, listening to Benny Goodman and Glen Miller. But she always ended up with that same record over and over. She would pull it out of the colorful jacket, the one with the picture of Humphrey Bogart and Ingrid Bergman. The soundtrack for the movie. She must have played it a thousand times.

She would remember the magic of that night. And she would gaze up at the mural on the wall where the two faces of the horse looked at the past and the present, listening to the words of the song as it spoke of the passage of time. And it continued to fly by; everything changing, always changing.

~~~

It was the first time Grace had attended a race since it happened. She didn't want to go out and face all those people, but she knew that if she was to remain at Janus, she had better show up. This was the only race that had been held here and there was no getting out of it. And anyway, she didn't want Papa asking questions.

When the gates opened out by the road that afternoon, cars were lined up down the highway as far as she could see. She stayed in her room for a long time, just watching.
~~~

Even as angry as she still was, she was glad that things were turning around. This had been a good business decision, she realized. No matter what had happened, she didn't want to see the track at Janus shut down. The men had been right. All their efforts were going to pay off. Even if they didn't win today, at least their track was back open and doing business again.

When she started to get dressed, she realized there was nothing in the closet that would be appropriate for the race. If they did win, there would be photographs in the winner's circle and she would be expected to be up there.

Peeking out the window, she made sure she could see Phillip down at the stables. Only then did she go down the hall to the room they had shared to get an outfit. She rooted around in the closet for a few minutes, trying not to look over at the sitting room. She wanted to get out of here as quickly as possible, so she finally just snatched a garment down. It slipped off the hanger and it clanged loudly as it hit the hardwood floor and she ran back down the hall to put it on.

She dressed and looked into the mirror. The tailored suit flattered her figure and the big bow off to the side at the bottom of the jacket made it look stylish but elegant. Funny, she thought. How she always wanted to just be plain and unnoticed but right now, she did want Phillip to notice her. She wanted to be pretty. She wanted other men to look at her and tell Phillip what a lucky man he must be to have her for a wife. She pinned the hat on, pulled the veil down over her forehead and went downstairs.

When Phillip came up to the stands and sat down beside her, she tried to move away a few inches without being noticed. But she could tell he did realize she did it on purpose, even though he pretended not to know. But as everyone came in to sit, they were crowded closer together until her knee touched his calf. Her muscles clenched even tighter but there was nowhere to go unless she got up and left.

When Bounty Money came out onto the track paddock, he was calm and quiet, just as he had been the day she had seen him at Hialeah. He made his way down to the track walking steadily beside his exercise pony and Grace could see why the public liked him. Not only was he a great runner, but a beautiful horse, tall and muscular and his dark coat gleamed in the sunlight. Approaching the gate quietly, he offered no resistance, but walked in like a gentleman, giving Manning no trouble at all.

When Big Red appeared from the stables, it was a different story. He reared and pranced, spooking out as he passed the stands. Grady, beside him on Cloudy reached one hand out and grasped the side of his bridle as he tried to help Glover control him. Cloudy had to go into his awkward canter to keep up as the colt tried to twist away from Grady's grip.

As always, Runaway was fractious and trifling at the gate. Grace could see Buzz approach on foot down there. With him walking on one side and Cloudy on the other, they finally managed to get him in, and he acted up just as he always had, stalling the race by a good eight minutes before they could get him settled.

When the gate clanged open, Bounty Money shot out like the bomb that proclaimed his nickname, off and running. As the jockey fought to get Runaway started, his opponent had already gained a hundred yards or so and as his stride lengthened, the distance between them grew.

Even though they had drawn the post position, Red drifted a little but quickly pulled back over to the inside. Once he did, begin to stretch out and accelerate.

"And they're off for the race of the century!" cried the announcer. Bounty Money got off to a quick start. And Runaway Rapids still fights his rider but it looks like the late, great Hoot Harrison broke him of drifting so far to the outside. That's going to make a difference for Janus Farms here today. That's good for them because the Big Cash Bomb is hard to beat."

The pair battled down the track, Runaway a good ten lengths behind Bounty Money. He was starting to gain when he lost his footing and fell, throwing Glover up onto his neck. The colt regained his position and started again but Bounty Money had pulled out ahead. Grace peeked over at Phillip. His face was serious and she could feel the tension emanating from his body. Such an important race, she thought. After all, the announcer had just called it the race of the century. It was by far the biggest crowd that Janus Racetrack had ever seen.

"Now the Carolina Colt's starting to move up again," the announcer said. Glover is riding him well and the work that Harrison did with him is paying off. He's running straight, oh boy, he's booking it now. Just look at that big, red horse go! Did you ever see anything like it? Looks like he's going to catch the Big Cash Bomb, he's coming up fast on him."

Grace glanced over at Papa. He had taken his pipe out of his mouth and she could see that his teeth were clenched beneath his gray mustache.

"Now they're going into the far turn and The Bomb is still out front. Runaway Rapids lost a little ground here, folks. I just don't know…. looks like that turn threw him off. Is he going to come out of it or did it do him in? But look out, look out he's coming on strong now as they head down the backstretch and he's pouring it on. He's gaining, he's gaining with two hundred yards to go. Now he's coming up on Bounty Money's flank and still moving up. Now they're running neck and neck.

"Now they're fifty yards from the line and its hard to tell which one it's going to be. They are burning it up, moving so fast they're almost a blur. Look at them go!"

They were only twenty yards from the finish line when Runaway suddenly poured on a terrific burst of speed and began to move away from Bounty Money. Grace could see Glover look back as they widened the gap, two lengths, then three and then they swept over the finish line. It was Runaway Rapids, back on top!

Phillip turned to Grace and put his arm around her. She didn't pull away. Together, they walked down to the winner's circle to pose with Runaway as he pranced nervously in place, shaking flowers loose from the blanket draped across his neck. And for the first time, instead of holding the trophy with Papa, Phillip kept his arm around Grace. And she didn't want to move away.

Papa fairly beamed at the after-race party that evening.

Strutting back and forth, he grinned broadly, brandishing his cane as he shook hands with all the important people. Grace sat at the family table, watching Phillip as he mixed in a little with the race crowd. He was quiet, mostly listening as others talked but she could see a faint smile on his face. And he kept glancing over at the table where she sat with Mama. Maybe, somehow, she thought, life was going to be a little more normal again.

She could hear Papa as he came over near the table to speak to Mayor Sykes. Shaking hands and accepting congratulations, he boomed, "Yes sir, we showed them, didn't we? Roanoke Rapids may be just a small Southern town, but we're keeping her on the map. By God, we'll keep the fans coming to Janus Farms for the next two hundred years!"

~~~

The family was in the living room that night, watching the late news on the television. The race, of course, was the leading story. "The Carolina Colt takes the Cash Bomb," the voice came over the waves. "It was a race the country will never forget; this one will go down in history." They were showing footage of the race and they kept repeating the finish, over and over as Big Red swept across the line lengths ahead of Bounty Money. Then Grace saw herself, standing with Phillip beside Runaway as he held the trophy, Papa and Buzz on the other side. She looked over at Phillip and noticed that he was staring at her. Instead of looking away, she allowed her gaze to lock with his and he smiled at her. She sat quietly but she felt her lips turn up just a little at the corners as she watched her husband looking across the room at her.

She thought Mama had gone to bed but now she came in and sat down beside Papa for a moment. Grace noticed that she was unusually quiet. They watched the news for a bit. The broadcast was now covering the war.

"An air raid on Berlin took place today," the announcer was saying. "A strategic run on the capital, one of great importance."
~~~

The men were all glued to the television now, concentrating on the facts the reporter was giving. They barely noticed when Mama got up and motioned at Grace to follow her.

Mama took her by the arm and gently guided her into the music room down the hall. She could tell something was wrong and her stomach clenched a little. Mama sat down on the sofa, pulling Grace down beside her.

Instead of releasing Grace's hand once they were seated, Mama held it between her warm palms and was silent for a moment. Finally, she spoke.

"I know what happened Grace. All these months and I couldn't figure out what happened between you and Phillip. And I didn't want to pry."

"I know, Mama. But you were there for me the whole time, even though I couldn't talk about it. Thank you for not pushing me about it. I think maybe now things are going to be better."

"Grace." Mama hesitated and looked down. "I just found out a few minutes ago. Lorraine is pregnant."

THIRTY-FIVE

May 14, 1943

Janus track was, indeed making a comeback. They were holding races at home bi-weekly. Between those and the tracks they were traveling to, Phillip was busier than ever.

And Grace was glad. He was out of town a lot and she always stayed at Janus.

Her emotions had taken such abrupt changes recently. It seemed that her mind had gone a little numb since the night Mama talked to her. For a few days she had simply sat in her room, staring straight ahead. Breathe in, breathe out. Just breathe to stay alive. Don't think about anything else.

Except she did. After she came out of the initial shock, all she could see was a tunnel in front of her. A very small space. Filled with images of Phillip and Lorraine. And a child.

As far as she knew, Lorraine hadn't so much as peeked out of the door of her room. She wondered if Lorraine was showing yet. Was she wearing maternity clothing? Perhaps Mama had gotten some for her.

Whatever. Grace certainly didn't want to see her. It had occurred to her to wonder if Papa had found out. But that was silly. Of course, he hadn't. He wouldn't have held anything back; she would have heard him all the way upstairs. Not that he would care about her feelings. But the Masterson name would be dragged through the mud and he would certainly care a lot about that.

Phillip. Did he know? Grace hadn't been able to bring herself to talk to Mama about it anymore. When she had finally ventured out of her room, she didn't say much to anyone. She just went down for meals and then went back upstairs. She would wait until Phillip was out of town before she would go down to the stables.

And all the while, all she could think of was how she hated Lorraine. How she wanted her gone. How she wished her sister-in-law would disappear from the face of the earth.

~~~

Phillip and Papa had flown out to Hollywood for the big auction. Grace suspected that Mama had wanted to go. But she probably felt as if she should stay home. Because of her and Lorraine.

They had left yesterday and wouldn't be back for nearly a week. They had planned to visit several farms in California to look at the stock. No need in going all that way without taking a look, Papa said. There was one particular two-year-old that recently had a big win at the Santa Anita track that he wanted to see. If they ended up making a purchase, they would ship the horse home by rail.

Finally, Grace felt as though she could breathe again. She started going down to the stables after breakfast. She still avoided all the men, but she would take Cloudy out and ride until late in the afternoon. It made her feel a little better. Of course, it was good to get out of the house. But it was more than that. It was the riding, itself. Something about the rhythm of the horse's gait, soothing, familiar. Even though Cloudy wasn't a hot, temperamental horse, you still had to pay attention to what you were doing. She supposed that was what made it seem so therapeutic.

On the evening of the auction, Mama asked her to come in after dinner and watch it on television with her. She didn't really want to, but she couldn't let Mama sit in there alone. After all, she was part of the reason Mama had stayed home.

The coverage had already started by the time she went in to join Mama. The emcee was in the middle of explaining how the event had been put together in order to raise funding for the war effort.

The first item up was a fur coat, worn in one of the most popular movies from last year. The bid started at ten
~~~

thousand dollars and in a matter of moments had reached thirty thousand. The auctioneer kept working the crowd until it reached seventy-two thousand. "Going, going, gone! To the gentleman in the second row."

Next was an autographed baseball, then a necklace worn by one of the starlets. The auctioneer was talented, he kept the crowd whipped into a bidding frenzy.

"And now," said the auctioneer. "We have a rather unusual item. A set of shoes. I auctioned a pair of high heels worn by a famous dancer once, but these are horseshoes." He paused and a murmur ran through the crowd.

"Not just any old horseshoes," the auctioneer said. "No, these are a set of the special shoes worn by the most famous race-horse in the country. Runaway Rapids, himself. The set, in fact, that the Carolina Colt wore in his last race.

"Now, let's start it off at ten thousand." He held one of the shoes up. "Come on, now, folks. Who wouldn't like to hang these on the living room wall and show them off to company? Great conversation piece, they'd be. Why, a look at these brings to mind all kinds of stories about one of the greatest thoroughbreds of the century." He pointed out into the audience. "Yes, sir, thank you. We have a bid for ten thousand dollars!"

The camera panned across the audience and although Grace couldn't tell who was bidding, she could see the excitement on the faces of the people. Then it panned back across the stage and a huge image of Runaway Rapids appeared on the wall behind the auctioneer. Big Red was, indeed, a star, just like the Hollywood actors who were so famous.

"All right, let's make it fifteen. Fifteen-fifteen-fifteen thousand. Who'll give me fifteen? Come on now! Give it to me, give it to me, give it to me! Thank you, sir! Got it, right here. Come on, guys, can I see twenty? Yes, right here. Now, let's go for thirty. Thirty-thirty-thirty, can I get someone to get thirty? All right, thirty thousand.

"Come on, people. Just look at the big, red horse on the screen up here. Big Red, the Carolina Colt, himself! A legend, I would have to say. We've just been playing around. Now let's see some real money here. I need at least forty. Forty-forty-forty, can I hear forty? Come on now, give it to me, give it to me. Yes!" He pointed down into the front row.

"Now the ladies are playing too! Forty-five? thank you sir. Come on sweetheart, can you make it fifty? Fifty, will you go fifty?"

Silence from the crowd for a moment. Then the auctioneer brought down his gave. "Sold! For fifty thousand. The special shoes worn by the country's most patriotic racehorse. To the lovely lady in the fourth row."

The camera panned down, and they could see a glamorous woman with platinum blonde hair get up to sign the paperwork as one of the auction employees passed it down the aisle to her.

Then, the emcee brough out a shimmering, silk scarf. It was long and sheer, and he whisked it through the air, making it twirl and spin.

"Now here's something really special," said the auctioneer. "A scarf worn by Ingrid Bergman in one of the most popular romance scenes ever to come across the silver screen. She wore this in the movie, Casablanca.

Grace's stomach clenched at the memory of that night. Phillip and herself, Frank, and Lorraine. It had been such a grand evening and they'd had a glorious time. It had been such a special night that it was painful to remember it.

"Thousand, thousand, who'll bid a thousand? Yep!" He pointed out in the audience and kept going. "Now how about two? Two thousand, two thousand, come on." He beckoned with his free hand. "Come on, come on, give it to me, give it to me, give me two thousand now!"

The auctioneer continued, the pace of his voice increasing until Grace could barely keep up with what he was saying at times. From the best she could tell, after the price reached ten thousand, many of the bidders seemed to fall off and the battle continued between just two people. The battle went back and forth, and the camera would pan down into the audience, but with so many people it was difficult to see who was bidding.

"Twenty-eight, fifty, twenty-eight, fifty. Now who'll give

me thirty thousand?" The auctioneer stopped for a moment and picked up the scarf himself, running it through his hands and waving it to ripple through the air.

"Come on now, folks." He was talking in a normal tone. "I know there's someone out there that really wants this scarf... no, someone needs it. Ladies, just think, you could be the envy of your friends. Why, they would just turn green if you wore this to a party.

"And you gentlemen. Just think what a gift like this would mean to your sweetheart. Worn by the most sophisticated actress to ever walk across a stage. Come on, remember when she was standing there and she had this very scarf draped over her head and shoulders. Such a glorious moment in Hollywood history. In my book, this movie is going down as a classic, one of the best love stories that will ever come to pass."

He paused for a moment, and you could hear the crowd murmuring, then the auctioneer's voice rose again in a flurry.

"All right, we have twenty-eight fifty." He pointed down at the first row. Now who'll give me twenty- nine?"

The bids were flashing back and forth now, "Twenty-nine, twenty-nine, I've got twenty-nine. Now about twenty-nine fifty? Got it right here. Now," he paused as he looked out into the audience. "Surely, we can get a bid for thirty. Come on, give it to me, give it to me, give me the money!" He beckoned with his free hand. "Thirty, thirty who'll give me thirty?"

He stopped and pointed across the crowd. "We have thirty thousand. Can I get thirty-one?"

Silence for a moment and then he banged his gavel.

"Sold! For thirty thousand to the tall gentleman standing in the back of the room."

The camera panned across the room and Mama gasped as she grabbed Grace's arm. "That's Phillip!"

THIRTY-SIX

Summer 2021

With temperatures hitting over a hundred degrees every day this week, we are riding in the early mornings only. Not even eight o'clock yet and the humidity slaps you in the face when you step outside.

The kids don't seem to mind, though. They ignore the heat, as excited as ever to be riding. It takes a toll on us adults. I'm so thankful that I'm not sick like I was when I first came here. I'd never be able to tolerate these temperatures.

The horses don't like it either. Always slow and calm, they are almost lethargic in this heat. By this afternoon, half the herd will be wallowing in the pond, while the others stand in the deep shade of the big oaks.

Most of us are in the large arena. Jennifer and I are working with a new client. He is a little tense, but I can tell he is excited about being able to ride a horse. Drake is in the lower arena on Boogie. She is practicing for the show ring. She and Ransom Copeland's daughter have been spending a lot of time together. They have asked me to bring Drake out to the local 4-H shows.

Maggie-Mae rode for an hour or so. Now she and Valentine are walking around, side by side, stopping here and there to visit with parents who are watching, or anyone who doesn't happen to be riding.

We have been working with the new boy for about twenty minutes when I get a strange feeling. Only one thing has ever made me feel that way. I look over towards the gate and see Cole standing here, one foot propped on the railing as he watches.

My first instinct is to drop the reins and walk away. But there's no way I can do that. I can't leave Jennifer alone with a new client. I have to stay out here, keep doing my job and act as if everything is all right.

I make it until the thirty-minute session is over. I keep sneaking glances over at the fence and he is still there, watching silently.

When we start out of the arena, he opens the gate but doesn't say anything. He just watches as we go to the barn. As soon as the client is gone, he comes in. My muscles are tense, but I stand my ground.

"This is a good thing you're doing here, Jo," he says. "I've heard about riding therapy, but I've never seen it. I never knew what it was really like."

As I stand here, I realize I'm not so nervous anymore. I still love this man, but I feel different.

"Well, you're welcome to come out and watch," I finally say.

"I will. I'll come back."

"And next time you come; I want you to bring my horse. I've asked you before." I stand here looking at him.

"Jo, you could start a program like this at our place. I'll keep the reining business going, build you a separate arena. Just think, if they've been able to build a program like this in such a rural area, imagine what you could do with all the resources on the outskirts of Raleigh."

I open my mouth to speak but just then Drake comes in. "Jo," she calls. "Did you see Boogie?" She puts him in the crossties and loosens the girth.

Cole takes my hand in his and looks at me for a moment. Even the callouses on his palms where he holds the reins feel familiar. "Think about it, Jo. We'll talk more about it." And then he is gone.

~~~

I do think about what Cole has proposed. I go through the motions of my work for the rest of the long, hot morning but my mind wanders.

There is much to ponder. It's as if something has shifted. Even though the feelings are still there, I am no longer afraid of being under his control. And what he has
~~~

offered to do has amazed me. Cole never was one that was very comfortable with children. It's such a shock that he would come up with this idea.

"Jo-Jo." I look down and Maggie-Mae is tugging on my jeans. "Can I stay with you and Miss Grace this afternoon? You can call my mom and ask her. She can come get me after work."

"I think we can arrange that," I say, glad for the distraction.

~~~

I sit in the library with Grace and Maggie-Mae. The huge room with the high ceilings is always cool. And besides, after what I saw with that painting in the office, I don't like working in there anymore alone, so I bring my paperwork in here.

Maggie always likes to go over to the children's section in the corner nook. The first time she came in, she wanted to know where the Pony Pal books were. Grace had no idea what she was talking about. I had explained that it is a popular series for kids.

"I'm afraid you won't find that in here, honey. All these books are pretty old."

Maggie brings her a thick book with a mare and foal on the cover, entitled Album of Horses. I remember getting that book for my birthday. The front cover with the beautiful picture of a mare and foal takes me back to my own childhood. My parents had put in a special inscription to their "favorite horse girl." Grace flips through and they look at pictures of the different breeds.

Soon Maggie hands Grace another book. Even with her glasses, Grace can hardly see to read but she tells the story of National Velvet. "I read it so many times I know it by heart," she says. She explains how a steeplechase is a race with obstacles that the horses must jump.

The child listens, quiet and wide-eyed.

"Now, if I remember right, Velvet had to disguise herself as a young man," Grace says.

"Why did she do that?"
~~~

"Well, back in those days, they didn't want to allow girls to ride in the races."

Maggie pokes out her top lip. "That wasn't very fair."

Grace looks over at me and smiles. "Well, girls can do a lot of things nowadays that they weren't allowed to in the past. In fact, they seem to be doing just about anything they choose to."

Maggie smiled. "That's good. Maybe I'll be a jockey when I grow up."

Grace gives her a little hug. "Maybe you will."

~~~

That evening, after Maggie's mom has picked her up and Grace has gone to bed, I sit out on the veranda. It is still humid, but it has cooled off and a breeze is blowing. The sun has set but there is a full moon, and you can see almost as if it is daylight.

I pick up the laptop. I have a couple of messages from Denise. I should do some of my paperwork. I click into Quickbooks, but the figures just stare at me and I can't really concentrate. I look at Twitter and then Facebook. I sit here, procrastinating, putting off the accounting business.

For some reason, I google Janus. The Roman god pops up on several sites and I click into the first one. The symbol of transitions, duality, time itself. He was supposed to have presided over the beginning and ending of conflict, hence war and peace. Barbarism and civilization. Greed and generosity. All these things, I thought. Janus Farms had seen them all.

I listen to the chains of the porch swing squeaking as I swing back and forth. So many things are going through my mind. What Cole said earlier had been so unexpected. I can't seem to wrap my mind around it. That he would do something like this for me. Almost as if he is a different person now.

I get up and wander down to the stables. The horses have all been turned out and they are grazing peacefully. I stand here thinking for a few minutes. I really want to take a ride, down by the river. I could take Boogie or Scooter;
~~~

they both give me a pretty fair ride. But I decide against it. The way the river has cut out culverts and freshets, it's really not safe to take them down after dark. If they stepped into one, we'd be in the river and I'm not taking a chance. I'll just walk down that way.

As I walk along, thinking about what Cole had said this morning, I realize the wind is blowing a little harder. I look up and see clouds scudding across the full moon at intervals. I pull my phone out of the back pocket of my jeans and look at the weather app. Looks like a storm is approaching but not a very bad one, just a few little pockets of rain. Maybe it will cool the temperatures down, I hope. It looks like I'll have plenty of time to walk down to the river and back before it hits.

I try to put Cole out of my mind and concentrate on the program. That new boy will be back tomorrow, and he needs a lot of attention. And the farrier is coming out, we'll have to catch all the horses that are due for a shoeing and shut them up. About a dozen of the horses are due for worming too. I need to get up extra early and get that done while it's still cool. I'll have to get it out of the way before we get busy with the kids.

Suddenly, I become aware of the sound of hoofbeats in the distance. Some of the horses must be running in the pasture. I look out across the fields but none of the herd is in sight. Just then, the moon goes behind a cloud, and it gets really dark.

The sound is coming closer now and even though I can't see very well, I can tell it is a large horse. Heavy. The earth shakes beneath my feet. The moon moves in and out of the cloud cover; one minute I can see as if it were nearly daylight and the next, I can hardly see the path in front of me. The sound gets louder. Closer and closer. So close that I step off the path, stumbling through the brush and fall across an old log that has rotted there.

And still, the hoofbeats grow louder. Now I can hear the sound a horse makes in his throat when he is winded, when he has been running for a while. A sort of grunting snort that comes up, no mistaking it; ugh...ugh...ugh... a little whoosh with every running breath. And then I feel a rush of wind as it passes me. The moon is out now but there is nothing to see except a shadow. I stand here, staring and the hoofbeats begin to recede in the distance. They grow fainter and fainter until I can no longer hear them.

Stepping back onto the path, I continue towards the river, walking quickly. I stop now and then to listen, but only silence meets my ear. Even though I am uneasy I really need to see what this was. The moon glistens on the white sand of the path and I can see hoofprints. The prints of a running horse, sand splayed out in all directions. A tremendously long stride. None of the horses here has a stride like that.

I follow the tracks until I can hear the running water of the river. But there is no horse to be seen. No shadow, no sound of hoofbeats anymore. And the hoofprints lead to the edge of the river and disappear.

THIRTY-SEVEN

May 25, 1943

Grace held the oversized polka-dot umbrella over Mama's head as she climbed out of the car, and they hurried inside for the Ladies' Circle meeting. It had been raining off and on for the last few days. Puddles stood everywhere and the ground was a soggy mess. They got inside, removed their galoshes, and hung up their wet coats.

"Grace, dear," said Hattie Birdsong. "We missed having you at the meetings. It's good to have you back."

As she sat, listening to the agenda, Grace thought it was good to be here. She was glad she had finally listened to Mama and started coming out of the house more. She didn't know what was going to happen, but she couldn't just stay inside forever.

The ladies really seemed to appreciate her efforts for the book and the Community Victory Garden. It had all made her feel more a part of things with this group.

Mama had already given them an account of the trip to the governor's mansion on her first meeting afterwards, but they were still talking about it. "I'd have just given anything to be in your shoes, Grace", admitted Martha Strayhorn. "I've always wanted to see the inside of the governor's mansion. Wasn't it fun?"

Grace nodded but she didn't say anything. She didn't like hearing anything about that weekend.

"It's just a shame you had to leave early," said Martha. "Just think, you would have been on television."

What if they hadn't come back, Grace wondered. She wouldn't have known what happened that night. Would it have been a one-time thing, or would it have turned into a drawn-out affair? A new thought occurred to her. Had that night been the first time, or had it happened before? Why had it taken her so long to wonder about that?

She hardly heard anything else that pertained to the meeting. But as she sat there contemplating it, she realized that it couldn't have happened before. That night was the one and only time that Phillip and Lorraine had been thrust into the situation of being alone there, on the second story of the mansion. And Lorraine could be so manipulative, she was an expert at making people feel sympathy for her. For some reason, being away from Janus for just a little while seemed to be helping her sort it all out.

And the scarf. She hadn't even known Phillip had gotten back from California in the middle of the night. She had woken to find the box on the foot of her bed. Wrapped in paper of the most beautiful lavender flowers. Iris. Her favorite. Like the ones he had filled their room with on that night that seemed so long ago. There was a note taped to the box. She put her hand in the pocket of her skirt and felt the edges of the paper. She kept it with her all the time.

Grace,

I know that material things were never of much importance to you. And that's not what this is about. It's about you and me; the night we saw her wearing it. We felt so close that night. I know I was busy and didn't pay enough attention to you. And I'm sorry. I was just trying so hard to make things better at Janus. Trying too hard to please Papa, I guess.

You told me once that you wished you could be like Bergman. How you thought she was so elegant and refined. And if I remember right, I just smiled and rushed off to work. But Grace, in my eyes, there is no woman, even a great Hollywood star, that has what you have. It's what attracted me to you in the first place. Your deep integrity, the feeling you have for others. And you're more beautiful to me than a whole room full of movie stars.

But Bergman was special to me. Because I knew how special she was to you. And that was why I wanted to bring this home to you.

I Love You,
Phillip

Grace sat through the meeting, hearing very little of what was said. She looked around the room at the other women, wondering what their relationships with their husbands were and wondered if their husbands had ever cheated on them. And what would their reaction be? She had long suspected that several of them had married for the social status and money. Would they simply be angry and embarrassed? Would they be relieved for their husbands to focus their attentions elsewhere so they wouldn't be bothered? Or would they feel the agony that she had been suffering?

And then she realized. If she didn't still love Phillip so much, the wound wouldn't be so deep. And yet, she didn't know exactly what to do about it.

When the meeting was adjourned and they went out to the car, the rain was still coming down. As they drove downtown, turned off the avenue and passed the river, Grace realized the water was so high that you couldn't see all the huge rocks anymore. She hadn't ever seen it that way before. She hoped the rain would hold off for a while. The water was so high it was nearly even with the banks of the river now.

~~~

Grace turned Cloudy onto the path beyond the East pasture. She hadn't been out on the trail for the last few days because the ground was so wet, but she just had to get away. They were still getting showers but now and then the clouds would blow out and the sun would appear for a short time so she wanted to get out while she could. Cloudy was sure-footed and he picked his way carefully around the puddles, never picking up the pace beyond a slow jog.

She had chosen this path because even though it was a long, winding trail, it was higher ground, away from the river. She was hoping the ride would clear her mind a little. Thoughts just kept coming at her.

As for the farm, and especially their track, things had
~~~

been looking up. Even though no one would ever compare with Hoot, the new jockey was doing well. And the crowds were flocking into Janus for the races held there nearly every other weekend. She sensed that Phillip seemed to be a little more relaxed. And it was the first time she had seen Papa this happy since Frank had left.

But last night, everything had changed. They had been watching the evening news when they heard it. The new law was going through. Parimutuel wagering was definitely going to be outlawed in North Carolina.

Phillip hadn't said anything at first, but she had sat there and watched her husband as his face crumbled. She remembered seeing him crush his cigarette into the ash tray and stare silently at the television.

They were all quiet for a moment, wondering if they had heard it right. Then Papa exploded. Standing up, he threw his whiskey tumbler across the room where it smashed into the bricks surrounding the fireplace.

"Blast it!" he had thundered. "They can't do this to us." He stalked about the room as Grace and Mama stared up at him. "I'll talk to the governor, we'll get up a petition, we'll get it changed. This is where thoroughbred racing started, it all began right here. How do they think they can do this to us?"

Phillip had gotten up and gone out of the room, shoulders slumped and staring at the floor. Grace had looked out the window of her room a little later and seen him in the moonlight, standing down in front of the stables. Looking into the water of the fountain where the statue of the two-faced horse watched the change they were about to go through in the near future.

What was going to become of the track, Grace wondered as she rode along. They would be all right; she had heard Phillip say that often enough. They would continue to ship the horses to other tracks. And Runaway's stud fee alone would keep them afloat for years to come. She supposed it was mostly a matter of tradition, of pride in the farm and their track.

No more racing in North Carolina. So strange. They were less than a mile from the Virginia border, where the betting system was still legal. And no betting meant no reason for people to come to the track. Talk about your bad luck, she thought. It was hard to believe that a race would never be held there again. No crowds of people in the stands, jumping up with their binoculars, jostling to see what was happening. It was just killing Papa. And even though Phillip didn't let it show, Grace knew it was hurting him, too. Even as angry as she was with him, she felt a sense of loss over what was happening.

Cloudy pricked his ears now and she saw something in the path up ahead. As they came closer, she could see that it was a red fox. Just as it turned to scurry into the brush, she realized it was holding a kit in its mouth. It was moving to higher ground, she thought. They had dens all along the riverbank and she supposed their dugouts were filling up with water.

Just the thought of a mother and baby turned her thoughts back to Lorraine. Carrying Phillip's child. She let the little horse walk on, paying no attention to where he was heading. How on earth were they going to all continue to live in the same house? Lorraine couldn't spend the rest of her life holed up in that room. And what about the baby? Something like this could only be covered up for so long. People would find out.

And how was she going to feel towards that child, Grace wondered. Even though it would be completely innocent, could she find it in her heart not to blame it? A daily reminder of that awful night.

She could never hate a child, she knew that. But she *did* hate Lorraine. Just hated her guts. The very thought of Lorraine made her feel sick to her stomach. She wished... she didn't know what she wished. That was the least of the evil thoughts Grace was having right now about her sister-in-law. Or maybe Frank would come back long enough to get her and carry her away with him. That didn't seem likely, though. They still hadn't heard a word from him.

All through their relationship, Grace had always tolerated her sister-in-law just as everyone else at Janus did. They had all become so accustomed to her high-minded ways and selfish displays that they had come to take it for granted. Amusing even, as they joked among themselves about it.

She thought now about some of the good times, though. How Lorraine had taught her to drive, how she had pitched in and helped when Spanky was sick. Loraine's tenderness for animals, which was the one thing that had really brought them together.

Suddenly, a loud clap of thunder boomed, drawing her out of her thoughts. She looked around and realized how dark the sky had become. A couple of seconds later, a flash of lightening raced across the center of the dark clouds.

She looked around and saw that she had ridden past the boundaries of Janus and was on the adjoining Weaver farm. She could see their house in the distance. She had never ridden this far before. She turned Cloudy towards home and urged him into a quick trot. He started back down the trail they had been on, but she turned him towards the right, knowing the river path was the quickest way back.

The wind started to blow, and she felt a light spattering of rain across her face. She bumped Cloudy a little with her heel and he went into his choppy, little canter. The mud was slippery out here, but she didn't want to get caught on horseback in a thunderstorm. She remembered Papa telling how six horses had been killed at once by a lightning strike when he was young, all standing beneath a big oak in the South pasture. She supposed the iron horseshoes would draw the lightening.

Thunder boomed again and the sky lit up. Grace saw the sparks fly when a firebolt hit a tall pine and she pulled her horse to a stop, just as the big tree crashed down across the path in front of them. Cloudy shied out really hard to the side. He had never done that before. She could tell he was picking up her fear.

She pushed the little horse with her legs, and he slowly picked his way through the brush to the side of the path, then they were around the tree and back on the path. The wind was blowing harder now, and the rain started to come down in sheets. Grace could see it, sweeping across the muddy waters of the river. She wished she hadn't ridden so far out. What had she been thinking? She knew they had been having thunderstorms nearly every afternoon. She just hadn't really thought about it.

Pushing Cloudy back into a fast trot, she posted in the saddle, looking out across the river. It had been rising so much in the last couple of weeks. They came to a spot where the banks had overflowed. Grace looked to see if they could go around the water, but the brush was so thick in this area that they couldn't get through. She turned Cloudy and urged him through the water. He balked at first, afraid to go in. Finally, he stepped gingerly into the edge of the water. Grace prayed he wouldn't step into a hole or catch his hoof on a branch. Debris was floating everywhere. They had nearly reached the point where she could see the trail when a water moccasin swam by, and her heart caught in her throat. But a few more steps and they were on the path again, picking the pace back up.

Finally, she could see the house and stables up on the hill. They were home. They would be safe. But as she pushed Cloudy into a canter, she looked back over her shoulder. The Roanoke was rising.

THIRTY-EIGHT

Fall 2021

I turn off Interstate 95 onto Highway 64, heading West towards Raleigh. I am driving the farm truck, towing the trailer behind me. I am tired of asking Cole to bring my horse to me.

I know the reason he keeps ignoring my request. He thinks she will bring me home. He knows how much I love her; he knows about the special connection I have with her. It's not about the trophies or the big money wins. It's how she works for me. Always willing. Ready to do what I ask. All the time and miles I put on her, the way she moves under me. I didn't think I could ever set foot on that property again. But I need her. Out of our entire marriage, everything we built together with the business, that horse is the only thing I have asked for.

When I reach the outskirts of Raleigh and get into the heavy traffic, I realize that I have really grown accustomed to the peace and quiet of living near such a small, rural town. I had a flat last week when I was hauling one of the horses to the vet and a stranger stopped to help me. I was nearly done, could have finished it myself but that's not the point. I look around at all the vehicles surrounding me on each side, bumper to bumper and imagine having a breakdown out here. I'm pretty sure no one would stop to lend a hand.

I don't know what to say to Cole when I get there. Maybe he won't be there, I tell myself. But since that's where he works, the chances of his being gone are pretty slim. I had thought about looking at the circuit schedule. It would be pretty easy to figure out which shows he would go to. I am still considering his offer to start a program in Raleigh if I come back and I'm not sure what to do. But in

278

the meantime, I have decided that I want my horse. And I want her now. I will have to figure all that out later.

When I turn onto the property, I see several rigs parked out by the main arena, so I know he is probably working with clients. As I get closer, I can see a woman in the arena on a dark sorrel. A young woman. Pretty. I get a little twist in my stomach.

As I watch, she does a rundown on the far side of the fence, slides to a stop and does an awkward sort of rollback. She looks like a good rider, but she must just be getting started at reining. Oh well, I think. Why else would she be here? That's what he does.

I park the rig and take a deep breath. I'm still watching the woman ride when I walk around the corner of the barn and come face to face with Cole, who is leading a bay gelding. His eyes widen with surprise.

"Jo!" He stops and stands there holding the horse as it stomps at flies. "What are…" He trails off and I meet his gaze squarely.

"Why didn't you tell me you were coming?" he asks. "I would have cancelled my appointments."

I start to speak, and my throat closes up for a moment. Just for split second, I am nervous. The way I used to be.

Then I see his gaze shift out into the barnyard and he sees my rig. The trailer tells him why I am here. He shakes his head. "Jo, don't. Can't we talk?"

I straighten my shoulders and look him in the eye. "We can," I answer. "But right now, I'm taking my horse. I want to get back and get her settled in before dark. Make sure she knows where the perimeters of the fence are while there's still enough light to see by. Then I'll give you a call."

"Jo, please." He tries to grasp my arm, but I pull away. He comes around in front to face me. "I'll bring her out this weekend."

"No, Cole. I'm taking her now. You and I can talk later. I've been considering what you said you were willing to do. A program for the kids. Here in Raleigh. But I've got to really think about it. And in the meantime, I want to do some riding."

He shrugs and helps me get my horse loaded. There is

nothing else he can do. If I come home things are going to be different. A lot of things.

~~~

Back at Janus, I open the trailer door and back my horse out. She stands, head up and ears perked, alert. Looking, listening, sniffing the strange smells of her new surroundings. I lead her into one of the small paddocks, walk her around until she knows where the boundaries are and release her.

Immediately, she bolts across the grass and my throat tightens a little as I watch my mare floating through the air. The long, white mane flowing out from the dark, golden body. The crest of her neck arches and her long, silky tail drags the ground. Hot Smoking Butterscotch is her registered name. My Scotty girl.

I can hardly wait to be on her back, to feel her beneath me. But for now, it is enough. Enough to simply stand here and watch her.

~~~

I am sitting at the big table in the library, going through a stack of bills to make online payments. Grace sits in one of the wingback chairs with Maggie Mae perched on the arm. During the late afternoon session, she had begged to come and stay with us while her mom goes to a meeting at her school. After we assured her mother about a dozen times that we wanted her to stay, she had finally given in. After I finish my work, we're going to make hot chocolate with marshmallows.

They are looking through a book at the illustrated pictures. I can see a black horse on the faded cover.

"This is the story of Black Beauty," Grace explains. "It's a really old book about a horse that keeps getting sold over and over. He had some owners that were so cruel to him and just didn't take care of him one bit."

Maggie's brow furrows. "What happened to him?"

"Well, now. That's the good part. It was a happy ending.

Black Beauty had a hard time with some people that abused him. But he finally got a good home with people who loved him and took real good care of him."

Maggie picks up the book and looks at the cover. "That sounds like some of the horses we have here, right?"

Grace looks over at me and smiles. "That's exactly right, honey." She kisses the little girl on top of the head. "Just like the horses we have here. The way it ought to be."

Maggie has grown tired of looking at the book. She hops down and begins to ramble around. She goes to the children's section and pulls out a few books. She piles them beside Grace's chair, but she is restless. She wanders around and I see her looking at the trophies. She asks Grace who won them. I am half-listening as I click in to pay the bill at the Feed and Seed store.

I hear a little squeaking sound. Maggie has found the liquor cabinet inside the big globe. I am wondering just how Grace will explain liquor cabinets, but Maggie closes it and doesn't say anything. She is off looking at more books on the shelves.

She pushes the ladder, and it moves a little on the tracks. She puts a foot on the bottom rung.

"Let's don't get up there, honey," Grace says. "You might fall."

Never one to argue, Maggie quietly does as she is told and continues her journey around the big room, stopping to look at each of the shelves that are low enough for her to see.

I am checking off receipts for grain against the monthly invoice because the bill is a little higher than usual when Grace says, "What in the world?"

I look up. Maggie is bent over, peering at one of the bottom shelves and at first, I can't see what she is looking at. But she moves to the side a little and it takes a moment for me to realize what it is. She has pulled open the door to what looks like a secret compartment.

When the door is closed, it looks like any other row of books. But they are not books at all. They are simply painted-on book spines that disguise the door. You would never have a clue that anything else lurked there.

I watch as Grace stands up, takes her cane, and walks over to Maggie. "Why, I never..." her voice trails off.

"What's in there, honey?" she asks.

Maggie moves aside and even from where I am sitting, I can see a small pile of papers. Newspaper clippings, photographs, things like that.

"Hand me those papers," Grace tells Maggie. "Here, sit them over there on the table for me."

Maggie piles them onto the table beside me and Grace comes over and begins to look through them.

"Oh, I remember that day," she says as she picks up a photograph and shows it to the little girl.

"This was when our horse, Runaway Rapids won a really big race."

The little girl nods solemnly as Grace continues to stand there, leaning on her cane, looking through the pile of papers.

Suddenly, she stops. The hand that isn't holding the cane comes up to her chest and I hear her give a little gasp. I look up and her face has gone pale.

Standing up, I grasp her arm. "Grace, are you okay?"

But she doesn't answer. It seems as if she doesn't even hear me. She is gazing down at the papers on the table. Her breath is coming in short, ragged gasps and I begin to really become concerned. After all, she is nearly a hundred years old. I stand here looking at her and my own heart begins to thump heavily in my chest.

"Grace! Grace, what's wrong?"

She continues to stare at those papers.

"Grace, I'm going to call nine-one-one." I pick up my phone. "We're going to have to get you some help."

Finally, that gets a response. "No!" Her voice is sharp. "Just let me sit down for a minute. I'll be all right."

Taking her arm, I help her over to the sofa. She sits down and leans back, closing her eyes. Her face is pasty-white now and I can see where perspiration covers her forehead.

"Are you sure you don't want to go to the hospital?"

She shakes her head. "Just let me lie down."

As I ease her feet up onto the sofa, Maggie appears at

my elbow. She has taken a cushion from the wingchair and slips it under Grace's head.

Grace takes the little hand. "Thank you, honey. I'll be all right."

"Jo-Jo." Maggie tugs at my shirt. "What's wrong with Miss Grace?"

"I'm not sure, sweetie. Let's just give her a minute."

Maggie stands at the end of the sofa, her little hand stroking Grace's hair. Grace lies there with her eyes closed and I can see a blue vein throbbing in her temples.

"Jo." She finally opens her eyes. "I'm all right. Maybe if you could just get me a glass of iced tea?"

I hesitate. It's a long way to the kitchen in this house. But if that's what she wants, maybe I should get it.

I trot down the maze of long hallways, darting around the corners, snatch open the door of the fridge and pour a glass of tea. My hands are shaky, and I spill half the pitcher. No matter, I'll mop it up later. I grab a dishcloth and dampen it with cold water. It drips on the floor as I run back down the different hallways.

When I get back to the library, Maggie is still standing beside Grace. I gently lay the cool cloth on Grace's forehead, and she opens her eyes.

"Oh, that feels nice."

I help her sit up and she takes a sip of tea, then takes the glass in her hand. I can tell she is feeling better now.

"I think I just need to go up to bed," she says.

"All right. Just let me shut the computer off."

I hit the power button and click on shut down. Just as the laptop is closing out, I glance over at the pile of papers sitting next to it. On the very top is a torn clipping from a newspaper. It is just the title of the story but now I see what upset Grace so much.

SCANDLE AT JANUS FARMS. FAMOUS TROPHY USED AS MURDER WEAPON.

THIRTY-NINE

May 28, 1943

Grace sat in the back seat of her car with Mama. Henry was driving them into Roanoke Rapids to help the Ladies' Circle. The rain had kept getting worse over the last week. The flooding was so bad in town, all the men in the area were working, trying to protect the businesses on the avenue and the women were keeping them fed. Even though Grace had grown accustomed to driving into Roanoke Rapids, Phillip had instructed Henry to bring them. The roads could get dangerous as the day went on.

Henry had apologized for having to take Grace's car out in this mess. Nearly every vehicle from Janus had already gone into town. All the house servants and most of the stable hands had gone in to help.

The flooding wasn't bad at Janus Farms yet. The track and some low-lying parts of the pastures were under a few inches of water. The house and stables, being on the hill were fine. Some of the farms upstream hadn't fared as well and Phillip had invited several of them to stable their horses at Janus.

The closer they got to town, the deeper the water was. The bridge at the North end of Roanoke Avenue had broken loose and was blocking the water. When they reached the avenue, Grace could see how bad things were.

Cars were crawling along, water up over the doors. Several had stalled and been abandoned. As they passed Bella's Boutique, she could see through the storefront window how the muddy water had seeped in and the bottoms of many of the dresses were soggy and wet. Dr. Joyner's office, across the street was flooded as well. As they passed by the funeral parlor on the next block, she saw a casket floating down the sidewalk. She hoped it was

284

empty.

As they continued uptown, away from the river, she could see a group of men stacking sandbags in front of a storefront. Phillip was on a flatbed truck, handing the bags to those waiting below. He stopped and stared when he saw her car, but Grace turned her head and pretended she didn't see him.

They finally reached the Baptist church. She could see Paulette on the far side of the fellowship hall, spooning bacon and eggs onto plates. As they took off their cloaks and hung them in the kitchen, she saw Cook, elbow deep in a huge bowl of biscuit batter.

They worked through the morning, plating up food. The men ate in shifts. As soon as a table cleared out, they cleaned it and a new crew would sit down to eat.

Grace kept watching for Phillip. Finally, she saw him come in with Papa and the stable hands. She helped Paulette take their food over. As Phillip took his plate from her, his hand rested on hers, lingering there for a moment. She swallowed hard and started to pull her hand away, but he held onto it until she looked him in the eye. He looked so tired and worried but then he smiled, and a feeling stirred within her. She hadn't felt it in a long while, but it was still there.

Grace saw that the other men at the table were watching them. Blushing, she went back and busied herself serving more plates. By the time she had finished helping back in the kitchen, he had left.

Around mid-morning, one or two men would trickle in at the time. Everything was fairly quiet, and they would have an hour to rest before it was time for the noon meal.

Grace was sweeping mud off the floor when half a dozen men came in.

"Can somebody get Doc Joyner over here?" one of them asked. "We've got some injuries here. Just minor ones, a few cuts and bruises."

One of the girls went to find Dr. Joyner. Someone had seen him, out helping with the sandbags.

By the time he came in, the women were wiping down the wounds with kitchen towels. The roof at the mill had collapsed, they were told. But thank goodness, no one had been hurt badly.

Most of them had lacerations and several were pretty deep. The women had temporarily staunched the bleeding with their potholders and dishcloths. Dr. Joyner stitched up the two that were the worst before he ran out of suture materials from the bag he always carried.

"I guess I'm going to have to send the rest of you to the hospital," he said. "I hate to do it, as minor as these cuts are. But we need to get the bleeding stopped and everything in my office is underwater."

One of them shook his head. "You know we don't have time for that, Doc. We need to get back out there. This town is about to lose everything and the water's getting deeper."

Grace stepped over to Dr. Joyner and said in a low voice, "Doc, I've got some shepard's purse at the house."

He looked at her, his face blank.

"It's an herb," she explained. "Slows down bleeding. If you can get them to stay here long enough for me to go get some, it'll help."

He nodded. "Go ahead. That's all we need to do for right now. I can get some tetanus shots and penicillin and give it to them later today. I'll get the ladies to feed them and maybe they'll sit still until you get back."

Once she got out of town and there wasn't so much water on the road, she thought it would be an easy drive. But she hadn't gone a mile before she saw water running everywhere.

It didn't look like it was very deep yet. Slowing down, she inched forward a few feet at the time. When she was halfway through, she suddenly felt a strange sensation and realized the car was floating. Panicking, she gunned the motor and felt the tires catch traction in the mud. The car slewed to the right and she couldn't tell where the road stopped and the ditch began. Steering hard to the left, she managed to bring the car back to what she thought was the middle of the road.

Her heart thumped when she heard a clunking sound. What if the car stalled? Then she saw a large tree branch float around the driver's side and in a moment, it was gone. Now, only a quarter mile to go and she should be back on solid ground.

She drove slowly, peering hard through the windshield as she looked for more floating debris. Leaves and sticks drifted past, along with pieces of trash. But she didn't see anything large. The waters began to subside and now she could see the road again.

She went through a few more places where the water covered everything but none of them were deep. And then, she was turning in at Janus.

She would hurry and get back to town before the water rose much more. Henry could drive them home tonight. When she got to the house, she went up and got the jar of herbs. Then she went down to the big pantry just off the kitchen. They were running low on coffee at the church and Mama had told her to bring all she could find. Just like everyone else, they didn't have much here because of the rationing. All she could find were two containers. She was loading them into a bag when she heard Lorraine running down the stairs.

Grace looked up as she burst through the kitchen door, eyes wide with fear.

"Grace! You have to help me. It's Frank, he just drove up!"

Grace just stared at her.

"I saw him from upstairs. He went into the stables. What are we going to do? No one in the house but us."

"What about it?"

Lorraine's eyes darted back and forth across the room. "Grace, you don't understand how vicious he can be."

Grace tied the top of the bag of supplies.

"Please Grace, I've got to get out of here. Before he comes back out of the stables."

Grace turned to look at her, brow wrinkled in disgust. "Leave me alone."

She turned away but Lorraine grabbed at her arm, her hand closing down so tightly that her nails dug into Grace's flesh. "When he sees what's happened..." Her voice trailed off and Grace looked down at the place where her belly had begun to swell. A small bump but it was there. And it was noticeable.

"I don't know what you want me to do."

"The keys to your car. Where are they?"

"Why?"

"All the other cars are gone. With everyone in town, there's no one else here but us. Even the servants are gone." Her eyes darted back and forth across the room, settling at the window that looked out on the stables.

They heard footsteps on the side porch and Lorraine looked up. Whirling, she ran from the room and Grace could hear footsteps in the hall. For a moment all was quiet except the squeaking of the door that she had left swinging.

It's nothing to me, Grace thought. I don't really care what he does. Why should I want to help her? I need to get back to town. But now Grace was beginning to pick up her fear. Not really afraid, just a little anxious. This is silly, she thought. I'm allowing her to make me paranoid. But she couldn't shake the feeling. Going over to the door, she turned the lock. She could see him through the window. He tried the lock, and she could see the doorknob twist a little, making her breath catch in her throat. She watched as it turned slowly, back, and forth. Finally, it stopped. She stood there, afraid to move.

B-A-A-A-M! The door burst open as he kicked it in, shards of glass flying across the room.

"Hello, Grace." He stood in the kitchen now, grinning. As handsome as ever, but that look in his eyes. It was chilling. "It's been quite a while."

"What do you want?"

"I heard what's going on. What Janus has been doing. All the big hoop-la to support the war effort. How you had the horseshoes auctioned off. It's all they talk about on the radio, television. You can't even go to a movie without them announcing how great it is. And those special shoes were my idea in the first place. No one else even wanted to do it. And now that I'm gone, you're all trying to take the glory for it."

So that's it, Grace thought. That's what it took to bring him home.

"Where is she?"

Grace turned to leave the room. She wasn't going to allow herself to be dragged into this. As she passed the open door facing, she saw someone running towards the stables. A flash of green skirt.

He caught Grace by the arm. Pulling away, she opened the door to the hallway, but he grabbed at the back of her blouse, ripping it. Up until that point, Grace had mostly felt contempt for him but suddenly she was terrified. Turning to face him, she kept her back to the wall, trying to hide her naked flesh.

Now he placed his hands on her shoulders and pulled her face close to his. The lock of dark hair that he always kept slicked back had fallen over his brow. He was so close she could see specks of brown in his hazel eyes and smell the sour whiskey on his breath.

She stood there, her lips pressed together, trying to hold her breath.

"Answer me! Where is she?" He shook Grace like a rag doll.

She looked at him silently, her eyes wide with fear. Drawing his hand back, he slapped her across the face. Hard. She gasped. He hit her again, this time with a closed fist. She felt blood spurt from her nose. He drew his fist back again, stopped, grabbed her under the arms and lifted her off the floor. She hung there for a moment, feet dangling, afraid to move. Then he slammed her against the wall.

She tried to breathe but nothing happened. She lay there, half propped up against the wall, feet splayed out in front of her, watching as he started out the door.

But he had forgotten about her. She could see him going down the steps, taking them three at a time. When he reached the ground, he stopped and looked around. After a moment, he headed towards the stables. Grace stood there trying to catch her breath, watching as he hurried down the hill.

When he sees that she's pregnant, there's no telling

what he's going to do, Grace thought. No doubt he's going to really hurt her, maybe worse. If only Phillip was here. Or Papa. They were the only ones who had ever been able to handle him.

Then a thought occurred to her. Buzz! She had seen Buzz stand up to him before. The only employee who had ever dared. And she had heard Phillip say he had told him to stay here with Grady and keep an eye on the farm. If only he was still here. She craned her neck, eyes searching for the red truck that belonged to the trainer. There it was, down by the jockey's quarters, he was still here!

Pulling at the shoulder of her dress to try and hide her nakedness, she hurried out the door. If only she could find Buzz before it was too late. But she hesitated at the edge of the porch. She didn't want to be seen. Perhaps she could make it to the big grape arbor. Scuttling across the yard, she ran under the canopy of the thick vines and stood watching, looking for any signs of movement. The grapes were just beginning to come in, their fragrance drawing bees that buzzed around her face. One landed on her, and she just stood there, frozen with fear. She could feel it crawling and braced herself for a sting, but she didn't swat at it, afraid she would draw attention to herself. She simply leaned on the heavy corner post, watching. But the only thing she could see moving about down there was the horses in the paddocks. Heavy clouds still lingered, and she wished the sun were shining.

The line of cedars running alongside the path. If she stayed near them, maybe they would hide her a little. But she hesitated there under the cool shade of the arbor. Why should she risk being hurt again, just to help someone who had done such an awful thing. I won't get involved in it, she thought. I'll just get Buzz and let him handle it.

She ran from tree to tree, taking shelter under the branches, just in case Frank was looking this way. When she reached the front stable, she heard something just inside the door and her heart jumped into her throat. But it was only one of the horses, shuffling through the straw. She stood there for a moment, trying to calm down, heart pounding, hands shaking.

Then a thought occurred to her. Perhaps Buzz had ridden with one of the other trainers. Just because his truck was here didn't mean he was.

She fairly flew past the other stables and around the corner of the last one. The jockey's quarters looked deserted but maybe Buzz was in there. Running up the steps, she didn't even hesitate to knock, just burst through the door.

Grady sat alone at the long table in the main room. He was wearing nothing but his boxer shorts and he jumped up, knocking his chair over. Grabbing the newspaper he had been reading, he thrust it in front of himself, as a deep purple blush crept across his face.

At any other time, Grace would have burned with shame at the sight of his muscular body but right now she was too scared.

"Miss Grace, what in the world?"

"Where's Buzz?" she managed to choke out, gasping for air.

"I don't know, he's around here somewhere. I think he went out to the stables when most of the other guys went into town. Why, what's wrong?"

But as Grady was struggling into his pants, she was already out the door, running back towards the stables. Her eyes searched the grounds but there was still no sign of human movement. The work room!

Sometimes when Buzz was worried, she had seen him go in there and just sit for hours, oiling the tack instead of ordering the hands to do it. He would even take down freshly cleaned saddles and polish them again. He had told her once that it was soothing, the repetitive motion, caressing the leather over and over. Maybe he was in there, working on them now. She heard footsteps running behind her but kept going. She knew how strong Grady was, she had seen him at work. And she knew how much Grady hated him, God knows he had reason to. But Buzz was the only one he was really afraid of.

Please, please let Buzz be there she thought as she ran towards the work barn. She slowed down as she reached the doors. The dimness inside prevented her from being able to see much. Creeping through the door, she was met with complete silence. As her eyes adjusted to the darkness, she could feel her heart pounding. Tiptoeing down the aisle, she stopped at the door to the work room, listening. She put her hand on the doorknob and turned it, ever so slowly. The squeak it made seemed to her ears as if it could be heard all over the farm.

But the room was empty. The fresh odor of linseed oil told her that someone had been working in here recently. She turned, closing the door behind her.

"Miss Grace! Where are you?" It was Grady. It sounded like he was in the next stable. But she ignored him.

She darted now from building to building, searching for the trainer. As she looked, she became more and more convinced that he would be the one to put a stop to all this. After all, Buzz was the one who had had the courage in the past to stand up to him.

But she scoured all of the barns and Buzz was nowhere to be found. Grace stood by the last stall of the second barn, holding onto the top railing as she tried to catch her breath. She was trying to think what to do when her eye landed on a flat-bottomed shovel leaning against the wall in the empty stall. Unlatching the door, she grabbed the shovel. She should have taken Lorraine away from the farm. If only she had, none of this would be happening. She had to do something herself. She shifted the shovel in her hands, it had a good heft to it. Solid. Heavy.

Straightening her spine and lifting her chin, she started back up the aisle and turned to run out when she heard voices coming from the main stable. She stopped for a moment, concealed by the fountain and the ridiculous thought ran through her mind that the statue was observing as the events unfolded before its eyes, gazing into the open doors of the building. Running to the doorway, she heard the voices again. They were up at the front, near the door to the tack room. Creeping up to the opening, she peeked in. In the dimness, she could see Frank standing there, his back to her. Another figure faced him. The figure that held the reins of the big chestnut stallion in one hand and the special trophy in the other. Heavy, made of solid silver. Adorning the top was the two-faced horse, one face looking in each direction. Grace had picked it up once to clean it with silver polish and the weight of it surprised her. Had to use both hands to move it to the worktable. He stepped closer to the other figure and the stallion snorted. The horse had always been afraid of him, and Grace knew why. The way he handled the horses, no one else on the farm was like that. The stallion dragged the figure holding him backwards as he approached. The horse continued to back away, until his hindquarters rammed into the wall.

"You might as well stay where you are," the deep, gravelly voice commanded. "I'm going to..."

"Stop!" Grace shouted as he drew his right arm back. She had felt the power in that fist. Heart hammering in her throat, she lifted her shovel, ready to swing. "She's my sister! Let her go!"

As Frank turned to look back at Grace, the sun suddenly came out from behind the hovering clouds. Grace saw the light glint on the pure silver horseshoes slicing through the air as Runaway reared above Frank's head.

Someone was screaming and it took Grace a moment to realize that the sound was coming from her own mouth. But the silver flash of the shoes rose higher, and she rushed forward just as all of the stallion's twelve hundred pounds came down on the back of Frank's handsome head, splitting his skull. Blood flew through the air and spattered on her face. A big glob of it went into her right eye and for a moment, she squinted, trying to see what was happening. Wiping it away with the back of her hand, she saw Frank still standing there in front of her with a look of surprise on his face. It lingered there for a second until he took a few steps backwards and for a moment, she thought he was going to be all right. Then he crumpled and fell to the ground.

Lorraine dropped the trophy into the straw beside him. Swinging up onto the stallion's bare back, she clung tightly there as he rushed out of the barn and down the path towards the river. The further they went, the longer the great horses' strides grew. Faster and faster, totally out of control. Grace could see Lorraine trying to pull him to the side, but it was futile. She watched helplessly as they hit a culvert and went into the river. The current took them, sweeping them beneath the waters. After a few moments, the horse's head popped up and Grace watched as he clambered out on the other side of the river. But she didn't see her sister-in-law again.

EPILOGUE

I ride by the river, watching the trail between two golden ears. They prick forward, as my horse listens, watching for the least little excuse to spook. Scotty is a reiner, not a trail horse and she is a little nervous out here in the open. When we started downriver, a covey of quail had burst up in a flurry out of the brush and she had nearly unseated me, fighting hard for her head, trying to turn and run towards the barn. But she has settled down a little and we are okay. More than okay. Tears prick at my eyes and threaten to overflow. It feels so good to be on her again. I've had a lot of good horses, but I believe for every rider there is that one special horse. Your heart horse. The one that can never be replaced. You know each other so well that there is hardly any need for cues. All I have to do is think, canter. And just like that, we are floating along. No spurs, no push, no squeeze. I just think it and she does it.

Drake is riding my horse some now. Only when we are alone and there is no one else around to see. She wants me to train her for reining and I believe she can do it. All the quick movements and turns are so different from anything she has ever done. She has taken a couple of tumbles but that's no surprise since she's never been on a reining horse. The first time she pulled the reins back to stop, Scotty sat down on her haunches and went into her ten-foot slide and Drake flew over her neck. But she bounced up out of the soft sand laughing, as my good horse stood waiting patiently for her to remount. And when Drake put her into a spin, she lurched to the side, hanging off the saddle, but caught her balance and was able to pull herself upright. We've got a lot of work to do, but as long as Drake is willing, so am I. In the meantime, she continues to use Boogie as her main horse and is taking him to small local classes.

WHERE THE STATUE WEEPS

I had walked up behind them the other day as Drake was grooming the Saddlebred and she didn't know I was there. I watched quietly as she stopped to scratch behind his ears and he leaned into her. She spoke softly to him and I could barely make out the words. "Now just because I'm going to ride Jo's horse some doesn't mean I would ever leave you," she said. "I'm only going to try a little western work. You will always be my boy and I'll still be riding you, too. My Boogie-Woogie-Boy. I love you so much." She leaned in to plant a kiss on the scarred nose and I turn away, almost embarrassed. I feel as if I was spying on something that should only be between a girl and her horse.

Denise will be returning in a few weeks, but she has asked me to stay on as her assistant. The program is growing so fast we can barely keep up. She has been working from her mother's house on grant proposals and some pretty hefty ones are starting to come in. We will be renovating a wing of the house so that kids from out of the area can come and stay for a week at the time at horse camp. I am also working on a certification in therapeutic riding. Denise said she had kept planning to do it herself because it will help bring in more grant funding but hasn't been able to find the time. With her writing proposals and me providing a certification, we are hoping to grow even more.

When Cole texts or calls now, I usually answer. I'm through with running away. It feels good not to be afraid anymore. I suppose the pain will always be there but it's no longer controlling my life. I'm not going back but I have forgiven him. That day, the woman I saw training there, the pretty one. The sensation I had gotten in the pit of my stomach when I saw her. Because I knew it had happened more than once, even after he had sworn that it never would. The feeling I had made me realize; I'm not going to live that way again. And I'll never, ever take another pill just to control my emotions. I can do that myself now.

Maybe one day there will be someone else, I don't know. If not, I'm okay on my own. I do watch some of the couples that come out and sense the invisible thread that binds them together over their children. I've been hauling Boogie and Drake to the local 4-H shows and I usually sit in the stands with Ransome Copeland, sharing hot dogs as we watch the kids. He is a man that makes you feel comfortable, at ease. Not what you would consider really handsome, but he is a good man. Solid. Always there, always the same.

I look up at the big house on the hill as I ride back towards it and think of Grace's past...the things she finally told me. I suppose it was a very different time. Women didn't have the same choices we do now. It couldn't have been easy to leave your husband back then. But I do believe that Phillip was a good man who usually put others before himself. He made one slip, out of overwhelming empathy for a woman whom he had watched suffer. But I think that some men are doomed to repeat that sort of mistake over and over, while others are not.

Grace had a reason for not saying what she had seen that day. After her incident when we found the newspaper clipping in the secret cupboard, she had told me the entire story. At first, her words were broken and hesitant, said she had never spoken of it. To anyone. She told me that she knew if Papa found out it had been the stallion that killed Frank, he would have gotten his rifle and shot him. Lorraine's body had never been found. The sheriff's department had assumed that she had done it and run away from home. They never even knew she had been the one that had taken the stallion out of his stall that day. After a few months, the search had been abandoned and the case had been closed. But all the sensationalism it had caused for the family had been devastating. Between that and the loss of the racetrack, things had never really been the same at Janus again.

We jog smoothly down the path, and I gaze out over the river, at the place it all happened. A chill runs down my spine. A couple of decades after Lorraine lost her life there, they put in a dam a few miles upriver from Roanoke Rapids in order to control the flooding. In doing so, they created beautiful Lake Gaston, which is now the number one tourist attraction in the area. But it is still a dangerous river, especially where the elevations drop drastically and the whitecaps rush around the big rocks.

I ride up to the barn and start to dismount. Instead, I guide my horse into the arena. We canter around the perimeter of the fence a couple of times and then we cross diagonally and begin working figure eights, with the circles becoming smaller and smaller. At the junction where we switch directions, she does a flying lead change, so the correct front leg is always reaching out towards the inside of the circle. Forty paces, change. Twenty paces, change. Twelve paces, change. Change, change, change. She performs it so smoothly that I can barely feel the transition, but it is always correct. Left or right, always changing to the correct lead. We are going in the right direction.

After a few more rounds, we slow to a walk to cool down. As we circle the arena slowly, I look out over the herd grazing in the pasture and realize that I have such a tender spot in my heart for every one of these horses. Not the fiery, spirited horses of the show world but such kind and gentle creatures. Generous to a fault. They give of themselves completely and I believe that is what helps the children so much. Even the ones that were so mistreated in their former lives, they hold no grudge. Just quiet and honest, horses to be trusted completely.

I look around in the silence of the fading twilight and imagine what this arena will look like tomorrow morning. Kids and horses, everywhere you look. And I love every one of them. With all my heart and soul. Everything, just everything has changed. Janus Farms is where I belong.

And the statue of the two-faced horse at the fountain continues to look over the farm, one face staring back on the past as the other gazes forward to the future.

Lenn Roberson was raised in Northampton County of N.C. She was always fascinated with Sir Archie, known as the "Foundation Sire of the American Thoroughbred." He and Janus, one of the earliest imported thoroughbreds ruled the history of the area. These factors led to the author's interest in local history, as well as a passion for horses. With a background in nursing, she has worked with many elements from her novel, including disabled children and battered women. She grew up boating and swimming in the Roanoke, named by the Native Americans as the "river of death." She had the delicious experience of living in an old Southern mansion which was said to be haunted and hearing things go bump in the night.

Roberson has been active with the Halifax County Horse Council and 4-H. Her family hosts an annual equine-centered event which has raised over $200,000.00 for patients facing a medical crisis. She co-founded the Roanoke Valley Writer's Group and started Rainbow Readers Literacy Program. She has published magazine articles and enjoys writing stories with rich local atmosphere and historical details.